Special thanks to the following people for helping breathe life into the Godsverse:

Amba Nevell, Andrea Johnson, Anij Fallows, Ashley, Beth Barany, Brad Com, Burnel Smith, C, Caledonia, Cat Fleming (MadCatter), Catherine Leja, Chad Bowden, Chris Call, Christina Lopez, Christine Chandra, Christopher Stillwell, Cristian Dinu, Daniel Groves, Dave Baxter, David Irgang, Dr.Salt, Earl Weiss, EconKelly, Elizabeth Noel Bennett, Emerson Kasak, Emily, Emily, Eric Williamson, Erica, Erica Hecker, Erica Jordan, Eva Jayet, Garry James Watts, Gavran, Genevieve Perosa, Gerald P. McDaniel, GMarkC, goodmancoming, Greywolfe, Isaac "Will It Work" Dansicker, James Kralik, Jason Crase, Jason 'XenoPhage' Frisvold, Jeff Frisone, Jeff Lewis, Jeremy Reppy, John "AcesofDeath7" Mullens, John Idlor, JohnDoe, Joshua Bowers, Joshua McGinnis, Juanita Nesbitt, Katrina Kunstmann, Kenny Endlich, Laura Ann Moylan, Lia, maileguy, Manic, Martin Nehmiz, Matthew Johnson, Maxi Organ, Melissa Showers, Michael Di Salvo, Nathaniel Adams Jr, Nick Smith, Paul Nygard, Paul Rose Jr., Pavlos Chatzipantelidis, Peter Anders, Peter Tarasewich, Randy Graham, Rebecca Carter, Rebecca M. Senese, Rhel ná DecVandé, Robert Brown, Robinflight,Rowan Stone, Ryan Scott James, Scantrontb, Scott Chisholm, Scott Kilburn, Shannon Carlin, Sil, Snir Kolodni, Stephan Szabo, Stephen Ballentine, Sunny Side Up, Venron, Victoria Nohelty, Walter Weiss, Winter, and Xavier Hugonet.

GODSVERSE PLANETS

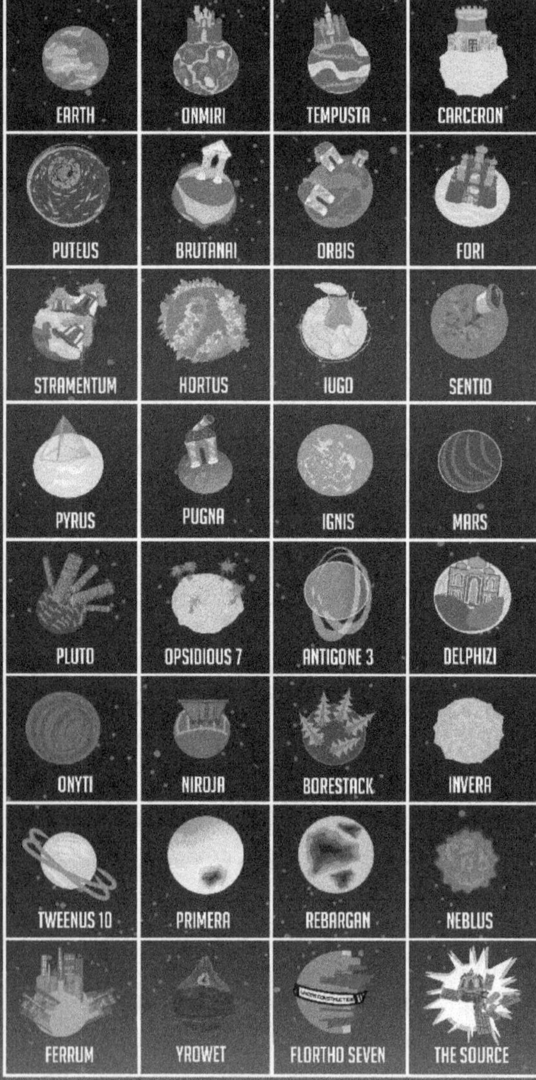

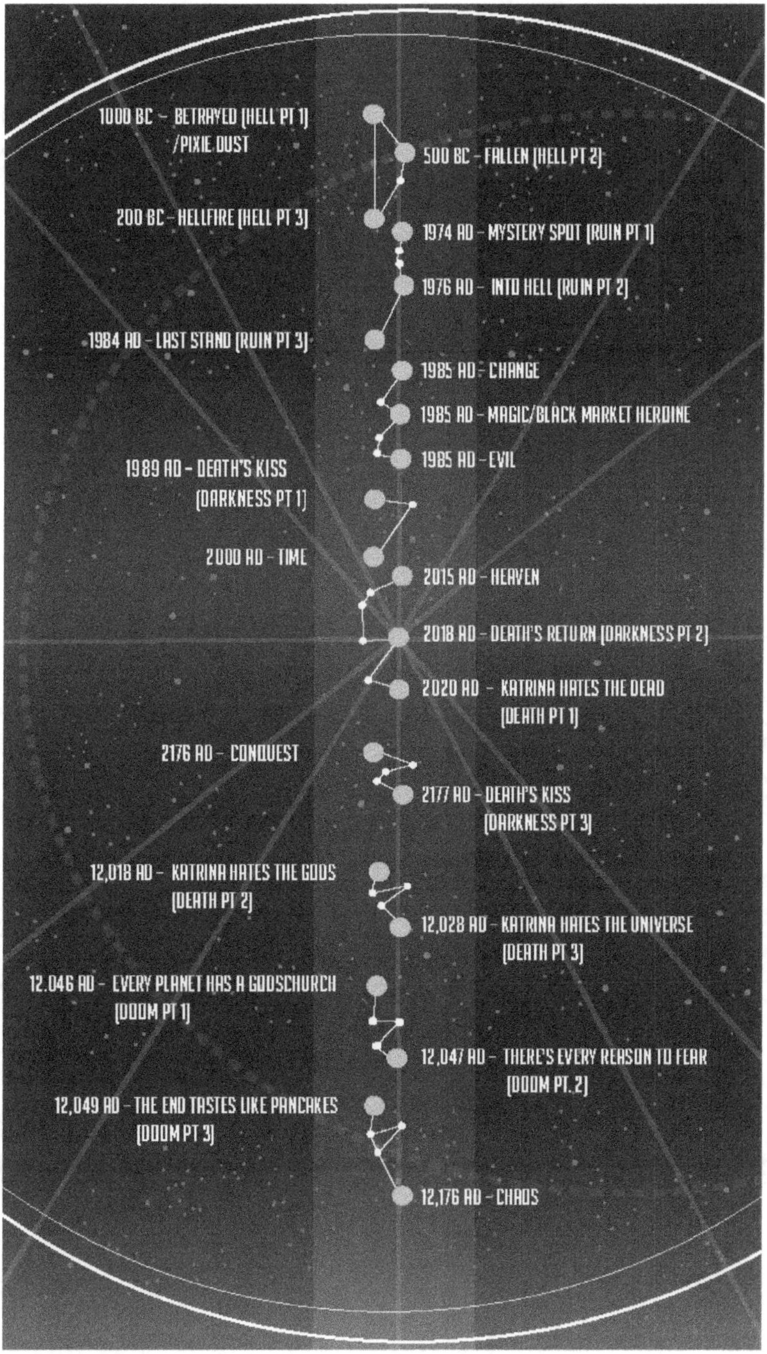

1000 BC – BETRAYED [HELL PT 1]
/PIXIE DUST
500 BC – FALLEN [HELL PT 2]
200 BC – HELLFIRE [HELL PT 3]
1974 AD – MYSTERY SPOT [RUIN PT 1]
1976 AD – INTO HELL [RUIN PT 2]
1984 AD – LAST STAND [RUIN PT 3]
1985 AD – CHANGE
1985 AD – MAGIC/BLACK MARKET HEROINE
1985 AD – EVIL
1989 AD – DEATH'S KISS
[DARKNESS PT 1]
2000 AD – TIME
2015 AD – HEAVEN
2018 AD – DEATH'S RETURN [DARKNESS PT 2]
2020 AD – KATRINA HATES THE DEAD
[DEATH PT 1]
2176 AD – CONQUEST
2177 AD – DEATH'S KISS
[DARKNESS PT 3]
12,018 AD – KATRINA HATES THE GODS
[DEATH PT 2]
12,028 AD – KATRINA HATES THE UNIVERSE
[DEATH PT 3]
12,046 AD – EVERY PLANET HAS A GODSCHURCH
[DOOM PT 1]
12,047 AD – THERE'S EVERY REASON TO FEAR
[DOOM PT 2]
12,049 AD – THE END TASTES LIKE PANCAKES
[DOOM PT 3]
12,176 AD – CHAOS

ALSO BY RUSSELL NOHELTY

NOVELS
My Father Didn't Kill Himself
Sorry for Existing
Gumshoes: The Case of Madison's Father
Invasion
The Vessel
The Void Calls Us Home
Worst Thing in the Universe
The Marked Ones
The Dragon Scourge
The Dragon Champion
The Dragon Goddess
The Obsidian Spindle Saga

COMICS and OTHER ILLUSTRATED WORK
The Little Bird and the Little Worm
Ichabod Jones: Monster Hunter
Gherkin Boy
How NOT to Invade Earth

www.russellnohelty.com

MAGIC

Book 1 of The Godsverse Chronicles

By:
Russell Nohelty

Edited by:
Leah Lederman

Proofread by:
Katrina Roets & Toni Cox

Cover by:
Psycat Covers

Planet chart and timeline design by:
Andrea Rosales

BOOK 1

"Black Market Heroine"

CHAPTER 1

Orcs smelled like moldy cheese.

Even if I couldn't see under their thinly-veiled illusion charms to their true faces, I would be able to smell them from across a room because they reeked of cheese. Every race had its own smell. Demons smelled like charred meat. Not pleasantly charred meat, but the kind that you left in the oven for an hour too long and caused a visceral, uncontrollable wretch in your gut.

Elves smelled like lavender and not in a pleasant way. More like that "why did you fill a room with lavender and then close all the windows for a week, so the lavender plumed out all at one time and kicked me in the face" kind of way. Dwarves smelled like stale grog, even if they hadn't been drinking.

Humans smelled the worst of all. They smelled of death, like a corpse trying desperately to mask their rotting flesh with perfumes and cologne.

My sensitive nose was only one of the many curses my parents heaped on me. I was also cursed with second sight, which allowed me to see through any illusion charm to the true nature of something, even if I didn't want to see it. They also bestowed on me a hatred of everything on either side of the divide, angels and demons alike, though that was more a function of nurture and not nature.

It's amazing I turned out as stable as I did, given the truckload of garbage heaped on me as a kid. On second thought, though, perhaps working in the underbelly of Los Angeles, trafficking in magical weapons and trinkets wasn't the best way to prove that I turned out well-adjusted.

Most people who don't know any better call it the black market, but to me, it was just the market. If you needed a hard-to-find weapon to kill a lasa, or a spell to impress a girl, or just a charm to make you smarter to pass an upcoming test, I was your girl.

I wasn't a drug runner, or an arms dealer, or an assassin, but those were the types that filled my Rolodex. I preferred to think of myself as a facilitator. Somebody who could introduce you to the right monster at the right time for the right job at the right price.

Sure, you could search for what you need yourself, and you might even find it, but you'd more likely get your face busted, ripped off, or killed, than if you'd hired me. I wasn't cheap. I was absurdly expensive, actually, but I got the job done, and I kept you out of the fray. *How much would you pay for that kind of peace of mind?*

My clients paid a lot for it, and I made a good living working with bad people. I knew they did bad things, but they never did it in front of me. To me, they were perfectly pleasant, sweet even, sometimes to a sickening extent. Maybe it's because I wasn't bad to look at or because I could slice their throat with the flick of my wrist. Either way, I never had issues with my clients or my suppliers.

Or, I rarely did.

My latest client was a complete pain in the ass. He buzzed my beeper every two hours asking for updates on the location of the precious dagger he had contracted me to find. Usually, it could take me months to track down a specific piece, but he was paying me three million dollars to find it in a week, forcing me to push my contacts to push their contacts, and well, in the end, everyone was on edge, and I hadn't slept in three days. I hadn't slept in a month before that, honestly, because I didn't sleep much. The past week was because of stress, and I didn't like stress. Though

I operated in a very dangerous profession, I went out of my way to only work with and for people who reduced my stress, or at least didn't add to it.

This was the exception to the rule. I had no idea who my client was, which was completely against protocol. However, three million was too much to turn down, even for me. Even after I had greased every palm in Los Angeles, I would still be left with two million, free and clear, for a week's work.

It had been a hellish week, but I had finally tracked down the dagger to an orc named Blezor. Of course, he was only an orc to those in the know. To almost everyone else, he was just an eccentric art dealer. A smaller group of misfits knew he laundered drug money through his art collections, but even those people knew him as a human.

It was a special kind of person that knew who we were, which was how we all lived in plain sight for thousands of years. We were your bank tellers, your grocery store clerks, and your doctors. If you've ever had a strange interaction with somebody that didn't seem quite human, that was probably one of us.

I preferred to do my work through proxies rather than get my hands dirty, but when the money was right and the timetable was tight, I didn't have any other options. I took it upon myself to make a move on Blezor. Orc males run hot, and it was particularly easy to seduce them. I wasn't the most sexual person in the world, but for three million dollars, I was willing to bed just about anything. I had no problem being a whore, especially a rich one. We're all whores for something.

Blezor wasn't a bad lay. He wasn't great, but his problems lay with being a selfish lover and not in the stamina or aptitude departments. The whole time I couldn't get over the fact that he smelt like rancid Limburger cheese, and when he was done, his musk had oozed all over me. At least he tired himself to sleep.

After I screwed him into a sex coma, I slid his arm off my naked stomach and rose slowly. I dressed in the leather pants and crop top which I had worn to get his attention. I reached into the pocket of my leather trench coat and pulled out my sunglasses. I never took them off if I could help it, but Blezor insisted, and…again, three million dollars, so I relented.

I slung my black leather coat around my narrow shoulders and walked out of the bedroom. Blezor was all too happy to regale me with stories about his collection of art and weapons, including the gnarled, sinewy, black dagger I was after, mounted behind a glass case in the study set off from the main foyer.

I pulled my willow bark wand from the interior pocket of my coat. *"Toddi gwydr."*

Most witches and wizards used standard Latin to cast spells, though they were effective in any language, especially if it held specific significance to you and your wand. My mother had given me my wand, one of the few things she ever gifted me. She'd made it herself with the core of a unicorn hair she plucked herself from her beloved Welsh countryside.

Of course, you didn't need a wand to cast spells, at least not when you were as powerful as I was; it just helped focus your power for more delicate or powerful spells that you needed to be concentrated in a specific area. I wasn't interested in blowing the case to kingdom come, so I needed the deft touch only a wand could bring.

A thin stream of orange light came from the end of the wand, and I used it to cut the glass case protecting the knife. When I had cut a circle big enough for my hand to fit through, the glass popped off into my hand.

"*Dyblygu*," I whispered to the wand, and it made a perfect replica of the dagger in the display, hovering above it. I jammed my hand into the display and picked up the dagger, placing the duplicate behind it to complete the illusion.

When I pulled the dagger free, I replaced the piece of glass and melted it back in place. It wasn't perfect, but it would do in a pinch. Hopefully, Blezor wouldn't be able to tell it disappeared until I was long gone.

"What are you doing?" I heard a gruff voice grumble. I turned to see Blezor scowling at me. "Are you stealing from me?"

Well, this wasn't good.

"Oh, this?" I said, stepping backward. "I can see how you would think that, but… *FFLACH*!"

I closed my eyes, and a flash of white light escaped the end of the wand. Blezor screamed, and I barreled over him, rushing for the exit.

Outside, I flung open the door to Lily, my 1968 Plymouth Barracuda, tossing my wand and the dagger into the passenger's seat. It would be a pain to fix this mess now that he'd caught me stealing, red-handed. There wasn't time to worry about that. I looked down at my watch. I had less than an hour to get to the meeting spot and make the exchange. *Cutting it close, Ollie. Real close.*

I gunned the engine and sped off into the night, wheels squealing as Blezor rushed out into the driveway. He screamed something at me that I couldn't hear over the blare of Lily's engine, which was probably for the best. Whatever he had to say couldn't have been pleasant, and I didn't need that kind of negativity in my life.

CHAPTER 2

The docks in San Pedro had one thing going for them—it was easy to keep everything in front of you and avoid being ambushed from behind if you planned it right. After some deft maneuvering and a dash of lead foot, I arrived at the dock from Burbank twenty minutes before my scheduled meeting, allowing me to position myself perfectly for a quick escape if I needed it. I had never worked with this client before, and the people who hired me had a higher propensity than most to be bottom feeders. Even if most of the bottom feeders I knew had ethics, it paid to take precautions.

I kept the car running while I rummaged through the mountain of weaponry and armor in the trunk, looking for a sheath big enough to hold the curved dagger. *Three million dollars for a stupid dagger.* I couldn't believe it, but I wasn't complaining either. I slid the now sheathed dagger into my coat, slammed the trunk closed, and exited the dock.

Lily and I had been through a lot together, and I loved her more than anything else in my life. She was the only thing that never let me down and had saved me more times than I cared to admit. Even when you are careful, in this line of work, you got into plenty of hairy situations. It paid to have somebody to watch your back—my somebody just happened to be a car.

A 1985 Oldsmobile Cutlass pulled to a stop a dozen yards from me. I pulled down my sunglasses to get a better look at it. It must have been barely off the lot because even in the darkness, it shimmered. I hated the boxy look of 80s cars, which was why I had no desire to get rid of my '68

Barracuda, even though it was almost twenty years old. They didn't make cars like Lily anymore.

Neither of the demons who exited the car was my client. I had never even spoken to him except over the phone, and none of my contacts knew anything about the smooth-voiced stranger, which put me on edge. Still, he had already given me five hundred grand in cash as a down payment, which gave me all the confidence I needed to take the job.

The driver was Balaam, a six-eyed demon with an underbite disguised as a black, square-jawed ex-wrestler. The other demon was Moloch, whose horns were tall enough to give him trouble getting in and out of cars. Moloch fancied himself charming, but he was as vile as any demon. They were both bulky and muscular and always chose to remain shirtless, perhaps to show off how ripped they were. I had lived long enough to know that muscles don't mean much in the grand scheme. A small girl like me was stronger than both of them combined, and I looked like a swift breeze would blow me over.

"Ollie," Balaam said. The duffle bag slung over his shoulder could have only been my money, even if it looked too small for three million. I knew that money was a lot slimmer than they made it seem in the movies.

"Boys," I said with a confident smile.

"Do you have it?" Moloch said.

I walked toward the demons, hand tight on the dagger's hilt under my coat. "Of course. It was a real pain finding it."

"That's why it cost three million dollars, right?" Balaam said, gruffly, as if it was his money he was spending and not his boss's. "We didn't think you'd show."

"I always show." I pulled the dagger out of the sheath as I removed it from my jacket. I felt the power of it in my hands then, which I hadn't quite appreciated before. My heart began beating faster, and I took a deep breath.

"Impressive," Moloch cooed.

"I should have charged you double," I told them, holding out the dagger for them to see.

"We would have paid it, too." Moloch beckoned me forward. "Now, give it to me."

I shook my head and slid back a step. "That's not how this works. You slide the money over, and then I hand you the merchandise. We talked about this."

"Afraid we can't do that," Balaam said. "Just do as he says."

Something's wrong. Sure enough, a moment later, they pulled out their guns, massive hand cannons with barrels nearly as big as my head. The kind of thing impotent and feckless men used to compensate for their inadequacies.

Moloch looked down the barrel of his gun. "Now, hand it over."

I couldn't help it. A big grin rose on my face. I was most at home in a fight. Subterfuge wasn't my jam, even though it was almost always called for in my line of work. I preferred to punch my fist through something squishy when given the chance.

"You don't want to do this," I said. "All you're gonna get is dead, and then I'll have the knife and the money."

Balaam's trigger finger twitched. "I'm sorry about this. You seem like a fine person, but we have orders."

"So did the Nazis, and they still fried. This is your last chance."

"Enough!" Moloch screamed.

"Yes, I agree," I replied. "I have given you enough chances."

I leaped high into the air as their hand cannons fired, sending several bullets into Lily's chassis. They would pay for that. I flipped around and landed behind the demons, where my smile dropped into a snarl.

"Now you've done it," I growled. *"Chwyth iâ!"*

A massive ice blast flew from my hands. It smashed into the two demons and sent them crashing into my car— my beautiful car.

"Lily! Dammit!" She was an innocent in all of this, but with the duffel bag Balaam dropped at my feet when I blasted him, I had the money to fix her up. "Now, look what you made me do!" I knelt and picked up the bag. "I'll take this as compensation for not killing you. It'll cost you another three million to get the dagger."

A shadow filled my vision, but not from the demons. This one was coming from the air in the form of a monster truck. "YOU BITCH!"

I spun out of the way, and an enormous monster truck, purple and red with tires at least six feet around, landed between the demons and me. Blezor popped his head out of the driver's side door, shaking his fist at me. "I loved you!"

"We barely knew each other!" I almost laughed. "I'm good, but I'm not that good!"

"I'll kill you!" Blezor screamed. "How could you steal from me?"

"It wasn't personal!" I shouted back. "It's just business."

"That's bull! Everything is personal!"

I had to get clear of these psychopaths. I couldn't reach Lily, but the demon's car sat idling behind me. I slid over the hood and ripped open the driver's side door. The car hummed under me as I slammed the gear in reverse. The tires screeched, and I took off backward across the dock.

Bullets pinged against the hood as Blezor fired an Uzi at me. *That little prick!* I looked into my rearview mirror to see a half dozen cars and trucks turn on their lights at the entrance to the dock. The way out was completely blocked by a string of Blezor's men.

Oh, poor Blezor. You really didn't know me at all, did you? No wonder we didn't last.

I slammed my foot down on the brake and spun the car until I was straight on with the blockade. Blezor was gaining with his monster truck.

"*Tonnau sioc!*" I shouted, and a shockwave echoed out from the car as I gunned it forward. Two cars in the center of the blockade flipped and crashed upon two other cars, giving me the perfect window to freedom. I slid through them and out into the night, Blezor hot on my heels.

CHAPTER 3

Blezor chased after me in his monster truck while two other cars that didn't care a lick about the rules of the road fired guns at my trunk. They were gaining on me! *Stupid car.* Lily would have dusted them easily. This awful Cutlass dragged like it was pulling a boat anchor behind it.

"Come on, come on, come on!" I urged as I felt around the passenger seat and in the grooves around the seat as well. "Wand, need a wand."

I didn't mind throwing magic around on the dock without a wand because there weren't a lot of buildings or pedestrians around, but after I turned onto the street, there were other cars and people that would be severely demolished if I let magic fly wildly everywhere. On top of all that, I was amped up and full of adrenaline, so my power would be even greater and harder to control. I definitely needed a focusing agent. *We couldn't all be as careless as Blezor's cronies.*

"Please, come on," I said to myself.

Then, a pen presented itself in my field of vision. "Will this work?" I heard from the back seat. I glanced back to find a demon girl in the back seat with big, green eyes and a disarming smile. "Hello?"

"Uhhh," I replied. "Who are you?"

"Anjelica, with a J. That's not a mistake. That's just how it's spelled." Her finger pointed to the windshield. "You should really keep your eyes on the road."

I had drifted into oncoming traffic, and a Mack truck was bearing down on me, blaring its horn. I screamed and swerved back into my lane. When I was steady again, I looked at the girl through the rearview mirror.

"Who are you, and what are you doing in this car? Are you working for those demon toadies? Do I need to kill you?"

"Um…okay. Like I said, I'm Anjelica, with a J and a C. I was kidnapped by those demon toadies, so I'm not working for them. In fact, I kind of hate them." She stopped for a second. "And for the last question, why would anyone say yes?"

"Touché," I said. "If you were kidnapped, then why aren't you tied up?"

"I was. I gnawed through it like a beaver and then burrowed through the back seat. If you look next to me, you'll see that there's a big frigging hole in it. Why would I rip a big hole in a car if I wasn't trying to escape?"

She was right. There was a roughly demon-girl-sized hole in the back seat. "I suppose I believe you."

"Good," Anjelica said, holding up the pen. "Because it's the truth. Now, you're looking for a wand. Will this work?"

I grabbed it from her. "In a pinch. Can you drive?"

"Kind of? I mean, I passed driver's ed but—"

"Then take the wheel."

I didn't wait for Anjelica to leap forward and snatch the wheel before I rolled down the window and aimed the improvised wand at the cars chasing me.

"*Nodwydd*!"

A thousand little needles shot from the end of the pen and popped the tire of the blue car in the lead, sending it careening into the white car that pursued me. Both cars crashed into the end median in a fiery crash. The monster truck drove right over them like it was nothing, crushing whoever was inside into a little flat pancake.

I fell back into the car and took the wheel again from Anjelica. "Thanks."

She grinned. "We definitely didn't learn that in driver's ed."

Bullets ricocheted off the car again. Blezor was firing a submachine gun out of his driver's side window.

"We have to lose him."

I spun the wheel of the car and hit the brakes, turning the car into a sideways skid before gunning it up the street. A monster truck could never take that turn, and I watched Blezor speed through the intersection. Halfway up the street, I spun up into an alley.

I pointed the pen out of the window. "*Trawsnewid!*" A green spark shot out and created a portal in front of us big enough for the car to drive through. "Hang on!" I shouted.

"What are you doing?" Anjelica asked, her eyes darting from the portal and back to me.

"Trust me," I said.

"No!" she yelped, covering her face.

The car glided through the portal. When it emerged on the other side, it was no longer a car, but an ice cream truck with a big ice cream cone on the top of it, playing Christmas melodies, as they often did for some unknown reason. *Seriously, there were all sorts of public domain music; why Christmas music?*

I slowed the truck to a stop at the end of the alleyway then looked in the back for Anjelica. She kicked her way out of a metal chest, holding a chocolate ice cream cone.

"This is so weird, and I am so cold."

"Just get down, okay?" I said, turning onto the street. "He should be going the other way on this road right about now."

Sure enough, I watched Blezor's monster truck race the other way down the road, missing us completely. We had avoided him, at least for the moment, and now I could figure out what the story was with my little stowaway.

"Phew," I said as I threw my car in park and caught my breath.

Anjelica peeled open the ice cream cone and nibbled at it. Her audacity made me chuckle. "You really thought of everything with this transformation."

"How is it?"

"Good." She smacked her lips and shrugged. "Not great, but good."

"That's what you get with a five-second spell cast under duress." I turned to her. "Now that the insanity's over, who are you again?"

She must have been starving because I heard her stomach grumble from the other side of the truck. "Can we do this over food? I haven't eaten all day."

"You are literally eating an ice cream cone."

Anjelica rolled her eyes. "Ice cream isn't food. It just slides down."

"I didn't know that."

"It's basic science. So, can we get some real food? Like a dozen hamburgers?"

"Sure, kid."

CHAPTER 4

When I was younger, I wanted to be a dancer. I spent nearly every afternoon taking classes until my feet bled and my muscles ached. When I wasn't in class, I was teaching them or helping somebody teach. I was good, too. So good that it got to the point where I really thought I had a chance at a scholarship to Julliard or perhaps the Sorbonne, in France, thousands of miles away from my nagging mother, where I could start over.

I was not much older than Anjelica when that dream began to fizzle and eventually faded from my life. My mother had stopped paying for my lessons, but I was determined to continue, so I got a job to pay for them myself. That's what led me to the lucrative and dangerous world of organized crime. It wasn't my life then, just something I did on the side. Steal something here, sell it to a fence there. It was just a taste, then.

It was only after I came home with gobs of money, enough to pay for lessons for the rest of my life, that Mom told me the truth: I wasn't human. I couldn't apply for the scholarship because it wouldn't be fair; I would always be stronger and faster than anyone else in any class. I tried to tell her that I was a great dancer because I worked harder than everyone else, but she insisted it had nothing to do with my skill and everything to do with my breeding.

She refused to sign the permission slip for my scholarship audition and swore that if I got in, she would not co-sign a loan for me. I couldn't do anything because I was underage. I swore that I would make enough money to pay my own way, but there were few jobs I could take that paid enough to get by, let alone get ahead.

Thievery, however, always paid, no matter who or when you were, and with my naturally lithe body, innate stability, superior strength, and small frame, I was a natural thief. I worked on my own terms, in my own time, and as long as I got the goods, I got paid. Sure, sometimes bad men tried to stiff me, but I was more than happy to knock teeth out if necessary.

I was sixteen then. By the time I lifted my head to look around, I was twenty-five. Even with all the money I'd earned, it didn't matter. My body was too old for professional dance. That's a younger woman's game. I never dance anymore, and while I take most of the blame for that, it all started with my mother telling me no when I was Anjelica's age. It wasn't fair that something that happened in your youth could derail your whole life and being kidnapped was not a small little thing. It had the potential to knock her out cold, and I couldn't let that happen.

"Feel better?" I asked, taking a sip of coffee as Anjelica stuffed another bite of burger into her mouth. Either she didn't have any shame, or she was already comfortable with me because there was mustard, ketchup, and grease all over her little demonic face.

"Mm-hmm," Anjelica replied, wiping her mouth with the one-ply paper napkin until it ripped apart in her hand. She used the sleeve of her shirt instead. "So much better. You build up an appetite, locked in a trunk all day. It was so hot. I feel like I dropped ten pounds from sweat alone." She took a sip of her milkshake. "Are you going to eat anything?"

I shook my head. "I don't eat. Coffee is fine with me."

Anjelica cocked her head. "What do you mean 'I don't eat'? Everyone eats."

"I'm not everyone." I didn't feel like explaining to her that I didn't have to eat unless I wanted to indulge. Another gift and curse from my dear, old parents.

"Ominous." Anjelica crammed a half dozen fries into her mouth. "You should try eating. It's awesome." She dipped another fry into her milkshake. "Mmmmm…sweet and salty. The ultimate flavor combination."

"That's disgusting," I said, wrinkling my nose in disgust. "Can we get back to you, please?"

"If we have to."

"We have to," I said. "Any idea why those monsters kidnapped you?"

"I know exactly why."

"Would you care to enlighten me?"

"All right." Anjelica looked around, then leaned forward to whisper. "But what I have to tell you is gonna shock you. It will blow your mind." Her eyes were wide. "You sure you can handle it?"

"Yeah, I'm good." I chuckled. If this girl knew even a hundredth of what I'd seen. "Hit me with it."

"It's really big news." Anjelica looked around again. "You sure this place is safe and stuff?"

I nodded. "I'm sure. I know the owner. Anything you say here will stay in our confidence."

She sighed before nodding slowly. "All right. Don't be scared—for I am—" She was so close to me I could taste the fries on her breath. "—a demon."

I leaned away from the table. "Oh, is that it? Cuz I already knew that."

Anjelica cocked her head, disgusted. "What do you mean you knew that? Nobody knows that. I didn't even know until those demon pricks told me earlier tonight."

I pointed to my glasses. "I see everything. The owner's a troll. The waitress is a changeling, and the barback, she's a gorgon, a real pretty one at that." I took another sip of coffee. "And you, you're a demon."

"You knew I was a demon, and you didn't say anything?" She glanced around the room one more time, this time with curiosity. "If all that is true, then this place is so gnarly."

"I don't come here for the weak coffee. I come for the company. It has a very monster-y clientele, and I dig that." I took another sip of coffee. "I'm surprised you didn't know you were a demon until somebody told you. It's not even a very good masking spell."

"Well, I didn't even know to look for it until tonight, did I?"

"I guess not, and it would take somebody like me to see through it."

"What are you?" she asked, cocking her head to the side.

I waved my hand. "This isn't about me. It's about you. Being a demon doesn't explain why you were kidnapped, so spill."

Anjelica pouted. "You suck. Did you know that?"

"I saved your life, didn't I?"

"I guess you did."

"And I'm buying all this food for you, right?"

"Well, yeah. That's true."

Now it was my turn to lean in, close to her face. "Look, I want to help you. If you want my help, I need to know everything."

"Fine." Anjelica sighed. "Just know this is no fun."

"More fun than being in a trunk." I smirked. "I can put you back, though, if you would prefer."

Anjelica stuffed another bite of her hamburger in her face and washed it down with more of the milkshake. "Fine, fine. So, I'm not just a demon."

"Obviously."

"I am…" she paused for dramatic effect, "the antichrist."

I paused, considering this. "Well, that is considerably more interesting, and it makes much more sense why you were kidnapped."

"Glad it could hold your attention, finally."

I slid the knife out of my jacket and placed it on the table. "Must be why they needed this."

"Holy sh—" She nearly spat out her milkshake. "That is a big knife!"

I nodded. "Big and powerful. I can feel the dark energy flowing through it. Any idea why they would take you today of all days?"

"I dunno."

"Think," I said. "It's important."

She threw her hands in the air. "Oh, you want me to think? Really helpful. Like I wasn't already. All they said was I'm the antichrist, and I had to die tonight."

I finished my cup of coffee. "Well, that's good news."

She sighed and slammed her hands on the table. "How did you hear good news in the sack of dung that is my life?"

"Because if we can keep you alive until morning, you should be safe."

"Okay," Anjelica said. "That's good because I would very much like this not to be my last meal."

I shrugged. "You could do worse."

"Oh, it's delicious, but I definitely want my last meal to be sushi. No doubt in my mind."

"I'll keep my fingers crossed for you on that one."

Anjelica looked up from her food. "Are you really gonna help me?"

I offered a tight smile. "As much as I can. Those pricks tried to kill me tonight, too, ya know. The least I could do is keep you alive to thwart whatever plans they had."

"Thanks."

"Don't thank me yet. You've never had to spend a whole night with someone like me." I held up my hand to ask for the check. "Now, finish that up. We have work to do."

CHAPTER 5

I hated the suburbs, especially in Los Angeles. At least in most cities, suburbs were outside the city. In LA, everything was stacked on top of and next to each other so that perfectly manicured and patrolled "suburbs" were nestled between crime dens and decrepit shitholes.

Suburbs were also nicer, cleaner, and better maintained in most other cities. There was some modicum of charm to them, even. Not in LA. In LA, suburbs sprang up with no rhyme or reason, like a nasty bout of herpes. It was as if a big, weird God of Housing and Urban Development pointed his finger and said, "The suburbs start here" and "Yes, I know the houses are EXACTLY the same as the ones on the other side of the street, but THESE ones are better for some stupid reason or another".

My mother's house was part of a small, gated community that the HUD god chose to build on that specific block even though it was beset by low-income housing in every direction. Still, she was very proud that she could afford that specific block, and she absolutely hated when I brought home strays, which meant I did so every chance I got. She fussed about my hoodlum friends from "the other side of the track" but, of course, in LA, that was a funny demarcation line. Everything in LA was arbitrary, including where the HUD god placed the train track. That didn't stop her from labeling all my friends. She only wanted me to bring home certain children from certain neighborhoods, which meant I fell into the wrong crowds again and again just to piss her off.

"Come on," I said, clicking open the door to the ostentatious house.

"Is this your house?" Anjelica gasped, looking around at the walls.

"No," I said. "I would never buy property in Los Angeles. I pay extra to be month to month on my apartment so that I can leave at a moment's notice."

"If this isn't yours, then—"

"Who's there?" My mother's shrill voice sounded from the second floor.

"If I were a robber, what good is asking who I am?"

"Ollie?" I heard footsteps upstairs, and my back seized up. "Hang on, I'm coming down."

My mother hadn't aged much in the thirty years since I'd popped out of her, except for the invading white in her hair. She had it pulled back in a ponytail and was wearing a white sleep shirt that fell to her knees. Even then, she was beautiful, which was the only thing she cared about.

"Hi, Mom," I said as she wrapped her arms around me. "You can let go of me now."

"Not until you hug me back," she murmured into my shoulder.

I grumbled and wrapped my arms around her. "Happy now?"

"I'm always happy to see you, sweetheart," she said before turning to Anjelica. "And who is this?"

"Hi," Anjelica said, waving. "I'm Anjelica."

Mom gave her an appraising look, and then her face dropped. Another stray. "Well, come on. I'm guessing you haven't eaten yet."

"Actually, I ate two hamburgers with fries." Anjelica stopped talking. "Oh, you meant Ollie. She said she doesn't eat. Who doesn't eat?"

"Exactly." Mom walked through a rounded archway into the kitchen. "My Ollie was always a brooding type, and thought not eating added to her mystique."

"I'm not hungry," I said. "And it's not like you're the paragon of health. When was the last time you—" I stopped myself. "Can we not do this?"

"Fine," Mom said with a smile that really meant "screw you." I was very familiar with that smile. "Well, come on. You will at least have coffee, won't you?"

"That I will do."

I felt a tug on my shoulder and turned to Anjelica. "She seems nice. Why do you seem to hate her?"

"Trust me, this is a front. She can only keep it up for so long."

"Why are we here then?"

"She's the most powerful being I know, and if you're gonna be safe anywhere while I figure this out, it'll be here."

I walked Anjelica into the kitchen. The floor was the same yellow linoleum with pink flowers from my youth. In fact, nothing had really changed. Something my mother cherished was consistency. I embraced chaos.

"Two sugars?" Mom said, spoon in hand.

"I've taken it black for a dozen years."

She set down the spoon and handed me the coffee. "Of course. Your taste for bitter things has grown in recent years."

"Truce," I said. "Just in front of the kid."

"What am I doing?" She scoffed. "I'm just saying that—"

"I know what you're doing, Mom." I placed the coffee down on the counter. I knew better than to accept a gift from her. She held every nicety she ever done for me cataloged in her head, ready to rattle off at a moment's notice.

"I don't see why you are so upset. I am not saying anything about the underage *demon* you've brought into my house. I'm just saying—"

"What does she being a demon have to do with anything?" I said. "She's a kid."

"A *demon* kid," Mom grumbled.

"No, a demon *kid*. She is having a really bad night, and she could really use a friend right about n—"

"Actually, I'm okay," Anjelica interjected.

"Stay out of this," I replied angrily, without taking my eyes off of my mother.

Mom sighed. "You know how I feel about demons after your fath—"

I held up my hand and spoke in terse syllables. "Don't. You. Dare." I dropped my head. "This was a mistake. Anjelica, let's go."

"You don't have to go." Mom shook her head. "This is ridiculous."

I grabbed Anjelica by the arm and led her toward the door. "You're ridiculous. I should have known better to turn to you when I needed help."

***

It was a stupid, desperate plan to think my mother could have an ounce of compassion for even a minute. I should have gone to Phil in the first place. He had been my only friend when I was in high school. He didn't care that I was—what I was. Hell, he was an alien and not a particularly handsome one, either. Even his holographic disguise was lumbering and awkward. I beat up anybody that messed with him, and he made me not hate my life so much. It was a good pairing.

"Can we please talk about what happened with your mom?" Anjelica asked, following me out to the ice cream truck. I brought the dagger and the duffel of money. Even though Phil lived in the same white bread, upper-class neighborhood as my mother, I was keeping my three million dollars close.

"No," I snapped. "Let me do the talking."

"Really?" Anjelica replied. "Because you are just about the worst talker I have ever met."

She wasn't wrong.

"Yes, really."

I knocked on the door. There was some shuffling inside before it opened. When we were younger, Phil masked his appearance behind a hologram, but as he aged, he became less concerned with hiding who he was, even if he was a green-skinned alien with a single, glowing eye popping out of his long neck.

"Hi, Phil." I smiled in spite of myself.

"Jesus Christ, Ollie. It's two in the morning."

I chuckled, but Phil didn't get the joke. "What's so funny?" he asked.

"Oh, blasphemy is particularly funny in this particular situation." I slid to the side to reveal Anjelica. "Phil, meet Anjelica. The antichrist."

"Jesus Christ," he repeated, eye wide.

"Not exactly," Anjelica said with a curtsy. "But I appreciate the comparison."

He shooed us inside. "Come on."

Phil had lived in the same house for the entirety of the time I had known him, and with every passing year, he seemed to just accumulate more stuff but never threw away anything he had acquired. Nearly every room was packed with garbage, and it stank something fierce. He said it was all research, but in truth, he was just a hoarder.

A trail of green ooze marked Phil's path into his office at the front of the house. It contained just about every piece of electronic equipment that RadioShack ever sold and several they couldn't even imagine. Phil's race was a million years more advanced than us, which meant even our distant descendants couldn't dream up the tech that Phil found banal.

"Aside from this thing—no offense, sweetie—did you bring me anything else?" Phil asked.

I pulled out the dagger and placed it into his gooey hand. "This dagger was supposed to kill her, I think."

Phil squinted at it. "Looks the type. I'll throw it under the magonomascope."

The magonomascope looked like a standard-issue microscope, only a billion or so times more advanced. If anyone on the planet could figure out why the dagger was needed to kill Anjelica, it was Phil.

"This place is cool," Anjelica said, poking at something that looked like a VCR. "Why didn't you bring me here first?"

"I didn't want to drag Phil into this or get him hurt."

"That's very sweet," Phil said, looking into the eyepiece of his magonomascope. "But nothing yet has hurt me on this stupid planet. Of course, I suppose your survival rate is 100 percent until the day it isn't, and even then, your survival rate is still 99.9999999 percent. Although, if you look at it on a universe level timeframe, I suppose any survival rate is indistinguishable from zero on a long enough time horizon." He looked up from his microscope with a whimsical look in his eye. "Isn't science fun?"

"No," I said. "See anything in that thing?"

"Patience. Science is an inexact science."

"That doesn't make any sense," Anjelica said.

"Precisely." He swung around and began typing on his keyboard. "Your technology is too primitive. Luckily, I was able to supe up your 'advanced' tech with my own modifications." A bunch of numbers and letters flew across the screen. "Ah yes, it's what I feared."

"What is it?" I asked, moving closer.

"This dagger was made in the pits of Hell. I need to call in backup."

"Backup? You always told me you know everything."

"Only what is and will be, not everything that ever was. That's my friend's department." He picked up the phone and dialed a number. "I know it's late…yes, I know it's late…of course it's important…sorry for waking your mom…Okay, thank you." He hung up and looked at me. "She's coming, but she's pissed, and she's surly even in the best of times."

A giant puff of purple smoke plumed into the room, accompanied by a flash of purple light. When it dissipated, a tall girl, not much older than Anjelica, floated in the air. Her hair was dark like her skin, and she was built like a ballet dancer with hard, strong legs. Long, blue wings fluttered behind her as she touched down lightly on the floor.

"Thank you for coming, Kimberly," Phil said.

"This better be good," she growled. "I'm so getting grounded for this."

CHAPTER 6

Kimberly and Phil worked on the dagger for hours, running it through every database in the known universe to find its ancient origin. Phil was nothing if not thorough, and while I didn't know Kimberly, she seemed equally intense in an off-putting, punchable way.

While they worked, I had a chance to call around to my contacts and try to figure out what was happening and, more importantly, who was trying to kill me. Luckily, Phil had an untraceable quantum number generator which allowed me to call anywhere in the world without it being traced back to me, and I had a Rolodex full of contacts that didn't sleep.

"Thanks, Skyler," I said to one of my informants. He was a police officer who would provide me with any information I wanted—for the right price. I paid him handsomely for the privilege, but he also got off on the thrill of the subterfuge. Police officers were often adrenaline junkies, and spycraft was the ultimate high. "I'll call you back later to see if you found anything."

I slammed the receiver down in anger. Halfway through my Rolodex and I still had no clue about the loser who was trying to kill me. I was hot as a pistol and inches from ripping somebody apart with my bare hands. I hoped it would be the jackasses who were on my tail, but if not, it would be the next person to cross my path.

I stormed back into Phil's office. The hum of computers and the glow of green screens filled the room. Anjelica was half asleep, and I pushed her toward the edge of the cot when I dropped down on the bed, the duffel bag full of money under me. It occurred to me that I'd been so concerned with figuring out what happened, I never even opened up the bag.

"Did you find anything?" Anjelica kicked me lightly as she stretched.

"Nothing. Apparently, whoever is trying to kill us both is a ghost."

"That's a distinct possibility." Anjelica rubbed the sleep out of her eyes. "Given who you associate with, after all."

"Funny," I replied with a chuckle. "But you're right. Saying they are a ghost is an insult to ghosts, ghouls, draugrs, lich, and spirits of all types. Those guys would have the decency to leave a trail, at least."

"So, there's nothing you can do?" Anjelica yawned through her words. "I thought you were good."

"I am good. It's very frustrating." I pulled the duffel bag close. "At least I'm rich now." I opened the bag, thinking that maybe looking at the money would cheer me up.

There was nothing inside the bag but gym socks and phone books, cut to feel like the shape of money. I dumped the whole thing out on the floor and searched through it, but I already knew the truth. I was boned.

"Gross," I grumbled, picking up a foul-smelling sock.

"That doesn't look like money," Anjelica said.

"No, it doesn't, and now I am a level of anger I have only reached twice before in my life. The monsters who did this are very, very dead."

I had leveraged everything for this job, emptied every account, and called in every favor. Even with the advance, it wasn't nearly enough to buy the information I needed, but I hadn't minded the expense because this was going to be "the big one," the one that would let me stop doing tiny, little jobs and move up to the big time. Now, I was flat broke.

"I'm going to kill them." I spoke through clenched teeth. "I'm going to find them, and I'm going to kill them so hard."

"You have to find them first, though, right?" Anjelica said.

"I do." I whipped around to Phil and Kimberly. "Anything yet?"

"Not yet," Phil replied.

"We're getting close," Kimberly added, typing furiously. "But a word of warning, bugging us isn't going to make us work any faster."

"Ugh!" I flopped back on the bed. "This sucks. Not only do I have no money, but if I can't find those scumbags, I can't make them pay. If I don't make this right, my name is dirt in every crime syndicate on the West Coast, and they'll all be gunning for my head. I'll have to go into hiding. Change my name—become a hermit."

"Ollie is a weird name anyway. Maybe you should change it." Anjelica was a little too perky for me at the moment.

"That's not the point," I groaned.

"I know. I'm just trying to distract you. Is it working?"

I sighed. "Kind of."

"Good," Anjelica said with a smile. She seemed to smile at everything, no matter the situation. "What's Ollie short for, anyway? Oh god, it is short for something, right? No offense, but I met your mom, and she doesn't seem to hate you enough to name you Ollie."

I chuckled. "Oh, you would be surprised. Ollie is short for Oleander."

I was surprised when Anjelica paused before saying, "That's unusual but pretty."

"My mother's last name is White, so she thought it was a funny joke because I poisoned everything I touched. Even her."

"I don't get it."

"White oleander is a highly poisonous plant," Kimberly said without looking away from the computer screen. "Effective, too."

"Exactly." I turned to her. "So yeah, she hates me plenty."

"Hey!" Kimberly shouted, cutting through the sudden, sad silence. "I think I have something."

"Thank god." I pushed myself to stand. "You found who's trying to kill me?"

"No," Kimberly replied. "I think I know what Apocalypse they are trying to start, though."

I glared. "Oh goodie, the least important part of all this."

"Not to me!" Anjelica's eyes bulged when she spoke, and she scrambled over to the computer. "So, hush. Kimberly doesn't have to help us. She's doing it out of the good in her heart." She placed a hand on Kimberly's shoulder. "Don't worry about Ollie. She's just grumpy because she lost three million dollars, and her mom gave her a stupid name. Please, continue."

I raised my hand in the air to protest but faltered. She'd kind of nailed it.

"Thanks for the permission I didn't need," Kimberly said. "A few months ago, I loaded all the information I have ever found about every apocalyptic scenario into this computer to help me find some connection between them." She typed something else, and the text changed. "I fed everything we know about you into the system, and it did whatever computers do—"

"—processed information," Phil added, though I was very sure Kimberly knew exactly what they did.

"Yeah, that," Kimberly said, her words dripping with sarcasm. "A Wudi philosopher named Lui predicted the end of the world would come 'when the Fire Eye ran around the world in the year when the marked leader rises in the West'."

"Very ominous, definitely," Anjelica said. "This whole night has been filled with ominous signs. I had a grand total of zero ominous signs in my life before today. I miss those days."

Kimberly waited for Anjelica to finish. *"Anyway,* I thought he was talking about Europe or even the USA, even though it wouldn't exist for thousands of years, but then I realized almost everywhere is west of China since it borders the ocean on its eastern coast. What if he was talking about the Soviet Union? He could have been talking about Gorbachev, who has a huge birthmark on his head and just came to power. It all fits."

"Except for the comet," I said.

Kimberly smiled. "Actually, a pretty big comet is going to come dangerously close to hitting Earth in two hours, right before sunrise."

"Bull plop," Anjelica said. "I haven't heard about any comet. Wouldn't something like that be on the news?"

"Yeah." I nodded in agreement. "Why haven't we heard about it?"

"Because nobody has," Phil said flatly. "My tech is far superior to anything on Earth. One day, you primitive monkeys will realize there is almost always a comet circling Earth."

"That's good news!" I said. "If the comet will pass by in two hours, then she should be safe if we get her to tomorrow morning, right?"

Kimberly shook her head. "It's not that easy."

"I didn't say any of this was easy. We have a bunch of murdering demons after us. Surviving until morning will be a pain. But it's doable."

An orange glow came from the window, and I heard a familiar voice calling from outside the house. "HEY, OLLIE! Get out here!"

I peeked through the blinds to see Moloch and Balaam, holding a rocket launcher and a Gatling gun between them. The ice cream truck was on fire behind them.

"And bring the whelp!" Moloch screamed, resting the rocket launcher on his shoulder.

"You have ten seconds!" Balaam added, spinning up the Gatling gun.

"Speaking of, guys…" I turned around. "We have a problem."

CHAPTER 7

Even at my best, I wasn't confident that I could dodge a rocket launcher and a Gatling gun at the same time. *Also, what idiot burned their own car?* That ice cream truck they burned was their cruiser. It was clear now that they were more brawn than brains.

"Oh my god, oh my god, oh my god," Anjelica was repeating as I tried to think. Between her and the countdown from the moron twins outside, it was hard to concentrate.

"Nine," Moloch growled.

"What should we do?" Kimberly asked.

"Relax," Phil said, throwing his hands casually behind his head. "They can't get in here."

"Eight."

"How sure are you about that?" Kimberly asked.

"About exactly 86.4 percent," Phil said, scrunching his face for a moment while he ran numbers in his head.

"Seven."

"That's not very reassuring." I frowned.

"Six."

Anjelica peered out of the window. "Yeah, if somebody told me my birth control was only 86 percent effective, I would not trust it."

"Five."

"Amen," Kimberly said approvingly.

"Four."

"We need a plan!" I shouted.

"I don't see what you're worried about," Phil said. "My shields protected me from a Gamrillian laser cannon and got me through the Hygof asteroid belt. The only reason my confidence isn't higher is because I haven't tested them against Earthen weaponry."

"Three."

"Why not?" I asked.

"Two."

"This is a residential area," Phil said, throwing his hands in the air. "And loud noises are frowned upon."

"One!" Balaam screamed. "I'm looking forward to this!"

"Me too, brother!" Moloch shouted.

"I guess we're about to find out," Anjelica said, diving under the bed like it would save her from anything if a rocket launcher exploded in the room. "God, I hope you're right!"

"God has nothing to do with it. This is science, which means I actually trust it." Phil finished typing and pressed the escape key on his keyboard with a flourish. "Just watch."

I did watch, stomach tight in my throat, as the two demons unloaded their weapons at the house. A blue forcefield protected us from every bullet and absorbed every explosion until they had exhausted their supply and simply looked at the house with a confused expression. I turned to Phil, who seemed very pleased with himself.

"My turn," he said.

"What does that mean?" Kimberly asked.

"You'll see. Humans are so impatient."

Sure enough, he was right again. The earth quaked, and a half dozen submachine guns rose from under the house and began to fire on Balaam and Moloch as they ducked for cover.

"Getting the permits was extremely complicated for these weapons, but they turned out to be worth it."

"Are any of those bullets blessed by a priest?" I asked. "Or forged from the black metal of Hell?"

"No," he replied. "I didn't think I would have to ward off demons. Gangs and aliens, yes, but not demons. Perhaps, given our close working relationship, I should have. An oversight I will correct in the next build."

"You know those won't kill them, right?" Kimberly said.

"It doesn't have to kill them to be a deterrent," Phil said. "It just has to hurt."

"You are amazing!" Angelica said, throwing her arms in the air. "I vote we stay here until morning. Who's with me?"

"We can't," Kimberly said.

"What do you mean we can't?" I asked. "They're out there, and we're in here. Safe and secure."

"You haven't dealt with many Apocalypses, have you?" Kimberly said, raising an eyebrow.

"No, I haven't. Thank the gods."

"Lucky you." Kimberly sighed. "Let me explain, then. Anjelica is *an* antichrist. Sh—"

"Excuse me?" Anjelica said. "I am *the* antichrist."

Kimberly shook her head sadly at Anjelica. "Oh, honey. No. No, you aren't. There are dozens of you. This isn't even my first time this year dealing with one of you."

"It's true!" Phil added. "We have a whole database devoted to antichrists. Wanna see?"

"No," I replied. "That doesn't sound like a good time."

"Speak for yourself!" Phil exclaimed.

"You look sad," Kimberly said to Anjelica. It was true. The poor girl looked like all the wind had been knocked out of her sails. "What's wrong?"

Anjelica kicked at the floor. "It's stupid."

"Try me anyway."

"I just…kind of thought I was special, and now…I know I'm not."

Kimberly wrapped her in a hug. Neither of them looked comfortable in it. "Oh, honey, that does sound stupid. So, so stupid. And vain, but it's okay. If it makes you feel better, you are special. Out of like four billion people in the world, you are one of a small number that could end everything with your crazy powerful blood. Even though there are hundreds of antichrists in the world, that's still just a fraction of a fraction of a fraction of a percentage of the number of people in the world." She let Anjelica go. "Feel better now?"

"Yes." Anjelica dropped her head. "And that makes me shallow, which makes me feel worse."

"All right," I said. "Enough feel goodery. Explain why we can't just stay here until morning."

"Right," Kimberly said. "So, here's the thing with antichrists. They're like time bombs. If you use them, they can end the world, but if you don't—" Kimberly made an explosion sound with her mouth and mimicked a bomb explosion with her hands. "—they still explode. It's just they only take themselves out."

"Wait," Anjelica said. "Are you saying I'm going to die tonight whether I start the Apocalypse or not?"

"Not necessarily," Kimberly said. "You'll only die if we don't work fast."

Phil snaked over Kimberly's shoulder. "There's a potion that can rid you of the explosive quality in your blood—if you drink it before sunrise."

"Explosive quality?" Anjelica asked, holding out her hands and looking over her limbs.

"Think about how much energy it would take to open a portal to Hell. All of that rests in you right now. We have to diffuse it, quickly."

"Then why are we still talking about it?" I clapped my hands together. "Let's get to fixing it."

"Good plan." Kimberly looked over at Phil. "Can you pull up the Apocalyptic Apothecary, please?"

Phil tapped on his computer, but it was dead. The lights in the house went out. "Bad news. That little attack seemed to have fried my system and drained my generator. It will take some time to reboot everything."

"How long?" Kimberly asked.

Phil shrugged. "I don't know. Human technology is fickle. If you recall, this system has never been properly tested."

"Then we'll have to do this the hard way."

"What's the hard way?" I asked.

Kimberly stormed for the door. "I have a backup library filled with everything I've ever found about the Apocalypse and Hell. The Apocalyptic Apothecary is a book in that library, so I just have to do the legwork to find it and copy the recipe."

"Great!" I said. "Let's go."

"No way," Kimberly said, pulling open the door. "You are both demons, so you can't come with me. I don't want you memorizing the location of my secret lair and jumping to it with your demon buddies."

"I don't have demon buddies!" Anjelica said, indignant.

My eyes narrowed. "How do you know I'm a demon?"

"I can smell your kind like burnt bacon." She tapped her nose. "I've been killing demons for years." She took a pinch of pink powder from a pouch on her belt, where she also kept two daggers. "Phil has the address where to meet me. Give me thirty minutes."

"Why can't we just stay here?" Anjelica asked.

"I don't know when Phil's system is going to be back online, and I don't want to leave you here like sitting ducks."

"We're not sitting ducks," I said. "I could fight those two goons with my bare hands if they came back."

"I'm sure you can, but how about this?" She leaned in toward me. "I don't want to put Phil in danger. I know he can handle himself, but I worry about him, okay?"

I looked over at Phil, who was waving at me. "Fine. We'll meet you there. Don't be late."

She dropped her pink powder and vanished. I knew that it was pixie dust from the saccharine smell that lingered in the air when she was gone. The stuff was notoriously hard to come by. An ounce of it could fetch $100,000 on the open market, and she had at least two pounds of it. If I were a different kind of person, I might jump her and take the dust, but alas. I actually had morals.

I walked back to Phil, who handed me a sheet of paper with an address on it. "You've been here before, yes?"

"The Palomino?" I recognized the address immediately. "Oh yes. I know it well." I looked back at him. "Are you going to be okay?"

He nodded. "Of course. I have plenty of analog weapons inside, and they have a simple point and click interface."

"Okay," I said, turning from him against my better judgment. "I'll see you soon. Don't take any stupid risks."

"That's more your domain," Phil replied. "I prefer chances that have a high probability of survival."

I grabbed Anjelica and walked toward the edge of the yard, reaching into my pocket along the way. It would have been much easier to have a wand, but I could create a portal with just my hands.

"*Porth i'r 46ain ganolfan.*" I held out my hands, and a green, swirling portal appeared in front of us. "Come on."

I pushed Anjelica through the portal, took one last look at Phil, who yawned and stretched, and then I disappeared into the ether.

CHAPTER 8

The portal led us into an alley between the 46th police precinct and a sandwich shop. It always smelled of fresh-baked bread and roast beef around there, which was a big improvement over the usual piss and garbage that perfumed most alleys in the city.

"Why would Kimberly want us to meet her here?" Anjelica asked as I pulled her toward the entrance.

"She wouldn't. I have to make a stop first."

A pair of buttoned-up officers sauntered out of the precinct. I turned away from them as they brushed past me. I didn't have any outstanding warrants, and technically, I wasn't breaking any laws, but I was certainly criminal adjacent and didn't want to be recognized. I spent most of my time avoiding the police, so walking into the belly of the beast meant I was really desperate.

"Why are we here, then?" Anjelica asked.

"Do you always ask so many questions?" I snapped.

"Always," she replied. "Even if I didn't, it's a valid question. I mean, yesterday I didn't even know I was a demon, and now I'm walking into a police precinct with one after coming out of a frigging portal. How is that not a cause for questions?"

"You're right. It is. Now shut up." I turned from her to the desk jockey. "Hello. I'm looking for Officer Skyler Vogel. Can you tell me if he's working?" I knew he was, but it seemed like the polite thing to do. I was laying on the politeness thick.

The slovenly young woman behind the desk stopped stuffing her face with a powdered donut like a frigging cliché and turned to her computer. The dust coated the front of her uniform like snow on Christmas morning. "Yeah, he's working. Third floor. I'll buzz you in."

"Just like that?" My eyebrows shot up. "Don't you need—you know what, thank you." There was a loud buzz in the hallway, and a gray door clicked open at the end of it. I flung it open and climbed to the third floor. Most districts in the country didn't have any computers, but Los Angeles had invested early and then tasked Skyler with implementing the system, giving him a back door to every case file and dirty little secret in the whole city.

There were a half dozen buzzing servers and hundreds of wires hanging everywhere on the third floor. I couldn't help thinking we had stepped into a bad sci-fi movie instead of an annoying action-adventure one, which was what my life felt like at the moment.

I made my way through the cramped room until I heard skittering sounds up ahead. Skyler was an Arachne, blessed with eight arms and a thousand eyes—a perfect candidate to have eyes on the whole city. His disguise was particularly good, but he really hated wearing it, which meant he had probably taken it off when he was alone.

"Skyler," I shouted. "It's just me. Ollie." I looked over at Anjelica. "And a friend."

"Aw," Anjelica said. "I'm glad we're friends."

"What did I say about shutting up?" I growled.

"Jesus Christ, man." His bucktoothed face popped out from behind a filing cabinet. His thick glasses, three sizes too big for his face, made his eyes look enormous even inside his costume. A second later, my eyes refocused, and I saw the hairy arachnid under the mask.

"What are you doing here, man?" He was frowning. "I told you never to come to my place of business."

"And I respect that, but people have tried to kill me twice tonight, and the last place I called you from got shot up by two demons, so you'll forgive me if I'm not in a rule-following type of mood."

"I don't like it, man," he said. "I'll have to fine you. There will be a 30 percent increase in price for all jobs until the rest of the year. That way, you learn your lesson."

"Whatever. I'm good for it." I wasn't good for it, not until I found the demon trying to hunt me down and shook the money out of him with extreme prejudice, but I wasn't about to say that. "Did you find anything?"

Skyler pushed up his glasses. "The monster you're tracking—it's like he doesn't exist." He slid across his cluttered desk and pulled out a file. "At least not on any system connected to the grid. The demons you told me about, though, Balaam and Moloch? They're your standard guns for hire. Go to the highest bidder."

I grabbed the file from his outstretched arms. "So, they wouldn't stay with this guy if he wasn't paying?"

"Not even for a couple of days. These two are the real deal. They go back to the beginning. They were there for the Garden, Sodom, Gomorrah, and even followed Lucifer out of Heaven. Real badasses." Skyler saw Anjelica behind me. "Is that her? The antichrist."

"An antichrist," I said, examining the file Skyler handed to me. "This says their last known residence was Seattle. Do you know who they worked for?"

"A rat king named Benny. He was pissed when they left, too. They went right in the middle of a big score. Really blew up in his face. His crew's been recovering ever since."

I smiled. "Sounds like he has reason to talk to me."

Skyler shrugged. "As good as any, though I doubt he'll enjoy it any more than I do."

"Thanks."

"Address is in the file." He grabbed me when I turned away. "And my fee?"

I swallowed. "You'll get it this week. Come on. Have I ever stiffed you before?" I reached into my pocket and pulled five hundred out of my stash, and put it on the desk. "This is a down payment. Once I handle this, I'll be back."

"And what if you die?"

"If only, Skyler. If only." I sighed. "Do you really think I would be that lucky?" I didn't have much time before we had to meet Kimberly, so I rushed Anjelica down the stairs and back into the alley.

"Porth i 604 10fed rhodfa, Seattle."

"Stop!" Anjelica shouted, pulling free. "This is not okay. You can't just drag me along like a lost puppy."

"Can't I? I wouldn't even be in this mess if it wasn't for you."

"That's not true!" Anjelica squealed. "You were being shot at way before you met me."

I sighed. "You're right. I'm sorry."

"You say that too much. Just…stop treating me like a kid. I am going to die in a few hours, and I'd rather not be dragged around like a lost lamb."

"All right." She was right. "That's fair."

"Where are we going?" she asked.

I was so used to just doing things without having to justify myself, but she deserved the truth. It was annoying.

"To talk to this rat and try to figure out who this demon is who's trying to kill you."

"But we're still going to meet, Kimberly after?"

"Of course," I replied. "I promise."

"Good, because I don't want to die."

"I don't say this to many people, but I don't want you to die either."

Anjelica smiled. "That was almost nice."

"I'm trying. Now, can we go?"

"Absolutely."

We walked into the portal and reappeared in front of a drug store surrounded by nothing but the night air. I wasn't surprised to see the lights on inside, but I was surprised that a mobster would be so blatant as to use the word "drug" in a huge sign hanging over their shell company. Some criminals just liked thumbing their nose at the law, while others were so powerful, they really did rise above it. I liked the first type but hated the second. I wondered where Benny fit into that spectrum.

"Ten minutes," I said to Anjelica. "This is the last stop, okay?"

"Then we'll find Kimberly?" Anjelica asked.

"I promise."

She followed behind me as we walked into the store. A bell jingled when I pushed open the door, and a smiling woman in a white lab coat waved from behind the counter, her bun pulled so tight it nearly gave me a migraine just looking at it.

"Welcome to Ratinger Drug, Seattle's only all-night pharmacy. Do you have a prescription to pick up or a new script we need to fill?"

I shook my head. "Neither, I'm afraid. We're looking for Benny."

She pursed her lips. "Oh, I'm sorry. There's nobody named Benny working here. You must have the wrong place. Just little ole me, I'm afraid."

"I know you're lying." I stepped toward the counter. To her credit, she didn't flinch or back into the shelves of drugs that hung behind her, packed with everything from Nyquil to codeine. "We're not cops. We just need to see Benny. It's about two of his me—"

Her smile dropped. "I told you there's no Benny on the payroll here."

"Oh really? Not even if I have information about Balaam and Moloch?"

Her face was hard and stern, nothing like the warm, gentle welcome we received. "How do you know those names?"

"Because they're trying to kill me, and I know where they are right now, to a degree of accuracy I think would be very interesting to your boss."

"That changes things." The woman reached under the table and a secret door unlatched in the row of drugs behind her. She pulled it open. "End of the hall."

"Thank you."

I followed the hallway downhill as it jutted to the left and then twice to the right before it broke into a big underground room with three sewer pipes leading out into different directions. The stench was overwhelming, but it covered the odor from the ball of rat parts and hair that made up the rat king in the center of the room, sitting behind a rotted and warped wooden desk. At least fifty rats skittered and crawled around to make up the shape of the mutant rat that turned to me.

"I hear you have information on two traitors." When it spoke, three different pitches echoed and melded together like a bad anime overdub. "Tell me where they are."

"I will, but first, I need your help."

"Of course. Turnabout is fair play, after all. What can I help you with?"

There wasn't time for tact. "Who hired them away from you?"

"That is a long, complex story, filled with many twists and turns, but in the end, we do not know. We thought we had him, then he slipped through our fingers in Budapest. As of yet, we don't know where he popped up again. I have a feeling you do."

"I do," I answered. "But if I know more than you do, then I think we're done here."

Benny let out a horrible squeak, and a hundred rats appeared from the sewers, filling the room in every direction. I had never fought a hundred rats before, but I took a fighting stance and prepared to be attacked.

"No fighting," Anjelica said. "You promised. Ten minutes."

I sighed. "Okay, you're right." I dropped my fists. "I'll tell you where they are. Hell, I'll take care of them for you, but I need to know who hired them and who's trying to kill me."

Benny let out a whistle, and the rats receded. "I promise, if I get my revenge on these two pieces of dirt, I'll get you your name and an army to chase their boss down. I guarantee it."

I nodded. "Good. They're in Los Angeles."

"Wonderful," Benny squealed. "And you're certain you can take care of them?"

"They'll be dead by morning."

"I would be most appreciative. Their blatant disrespect has caused me all sorts of headaches."

"Don't call me, I'll call you. I have work to do."

Back outside, I looked down at my watch. "See, that wasn't even ten minutes. I'm very efficient."

"Yes, yes. I'm so glad you are playing fast and loose with my life," Anjelica said.

"Fast and loose?" I scoffed. "Kimberly said thirty minutes, and it's only been twenty."

Anjelica grabbed my hand. "Let's just go, please. My insides feel like they are ready to explode."

"You got it. *Porth i Palamino Lankershim.*" The portal opened in front of me. "Come on, kid. Let's fix you up."

CHAPTER 9

When I was eighteen, I left home to make a name for myself. Mom didn't much care as I was well-built to survive and thrive in a world of humans, even though she didn't much like the way that I did it. That was important to her—not just that I did something, but that I did it in the appropriate way. I thought the right way could suck an egg. After all, she did everything right and still ended up with me, the bane of her existence.

I hadn't been on the street for long before I got in a fight with a group of teen toughs and beat their asses something fierce. That's when he found me and brought me to the Palomino. He wasn't relevant to the story except as a catalyst for my new life. I didn't even remember his name, but I owed him everything. He brought me to the hub of monster underworld activity in Los Angeles and introduced me around to the right people at the right time. Somebody noticed when I knocked out his teeth for trying to slip his hand up my shirt, and they offered me a job. That job led to another, which led to another, which led to a half dozen more, and soon I was making more money as a street urchin than I would have if I got proper work.

Naturally, Mom didn't approve and said that it must be the demon in me who was comfortable making money the slimy way. She really hated demons, which was probably why she hated me so much. Point was, I knew the Palomino and its reputation quite well.

Nobody in front of the Palomino batted an eye at the fact that Anjelica and I just emerged from a portal, which was why I loved it there.

"I gotta say," Anjelica said when she stepped out of the portal, "that is so cool. You can just do that all the time?"

"I can," I said with a stiff nod. "I prefer to drive, though."

"Why?" she asked. "I would never ever drive if I could just portal everywhere."

The Palomino was a safe place, and there were frighteningly few of those. Even fewer that existed out in the open. Billy and Tommy paid good money to keep it that way. It wasn't that there weren't normals that came into the bar, they just tended not to remember what they saw when they left the parking lot, except that they had a good time.

"You get bored of it sooner or later, like with all magic. I like having the time to think, and Lily gave me that."

"Lily…was your car?"

"Is my car. She's not dead yet. I just don't know where she is right now." I sighed solemnly. "She was the best car I ever had. Those monsters better not have ruined her."

There weren't a lot of places for a country music fan to have a good time in Los Angeles, and the Palomino was the best one for fifty miles in any direction. People came from all around to play the stage, and it was known that if a big act was playing, the monsters laid low, but most other nights, it was a free-for-all.

"Hey," Anjelica said as we walked up to the entrance. "You aren't really a demon, are you?"

The bouncer at the front had gills like a fish, and he didn't raise an eyebrow when he overheard Anjelica's question. I paid him with part of the wad I got earlier, and he stamped our hands.

The band was a country music act called the Whosiers, which I assumed meant they were from Indiana, probably traveling across the country building a name for themselves. Either that or the poor shmucks uprooted themselves and moved to Los Angeles, city of dreams—a thousand dreams dashed every day. Of course, it could have also been some stupid writer who liked puns and decided to try his luck in a band in his copious spare time from not having a job.

"What'll it be?" a squid monster said from behind the bar.

"Two whiskey cokes," I said, holding up two fingers.

"No way that girl is 21," he said, walking over with an eye on Anjelica.

"They're both for me," I replied. "What do you want, Anjelica?"

Some girls have resting bitch faces. She had a resting sweet smile face. "Can I have a Shirley Temple?"

"Sure, kid," the squid monster replied with a curt, abrupt smile.

I rolled my eyes. "You gotta be the least demonic demon I've ever met."

"Well, I only found out I was a demon this morning. Before then, I was just a kid and a pretty happy one at that."

"That's gotta be rough."

She shrugged. "It was rougher being kidnapped, and it will be rougher if I die by sunrise, but yeah, it's not the best night of my life. I did meet you, though, and that's been rather pleasant, except when it hasn't been." She took a cherry from the bowl behind the bar and sucked on it. "What about you? When did you find out you were a demon?"

"I've always known," I said. "My mom wouldn't let me forget it."

The bartender placed the Shirley Temple down in front of Anjelica.

"Thank you!" She pointed to the cherries behind the bar. "Hey, are those free? I'm starving."

The squid monster rightly chuckled that time and slid them toward her. "Eat away."

"Thanks, mister," she said with her mouth full of cherries, then turned back to me. "What's with you two anyway? Why does your mom hate you?"

I grabbed one of the two drinks the bartender put in front of me. "My family situation is complicated, kid."

"And mine isn't?" She swallowed her mouthful of cherries. "I'm the antichrist, for crying out loud. No, correction. I'm AN antichrist." She looked down at her lap. "I know you hate questions, but I'm just trying to figure this out. Can you please help me?"

"I'm already helping you."

"More. Can you please help me more?"

"All right, kid." I tilted my head back and finished my first drink. "But I'm going to need more than this." I picked up the second drink. "Luckily, I have another one." I sighed loudly. "The truth is I'm not quite a demon. Not really."

"What does that mean? You either are a demon, or you aren't, right?"

I shook my head. "I'm a Nephilim. Half angel, half demon. The ultimate bastard child of the universe. Heaven doesn't want me. Hell won't keep me. Cursed to roam the Earth forever."

"That's terrible. Which parent was the angel?"

"My mom."

"I can see that." Anjelica nodded. "She looks like the type. She has a real ethereal way about her."

"She knows it, too." I took another sip of my drink. "When God found out what she'd done, he flipped out and kicked her out of Heaven."

"Why would he do that?" Anjelica asked. "I thought God was cool."

"He is decidedly not cool." I took a longer drink this time. "Angels are supposed to be pure. Not only did my mom have sex, she had sex with a demon. It's bad enough when a male demon has sex with a succubus or inferi and creates a half-breed. At least they can hide their shame with denial. My mom, though, she brought her shame with her everywhere for nine months. God couldn't abide that. So, he booted her." I finished my second drink. "That she didn't abort me was a minor miracle. Another thing she will never let me forget."

Anjelica placed her hand on mine. "I'm so sorry."

"It's okay," I replied. "It was a long time ag—"

"Well, well, well…" I spun around to see Blezor holding a shotgun a foot from my tits. "Fancy seeing you here. Where's my dagger, honey bear?"

Couldn't I catch a single break?

CHAPTER 10

Disarming an armed assailant in a crowded building was a dicey move, especially one as unhinged as Blezor. If I spun and grabbed for the gun, it might go off and harm an innocent monster or even Anjelica. I couldn't risk that. I had to play it safe and look for an opening when I could thrash him without injuring anyone else.

"Hey!" the squid monster bartender shouted. "Take it outside."

I almost laughed, but that was the kind of place the Palomino was. The bartender was never going to help me. He just wanted to make sure that if I was going to fight, it didn't start a riot—or make a mess. The sea of people parted as we made our way toward the front door. Everybody we passed acted more inconvenienced than scared by a gunman with a hostage. Anjelica trailed behind, her eyes bulging. Outside, Blezor pressed his gun into my back. "You're going to wish you never met me."

"Honestly, I already wish that," I said. "I wished that less than ten minutes after I started talking to you."

He jabbed me with the barrel of the gun. "Then why did you sleep with me?"

"Ew, you slept with this creep?" Anjelica said. "I thought you had standards."

"Why would you think that?" I said. "Okay, I do have standards, usually at least. It's just that—"

"Shut up!" Blezor said, his voice breaking like he was about to cry. I looked back at him, eyeing his hands in the hope he would let up his grip on the gun, but he was white-knuckling the grip.

Blezor's monster truck towered over the rest of the cars in the parking lot.

"I kind of feel like I should have seen that when we came in," I muttered to Anjelica.

"Yeah, we really blew that one," Anjelica replied, nodding.

"I just don't understand, honey bear," Blezor said, his voice trembling. "Why would you betray me?"

"Don't call me that." I wheeled on him. "I already told you, it wasn't personal. I needed the dagger. You had the dagger. It was as simple as that."

"I can't believe I was nothing but a mark to you. I shared things with you that I never shared with anyone else."

"I never asked you to do that. And also, really? I mean, we barely talked."

"We had a connection!" he screamed, the gun shaking as I inched backward. I wanted to put Anjelica behind me. A shotgun blast wouldn't hurt me much, and I doubted Blezor went to the trouble of dousing them in virgin blood or using consecrated bullets. He seemed too impulsive for that. But Anjelica was new at this, and she wasn't taking the hint. Her wide eyes were simply staring at him, transfixed with fear, out in the open. She was half-demon, so she might have been fine, but there was an equally good chance that the human side of her bled out, and I didn't like those odds.

"Tell me I was more to you!" he shouted.

"Just do it," Anjelica whispered. "Even if it's a lie."

"It's not a lie!" Blezor stomped his feet like a tantruming child. "It's not a lie!"

"I'm sorry," I said, looking him in the eyes through my sunglasses. "I don't know what you think I am or what you want from me, but I'm not that person. I'm not a good person. I never claimed to be. I'm just trying to survive. So, no, you were nothing more than a mark to me."

Blezor took a step forward. "You're a bit—"

The top of a metal trash can smashed into Blezor's face with a big clang. Kimberly stepped out from the shadows outside of the club. "I thought he would never shut up."

I looked down at the unconscious Blezor. "That's not even the worst thing about him."

"Should we kill him?" Kimberly asked.

"If I wanted him dead, I'd have already killed him. He still has some use to me."

"How?" Anjelica asked.

"He still loves me, and I can manipulate that."

"Wow," Kimberly said, shaking her head. "You really are a terrible person."

I shrugged. "Except I'm really not a person at all." I turned to her. "Did you get what we need?"

She pulled the list from her pocket. "Yup. Here it is. Ingredients and recipe."

I snatched it from her. "Took you long enough. I thought you said thirty minutes. It's been almost forty."

"Oh, I've been here," Kimberly said, her eyebrows raised. "I just wanted to see if you were good enough to save yourself. You aren't."

"I was biding my time."

"Sure you were."

"I was jus—"

"Hey!" Anjelica said. "Not to make this all about me, but I'm the one who's going to die when the sun comes up, so it's really not cool to hear you arguing about taking your sweet time. God, you are both so selfish."

"You're right," Kimberly said. "I'm sorry."

"Ugh. I am so sick of you two saying you're sorry. I don't care. Sorry doesn't matter. Words are meaningless." She slapped her hands together. "Let's have some action."

"I mean, did you already forget—again—that I saved your life?" I replied.

"And you put it in danger just as much!" Anjelica said. "I don't even care. I know you are both doing your best…I just was hoping it would be better."

"We have the list for the potion," Kimberly said. "That's something."

"You're right." Anjelica pressed her fingers against the bridge of her nose. "You guys are doing great. Well, maybe not great, but better than I could do by myself. I'm just crabby because tons of people are trying to kill me, I haven't slept all day, and my insides feel like they are about to explode."

"That's fair," Kimberly said, nodding. "It must be hard."

"It's so so so so hard!" Anjelica whined. "But now I'm over it. What's on that list you brought us, anyway?"

I held it into the light. "Four ounces boiled intestine from a monstrous spider, three teaspoons pureed werewolf bane, five saffron stems from a dragon's garden, two tablespoons coarsely ground wraith liver, one-ounce peeled skin from a zombified human, and a pinch of pixie dust."

Anjelica grimaced. "I'm supposed to eat that?"

"Only if you don't want to die," Kimberly said with a shrug.

"I super don't want to die. But I also super don't want to drink that."

"Tough decision." Kimberly's words oozed with sarcasm. It was one of the few moments that I thought I could actually like her.

"Most of this shouldn't be a problem," I said. "But I haven't seen a dragon in ages."

"I have that covered," Kimberly said. "I picked some up from my dragon friend."

"You're friends with a dragon?" Anjelica asked in awe. "That's so awesome. Man, this night is a roller coaster of emotions."

"He's more like a father to me," Kimberly replied. "A very annoying father."

"*Porth i Fasnach apothecary Mortar and Pestle*," I said, and a portal opened in front of me. "Shall we quit complaining and get this over with?" I stuffed the list in my pocket and pushed Anjelica toward the portal. "You're a pain in the ass, but I don't want you to die."

"That's sweet, in a weird way," Anjelica said.

I smirked. "That's not a very common sentiment, so I appreciate it."

CHAPTER 11

"No way, Ollie," the grizzled old hound said from behind the counter of his shop, shaking his floppy ears in the air. "You are like toxic ooze. Get out of my shop."

It was the third apothecary shop I'd been to in a row that refused to work with me. Whoever was trying to kill me was foreboding enough to put the fear of the gods into some of the most powerful monsters in town.

"Come on, Digger," I replied. Digger used to be a burrow hound in a previous life before a magical fungus gave him sentience, and the ole dog was never the same. Licking himself wasn't a good enough life for him, so he set out across the world, winding up in Los Angeles. The city was a magnet for the broken and the forlorn, and nobody found salvation within its borders.

"I'm staying out of this, kid," he grumbled. "I know I'm on my way out, but I still got a couple of good years left, and I'd like to use all of them." He came around the counter. "You're lucky I don't call the scumbags that threatened me and tell them you're here." He pointed his paw at me. "You should be thanking me."

"Thank you for screwing me over," I said. "You realize this girl is going to die, right?"

Digger looked from me to Anjelica. "I'm sorry for that, but better you than me."

"Cold," Anjelica said. "I guess I can't argue with that, though. I would rather you die than me, too."

"Don't be so understanding," Kimberly snapped. "You're supposed to get mad."

"I want to," Anjelica said, gesturing towards Digger. "But he's just so cute."

"It's a blessing and a curse." The old dog rubbed his ears. "I really am sorry."

"Where am I supposed to go then?" I asked. "If you're not going to help me, who will?"

The dog's ears perked up. "What about Greta? Or Sal? They always did like money more than their lives."

I shook my head. "They turned me away, too."

"I was your third choice. That hurts, Ollie." He hobbled forward, his old bones creaking. "There's only one other shop I can think of that would even have a chance of carrying everything on your list."

He couldn't have been talking about— "Kitsune."

Digger wagged his tail. The two of them once had a thing. "I know you don't get along, but she's hard up for cash, and she's not picky about her clients these days."

I rolled my eyes. "She's also dumb."

"All the better," Digger said.

"Thanks for nothing." I waved him off on my way out the door. Anjelica and Kimberly ran after me.

"This isn't going well," Kimberly said. "We're running out of time, you know?"

"I know!" I shouted. "I'm trying here."

"Does anyone in this town like you?" Kimberly asked.

"Not as much as they like their lives, clearly. I have another beat on a place, but the owner…she and I aren't the best of friends."

"See my previous question," Kimberly said. "Does anyone like you?"

I opened a portal, and we headed to the only other apothecary in Los Angeles worth anything. There wasn't another quality one until Portland, and it didn't have nearly the selection. I was getting desperate, and if Kitsune couldn't help me, then I would have to take more drastic measures.

I will admit that the main reason I didn't love Kitsune was her name. You can't just name yourself the thing you are. That would be like me being named Nephilim or Kimberly being named Pixie. It was just dumb.

Kitsune had her head stuck so far up her own ass that she named herself the thing that she was so that everyone knew she was a fox-human hybrid whose Kitsune soul bonded with her as a baby, giving her foxlike ears and three tails—and she was so smug about it. On second thought, it wasn't the name. It's just that the name stood for every conceited part of her that I hated.

She owned Kitsune Apothecary in Koreatown, and her shop stank like incense even more than a normal apothecary. She stood tall as she glared over my list. "I think I have most of this stuff, but I haven't seen a dragon in ages."

"Don't worry about that or the pixie dust," Kimberly said.

"We should really cross those off the list," Anjelica said. "To stop confusion."

The Kitsune looked through the shelves behind her, moving boxes around and looking behind them. "What are you brewing, Ollie? You and your…friends."

"That's none of your business," Kimberly replied.

Kitsune paused her search. "I know. I was just being polite." She continued rooting around on the shelf. "Besides, I already know what you're making."

"How?" I asked.

"Would you say you're good at your job?" she asked.

"The best."

"So am I," she replied. God, she was conceited. "Which one of you is the antichrist?"

"Uhhh, should we really answer that?" Anjelica asked. "Cuz—"

She waved her hand dismissively. "Never mind. I don't care." She placed a small vial on the counter. "Here's the wraith liver." Next, she set down a sardine tin. "And the skin." It was nearly rusted through, and the label was ripped off. "It doesn't say it, but you are going to want to julienne this skin. Otherwise, it's going to be slimy. Like a slug." She walked out from the counter. "I have to go in the back for the rest. I'll be right back."

She wasn't gone a minute when Kimberly turned to me with fear in her eyes. "I don't like this."

"Most people don't like waiting."

"I hate it," Anjelica added. "Especially since my tummy is on fire right now."

"I don't like it either, but that's not what I'm talking about," Kimberly said after a painfully long silence. "There's something about her that puts me on edge. Plus, she's taking too long,"

"It hasn't even been two minutes," I said, glancing at the clock. I was a little nervous, too. "She's gotta search for each one. It's not like these ingredients grow on trees."

"Thank god." Anjelica stuck out her tongue in disgust. "Those would be disgusting trees." She bent down to get a better look at the ingredients. "I seriously don't want to put that in my mouth."

"We'll blend it with kale, bananas, and peanut butter. It will taste like a milkshake."

She made a face. "But I'll know."

"Better than dying."

"Is it?" She rubbed her stomach.

Kitsune burst out from the curtain that separated the store from the back room. "Found it!" She placed a glowing blue vial on the table. "Werewolf bane."

"Wonderful," I said.

"That's the good news," Kitsune said. "The bad news is that I don't have any boiled spider intestine. Only dried. I put in a call to my friend, who confirmed she got some fresh this morning. She's boiling them up as we speak." She typed into her register. "That'll be thirty-two thousand. I rounded down because you're a good customer."

I certainly wouldn't call me that, but I didn't have the kind of money to pay full price. Not anymore. I pulled out the only card that wasn't maxed out and hoped it swiped through. Anjelica better appreciate living.

"Are you kidding?" Anjelica said. "That's a fortune! And for what? This gross stuff?"

"It's very rare, and it's the best."

"Do you know what that word means?" Anjelica asked. "Cuz this stuff definitely doesn't look like the best."

"It'll fix you right up and prevent you from dying, so...It does look disgusting, though," I said.

"Will it fix me, though? Cuz I definitely don't want to do this only for it not to work. I would rather die than have this be my last meal."

Kitsune folded her arms across her chest. "Of course, it will work. Just make sure to drink every last drop, antichrist, and you'll be right as rain come sunup."

"Oh man, I'm glad you finally said it," Anjelica said. "I was getting so nervous you didn't know what we were trying to do, and I was going to take some mystery liquid and turn into a chicken or something."

"I told you I knew." Kitsune eyed the clock behind her. It was four-thirty in the morning. "Oof. You're cutting it close. You're lucky it's the Solstice. That'll buy you a couple more hours."

"Thanks for the kind words, but nothing about tonight is lucky."

"I don't know about that. My friend owns the best sushi restaurant in Santa Monica. Play your cards right, and she might even make you some food and It. Is. Divine!"

CHAPTER 12

The portal let us out in front of the sushi restaurant of Kitsune's friend. There was a big window in front of the shop that let us see inside. Cars passed quickly on the street behind us, and the light from their headlights illuminated the dark restaurant, where a funny-looking parrot stood prepping for the next day.

When I went for the door, Kimberly stayed my hand. "I really don't like this."

"I'll admit it's not ideal," I replied. "But unless you want to fight a monstrous spider yourself, this is our best bet."

She crossed her arms over her chest. "I could beat a monstrous spider."

"Me too, but I can't find one, beat it, and boil it proper before sunrise. Could you?"

Her arms dropped back to her sides. "Good point."

"Then this is our option, even if it is a trap." I pushed the door open.

"Please tell me they don't put spider intestines into their sushi," Anjelica said. She was looking a little green.

Kimberly rubbed Anjelica's back. "Some people like exotic meat, and I've had tripe before. It's not so bad."

"That seals it. I'm never eating again."

"I thought you wanted sushi for your last meal," I teased her. "This might be it."

"She's right." Kimberly pushed the girl inside. "If we don't get that intestine, you won't have to worry about whether it's disgusting cuz you'll be dead."

"I don't like either of those options."

The harried-looking parrot stood six feet tall behind the sushi counter. She looked up from the halibut she was cutting. "You Ollie?"

"I am."

She pointed her knife to the back of the restaurant. "Intestine has to boil for three more minutes." She pointed to one of the red leather-covered wooden booths against the wall. "Meanwhile, sit, and I'll bring over some fresh sushi."

Anjelica held up her hand. "I'm not hungry."

The parrot aimed her knife at Anjelica. "I wasn't asking."

Kimberly pulled Anjelica toward the booth. "Thank you. We would love your fish."

"What if it's poisoned?" Anjelica whispered.

"It's not poisoned," the parrot replied with a glare. "It's delicious. People wait six months to eat here. This is your lucky night." She swung around the counter and brought over a plate of tuna, salmon, yellowtail, octopus, and eel. "Enjoy."

"Thank you," Kimberly said.

"It looks scrumptious," I added. It was the type of white lie that didn't hurt anyone.

"It is. I guarantee it," the parrot said with a bow. "I studied under Jiro Ono for five years."

"Who's that?" Anjelica said, confused.

The bird looked visibly distraught and sighed. "Just eat."

Kimberly reached across the table and grabbed a piece of tuna with her bare hands. She smelled it carefully, shrugged, and downed it in one bite.

"How does it taste?" I asked.

"Not like poison."

"You sure you don't want any?" I asked Anjelica. "You said you love this stuff."

"I'll eat if you eat," she replied. "But otherwise—"

"Might as well." I picked up a piece of yellowtail and took a sniff. I didn't trust Kimberly's pixie nose, but mine was more sensitive than hers. I could smell a dog pooping a half-mile away. The fish didn't smell like any poison I had ever come across before and, not to brag, but many people had tried to poison me.

"This really is great," I said, chewing loudly. "I mean, I don't normally like human food, but this is delightful. Is this why humans are always eating?"

"Duh," Kimberly said.

"You should try it," I said to Anjelica. "It is, dare I say, delectable."

"You really shouldn't talk with your mouth full," Anjelica said, eyeing a piece of tuna with desperate intent. "It's disgusting."

I covered my mouth and swallowed. "I'm sorry, but turnabout is fair play, after all. You did it to me earlier."

Kimberly grabbed another piece of sushi. "Your next meal is going to be disgusting, so you might as well have something delicious for balance."

"Well, all ri—"

The parrot squawked and emerged from the back room, holding a paper bag. "Here you go, one boiled spider intest—"

BAM! BAM! BAM! A spray of bullets crashed through the window and peppered the parrot with a dozen holes. I pulled Anjelica down under the table as the hail of bullets continued relentlessly.

"Holy Hell!" I screamed, knocking over the metal table and sliding it across the floor. "Get her into the kitchen!"

Kimberly grabbed Anjelica's hand and dropped a pinch of pixie dust, disappearing and reappearing behind the kitchen wall. The parrot's dead body sprawled in front of me, seeping blood onto the floor, her dead, glassy eyes staring at me, helpless. I waited for a lull in the gunfire, then inched across the floor, taking the paper bag from her cold, feathered hand.

"Are these the same demons from Phil's house?" Anjelica asked.

I popped my head up cautiously, but their headlights were blinding. "Probably. I can't be sure."

"What about Blezor?" Anjelica said.

"I think he would be crying more if it were him," I replied. "Besides, he's probably still unconscious."

"Oh yeah." She nodded. "You're probably right."

The gunfire stopped for a second, and I poked my head out again, this time catching the outline of what looked unmistakably like Moloch. "Yeah, it's those two demon dickheads."

"I guess that firefight at Phil's didn't kill them."

"I told you it wouldn't."

"Can we kill them now, please?"

"Working on it!" I kicked the table away and rose to my feet, mustering every ounce of energy I had inside of me. *"Gan yr hen dduwiau a'r newydd, teyrnaswch eich dialedd i lawr trwof fi!"*

A torrent of energy ripped through me and exploded out toward the demons. When it was over, there was nothing left of the storefront, and from where I stood all the way to the front door, the tiles were ripped completely out.

"That was awesome!" Anjelica said as I fell back, drained of all my energy.

"Thank you." I struggled to keep from collapsing onto the ground, until I couldn't.

"Ollie!" Anjelica wrapped her hands around my shoulders and lifted me off of the sticky floor. "Are you okay?"

"I'm fine," I lied. I felt like I had just had my soul ripped from my body. "I just need to rest for a minute."

"Unfortunately, I don't think we're going to have that chance," Kimberly said. The three of us watched as the light from a dozen cars flooded the restaurant, and shadowy demons with massive blasters emerged from them.

"I can't do that again," I said. "We need to go now. You have to take us."

"That I can do." Kimberly wrapped herself around us and threw a pinch of pixie dust. We vanished just as the bullets whizzed toward us. We reappeared in front of the Hollywood sign.

"Why are we here?" I asked. "How is this helpful?"

"I don't know!" Kimberly said. "I panicked, and it was the first place I could remember."

"It's a nice view of the city," Anjelica said, looking out on all of Los Angeles.

"Yeah," I said, pointing at the sun poking through the horizon. My stomach turned over inside my body. "And it's almost sunrise. Come on."

"Where are we going?" Kimberly said.

"Well, we can't go to your house, and I don't have a blender…so I guess we're going back to Mom's. This should be fun." I stood up. The blood rushed to my head, and I listed to the left for a moment before catching myself. "*Port i dŷ mam.*"

When the portal appeared, I fell into it, and on the other side, I stumbled into my mother's kitchen. She was standing at the counter, staring into her coffee pot.

"Jesus Christ!" Mom shouted, jumping six inches into the air. "We really need to lay some ground rules about how you enter my house."

"Tomorrow," I replied, trying to stop from vomiting. "We can talk about this tomorrow."

"What are you doing here?"

"Nice to see you, too, Mom," I said wearily. Kimberly brought Anjelica through the portal. When she was through, Anjelica grabbed her stomach and fell to the ground. "We're in bad shape, and we need your help."

"Of course you do. You only come when you need something. What is it this time? Spell gone wrong? Potion concocted—"

"Yes, a potion. It's a potion," I said breathlessly. "Quit guessing. I know potions are kind of your thing."

"Why do you say it like that?" she asked. "Such bitterness."

"I'm not bitter," I replied. "I've just had a bad—I need your help, Mom, and for once, I need you not to rake me over the coals for it."

She pointed to Anjelica. "I suppose this is to help your little demon friend?" She didn't wait for me to answer. "You know how I feel about demons."

"She's fifteen. She had no idea she was a demon until this morning when she was kidnapped, and she doesn't deserve to die. She's an innocent."

"HA!" Mom screamed the word, but she didn't laugh. "That's funny, coming from a demon."

"You know what, forget it."

"No," Mom said. She flipped her perfect hair back and let out a sigh. Then she swished her pink nightgown like it was a cape. She always had a flair for the dramatic, even in the dead of night. "I'll help. Where is the potion?"

"Right here—" I reached into my pocket. "Wait, where is the piece of paper?"

"Did you leave it with that miserable Kitsune?" Kimberly asked. "Do we really need it?"

"Absolutely," Mom said, indignant. "You have to add each ingredient in the right order, or it could destroy everything. Don't you know anything about potion making?"

"No," Kimberly said. "Not really." She looked at Anjelica, who had suddenly gotten very pale. "She doesn't look good. We don't have much time."

"Let's just hope it's with Kitsune and not burned up at that sushi restaurant." I called another portal and pulled Anjelica to her feet. "Come on, sweetheart. We're going to get you some help."

"Good seeing you as always," Mom said, turning back to her coffee pot. "I do hope you'll come for dinner soon."

"If I'm alive in a couple of hours," I replied, barely able to keep the room from spinning, "I might take you up on that."

CHAPTER 13

If there was one thing I could not abide, it was dishonesty. *I knew there was a reason I hated Kitsune.* I worked in a dangerous business, but there was honor among thieves. There had to be, or it was chaos, and yet I had been double, triple, and quadruple crossed enough times in one night to last a lifetime. If we could save Anjelica, I would make sure they all paid with their pound of flesh. Every last one of them.

But first, we had to save her.

We went through the portal and jumped into the shop of the duplicitous Kitsune who had stabbed us in the back. I knocked over a stand full of incense as I fell through the portal onto the ground. When I stood and caught eyes with the Kitsune, she snarled at me. "You! But how—"

"I was going to ask yo—" I pressed my hand against a stand.

"You sold us out!" Kimberly screamed at the Kitsune. I didn't have the energy to do so.

"I know that!" Kitsune screamed. "I was there! The question is, how are you still alive?"

"Because we're awesome. Where is the spell?" Kimberly pulled out a dagger from her belt. "Tell me, or I will rip you open!"

"I—I—I burned it when you left, okay?" Kitsune said.

"I am so going to gut you like a fish!" Kimberly screamed as I fell onto the table, the effects of the last few hours taking their toll on me.

"Uhhh," I groaned. My head was light and fuzzy.

"Are you okay?" Kimberly asked, holding a knife to Kitsune. "Cuz I really want to cut a bitch."

"Wait!" Kitsune shouted. "I can help her. I can help both of them, but not if I'm dead."

"How?" Kimberly grumbled.

"I know the potions they need." She tapped her head. "They're both in here, so if you kill me, they die with me."

Kimberly looked at me, then back at Kitsune. "Do it, and hurry, but you're not leaving my sight again. If that little girl dies, you do, too."

I rolled over, my face on the cool tile floor. It felt good against my burning skin. I had never used so much energy as I did with that spell in the sushi restaurant. Most days, all I would be thinking about was how I could return to full strength, but tonight—I turned my head to see Anjelica writhing on the floor, moaning, her demon face no longer a deep red but a light pink. *She was dying.*

"Hang on, kid. We're almost there."

"It hurts so much," she whimpered.

"I know, but we're so close. We're so close."

Kitsune shuffled out of the back room with a steaming cup of white goo. She yelped as Kimberly, following behind her, prodded a knife into her back. "Drink this."

She handed it to me, and I warily took it. "This is bull semen, isn't it?"

Kitsune reeled back, horrified. "Absolutely not. This is an ancient—it will restore your manna. It does taste a bit salty, though, if I'm being honest. The main ingredient is a special salt from the top of the—" She realized that nobody cared. "Just drink it. Every drop."

I looked over at Anjelica. "Looks like you're not the only person drinking something disgusting tonight." I tipped my head back and let the warm liquid slide down my throat with as few sips as possible. The quicker it was inside my gullet, the less I had to deal with the foul taste.

When it was all gone, I dropped the cup on the floor.

"How do you feel?" Kitsune asked.

"My head's no longer trying to spin off my body, so I think a little better. Thank you."

"Don't thank her!" Kimberly shouted. "She's the reason you ended up like that!"

I pushed myself to stand. "She's also the reason I feel better."

The Kitsune stammered. "I am really sorry. It's just so hard, all of this. The business is going under, and I—the reward was substantial. You must understand."

"That's no excuse," Kimberly growled. "It just shows your soul has a price."

"I never said it was." She sucked in a deep breath. "It's not an excuse, but it is my reason."

"One down, one to go." Kimberly pressed her dagger into Kitsune's cheek. "I sure hope you have a good memory. Otherwise, I'll splash your intestines all over this dusty floor." She looked at Anjelica, who was still whimpering, barely moving. She was not going to make it much longer. "Come on, we still have work to do."

They disappeared again behind the curtain, and I slid over to sit next to Anjelica. I pulled her head onto my lap, and she looked up at me, hopeless. "Can you take those stupid glasses off?"

She pawed at them. She had almost no strength left. I placed her hand in mine. "I don't like to do that. For anyone."

"I'm not anyone…" she eked out. "I'm me."

I smiled grimly at her and took off my glasses. I didn't show anyone my eyes—one crystal blue and the other a swirling red, demon and angel, a reminder every time I looked at myself in the mirror that I was a freak.

"Your eyes are super pretty," Anjelica said with a soft smile.

I snapped my head away from her. "You don't have to lie to me."

"I'm not lying." She took a deep breath. "They really are lovely. Striking, even."

It was hard, but I smiled at her, tears welling in my eyes. I didn't get attached often and never this quickly. I desperately didn't want Anjelica to die. "Thank you. My mother hated them."

"I'm sorry she screwed you up so bad."

"I hated her for it my whole life. She was just being her, and I'm just being me. We can't fight our nature. I can't hate her for that."

"You sure about that? What about Moloch and Balaam? Were they just being them, too?"

"Oh no, they suck. I hate them."

"…good." She struggled to speak, but it seemed to help her fight drifting away. "I thought angels were supposed to be all 'sugar and spice and everything nice' until tonight."

"She's not that kind of angel," I said, brushing the hair out of her face. "She's more the fire and brimstone reigning destruction on Sodom and Gomorrah type of angel."

"Ah. Those ones were less nice."

The drapes rustled, and Kimberly led Kitsune back into the room. She was holding a cup of black juice. "It's ready."

Anjelica was mostly dead weight, but with a grunt and the force of brute energy, I got her to her feet, stumbling forward. "Great. Let's end this."

She slammed into the counter as she tried to lift herself on wobbly legs, and Kitsune placed the glass in front of her. "Here you go."

"So, I just drink this, and it's over?" Anjelica slurred.

"No," Kimberly said. "Once you drink it, you won't die at sunrise, and you can't destroy the world. There's still a pack of bloodthirsty demons hunting you."

"Oh, right."

Kimberly patted her on the back. "One thing at a time, okay?"

"Right." Anjelica grabbed the drink. "One thing at a time."

I helped her lift the cup to her lips. "Bottoms up."

Anjelica tilted her head back. "Bottoms up."

The drink slid down her throat, assaulting my nostrils with its rank odor as the slimy liquid drained. I felt bad for the poor girl, but I still helped guide the glass higher into the air.

Finally, when it was done, Anjelica slammed the drink on the counter. "Done!"

I rubbed her back. "Feel any better?"

"Not really," she replied. "Except I really want to barf right now."

"Fight the urge," Kitsune said. "It takes time for the tincture to work, and if you throw up, this will have all been for nothing."

Kimberly pulled Kitsune toward the back room. "Stay with her. We have to call the demon who's trying to kill you."

"No way," I replied. "I've been looking for this son of a bitch all night. He took three million dollars from me. I am going to listen to this conversation."

"That's why you shouldn't come. You're too emotional."

"That wasn't a request. I'm coming. Deal with it."

"Fine," Kimberly sighed. "Let's go, then."

They led me into the back room of the apothecary. It was barely big enough for one person, let alone three of us.

"We're listening," I said. "Don't mess it up."

"And if you mess this up," Kimberly said, pushing the dagger into Kitsune's side. "We'll—"

"Kill me." Kitsune rolled her eyes. "I get it. Trust me, I have no interest in dying."

She picked up the phone and dialed a number into her rotary phone, a relic of a bygone age. Push-button phones had been out for over a decade.

"They came back," Kitsune said into the mouthpiece. I leaned in to hear the other end of the conversation, and for the first time, I heard his voice.

"Are they there now?" he asked, smoothly and casually, like he wasn't a sadistic, bloodthirsty prick.

"They are," Kitsune replied, trembling. "They're in the front, taking care of their friend."

"So, the demon girl is with them?" There was barely a hint of interest in his voice.

Kitsune nodded. "Yes, she's here."

"Do they suspect you?"

"No," she said. "I don't think they suspect me."

"We'll send men right now to yo—"

"No," she whispered. "If you do, they'll know it was me."

"But my love," the voice changed, from smooth to agitated, anger bubbling up with each passing word. "They already know it was you because they are there with you, listening, right now, to this very call. Tell your friends that they are not as clever as they think they are."

"No, but I di—" It was too late. Kitsune wasn't as good a liar as she thought she was, which made me like her slightly more.

"It's not your fault, my love, but duplicitousness must be punished. I promise not to hurt you…much." The man cleared his throat. "Now, this is very important, so I will say it slowly. My patience has worn thin with this charade. It ends now. Do you understand?"

"Yes," Kitsune replied, her eyes bouncing between each of us for confirmation. I had no idea what to do except listen to him talk. "I understand."

"Good," the voice continued. "Now, if you want to see your alien friend again, come to Griffith Park, in the parking lot of the observatory, in forty-five minutes."

Phil. They had Phil. I grabbed the phone from Kitsune. "Listen to me, you little shi—"

But it was too late. All I heard was the dial tone.

CHAPTER 14

Forty-five minutes was not a lot of time, but I could do a lot of damage with it given the proper motivation, and I was intensely motivated. I opened a portal and left Anjelica to recover with Kitsune and Kimberly while starting on a list of errands I needed to finish before my final battle with this prick who had kidnapped Phil and was trying to kill me.

First, I stashed the knife in a storage locker Kimberly kept in the city. That way, the demons couldn't just kill us on sight. Then, I teleported back to my apartment to recover a secondary wand I kept stashed within a pocket dimension in my bedroom. I would need it if shit hit the fan.

I lived in Santa Monica, in the penthouse of a nice building overlooking the ocean. The thing I liked most about the neighborhood was people smiled all the time like they were actually happy—contented. These were people who had found some secret to life and lived the life of their dreams. When I came around, their smiles faded, their shoulders shrunk, and their faces scrunched as the air left the room. I tried to be nice, but I was a dark cloud over their bright outlook. I was only capable of being so nice.

They whispered about how I could afford such an apartment. Little did they know I paid double their rent, in cash, so the landlord wouldn't ask any questions. Money wasn't an issue for me—at least not until today.

There was a bellman waiting in the elevator, but I took the stairs up to my apartment. I noticed something was wrong the minute I exited the stairwell. My door was hanging wide open, and the lock was busted. The edges were frayed and snapped, and the middle of the door had a dent in it where it had been smashed with something heavy.

Everything inside had been turned over and torn apart. I had nice taste in furniture. Some might have even called it elegant if I'd ever let anyone ever see it. I was quite particular that everything had its place. Sometime in the last day, somebody had ransacked the place. The couch had been gutted with a knife, and so had the bed. More importantly, they had somehow found my pocket dimension and snapped my wand in half, leaving it on the ground as a message that I was powerless against them. *I'll show them powerless.*

I looked down at my watch. Eighteen more minutes until the rendezvous. If I didn't have a wand, maybe I could raise an army. I made a portal and arrived back in Seattle at Benny's drug store. I didn't have time to be polite, so before the pharmacist could even address me, I leaped behind the counter. She wasn't quick enough to stop me before I pushed the button to unlock the secret door in the shelving and rushed down the hallway.

Benny hadn't moved from behind his warped desk. Even though I had been there just a couple of hours earlier, I had forgotten the horrendous stench. It made my eyes water and knocked me off balance at the sheer heinousness of it.

"You're back," Benny said, his voice echoing in a half dozen octaves at once. "Should I take that to mean what we agreed on is done? If so, I must commend your efficiency."

"Honestly, I don't know if I killed them yet. There was an explosion, and I vaporized two demons, but I'm not sure if I got them or not. And actually, I'm not here for that."

The rats skittered around inside Benny, forming two hands which Benny placed on his desk. "What are you here for, then?"

"I know where the snake that poached Moloch and Balaam is going to be in—" I looked at my watch, "seventeen minutes. You can have your revenge right now if you get your men to come with me."

Benny tented his rat-made fingers. "Interesting. And this person who stole my associates from me will be there?"

"I don't—I mean—"

"He explicitly said that he would be there?"

"Well, no, but—"

Benny rocked back. "Then I'm afraid I have to decline. I will not send my men into a turf war without a very good reason."

"The reason is revenge!" I screamed. "What better reason is there to do anything?"

Benny chuckled slowly. "A wonderful reason to be sure, especially in my younger days, but I run a business here. Starting a gang war is not something I'm interested in doing at this moment with my budget stretched thin. These things have to be taken care of delicately."

I stomped toward the desk. "So you're saying you're a wuss, then."

"How dare you!" Benny's voice changed. Anger vibrated off every squeal. "I have killed people for less!"

I leaned over the desk to get in Benny's many faces. "You are a coward. I am serving him up on a silver platter, and you refuse to do anything! What else could that possibly make you?"

"Smart!" Benny screamed. "It's how I've risen to be king of the Pacific Northwest, by being smart and, frankly, letting others do my work for me."

"You want us to attack him alone? What if we die?"

"Why would I care about you? I only just met you. If you succeed, it will be a great victory for us both. Come back, and we will toast together. If you don't, then there will be many more chances."

I slammed my hand on the desk, cracking it in the middle and sending both sides crashing onto the ground. "I'll remember this." I spun and walked toward the entrance.

Benny cackled behind me. "I wasn't lying. If you do happen to survive, come back, and we will celebrate."

Men. They were always the same. I looked down at my watch. Less than ten minutes left now. I needed to get back. I stepped through the portal back to Kitsune's Apothecary. Kimberly, Kitsune, and Anjelica were gathered around the counter.

"You're back," Kimberly said. "Just in time. Did you do it?"

I reached into the pocket of my trench coat and pulled out a key. I tossed it to her, and she put it in her pocket. "Yup. Just like you said."

"Good," Kimberly said. "You didn't take anything, did you?"

"Of course not," I replied, smiling. "Don't you trust me yet?"

"Not even a little bit. Did you find anything else helpful in your travels?"

"Nothing. You?"

"Well, I've been sitting here watching our new friends, and no, absolutely nothing. I assume nobody is interested in risking their lives for a teenage antichrist and a petulant alien, right?"

"Exactly. I don't blame them, I guess," I said. "Not a lot of tactical advantage there."

"Hey!" Anjelica shouted. "I'm right here, you know. Quit talking about me like I'm somewhere else. It's super weird."

"You're right. How are you feeling?"

"I mean, I would rather not die if that's what you mean. I'm fine, aside from a little nausea."

"That's common," Kitsune said. "It will pass if you live."

"Are you sure you want to come with us?" I asked. "We can do this without you."

"She's right," Kimberly added. "You don't have to put your life in danger to protect him. He's our friend."

"And what will happen if you show up without me?" Anjelica asked. "I'm integral to the plan."

"This plan, yes," I said. "But we can come up with another plan."

"In what time?" Anjelica said. "There is no more time. This is the best chance we have of getting Phil."

"I'm not saying it wouldn't be a lot easier if you came," Kimberly said. "Only that you don't have to. You've been through enough tonight."

"No way." Anjelica shook her head vehemently. "He helped me when he didn't have to. Least I could do is return the favor."

"The least you could do is nothing," I corrected.

"I'm coming."

I grabbed a length of rope that Kimberly had procured from the counter and walked around Anjelica's back, wrapping her arms.

"Just don't make them too tight." I yanked the rope taut, and Anjelica yelped. "What did I tell you? Ow."

"Sorry, but it has to look real."

"It is real," she replied. "You're really giving me to them, right?"

"Just for a little bit."

"We'll find you before they kill you," Kimberly said stoically. "I promise."

"Don't promise that," Anjelica said. "I know the risks and how stupid it is." She turned to me, her big, puppy dog eyes tinged with sadness. "Is this going to work?"

"I don't know. It's best not to ask those questions." I opened the portal to Griffith Observatory. "Let's go."

We ended up in the parking lot with the observatory in the distance. Between us and the entrance, hundreds of demons and other monsters readied their weapons. In front of the horde stood a tall, slender, snake-like demon in a well-tailored suit, no weapons, holding out his arms reverently like he was a prophet.

"Crud," I sighed.

"This just got a lot more complicated," Kimberly replied.

CHAPTER 15

The hardest part of a prisoner transfer was that you had to trust the other party to behave themselves. That was complicated by the fact that it was impossible to trust the other party; they were, simply by the fact that they had one of your friends, completely untrustworthy.

You had to hope that your hostage was important enough that your enemy would find their honor, despite being completely dishonorable. That meant the scariest part of the transfer was after the exchange took place, when you had what you wanted, and they had what they wanted.

You could usually tell how good your chances were of surviving the exchange by the number of men they brought. If there were only a couple of men and it was in a public place, then the odds were in your favor. But if you showed up to a prisoner transfer in a place as public as Griffith Observatory and there were at minimum a hundred thugs on the other side, and all you had in your corner was a pixie, a demon, and yourself, the odds of getting out of the transfer with your life were severely lessened.

We would have to leave quickly, so I left the portal open when we stepped toward the snake monster in the impeccable suit. Phil laid under the snake's shiny loafer, beaten and bruised, but breathing.

"Quite the entourage," I said.

His tongue flickered as he spoke. "I sssssssee you have her."

"You sound different than the guy on the phone," Kimberly said.

"Sssssssilly girl." The snake laughed. "My bosssss does not ssssully his hands on sssssuch things."

The demon who had double-crossed me wasn't there, which meant Benny was right not to risk his people, and suddenly I hated him less for not walking directly into a trap and more for proving me wrong. I wouldn't have walked into it, either, except that I was compromised, tainted by my feelings.

Kimberly stuck her hands on her hips, unimpressed. "Except answer his own phone, that is."

"Enough, Kimberly," I said. "Who is your boss, then?"

"Not important," the snake said.

"I think it's important." I stepped forward. "How else will I know who to kill for hurting the girl?"

"You do have ssssssspirit." The snake chuckled. He was having a grand ole time for a moment, but then his face grew deadly serious. "I hate that. Now, the girl."

"Not so fast. What's to stop you from killing us when you get her?"

"Nothing, exccccccccept my honor."

"Is that the same honor that has you sacrificing a little girl?" Kimberly's eyes narrowed. "Why do you even want her? It's almost sunup."

"My bosssssss has his own reassssssssons." The snake looked back to his army of monsters. "As for your former query, I could ssssssssimply kill you now and take the girl if I did not have honor. Is that what you would prefer?"

"If you kill us, you'll never get the knife."

"Where is it?"

"Hidden," Kimberly said. "And we'll only tell you where after you give us Phil back."

"The deal was the knife and the girl for the alien. No knife, no deal." He raised his hands in the air, and the monsters lifted their guns.

"We can just retreat into this portal and do this later," Kimberly said, squeezing the hilts of her sheathed daggers. "We're not the ones who need to sacrifice her before sunrise."

"Sssssssssshe's no good to ussssssss dead. You, on the other hand—"

"Wait, that doesn't make sense," Kimberly said, holding up her hands. "Isn't dead the only way she's good to you?"

"Look, it's easy," I said, stepping between them. "Once Phil's safe, we'll tell you where to get the knife. Come on, you couldn't have thought it was going to be that easy, did you?" I pointed to the horizon and the sun creeping over the edge. "Tick tock."

"I don't like it…but I accept it." He beckoned Anjelica over. "Send over the girl."

I leaned down and whispered in her ear. "Be strong. We got this."

"I know," she whispered back.

I felt her back tense as I pushed her forward. She might have said she believed us, but her body thought differently, and I didn't blame her. It was one thing to intellectually think about going into the belly of the beast bravely, quite another to do it for real.

"Now, give us Phil," I called out once two demons ran forward to grab Anjelica.

The snake bent down and kicked Phil to us. He was struggling to get free as I pulled off his gag. "Welcome back, buddy."

His eye was bloodshot and bruised. "You shouldn't have done that. They're crazy."

I pulled Phil to his feet. "So are we. C'mon, let's get you home."

As I trudged toward the portal with Phil strung over my arm, Kimberly called out to the snake monster. "The dagger is in the Quik Stor on Figueroa and Grant in Wilmington. Unit 25." She reached into her pocket and pulled out the key I had given her earlier. She tossed it through the air. "Here's the key."

She followed me quickly through the portal, and I closed it behind her after taking one look back at Anjelica, who was trembling under her proud exterior. I took a deep breath and turned away, appearing back in Kitsune's shop.

"You really shouldn't have done that," Phil said. He'd stumbled to the ground.

"Here," Kitsune said, giving him a concoction that she brewed up in our absence. "It will help, but it will taste terrible."

"Thank you," Phil said. "Thank you all, but really. You shouldn't have. You have no idea what they plan to do or what they're capable of."

"Start the Apocalypse. Rule the world. Sow carnage and destruction." Kimberly narrowed her eyes at Phil. "Some crap like that. Sound about right?"

"More complex than that, but those are the broad strokes." Phil shook his head.

"Demons are very predictable."

I grabbed some salve from the table and busied myself cleaning his wounds. "They won't get away with it."

"How do you know? They seemed pretty determined. They said they wouldn't stop until they killed the Devil and controlled Heaven itself."

"Well, that's slightly more ambitious than most demons, but we have it covered." I pressed the salve on a cut across Phil's shoulder, and he winced. "Did you meet the main boss?"

"Yes, he took pleasure in torturing me personally."

"Where did they take you?" I asked.

"I don't know. A mansion of some type. It was hot there. So hot. I could barely stay awake it was so hot."

"What did he look like? Any distinguishing features?"

Phil shook his head. "No, aside from having an impeccable smile. Demons all look the same to me."

"Hey!" I said. "I'm half demon."

"Now you know my secret," Phil said. "Humans look the same, too, for the most part. It's only after many years that I trained myself to see Kimberly and you as your own beings."

"That hurts, but I can't say I would be able to tell you apart from another alien."

Phil pulled away and looked at me. "I'm concerned you aren't concerned."

"It's not that I'm not concerned. You just have no idea what we've been through tonight. After this is over, I'll tell you all about it."

"I think I would prefer never to think about this again," Phil said.

"Fair."

We'd managed to get one of our friends back, but that was only half the plan. The dagger and Anjelica were still out there, and we had to get them back. That kid was not going to die. Not if I had something to say about it.

CHAPTER 16

I had no choice but to bring Phil to my mother's house. I couldn't bring him to my apartment, and I couldn't leave him with Kitsune without somebody to keep an eye on her. She could double-cross me again. As much as I disliked my mother, she wasn't a duplicitous shrew, just an annoying and manipulative one. I left Kimberly to look over the storage unit.

"I don't understand," Phil asked before we went through the portal I'd opened. "How can you hate your mother and still hang out with her?"

"How could you hang out on Earth for so long and not understand us at all?" I replied. "Just because I hate her doesn't mean I don't love her."

"Odd," Phil said.

"Yup, love is stupid."

The sound of Billy Joel played through the house when I entered. Mom was sitting on her leather sectional couch, reading a book, tapping her foot in time to "Uptown Girl."

"Three times in one day," my mother said when I entered her living room. "This is a record. What degenerate have you brought this time?"

"This one's not a demon," I said. "You even like him, if I remember correctly."

"Ah yes," she said, setting down her book. "Phil, right? I see you've stopped pretending to be human now. I'm glad. This is a good look on you. We should all be true to ourselves."

I dropped down on the couch with Phil. "I need him to stay here for a while. Since he's not a demon, I assume it will be fine."

"You could have left the girl here, too. It just threw me off guard to see a demon in my house in the middle of the night but look at me now. Completely on guard. Not even a little bit fazed by your entrance. It's just—you just know how your father—"

"The last thing I want to hear about is my father right now."

"So hotheaded. You're just like your fa—" Mom corrected herself. "Sorry."

I called open a portal. "I have to go. That little girl you turned away risked herself to save Phil, so please protect him."

Mom nodded. "That's very noble of her. I didn't think demons had it in them."

"I always told you, Mom, there are no good or bad beings. Just ones that make different choices." I put my hand on her shoulder. "Now, I really need you to say that you'll help him and protect him. Please."

She kissed me on the forehead. "I'll protect him like he was my own."

I turned away from her. "Please do better than that. We both know how I turned out."

I stepped through the portal and onto the roof across from the storage unit where the dagger was. Kimberly had set up two lawn chairs. I slumped down into the empty one. "Nobody's come yet?" I asked.

"Nope," she replied. "All good with Phil?"

"He's gotta hang out with my mom for a few hours, which sucks, but otherwise, yeah, I think so." I let out a gasp of air. "Which is a big deal considering how pear-shaped this day has become."

"Do you ever get tired of it?" Kimberly asked. "The life?"

"Oh god, all the time." I looked over at her child-like face. "I feel bad for you, a whole lifetime to go putting up with this garbage. I would tell you to stop, but I can see the fire in your eyes. The same fire I had when I was your age."

"Any advice for me?" she asked.

"You for sure don't want advice from me. If anything, look at everything I did and run the other way."

"You seem to be doing all right."

I laughed and then caught myself to avoid giving our position away. "I'm broke, tricked by a demon trying to start the Apocalypse, and now I have to save a girl who is way braver than I've ever been by ambushing whatever demon comes to get the dagger—one that's already cost me everything. I wouldn't say any part of that was all right."

Kimberly turned her attention back to the storage unit. "Who do you think they'll send?"

"Some peon," I replied. "It's always a peon. That's why they're so easy to turn. No creature getting paid a pittance is going to give up their lives for their boss."

A long shadow hobbled toward the locker. When it stopped to pull up the lock, it came into focus—an imp, about as peon as demons got.

"There he is," Kimberly said.

"Looks more scared than most."

The imp dropped the lock and disappeared into the unit.

"That's our cue," I said.

I leaped down from the roof and made my way toward the unit. When I arrived, Kimberly appeared next to me in a puff of smoke. The dagger was on a podium in the center of the room, and I cleared my throat as the imp reached for it.

"Hello," I said, clearing my throat again. "We have some questions."

Imps could teleport with the snap of their fingers, which made them impossible to catch unless you were fast as all hell.

I leaped forward and grabbed one of his hands while Kimberly grabbed the other. She reached into her pocket and pulled out a pair of gardening gloves, which we slid over his hands. I used a piece of rope to tie them together at the wrists.

"Where are they taking Anjelica?" I asked, trying my level best to stay calm. "Tell us what you know, or we'll make life very difficult for you. And trust me, I know how to make a demon's life a living nightmare."

"I ain't saying nothing!" the imp growled back. "You can't make me!"

"I'll bet I could." Kimberly grabbed the dagger from the podium. "Do you know what this is? What this really is? It's a weapon that can kill an antichrist." She held it against the imp's skin. "I'll bet it can kill an imp, too. What do you say we find out?"

"You don't scare me!" the imp screamed, but he was shaking like a leaf in a stiff breeze.

"Don't we?" I asked. "Because I would be very scared if I were you."

"She's right," Kimberly whispered. "I love knives. They are so versatile. I wonder how thin I can fillet your skin." She pressed the dagger closer against him. "Or you could play nice and go free."

"All right, fine," the imp cried. "You're both crazy!"

Kimberly slashed him across the cheek. "That was not nice, imp. Now, tell us where they are."

"The western edge of Kamokuna, in Hawaii, by the volcano. There's a gateway to Hell there, and they need it for the ritual. Now let me go."

I cut the rope off the imp and watched him scurry off into the distance.

"He's going to tell his boss, you know."

"Are you kidding me?" I laughed. "If any of his buddies found out he got jumped by two girls, he'll never live it down. No, if I had to guess, he's going home to Hell to cry in his piss warm beer."

Kimberly stood and followed me out of the unit. When she pulled down the door and locked it up, she had a wistful look on her face.

"Do you think that was too mean?"

"Not even close. You really do have a knack for this type of work."

"Thanks." She looked down at the dagger. "It was fun. Really easy, too."

"Told you," I replied. "Gotta love peons."

She handed me the dagger. "Well, let's go save the world."

"Don't you need this?" I asked.

"Too fancy." She pointed to the daggers on her belt. "I prefer these."

CHAPTER 17

It was dark when we flashed to West Kamokuna on the big island of Hawaii to rescue Anjelica. The ground was black obsidian from the lava that had flowed over it for eons. A cauldron of orange lava steamed up from the ground. On our left, the sea crashed against the cliffside. A half dozen demons surrounded the snake that had Anjelica strapped to an altar.

"Yup," I said. "This looks like the kind of place for a big final battle."

"Leave it to a demon to find three more hours of night by hopping to Hawaii."

"I disagree. It's way too brilliant for demons."

"Diabolically brilliant."

The snake demon chanted something loudly transfixed by all the demons with him. "*Gloria Causa SSSSSatani, et emittat illum, et inferus et mors diis, fructum armageddon translationem onto orbis terrarium!*" He turned to us, eyes trained on the sky. "And here is the main—" Its face dropped when he finally saw us. "Oh, it's you."

"It's us," I replied, deadpan.

"Thissssss isssss unfortunate." He snarled. "Though not entirely unexpected."

"Your plan isn't going to work."

"Yeah," Kimberly added. "We drained the antichrist right out of her hours ago. Now, she's just a demon like all of you."

"LIESSSSSSSSSSSSS!" the snake screamed.

"We have no reason to lie." I clenched the dagger. "Let the girl go, and we won't kill you."

Kimberly unsheathed the daggers around her belt. "I'm not making that promise."

"Get them!" the snake shouted. The demons broke out of their trance and rushed toward us at full speed.

"*Rhew*!" I screamed, and ice shot out of my hand, encasing two demons in a frozen cocoon. Kimberly disappeared to fight two demons lunging toward her. Meanwhile, I stabbed the final demon through the heart with the dagger, and it disintegrated into ash.

"Awesome."

The ice broke around the first two demons. The heat pulsating off their scalding bodies was too great for a normal spell to contain them. Luckily, their temporary encapsulation bought me enough time to readjust. One demon took a swing, and I ducked, jabbing it in the stomach with the dagger, and it also exploded into a million pieces.

"Well, that's fun," I said.

I looked over to see one of the demons near Kimberly fall to the ground after she stabbed it in the neck. I could smell the demon behind me, and I rolled backward as it slammed its fists on the ground I had just vacated. I took the dagger and stabbed it deep into the demon's back, kicking it off as it turned to ash and floated away.

Kimberly had killed her second demon, so I turned to the snake. "It's over."

"Nothing is over!" the snake screamed. "There are hundredsssss of Apocalyptic predictionsssss, and one of them will come true soon enough."

Kimberly slit her last demon's throat and walked toward us, wiping off the demon's green blood from her daggers. "I will fight with every bone in my body to make sure none of them do. You can count on that."

"You're just a little girl!"

"But I'm not," I growled. "And I'll be there every time, making sure scum like you never succeed." I walked closer. "Of course, not you personally." I jabbed the snake through the heart, and he grunted before the wind carried away his ashes. "Because you're dead."

"Couldn't he have helped you find the monster that tried to kill you?" Kimberly asked. "Seems like poor planning."

"I don't want his kind of help." I shrugged. "He'll show up again, and I couldn't hear that asshole's voice for one more second."

"Fair enough."

I walked over and untied one side of Anjelica's restraints, with Kimberly on the other side doing the same. Once free of her bondage, she pulled off her gag.

"Thank you," she said.

"No," Kimberly said. "Thank you for helping us."

"For trusting us," I added.

"So, is it over?" She jumped down from the altar. "Like really over?"

"For you," I replied. "But that snake had a boss who funded this whole operation, and I can't stop until I find him."

"And if there's one thing I know about the rich," Kimberly added, "they always have the money to try again."

"Oof," I said, sitting on the edge of the cliff, "that's the truth, but that's a problem for another day. Right, now, let's just enjoy a beautiful sunrise."

That's exactly what we did. We sat there on the cliff, laughing and talking like old friends, even though we had just met. It was corny and horrible, and I loved it. It was the first time in a long time that I actually enjoyed being in the exact place that I was, but even the best things had to end.

"I will hide her," Kimberly said finally as the sun rose high in the sky, kicking her feet over the cliff.

"Okay." I stood up first, and the others followed close behind. "It's for the best."

"Don't I have a say in this?" Anjelica asked. "Whether I fly off and leave everything in my life behind?"

"Of course," Kimberly said. "We're not monsters. Do you want to go back home and risk your family being targets of another crazy madman?"

"Will they come back for me, though? I mean, I'm free, right? My blood is useless."

"Not everybody knows that," I said. "And besides, magic is dumb. Who knows what some crazy demon can use your blood to do."

"It has rules, though. You said it yourself."

"Rules can change. That's one of the worst things about magic." I sighed. "It's your choice, but I think you should go."

"Will I ever see you again?" Anjelica asked, tears streaming down her face. "Will I ever see anyone I love again?"

"I can't answer that, kid," I said.

"I hate this so much." She was trying to choke back tears as if crying meant she wasn't strong. Actions were what mattered, and she was brave enough for ten people and about a hundred demons.

"Better than dying, though." I took a deep breath of the salt air.

"Which was a very real possibility," Kimberly replied. "Trust me, they don't all end this way. It's a gift that you have the choice. Most of us don't get one."

"Truer words." I turned to Anjelica. "So, what'll it be, kid?"

"I'll go into hiding, I guess." Anjelica leaped forward and hugged me tightly. "Thank you. I would be dead without you."

After a few seconds, it got awkward to have her wrapped around me, so I tapped her shoulder. "Okay, that's enough." When she let go, I turned to Kimberly. "Where are you going to bring her?"

"I think it's best if you don't know, but I swear she'll be somewhere safe."

Anjelica grabbed my hand. "I don't have to go with her, you know. I could stay here with you."

I couldn't help it. I laughed—laughed so hard a tear rolled down my cheek, and I wiped it away. She was trying to have a tender moment, but I just—couldn't. "Thank you for the laugh, kid."

"That's what I thought. I just had to ask," Anjelica said with a sad smile. "I'll see you around,"

"No, you won't," I said. "That's the point."

She let go of my hand and grabbed Kimberly's. I watched them vanish into a purple cloud. When they were gone, and I had collected myself, I called forth a portal and disappeared into it.

I reappeared in front of Blezor's house. His monster truck was parked outside. I couldn't believe he didn't get in trouble for having it. I guess he did have more money than the gods, just like he'd said when he was trying pitifully to woo me.

I knocked on the door, and after a minute, Blezor came to the door. He wasn't angry or happy. He just looked tired and sad.

"What are you doing here?" he mumbled.

I held up the dagger. "I don't need this anymore. Thought I would give it back to you." I placed it in his cautiously outstretched hand. "Call it even?"

"We're nowhere near even." He sighed. "You don't even know why I'm mad, do you?"

"I took something from you, and now I'm giving it back."

"Not even close." He turned from the door. "You want pancakes? You look horrible. You could use a home-cooked meal."

"No, thanks," I said. "I have plans." I had a traitorous scumbag to track down. Every moment I waited, he could put more distance between us, and I couldn't have that, now could I?

BOOK 2

"Blacklisted Heroine"

CHAPTER 18

After stopping the Apocalypse and saying goodbye to Kimberly and Anjelica, I set out to figure out who was trying to kill us. That "us" did not include Kimberly, of course, as she was simply sucked into my vortex, like so many other unfortunate souls. Most mortals didn't survive tumbling into my web of misfortune, but she did, and that was impressive.

The "us" was Anjelica and me. Kimberly had taken her to live in safety and anonymity, but if I could find the demon who was trying to kill us, maybe she could return home and live a normal life, though I didn't know what "a normal life" meant for demon spawn. She might become an accountant, die in her sleep at 200, or live to be 1,000. It was a shot in the dark. Whole schools of magic existed to exploit the inconsistencies in the underlying code of the universe.

Back in school, we had learned about physics, Isaac Newton, and the stupid apple that fell on his dumb head. Centuries later, Albert Einstein came along, and his theories and scientists were sure they knew exactly what made up the universe—then came 1964, and Murray Gell-Mann discovered quarks. Little tiny particles smaller than atoms that broke everything humans knew about the physical world. Particles that didn't act like anything else in the universe. Particles that acted like magic.

I always knew that the universe was chaos. I often felt like one of those quarks, unstable and unpredictable, going strange when I should go charm, and up when I should go bottom, affecting the universe in uncharted and often unwanted ways.

I supposed we were all chaos agents to everything we touched. Anjelica was surely that for me. She dropped into my life like a bomb, forced me to care about another person for the first time in a long time, and then evaporated into the ether. She upended everything.

I thought about her more than I imagined I would since she'd been hidden away from everyone in the world. I thought about getting in touch with Kimberly so that I could ask her about Anjelica, but she was right. It was better I didn't know.

Before she fell into my life, Anjelica was a normal fifteen-year-old kid. I mean, she was born a demon, which was highly abnormal, but she didn't know that. She was just a cheerleading, pep squad, honor roll student at Pasadena Prep. You could have used her as the standard by which normalcy was judged.

Yes, I looked her up. Yes, I went to her house. Yes, I watched her mother cry every night for a week when she didn't come home. I saw the cops come and take her statement. I witnessed the frantic calls she made to the whole world. I observed her summoning circle and the pleas she made on Anjelica's demon father, and I saw the light drain from her eyes when she ran out of options.

I didn't know why I went to Anjelica's house every day. It wasn't even about Anjelica, really. It was about the fact that I opened up for once in my miserable life, and she was the first in a long line of beings, celestial or otherwise, that didn't twist a knife deep in my back. I also realized that I actually enjoyed her company.

I had convinced myself that I didn't need friendship in my life, that I didn't need somebody to believe in me when I didn't believe in myself—but when it was taken from me, it left a chasm—aw Hell, what am I talking about? It was one night, and her leaving was for the best. Anyone can be sweet for a night, but over a long-time horizon, they all betrayed you if given a chance.

That's why you didn't give them a chance. *Remember that, Ollie.* That's why you allowed yourself to get lost in your work. Nobody was worth it. Look out for number one. There were things you needed to get done, for you.

Which was what led me to the port of Leixões in the north of Portugal, about ten minutes from Porto. It's the biggest port in Portugal, but normal people know it as the home to port wine, the delicious, fortified wine that I could drink by the gallon. I was looking for something that had been taken from me.

One of the advantages of being a Nephilim is that I could understand and speak every language fluently even if I'd only heard a couple of words of it. I wasn't sure exactly how it worked, nor did I care. I learned long ago not to question magic. All it gave you was migraines.

Speaking in tongues was handy, especially for somebody that arranged deals with all sorts of people and took all sorts of clients from around the world, traveling to them with the snap of a finger by ripping a hole in the fabric of space-time. That method of travel certainly saved money, which was an added bonus since the demon that stiffed me for three million dollars was elusive, and I was broke.

"Kalle!" I shouted at the dock manager. I'd been searching for him all over the enormous docks for the better part of an hour. Kalle navigated the docks like a five-star general, directing traffic like an air traffic controller, which meant even when he told you to meet him somewhere, there was only a ten percent chance he would actually show up. Today was no different.

"Ollie!" Kalle said. He had gained weight since the last time I saw him, but he wore it well, and now a thick, black beard covered his chin and hung down to his chest. He wrapped me in a hug, and the coarse hair bristled against my chin and itched uncomfortably. "It's good to see you."

I patted him on the back. I didn't like hugs, but I knew they were a part of doing business with people, especially Portuguese people, who were considerably touchier than my British and American contacts. "It's good to see you, too, my friend. You have something to show me?"

"Always business with you." He smiled with his whole face. "I haven't seen you in years. Aren't you going to ask me how I've been?"

"Must we with the pleasantries?" I sighed because I knew the answer was yes. "How have you been?"

"Fat!" He bellowed through a loud laugh, slapping his stomach and sending ripples across his belly. "Two children and a wife have me stress eating everything in sight, but it's wonderful. Would you like to see pictures?"

I really didn't care to see them. "No. I'm sure they are—"

It was too late. He was already digging in his back pocket for his wallet. When he unfolded it, a half dozen images sealed in plastic folded out. "This is Dada." He pointed to a very tiny girl with dark hair and eyes wearing a pink dress and smiling. "And this tiny one is Gael. What a blessing and a curse, but mostly a blessing…most days." I didn't know how to tell babies apart. The boy, I assumed from its blue jumper, looked exactly like a baby, with two hands, feet, and eyes.

"They're beautiful," I replied because that was the thing to say.

He flipped his wallet closed and stuffed it back in his pocket. "Enough small talk. We don't have time. You are so nosy." He gave me a teasing grin. He started to powerwalk down the dock. "Come, come. Or do you not want your prize?"

"Oh no," I said, following behind. "I'm coming. Lead the way."

CHAPTER 19

I followed Kalle as he ping-ponged between the containers like a rat looking for a piece of cheese, hitting a dead end and then doubling back on himself. He pulled a clipboard from the end of a row of containers and stared at it, scratching his head.

"I'm sorry about this," he replied. "I thought for sure that container 3-8-4-2-1 was in this—aha—" He pointed at his sheet and then pulled a walkie-talkie from his belt. "Operations, this is 623."

"Go ahead, Kalle," a gruff voice squawked back.

"This manifest doesn't have container 3-8-4-2-1 on it, but I'm sure it came in last night. I have the owner here, and she is pissed. Over." Kalle smiled at me. "Just play along, okay?"

"Oh, that won't be a problem, my friend," I said. "I'm always pissed, including right now."

The walkie crackled to life again. "I'm showing an override here to expedite the container for delivery. It has your code. Over."

"That's impossible. It hasn't passed through customs." Kalle's smile faded into an irritated scowl. "Where is it now? Over."

"They're loading it on a cargo truck at entrance thirteen," the walkie replied. "Over."

"Do not let that truck leave, operations. Do you hear me? Over."

"Roger, roger."

Kalle flagged down one of the many golf carts zipping back and forth across the dock and pushed its driver out of her seat. "Get in." I hopped into the passenger seat, and he took off, leaving the irritated woman flailing her hands in frustration.

"This doesn't make any sense," he said, shaking his head. "I would never—you have to believe me! I would never call you here and then—it doesn't make any sense."

"It makes perfect sense to me, my friend. You have a traitor and a liar in your organization."

He shook his head. "I don't believe it. My men are loyal to a fault."

"Nobody ever believes it. I have never met a good person that didn't vehemently deny one of their people was crooked. Anybody can justify anything given enough money, and the people who are messing with me have plenty of money—and they stiffed me, which makes it even more infuriating."

"This is very troubling."

"Do you remember when I slid you five thousand Escudo to get a look inside one of your containers?"

"Of course, but that was different. You were—"

"What? Beautiful? I don't—"

"I was going to say very annoying." He smiled. "But I get your point. I have not been perfect in my life, have I?"

"None of us have. That's part of the human condition, or the—" He didn't know I wasn't human, so I bit my tongue. "Maybe the most human condition of all. I remember your wife was sick, and she needed some surgery or another—"

"A new heart valve," Kalle said. "It was a horrible time, and I didn't have the money…"

"I played on that, the same way somebody is playing on you right now."

"I don't like this story."

"Think of it this way. You took that money, your wife is still with you, and you have two beautiful children. I'm sure you would say that was worth it, wouldn't you?"

He spun the wheel, and we turned left down another row of containers. "Of course. It saved her life."

"Just remember that whoever betrayed you, they have similar motivations. None of us are mustache-twirling evil henchmen, no matter what the storybooks say." It felt a little silly telling him that when I was looking for vengeance against my own betrayal, but we're all hypocrites.

The trucks idled near the entrance. A hairy, lumbering driver stood outside screaming at a poor woman holding a clipboard. She flinched with every move of his hands.

"Perla," Kalle said, bringing his cart to a stop and hopping out. "Having some trouble?"

The driver wore the stained blue hat of the FC Porto soccer team and a cut-off shirt that showed off his flabby arms. "This is such bull!"

"What seems to be the problem?" Kalle said, hands high and speaking in a calming voice.

"We're ready to go, and you people are saying we can't leave. I have shipments to make today. Time is money."

"I'm sorry, sir." Kalle walked around the truck. "Ah yes, 3-8-4-2-1. This is what I was looking for." Kalle turned back to the man. "I'm afraid this container was cleared in error."

"That's a you problem," the man said. "I radioed my boss saying I was leaving port. She expects me back there as soon as possible."

The pleasant smile faded from Kalle's face. "Then you need to call your boss back and tell her that you've been detained because this has become very much a you problem."

The trucker threw his arms in the air. "Why even call us to pick up, then?"

"Mistakes happen. I'm sure you understand."

"I don't understand, but what am I gonna do about it? Nothing." He kicked the ground and walked off. It wasn't the truck driver's fault he had something that belonged to me. He was just doing his job, but he had unwittingly aligned himself with forces that opposed me, and that meant, on some level, that he opposed me.

Kalle whistled to a crane operator, and though I didn't understand the gestures he made, I was able to figure out that he was telling the operator to pull the container off the truck. Even though Kalle was the boss, it still took half an hour to comply with the request and another twenty to haul the container from the truck. An hour later, the truck was gone, along with the pissed-off driver, and we were standing in front of the container, ready to open it.

I tried to contain my excitement as the door swung open, but when I saw her, my heart sang, and I rushed forward to hug my beloved car around the hood. "Lily!" She was the best lead I had in my search for the jerk demon that betrayed me, and I had tracked her all over the world. After I had my moment with Lily, I turned and hugged Kalle tightly. Rare tears welled in my eyes. Lily was one of the only long-term relationships I had which wasn't toxic, and now I had her back.

'Thank you, my friend," I said.

"It was my pleasure." Of course, it wasn't just his pleasure. I paid him for the privilege, using most of the money I had made since the night I stopped the Apocalypse. It was worth it. I hoped that maybe Moloch or Balaam would be too stupid to know how valuable the wand was, and it would be waiting for me in the passenger's seat. It wasn't, which was disappointing, though not unexpected.

Kalle called his people over and had them fill up my tank. For thirty thousand Escudo, it was the most expensive gas ever, but I would have gladly paid it twice over. Lily rode rough when I pulled her out of the container. She sounded like an old smoker coughing up their last bit of lung, but she drove.

"How are you going to get it home?" Kalle asked, resting his hand on my open window as I idled by the front entrance. He was sweet, but there was no way I was going to tell him the truth. Humans didn't need to know that I could teleport at will. "Do you need me to arrange a lift for you?"

I shook my head. "No, thank you. I've got it covered. Tell your family I said hello."

"Would you like to meet them?" Kalle asked excitedly. "Calandra is making Bacalhua tonight. I'm sure she wouldn't mind making another piece of fish for you."

"Absolutely not." I patted his hand. "I was just trying to be polite, Kalle. Now, can you please take your hand off my window?"

He smiled and brought his hand up in a wave. "Another time, then."

I appreciated Kalle, but I was never going to accept that dinner. It sounded horrible. I pulled out of the yard and turned onto the road on my way to the main street. There weren't many places to perform magic by the port, but Porto had plenty of blind alleys.

"It's good to have you back, girl," I said out loud to Lily. She sounded sick, like something had taken all the soul out of her and crushed it under their thumb. "Just hang with me, we'll have you feeling better in no time."

It was an uneventful trip back to the city, which I was thankful for. When I arrived, I turned into the first one-way alley I could find, which wasn't hard to find. I held my hand up toward the end of the alley. *"Porth yn ôl Los Angeles, a Phil."*

A green portal opened in front of me, and I disappeared into it with Lily.

CHAPTER 20

I wanted to take a long drive through the streets of Los Angeles. It was a driving town, which was one of the few things I liked about it. For public transit, you went to New York, or Paris, or London, or—well, just about anywhere in Japan or Europe, but if you wanted to drive, you came to Los Angeles. I loved to drive.

Lily was sick, though, and she needed some TLC before I could take her around the city. The only mechanic in Los Angeles I trusted with Lily was Phil, the only other non-toxic relationship in my life after my beloved car. *God, what a sad thought.*

I tried to convince Phil to move after he had been kidnapped and all, but he assured me that his capture was a statistically insignificant outlier data point and only came about because a.) he was defenseless after the attack on his house by Balaam and Moloch and b.) he was caught blindsided by the fact human guns were far more difficult to operate than he was led to believe. I couldn't force him to do anything. I mean, I could, but I wouldn't because that's not how you treated friends.

Lily puttered into Phil's garage, and he closed the door behind it. I popped the hood as I slid out of the car. By the time I walked around, Phil was shaking his little, green body and mumbling under his breath.

"Distributor cap is gone, fuel hose is leaking, carburetor is shot." He turned to me. "This is almost a complete rebuild. Are you sure it's worth it?"

"Would you say that about your best friend? Lily is priceless."

"Yes, that is what you always say to the thing I always say." We went through this same song and dance every time Lily needed repairs, which wasn't as infrequent an occurrence as I would like. "Do you have any idea who did this?"

I shook my head. "No, but considering I met those two idiots at midnight, they were dead by 4 am, and when I went back to the dock at 11 am, the car was gone. There aren't that many options. I talked to everybody I could find on those docks, and nobody saw anything useful despite my very persuasive interrogation tactics."

"Torture," Phil said. "Don't sugar coat it with me. You tortured them."

"I mean, yeah…" I shrugged. "I kind of tortured them."

"No qualifiers. You tortured them."

"Yes, I did," I replied. "And since I'm very convinced nobody on the dock saw it, that means the dum dum twins drove it off the dock after they defrosted."

"They weren't the dum dums that left the key in the ignition," Phil said.

"Watch it," I said. "I can hurt you."

"I'm just saying that they couldn't have driven it off if you didn't give them the means to execute it."

"Well, I didn't expect my former lover to interrupt us."

"You should always expect everything, even outlier scenarios." He touched a scar on his long neck that reminded him of the time he'd spent being tortured. "I'll never forget that again."

"You can't predict everything."

"Hrm." Phil cocked his head. "I wouldn't care to live if I thought that." We went back to fiddling with the engine block. "So, Jessica Fletcher, how is finding Lily going to help you figure out who's trying to kill you?"

"That's as easy as it is complicated, my good friend. Assuming Balaam and Moloch were the ones who took the car, they would have dropped it off somewhere quickly and quietly. It was somebody they knew well and somebody that could outfit them with a new car quickly. There aren't many people with that kind of pull who can load a car on a boat the same night. Which means all I gotta do is find a car thief that sells cars in Europe often and has easy access to the ports. How many places do you think have that kind of MO in Los Angeles?"

"My gut says very few, but my mind says that in a city of several million, it would be more than you think."

"Then I guess I should stop talking to you and get started, huh?" I walked to the front of the garage. "How long do you think it will take to repair her?"

"Using my replicator for parts, a couple of hours, maybe a day at most?"

"Why are you complaining when it's going to take less than a day?"

Phil smiled. "I like complaining."

I opened the garage door. "I'll never understand you."

Everybody in Los Angeles knew my 'Cuda and respected it. There was very little chance it would go unnoticed that a beat-up '68 black Plymouth Barracuda perfectly matching mine was on the market, so it had to be a really ballsy asshole who would try to take it.

It was easiest to start at the top of the chain and work down. If Candace didn't know what happened with my car, I bet she could direct me to the person that did. "Candy" was a car god on the west coast. Whether you needed to find a car, lose a car, or just wanted to talk cars, she was your girl. She was a firecracker, too. She had to be in the testosterone-fueled world of exotic cars.

She was a slight woman at barely five feet, and more than one man had been castrated for joking that she needed a booster seat to see over the wheel of her car. Those that laughed were humiliated when she rose from nothing to the top of the pack, first in Los Angeles, then the West Coast, and now she was expanding into Vegas.

The front for her whole operation was Cotton Candy Exotics, a combination auto body shop and car dealership that Candy bought to give her business an air of legitimacy. She specialized in big, bright paint jobs and rip-and-replace overhauls for high-end collectors around the world. She definitely had the skills to take Lily's busted body and bring her back to her glory.

During the day, Cotton Candy was a place where millionaire Joes and Janes walked around looking at the merchandise. It cost seven figures just to get into the door, and Candy ran background checks on everyone who booked an appointment with her. When I walked into her shop, she was talking to a buttoned-up couple that looked like they had a stick jammed so high up their asses that they could pull it out their mouths. It looked like it would take chopping them down with an ax to get them to move an inch, yet Candy swayed with the ease of a blade of grass.

Candy was anything but buttoned-up. She had purple and pink hair, with thick, hyper-saturated make-up, and bright pink lips. Her clothes were black leather, and she rocked two piercings in each of her nostrils. She was smacking her gum loudly while she talked with the couple.

"So, if you want Lago Grand Sport, custom, that's easily going to cost you an easy seven million, and that's without any customizations."

"How long?" the man asked brusquely.

She laughed and gave a casual wave of her hand. "Could be a day, could be a year. Either way, I take half up front and half on delivery."

"That's highway robbery. What if you don't find it?" The woman scoffed as if Candy would care. "Absurd."

Candy spun away with her chin in the air. "Look, my reputation speaks for itself. I know better than to work with people that don't have this type of money to burn. It just doesn't work out. I gotta bounce you."

"Excuse me?" the man said, indignant. "I'll have you know—"

Candy held up her hand. "Look, I said my peace, now get the Hell out. You've insulted me." She caught my eye and smiled, completely stonewalling and ignoring the rich pricks behind her. "Hey, baby girl."

"You really know how to talk to people," I said with a smile. "Those two are going ape." And they were, hissing and spitting in their fight with each other. "It's awesome."

"They are going to come back with ten million, and I'll sigh and agree as long as they don't give me any lip. You watch."

I had to hand it to her: She could play rich people like a fiddle. "I need your help."

"Sounds like you," Candy said, still smiling.

"Couple weeks ago, my car was stolen and sold. It just showed up in Portugal, of all places. You're the best at smuggling cars I've ever met. Know anything about it?"

She laughed again. "First off, I wouldn't touch that 'Cuda, and you should know that by now."

"Why not?"

"For a couple of reasons, first of which is you are a reckless wench who would kill me as soon as look at me, and two, it's hideous. I hate 'Cudas so much. I would never be caught dead with anything so pedestrian."

Candy was one of the only people who could insult Lily without getting decked for it. "Fair. Know anyone who would?"

She nodded. "I have a short list."

The couple approached. "We talked it over," the man said. "And if you're willing to help us, we'll bump you up to an even ten million to make up for the insult." The man pinched his wife. "Do you have something to say, sweetie?"

The woman looked down at her designer shoes. "I'm sorry for insulting you."

Candy shrugged. "That was very brave of you to say. I'll take your order. But I don't want to hear one more word of lip out of you, agreed?" They both nodded in silent agreement. She turned to me. "Gimme a second."

That was Candy, the rich prick whisperer.

CHAPTER 21

I was comfortable hearing no. I had to be in my line of work. Often, there was only one magical scepter or enchanted amulet of a certain type in the whole world, and tracking it down took tenacity. The reason something remained hidden was usually a matter of not looking hard enough. Once, a rich twatwaffle paid me to find a piece he had forgotten was already in his collection.

As much as I liked brute force, you generally got more bees with honey and more money with smiles than you did with being a thorn in somebody's side. I was great at my job because criminals were surly and suspicious of each other, and I made a lovely go-between. I was unceasingly patient when money was on the line. It was only when things went tits up that I relied on my other skills—which were equally impossible if I said so myself.

So, when Candy gave me a list of possible criminal masterminds who could have fenced Lily, I knew it would be a slog, but I was up for the challenge. Not a particularly long list, it was filled with people I didn't know. It had to be. Nobody we knew would pay me that enormous of an insult. They'd know I would be after them with fire and brimstone.

I spent the day going through Candy's list one at a time. Unfortunately, I kept striking out, and everybody I met was more and more punchable than the last one. Before I reached the end of the last nerve, Phil buzzed my beeper with good news, and I portaled to his house. He opened the garage, and Lily shimmered at me. The bullet holes and all of the dents Moloch and Balaam made in her were gone.

"She looks perfect!" I yelled.

Phil threw me the keys. "Runs perfect, too. Better than perfect, after I was done with her."

I slid into the driver's side and massaged the newly polished steering wheel. Breathing in the smell of new leather and lemon, I couldn't stop myself from smiling. Lily purred for me like a lap cat when I turned on the engine.

"I'm afraid it doesn't help you find the monsters who did this to her," Phil said, leaning against the car. "But as a little thank you from me, I juiced it up a bit."

"Juiced it up how?"

"Flip open the top of the gear shift."

I did and saw a big red button on it.

"That injects nitrous oxide into the fuel line for an extra boost of speed. I also lined the engine and interior with shock-absorbing technology, so if you have to use your magic powers…well, now you won't damage the tensile integrity of the car."

"Thank you," I said. "You have no idea how much this means to me."

"Actually, I know exactly how much it means. I calculated it, and it exactly correlated to the guilt I felt for you risking my life to save me, so this is a win-win in my book." He sighed. "I just wish I could do something to change the fact that demons drove your baby without you."

My eyes lit up. "That's it. Phil, you're a genius!"

"I know that…but how, specifically, in this instance?"

I hopped out of the car. "They had to drive the car somewhere. If I use a mimic spell from the exact place that I lost the car—"

"It would lead you to where it was sold," Phil finished the thought. "That is bloody brilliant, I must say. Kudos to me for thinking of it."

I hopped back into the car. "Sorry to dash and ditch, but I have to—"

"I know. He kidnapped me, too. I want you to find him as much as you do. Every time I close my eye, I see his face in my dreams, and…find him. For both of us."

"I will."

CHAPTER 22

I waited until midnight to drive Lily back onto the dock, just like I had when I met with Moloch and Balaam that fateful night when I stopped the world from ending. I had thought then that the docks, while not the greatest spot in the world, would at least prevent me from getting ambushed. That was before I was ambushed not once but twice, by two different groups of monsters, in the span of five minutes.

"Ysbryd fy nghamgymymeriadau yn y gorffennol."

The spell created a ghost, or a memory, of what happened to my car after I left it—a spell that only I could see. In order for it to work, I needed a strong connection with what was performing the memory—in this case, Lily—and I couldn't let go of my grip on it without breaking the connection, which meant no getting out of the car.

I took a deep breath. As I exhaled, smoke plumed from my nostrils and encased the car. Slowly, the smoke took shape, first little by little, then all at once. In front of me, I watched as the ghostly apparitions of Balaam and Moloch fired bullets at me that lodged into the hood of the car. A cloudy version of my body leaped over the demons, and they came crashing toward me, iced into the side panel of the car. Then, a massive monster truck crashed through the gate. *I had no idea how close Blezor was to crushing you, Lily.*

I rubbed the steering column tenderly as the ghostly version of me leaped into the demon's car and tore out of the dock and down the road. Our collective memories were done. Now, all I had were the car's remembrances.

The first five minutes were boring as sin, but then, the heat from the demons melted their ice, and they broke free. I couldn't hear anything they were saying since the spell memory didn't have sound, but they screamed at each other in silence as they leaped into the car. For a moment, the cloud version of Moloch sat right on top of me, and I just about wretched. Then it took off with the ghostly version of Lily.

I followed the cloud down the road, weaving through the real cars around me as I chased the speed demons. Los Angeles at night isn't very crowded, especially down by the docks, so tailing them to their first stop was easy. They parked at a gas station just over the bridge back into Long Beach. Balaam went inside while Moloch waited in the car. I touched Lily's roof gingerly. Moloch's horns would have scratched her something fierce, but Phil returned her to even better than her original glory.

They continued up the 405 for a while before stopping at an apartment complex in Inglewood. There was no way that the boss lived there, but I jotted down the address in case I needed it later. About ten minutes later, they came back down the stairs and sped off.

They continued down the 405 to the 710 and took that until it ended. They snaked around service streets and finally stopped in front of a shop. I nearly burst out laughing when I saw the sign, and I got a big, bold case of Déjà vu: *Cotton Candy Exotics*. It wasn't the main showroom in West Los Angeles, but one of the many expansions Candy had set up around the city.

Twenty minutes after they'd gone in, Balaam and Moloch walked out, waving through the office window before disappearing behind the corner. They never came back, and eventually, a short little thing with pink hair came out of the shop and hopped into the car.

I couldn't believe it. I thought maybe one of her people was working off the books, but there she was, nose rings and all—Candy, driving my precious car into her garage. I was going to kill her for touching my car, for insulting me, and for lying to me. She knew what had happened. She'd done it herself. There was one thing I couldn't abide, it was a liar, especially when they looked me in the face and called me a friend. *It was time to raise some hell.*

I kicked open the door to the shop, ready for a fight, but what I found was a bloodbath. A half dozen people laid on the floor with their organs turned inside out, oozing blood all over the shining tile floor. The office didn't reek of the acrid blood that rose from the bodies on the showroom floor. It smelled of fear and sweat—of salty tears. They hadn't even had a chance to go for their guns. It was vicious and brutal, the kind of thing that happened when someone wanted to send a message.

I rubbed my temples, thinking about my next move. That's when I heard a whimper coming from behind the reception desk, where a once-pretty girl with red hair was sprawled, head on her clipboard, eye wide open, blood from her slit throat dripping onto the floor. I followed the sound to a cabinet behind the girl along the back wall, a blue lacquered type that locked with a key.

I didn't have the key, but that didn't matter. I bent down and ripped the door off its hinges using a fraction of my strength. There, hidden in the cabinet, was Candy. Gone was all her poise and finesse. Mascara and eye shadow smeared all over her face, her tears making clean rivulets on their way to her chin.

"Demons," she squeaked. "There are demons. Demons!"

I almost felt bad for her. *Almost.*

CHAPTER 23

Candy could barely hold a cup of tea without spilling it everywhere, her hand was shaking so violently. She was white as a sheet, muttering to herself, and jerked away from me whenever I caught her eye. Humans were never meant to learn the truth—that demons walked among them, that monsters were real, and that they were right to fear things that went bump in the dark.

"We have to get out of here," Candy said, raspy-voiced. "We can't—we can't—"

"Candy," I replied softly. "Do you know where you are?"

I had wrapped her in my arms and carried her out of the shop over an hour ago. She was sitting in one of the few safe places in the city, Ginger's Diner. I brought all my strays to Ginger, and she took care of them. When I needed my space, she never asked questions, and since I never had answers, it was a perfect arrangement.

I bought Candy a plate of waffles, and the butter and whipped cream melted off of the top of it as it went unattended. She did take a sip of black tea, her favorite, but that was all I could muster from her without force-feeding her. I wasn't a hospice nurse.

"Hell," she whispered, finally finding my eyes. "I'm in Hell. We're all in Hell…and there are demons."

I clasped her hands together inside of mine. "I know there are, sweetheart, and I really need your help finding the one who did this to your people."

"H-h-h-how?" She said, blinking wildly, fighting to come out of her trance. "How do you know?"

I sighed. "Cuz I work with them, honey. I see them all the time." I pulled off my sunglasses, showing my blue and red eye, each swirling independently of the other. "I need you to look at me so I can help you. Can you do that?"

If I could get to her broken mind quickly, I could seal the fissures and repair it, but I needed them to have a flicker or consciousness in order to do it, and Candy hadn't been lucid since we sat down at the diner. Every second I waited, she slipped further and further from me.

Candy pulled her hands back and went back to her tea, staring into her cup. Her breath had been erratic since I found her, vacillating between hyperventilation and a slow heave that spasmed her stomach, and she hadn't stopped crying since we sat down. Staring into that cup, suddenly she seemed to snap back. Her pupils undilated, her jaw tensed, and her breathing returned to normal.

"Candy?" I whispered to her.

When she looked up at me, more tears spilled down her face, but she was resolute in a way I hadn't seen her all night.

"How can you just work with demons?" she said through gritted teeth.

"I will tell you." My voice was calm and steady. "But while you're lucid, I need you to look at my eyes. Otherwise, you'll be broken forever, okay?" She nodded and turned her attention to my eyes. I hated for people to stare at me too deeply, and an odd chill slid down my back when she did, causing it to arch slightly, but I fought the natural distaste for eye contact. "Good. Now, follow my voice, not with your eyes, but with your mind."

I needed to maintain complete concentration, or I could lose the thread of her consciousness forever. I couldn't quite explain how I was able to see into her, past her eyes, into the neural network that made up her brain, but then I couldn't explain much about magic. I tried to keep myself to asking "how" questions instead of "why" questions. If I didn't think too deeply about it, things almost ended up okay most of the time.

"You're doing great, Candy." I took a deep breath, and I was able to mentally project myself onto the surface of her mind—not her physical brain, which had not changed shape in the past day, but the consciousness of her mind, which was fracturing.

Inside her mind, hundreds of fragments of glittering rock floated free in the black abyss, held together by nothing, as if a giant rock collided with it and broke the whole thing apart. An intact mind looked like a singular, perfectly smooth mirror ball. Her condition was more advanced than I thought. I had to move fast.

"Candy!" I screamed into the ether. The first step was finding her projection of self. It was her sense of self that held the rest of her mind together. Without a strong sense of it, she would drift through the mental void forever, catching reality only in fits and starts. "Candy!"

I hopped across the fissures of her mind, one to another, searching for any projection of Candy. All animals had a mind, but few had a sense of self, which was what separated humans from most other life forms.

"Candy!" I screamed, seeing the outline of a woman. I leaped forward, past the shattered pieces that reflected myself back to me until I reached Candy. She let out a lethargic groan, slumped over like she was floating face down in a pool…but she was not dead. I saw her struggling to move.

I reached out and grabbed her hand, pulling her to me. When she fell into my arms, I brushed the black hair from her head so I could see her eyes. She smiled at me, a tepid, tired smile.

"Ollie? What are you—" Her eyes went wide. "Demons. Demons are real. You have to—"

I pressed my finger on her lips. "I know. I know. It's okay. Everything's going to be okay."

Candy craned her neck around to see the fragments floating around her. "How? This place—What is—How is Eddie? And Tina? And Janet? And…" Her voice trailed off.

Those must have been the people that worked with her, and the last thing I wanted was to bring up that piece of trauma. "Listen to me, Candy. I need you to pull it together. Quite literally."

"Your eyes—" Candy. "I've never seen anything like them before. How—how are you here?"

"Don't think too much about it, okay?" Groans came from the distance, in the dark. Her mind was trying to fight off invaders. It thought I was the enemy. If I lost her, then she would be gone into the darkness forever. If I wasn't careful, I would follow her into the abyss.

"Candy," I said. "We don't have much time. I need you to think about somebody you love dearly."

"Janet…" She rolled her head from side to side. "She was smooth."

Janet was dead, so that wasn't going to work. I needed her to run toward the memory, not escape from it.

"How about your mother?" I said.

"I hate her."

"I hate mine, too, but, but…just go with me, here." I knew better than most you could hate somebody and love them at the same time, especially a mother. "What was your mother like, back when you were a kid?"

"Loud, so loud. She never wanted me to start working on cars. Said it was undignified. She worked as a maid and told me that what I wanted to do was undignified. How funny."

"What do you remember about her, physically? What did she look like?"

"Her hands," she said. "They were so rough. It prickled when she touched me." She twitched. "So, she never did. She didn't want to hurt me, but she didn't touch me ever, and that hurt me more."

The groans were getting louder, and I saw the darkness shift around me as wisps began to form around us. Something else was happening, too. The glass-like pieces around us started to sway and move, too, as they collapsed back together. It was working.

"What was your favorite thing she cooked?"

"Orange chicken," Candy said with a little more energy. "She hated it. She said it wasn't real Chinese food, but I didn't care, and she was so good at it. She also knew how to cook fish better than anyone I've ever met. I didn't like when she ate the eyes, but she gave me the best piece, always, and she made this sauce, oh my god, that sauce. My sister used to—"

I could feel the pain coming again as the screams around us rose to a nearly deafening level. "What about a good memory?" Memories pulled the brain together, and I watched as the little pieces of her mind coalesced again into a mirror ball.

"She did tai chi every morning, and she would shout so loud it would wake every other apartment that lived around us. They yelled and hollered through the walls, but every weekend she would make pork buns and bring them around the complex. I went with her, and I saw how you could get away with just about anything if you brought food." She looked at me in the eyes for the first time. "I'm so sorry about what I did to you. I'm so sorry."

I stood up and helped her to her feet. The mirror ball of her mind had been repaired, but the screams weren't quieting. I took her hand and pulled her along until I saw a little hatch. I slid it open and led her toward it. "It's going to be okay."

She nodded and crawled down the ladder. When she was gone, I spun the latch closed. The monsters of the mind were on top of me now, ready to pounce, and I needed to leave. I closed my eyes, and a moment later, I was back in the diner.

I opened my eyes and watched the spark come back to Candy's face. "Ollie?"

"It's me."

"I just had the craziest dream."

"Don't worry about that now," I said, sliding the lukewarm waffles over to her. "Eat. You look like you've seen a ghost."

She took the fork and looked down at her plate. She thought for a moment and then took a bite. A contented moan escaped her lips when she chewed. After she swallowed, she stuck the fork in the waffles again and looked up at me.

"I don't deserve this," she said, disgusted. "I haven't been honest with you."

"I know," I replied. "I know everything."

"That car you're looking for—Lily. I did take it from them. I had no idea it was your car until they drove off. I swear."

I bit my lip, trying to stifle my anger. "I know you've been through a lot tonight, but don't lie to me. You knew exactly what you were doing."

"You're right." She nodded. "I knew exactly what I was doing, you're right."

"How long were you under their thumb?"

"It wasn't their thumb. It was their boss's."

"So, you met him?"

She shook her head. "Never in person, but he always paid and paid well. He needed clean titles, and then after a job was done, they would bring it to me for detailing and modifications. It was so much business, so much money, I couldn't say no, and that night…I couldn't say no to them, even though I knew exactly what I was doing. I'm sorry, Ollie. I'm so sorry."

My eyes narrowed. "Finish your food, and then you're going to take me to where you dropped off their cars."

"I don't—"

I held up my hand. "That wasn't a question. I'm in a forgiving mood right now, especially given what you just went through, but don't test me."

"You don't understand. They brought the cars to us or picked it up—" A flash of a thought ran through her mind. "Actually, there was one time—" She faltered.

"One time is all you need. Do you remember the place?"

"Yes."

"Then, finish your food and take me there."

"All right." She knew she didn't have any choice in the matter, and for somebody as proud as Candy, that was hard to swallow. Still, it was a far easier pill to swallow than her death.

"One more thing," I added, leaning forward. "Was there a wand in the car when you got it?"

She shook her head. "No."

Drats.

CHAPTER 24

After Candy finished wolfing down her food, we spent the next hour slowly driving Lily up the Hollywood Hills, working our way up and down switchbacks, rising high and then sinking lower into the mountains. The views in the Hills were majestic but getting there was like navigating through the favelas of a third-world country, with roads barely wide enough for one car. You were stuck going around turns at five miles an hour, and god forbid you missed a turn.

"STOP!" Candy finally shouted. "Pull over here. This is it."

"You're sure this is the place?" I asked as we idled outside a house high up in the hills. It was protected by a fortified gate, and a half dozen demon sentries patrolled the grounds. The lip of the house hung over the edge of the mountain, and wall-to-ceiling glass gave it a slick modern look. Unfortunately, the tinted glass didn't let me see inside, and I had a feeling it was reinforced with bulletproof glass.

"I'm sure." Candy's voice didn't waver. "He made me drive a Rolls up here myself once when all his drivers were busy. Said I was the only one he could trust."

I squinted, trying to get the best look I could. I didn't like what I saw. Even at my best, I couldn't take on an army of demons in a fortified place like that. Not without my own army. Maybe now I had a reason to call in an old favor. I found a safe spot to park and hid Lily on the hill as best I could.

I pulled Candy into an alley where I could be as hidden as possible in a residential neighborhood. "You're about to see some stuff you can't unsee. I need you to be cool, okay? Nothing is going to be as bad as what you've dealt with already tonight, okay?"

"Okay." Candy nodded, then put a hand on my arm. "Why aren't you madder at me, though?"

"Is this really the time?"

She shrugged. "If you're going to kill me at some point, I think I should know."

"I wouldn't save you just to kill you. We both have the same enemy for now. But after this, we aren't friends. I don't ever want to so much as sniff you in the same place as me. If I even hear your name on the wind, I will reign vengeance on you like a frigging archangel, do you understand?"

"I figured it was something like that." She nodded. "I understand."

"Besides, right now, I would rather have you close, where I can make sure you don't ruin my plans." I grabbed her arm. "*Porth i Ratinger Drug, Seattle.*"

A huge green portal opened in front of us, and Candy's eyes went wide for the hundredth time since I'd found her in that cabinet. "What is this?"

"Don't ask questions." I pushed her through the portal. When I arrived on the other side, Candy had stumbled on the sidewalk in front of Ratinger Drug, the front for Benny's criminal enterprise. I reached down and pulled her up. "Come on."

I led her into the drug store, the door jingling when I opened it. The same hard-faced woman with the fake plastic smile guarded the counter and the hidden door behind it.

"Can I—" Her face dropped when she recognized me. "Oh, it's you." She pushed the buzzer underneath the counter, and the door behind her clicked. "Maybe he'll finally kill you tonight."

"He couldn't kill me," I replied, moving past her. "He loves me."

I did more for Benny than I asked in return. In fact, aside from agreeing to help me take down the asshole who betrayed me, I'd never asked him for anything, and I hadn't even called in that favor yet. Meanwhile, I'd done more and more work for the Rat King to inch into his good graces, always cutting my rate by fifty percent or more to show I was reasonable and a team player. It was a trick I learned early. Even when you have a gruff personality, if you were valuable to somebody, they would like you—even if they didn't like you. Of course, it was a perilous dance. The minute you proved disposable, you would be disposed of. That's when it was good you were more powerful than just about anything on Earth.

We snaked through the sewers under Ratinger Drug until we came to a break in a series of underground sewer pipes where three lines converged in one room. The smell of rotting food and feces grew as we descended, but the worst of it converged in the room that Benny called an office. My nose was already sensitive to smells, and Benny's was the foulest I had encountered in a long time. I came prepared, popping in a pair of nose plugs. Too bad they couldn't do anything to stop the foul taste of death on my tongue.

"Ollie!" he said. "My good girl. How'd that tip work out for you?"

"Perfect, Benny. Thank you. Lily is back home safe and sound."

"Good, good to hear it." His voice was softer than in our first encounters, and the rats that formed his body were more relaxed than they had been in the past. "I'm glad I could help."

"That's what it's all about, isn't it? Helping each other."

"Absolutely. I scratch your back, and you scratch mine." He left me an opening, and I took it. "Funny you should say that." I rubbed the back of my neck. "Because it's about time I called in that favor, Benny. We got him."

"Got who?"

"The demon that betrayed us both." I pushed Candy forward. "This is Candy. She used to deliver cars to the creep, and she led me to his compound. It's guarded by a small army of demons, which is a good sign they are protecting something massive inside."

The rats that made up Benny's face turned it to a scowl, looking Candy up and down. "How certain are you of this?"

"A hundred percent," she replied. "Took me a second to remember, but I'm absolutely sure that's where I delivered the car." She dry heaved. "My god, how do you survive down here?"

"Evolution, my dear. Any who come to attack me gotta survive a natural barrier to doing so, and meanwhile, my rats bring me news from around the city. I control my whole army from here. This is the single most important room on the whole west coast." He scoffed. "You humans, thinking everything revolves around your sense of smell. Pitiful."

I pulled her back by the elbow. "I'm sorry. She didn't mean to offend you."

"I don't like to be insulted. Even if it's your friend, I will—"

"Whoa." I held up my hands in protest. "She is not my friend. She betrayed me. If she didn't have information I need, I'd kill her."

"Hey!" Candy shouted, collapsing on the ground. "Oh god, I got it in my mouth."

Benny growled. "If she's a traitor, then why should I believe her?"

"Because I do," I said.

"You're willing to stake your reputation on this girl?"

"Is there any other way you'll give me the men I need to mount an attack?"

Benny cackled in ten pitches at once. "No, I don't think there is."

"Whatever it takes. I'm calling in all my favors, and I'll stake whatever you need to get your men to help me."

Benny shrugged. "One hour. Be ready."

"We will be."

CHAPTER 25

An hour later, I was standing above ground with a group of Benny's troops. The three orcs, decked out in battle armor, would lead the charge with their snub-nosed shotguns. Behind them, a dozen goblins would scale the walls and lay down cover fire while the dwarves and I broke through the front gate after the changeling blew the door clean off with a carton of C4. Meanwhile, the pair of elves perched across the street would take out the guards on the opposite roof. The whole plan should take less than two minutes beginning to end once we blew the door.

Candy wasn't much of a fighter, so I convinced her to stay under armed guard with two troglodytes in Benny's office. If we all survived, I would deal with her later.

"Don't die," Candy said to me.

"Very little chance of that," I replied. "I'm quite hard to kill."

She smiled. "I'll bet you are."

"Remember that, Candy." I squeezed her hands tightly, almost violently. "That's as much a threat as a fact."

"I got it." She turned toward the troglodytes, who brought her inside the drug store.

I motioned for the rest of the attack squad to gather around me. "Killing demons is tricky," I said. "Benny equipped you all with special bullets made of black steel from the bowels of Hell itself. In a moment, I will bless and consecrate them. My mother was an angel, so I can do things like that." I stared into the faces around me. "Before I do, I want to remind you that demons are fast and strong. They respect a show of force, but it also infuriates them.

Demons are hard enough to kill when calm, and even if you do kill them, they just rematerialize in Hell. It might take them eons to get back out, but when they do, they'll come back with a vengeance. So, don't let them find out who you are, no matter what."

I tapped my chest, then my head. "Two shots in the chest. One in the head. That should do it. Now, drop your heads."

I held my arm up and chanted. "*Yn enw'r tad, spn, a'r ysbryd sancaidd.*" I made the sign of the cross and then spun on my heels. "*Porth i Lili.*"

I created a portal and, after the team had rushed through, closed it behind me. The elves were already halfway across the street by the time I stepped onto the hill, where I watched the changeling disappear from sight with his box of explosives. I brought the rest of the troops into an alley next to the compound.

A minute later, the elves flashed a light to signal that they were in position. I motioned for the others to follow, and we crawled slowly in the darkness toward the gate, hugging the wall. We were twenty yards away from the main gate when the door blew, sending fire into the air, just like we planned. We couldn't see her, but the changeling could see us, and I told her to blow it when we were just outside of the range of the blast.

"Go! Go!" I screamed, and we charged the door. Gunfire rang out over me as two guards ran out from behind the gate. "*Pigua obsidian!*"

Huge metal spikes flew out of my hand and embedded in the foreheads of the two demons, sending them crashing to the ground. When I reached them, I looked up to see the goblins on top of the walls, firing wildly at the demons below them.

"We're going in!" That was their signal to stop firing until we got to safety.

I rushed forward and took cover behind a black van as the bullets flew all around me. The dwarves met me as the orcs charged, blasting their shotguns across the front lawn of the house. A lawn sculpture of a swan made of bushes exploded inches from my head as I ducked to avoid the blasts. Automatic rifles sprayed bullets down on us like rain from the roof, pinging the van with dozens of shells in mere seconds. When they had to reload, we had a small window to advance.

"Now!" I screamed when the orcs were past the front door. The dwarves laid down suppressing fire while I charged in after the orcs.

I kicked through the entrance and fired more spikes on two demons crouching behind a couch in a makeshift barricade. I assumed a fair few demons were inside, I just had to find them. The dwarves entered and took over so I could investigate. I turned the corner of a wood-paneled hallway, and a demon rushed out of the bedroom to greet me.

"*Pigua obsidian*!" I shouted and a spike embedded in its forehead.

"Clear!" I heard the dwarves shout from the front room. Outside, the orcs screamed the same thing. I met the dwarves on the other side of the hallway and took turns clearing the rooms and cleaning up any demons who remained.

"Only one room left," I said. "Let's hope he's in here, and this hasn't been an exercise in vanity."

Something was wrong. It had been too easy, much too easy to storm this fortified compound. I didn't understand why until I opened the room. Inside, I didn't see a demon, but a woman, light skin, red eyes, and a smile that took up half her face when she opened her mouth.

"About time," she said in an unsettling growl. She snapped her fingers, and the whole room went up in flames.

"Firestarter!" I screamed. "*Porth i Lili!*"

I leaped through the portal and dove to the ground next to Lily outside the compound as I watched the whole compound explode into a million pieces. "NO!"

The dwarves never arrived through the portal, and I had to close it before the fire made its way through. Few things frightened me, but firestarters pulled their fire from the depths of Hell, and my mother once told me it was one of the very few things that could kill us.

The blast only lasted a second, but it was enough to tear through everything. I waited for somebody, anyone, to come out from the ruins. To meet me, but there was nobody. I went through the rubble and found the charred remains of goblins, orcs, dwarves, and even the elves, who'd left their position once the grounds were clear to help secure the compound.

They were all dead.

I was so screwed.

It took until sunrise for me to get the courage to face Benny again. How was I going to tell him I'd gotten two dozen of his men killed and didn't even get the demon bastard that had betrayed us both?

He was going to make my life a living Hell. He couldn't kill me. I wasn't worried about that, but that didn't mean he couldn't torch my standing with everyone in my Rolodex and then hunt me to the ends of the Earth. It would be a terrible inconvenience. Could you imagine drinking a coffee next to the Eiffel Tower and suddenly you had three armed gunmen chasing you down?

When I entered the drug store, the door to Benny's office was open. Streaks of blood lined the shelving.

The poor pharmacist was bleeding out on the ground, white as a sheet. *Another ambush.* There was no way this was a coincidence. This was a coordinated hit. I rushed down the stairwell to find Benny. Too late. No longer was the rat king assembled as one fluid being. Instead, dozens of dead rats lay strewn around the room.

Around him, two troglodytes bled out with their boss, but there was no sign of Candy. Of course, there wasn't, because she was a liar. *And I vouched for her.* Then I heard it—whimpering, coming from one of the sewer tubes.

I hopped up into it and followed the sound until it stopped at a sniveling Candy, who looked up at me. "It wasn't me. It wasn't—I would have died, but those two. They pushed me into the drain. Told me to be quiet. They—they saved me—"

I took her by the shoulders and shook her. "If you're lying to me, I'll rip you apart."

She sobbed. "I'm not. I'm not."

I grabbed her around the neck and shoved her toward Benny's office. She jumped down, and I landed behind her. When I stood up, I saw a bull elk in a suit, standing on two legs, looking at me.

"What have you done?" he said, his voice trembling.

"It's not what you think." I held up my hands, but it was too late. He pulled his gun and fired at us.

CHAPTER 26

"*Tarian grym!*" I screamed as the bullets fired from the bull elk's gun. A blue shield formed in front of Candy and me. I had no doubt that I could survive the attack, but bullets still stung something fierce, and I had no interest in getting the wind knocked out of me or nursing welts for the next two weeks. Besides, if even one of the bullets went through me and hit Candy, she would likely die. If anyone was going to kill that girl, it would be me.

"You won't get away with this!" The Elkman screamed.

"Get away with what?" Candy shouted behind me. "We were just standing here."

"Liars!" I heard footsteps charging down the stairs above me. "Die!"

I didn't want to get involved in a gang turf war, and I didn't want to kill a bunch of innocents, either. Not that a cadre of criminal guards was innocent in the grand scheme, but they hadn't done anything to me. I wanted to keep it that way. "*Porth i Lili.*"

A portal shot open from my extended hand. I pushed Candy backward so that she fell into it, and I walked through after her. We stepped out of the portal on the Hollywood Hills, and I closed it behind us. Dozens of cruisers filled the tiny street. Firefighters worked diligently to put out the blaze from the explosion while medics sifted through the wreckage for survivors. The denizens of the surrounding units were out in the street en masse, giving statements to the police and blocking the way in and out.

I certainly didn't want to get into it with the police, but I wasn't about to leave Lily either—not when I just got her back. "Follow me."

I turned from the alley down the street. Lily was parked several blocks from the carnage but within the radius of the police perimeter. I unlocked the door and pushed Candy inside. She crawled to the passenger's seat before I slid into the driver's and started the car. Lily's engine got the attention of a beat cop with a bushy mustache.

"Hey!" He shouted, flagging me down. "Nobody can leave."

"I'm not going anywhere." I rolled down the window to greet him. I had to think fast. "I just want to pull my car into the garage."

"You live here?" he asked. "I need to get a statement."

"I'm afraid we didn't see anything, officer. We heard some kind of explosion, and it rocked our apartment, but by the time we got outside, I think it was all over."

He flipped open his book. "And what apartment complex do you live in?"

I pointed to the building on the left. "That one. Unit 4."

The cop furrowed his brow and flipped his book. "That's the Gunderson's residence. I talked to them half an hour ago."

"Yeah," Candy said, leaning over. "We were staying there for the night."

"They didn't say anything about guest—" The officer mushed his mouth into a scowl. His hand went instinctively to his gun. "I need you to get out of the car."

"I don't have time for this." I pulled off my glasses. "*Anghofio.*" My eyes shifted and turned, hypnotizing the officer. "You never saw us, got it?"

He nodded. "Saw who?"

"Excellent," I replied. "Now, clear a path for me."

I put my glasses back on and put the car in gear. The officer shook his head and looked at me, concerned. "Hang on, ma'am. Let me clear a path for you."

"Thank you."

"Why don't you do that all the time?" Candy asked.

I pressed my forehead, trying to prevent a migraine from setting in. "It takes a lot of energy, and I don't like talking to people very much." I rolled the car forward, following the officer's lead until we had passed him. "*Porth i'm fflat.*"

A green portal arose at the end of the alley, and I gunned the car toward it. Inches before hitting the edge of the hill and careening off, we made it through the portal and into the garage under my townhouse at the other end. I had moved since the Solstice when a group of thugs ransacked my apartment. I didn't give notice. I just left. That's why I paid top dollar, so I could do things like that. I was getting sick of the beach anyway and moved back to Palms, which was more centrally located.

I backed into the parking spot and placed the car in park. "Now that we have a second, what just happened?"

"I was going to ask you the same question," Candy said. "Did you blow up that house?"

"No!" I said, indignant. "Somebody else did that. And they killed everyone. I expected to come back and grovel to Benny. But when I found him, he was dead, and you were alive, so I'm going to ask you again…what is going on?"

"I don't know!" Candy screamed. "I was down there with Benny, trying not to heave my lunch from the sewer smell when I heard a bunch of footsteps above me. Benny ordered his guards to be on alert, and then the shooting started. They must have had machine guns or something because I had never seen so many bullets go off so quickly before. One of the trobl—tribblin—"

"Troglodytes."

She nodded. "Right. Sorry. One of the—those guys pushed me into the sewer with his last bit of energy. I don't think they ever saw me, but I saw them—they massacred that poor rat."

"What did they look like?"

"I don't know."

"You said that you saw their faces!" I growled.

"No, I said I saw them. They were wearing masks or something, and it was only for a second before I went to hide. I stayed put until you found me."

"You know this looks bad for you, right?"

"How?" She lifted her hands in a hopeless gesture. "I'm a victim here."

"Well, Benny was alive before you came along, a known traitor, and since I started looking out for you, Benny is now dead, and the attack went tits up. And, hrm, which one of us was working with a known enemy of both Benny and me—that would be you."

"You've been with me every step of the way since you found me. How could I be working for them? Seriously, you wouldn't even let me pee alone."

I shook my head. "I don't know how you could do it, but I'm going to find out." I put the car into drive. "And I know the perfect alien to help us."

CHAPTER 27

I didn't want Phil involved in this whole escapade, but there weren't many people I trusted. I needed help. A gang of demons wanted me dead, and now I had Benny's crew breathing down my neck.

The garage door was already open when I arrived at Phil's house. He had a habit of forgetting to close it. He would probably forget his eye if it weren't attached to his head. Since he'd been kidnapped, he talked more and more about the stars. I worried he would leave me—and then who would I have left?

I pulled into the driveway and closed the garage door behind me on my way inside. The house wasn't the rancid pigsty I had grown used to over the years, and it knocked me for a loop to see it clean for the first time.

"Like what I've done with the place?" Phil said. "You haven't been inside for a couple of weeks. I know you've been bugging me to get rid of this garbage for years, but— but I knew they would have a use." He waved me onward.

"I don't really—"

He held up his finger. "As you would say, that wasn't a request, yes? I was just being polite."

He was right. I would say that. "Lead the way."

I followed Phil through the back of the house and into a small laundry room off the kitchen, where I had watched him learn to cook unsuccessfully when we were growing up. He turned the washer's dial to "delicate" and the dryer to "heavy-duty." The ground shook, and the washer-dryer combo dropped into the floor, revealing a small walkway underneath the house.

"I closed your garage," I said.

"Ah yes. That's nice. I should have… I've just been too dang excited to think about anything else. I've been dying to show you this—I've been dying to do anything, as it's the natural condition of every sentient, mortal being. Death, that is."

"Deep," Candy said from behind me.

Phil suddenly realized that we weren't alone, and his neck snaked around to get a look at Candy. "Who are you?" he asked, more curious than angry.

"This is Candy," I replied. "She's the reason we're here."

"Is she cool?" Phil asked.

"Absolutely not," I said. "She betrayed me, and I think she might have betrayed one of my clients, too."

"I didn't betray you!" Candy shouted before thinking better of herself. "Okay, so I kind of did betray you the one time, but I don't think that's as much a betrayal as lying to you."

"That's the same thing!"

"No, it's not!" Candy scoffed, offended. "They're in the same ballpark, maybe, but they are not the same."

"What's the difference, then?" Excitement bounced on Phil's voice. "This is a fascinating course of discussion."

"Intent, I guess?"

"Didn't you have something you wanted to show me?" I asked, trying to steer the conversation anywhere but with Candy.

"Well, not with a betrayer," Phil said. "I wanted to share it with my friend."

"I'd like to see it," Candy said. "And then maybe we can be friends."

Phil's eye narrowed. "Oh, honey…no. I'm sorry, but I'm not in the market for any new friends." He sighed and fidgeted, but he couldn't contain his excitement. "ARGH! Okay, I'm going to burst if I don't show you." He pointed his finger at Candy. "Don't betray me, okay?"

"I won't," she said.

I chuckled. "I'm old enough to know that on a long enough time horizon, everyone will betray everything."

"I haven't." Phil turned down the hallway. "Though you're right, perhaps we only need a long enough time horizon. That is a depressing thought—don't you betray me either, Ollie."

"Okay," I replied, following Phil down the stairwell. "I won't."

It had been years since I'd been in his basement. For the longest time, it was a repository for his various experiments. Now, however, it was clear that Phil had been busy. He had excavated triple the space and lined it with sleek, white plastic. In the center of the room was a generator, and next to it was a massive trash receptacle.

"As you may remember, since I crashed on this planet, I've been looking for a source of fuel abundant and formidable enough to power intergalactic travel, at least until the next service station on Alpha Centauri. Well, it took some decades, but I've finally done it."

"Wow," Candy said. "Is that a Ferrari engine dropped into the middle of that contraption?"

"Very good," Phil said. "I've tried every engine from your primitive automobiles, and this was the only one that could approximate the power I needed for escape velocity."

Candy rushed forward and slid her hand along the engine. "Does it still run on gas?"

"Well, no," he said. "Gas is unstable. This is part nuclear, and part my own design, which will allow me to take a stable, neutral piece of matter, convert its potential energy to kinetic energy, and use it for propellant."

I cocked my head and grinned. "And you chose trash, I assume."

Phil nodded. "I've been feeding it for the past weeks, trying to make sure it was stable, but yes. It doesn't have to be trash, of course. Considering what I had lying around, it was effective for testing."

"Whoa," Candy said. "So, this thing runs on nuclear power and trash?"

"Technically, the nuclear power is just a propellant to get me into the upper atmosphere. Once I have escaped the pull of Earth, I should be able to continue through the solar system with a minimum of energy, save for the life support." He turned back to me with a sharp look. "At least your friend is excited about what I've done."

"I'm sorry, buddy. It's very nice. It's just—well, it brings you one step closer to leaving."

"Yes," he replied. "But that won't be until I can fix the chassis of the ship, which could take—"

"Can I help?" Candy asked. "Cars are kind of my thing, and there's no way I could live with myself if I passed up the chance to work on a real-life, honest to god spaceship. I'm very good. Tell him, Oleander."

"She's very good until she betrays you." I glared at her before turning back to Phil. "Now, I appreciate that you're very excited, but I need your help."

He sighed. "I know, but I thought for one moment you could be excited for my thing…for a change."

"I'm sorry, the people trying to kill me—"

"Yes, I know," Phil said, touching the engine one last time. "I miss when people weren't trying to kill you."

"Me too, buddy," I replied. "There's nothing I want more than for things to get back to normal." I stepped closer to the engine and tried to look interested. "Did you hear they're working on a new video console system in Japan? It should be out by the end of the year. I promise when it comes out, I'll make some time to come hang out with you and play."

"That's if I'm still on the planet."

I nodded. "Let's not talk about that. It gives me a pang right in my stomach, the thought of losing you."

"That's nice." He turned to Candy. "Now, what are we going to do with you?"

I spoke up before she could say anything. "She said she wasn't helping the demon who betrayed me, but within an hour of introducing her to Benny, he was killed, and my attack was blundered like they knew we were coming and—"

"And I almost died!" Candy shouted.

"Yeah, it's a good deception," I grumbled. "People who almost die are almost never thought of as a suspect."

"Because they usually aren't responsible for almost dying!"

I got in her face. "Except when they are!"

"Ladies," Phil said, stepping between us. "I think I have a solution."

CHAPTER 28

Phil led us out of the basement and into the kitchen. He pulled a string behind the fridge. A medical table lowered from the ceiling and spread across the counters on either side of the room.

"Up," he said to Candy, patting the mattress. It wasn't so much a demand, but a strong request, and Candy acquiesced without question. She hopped onto the table and laid down. Phil opened the fridge and pulled out a collection of nodes that he placed on her temples, across her chest, on each wrist, and along her stomach and thighs.

"They're so cold," Candy shivered as he placed each one.

"I'm sorry, my dear," Phil said. He blew on the last node and shrugged before he placed it on the middle of her chest. "Unfortunately, I am cold-blooded, which means that didn't help much. It was a performative show at best."

"I still appreciate it," Candy said, bracing herself for the chill. "Sometimes, all we have is the performative."

"How right you are," Phil said. He opened the freezer and started typing on a computer console inside the door. A long metal cartridge as large as Candy descended from the ceiling. "Don't move. This won't hurt unless you move. In which case, it could lead to a nasty case of dead."

"Is it safe, then?" Candy asked. "If it could kill me?"

"Oh, gods no," Phil said with a smile. "Let's begin."

He typed away on his console while a red beam covered Candy's legs and moved up to her naval, then to her chest, and finally to her face, before making its way back down.

Three times it trekked from the soles of her feet to the tip of her head.

"Scan complete," Phil said. He turned from the console to watch the scanner work. "Now, the fun part."

The scanner let out a slow moan and then shot a thin, precise beam into the right side of Candy's stomach, two inches from her naval.

"What does it mean?" I asked.

Phil reached into one of the kitchen drawers and pulled out a thick marker, marking the position of the beam on Candy's stomach with it.

"That tickles," Candy said with a giggle. If I didn't know any better, I would think she was flirting with Phil. Not that Phil wasn't attractive, but he wasn't really human. I had never even seen a girl interested in him when he wore his human suit, let alone in his alien form.

"There is a tracker in Candy's stomach," he murmured, turning back to the console. "Though it's not a technology that I'm familiar with."

I shook my head. "It's not tech at all. It's probably a tag."

When you wanted to track somebody magically but didn't want them knowing about it, you used a tag. It let you keep tabs on anyone you wanted with a simple map spell. Of course, any witch, wizard, or magical creature worth their salt would know how to remove a tag. A human wouldn't even know to look for one.

"Well," I took a deep breath. "It looks like you might have been telling the truth."

Candy pulled down her shirt and shot me a look. "Duh. I told you. I'm a lot of things, but I'm not a narc."

"No, you're just a liar."

"It's better, though." Candy said. "I didn't snitch on you and get a bunch of people killed." She sat up. "How do we…get it out?"

"I'm going to need a wand." It was a delicate procedure, and skin was pressure sensitive. I would be as likely to blow her up as remove the tag. "At least this gives me a reason to go searching for it." I searched her face. "You are sure there wasn't a wand in the car when you got into it?"

"I don't know. What is a wand?"

Grrr, humans, especially humans that didn't read fantasy.

"It's like a long stick of wood," Phil said. "Unimpressive unless you know what to look for."

Candy shook her head. "Nothing like that. It was pretty clean inside."

I stroked my chin. "Balaam and Moloch were busy bees that night. If only I knew where they went after your shop."

"They told me they were going right to their boss's house. Something about you getting away and that he wouldn't be too happy about it. They seemed kind of nervous, too."

"If they still had my wand when I vaporized them, they would have used it. Even dummies like Balaam and Moloch would know what kind of power it could unleash on the world—on me. That means they had to get rid of it before the sushi shop." I thought back to everywhere Balaam and Moloch stopped. Before the car shop, they stopped at a gas station, and then—then they stopped at that apartment. That had to be it.

"Do you think you can watch this one here?" I asked Phil. "I usually wouldn't ask, but since she's pretty much been cleared, I feel a little better about it."

He shrugged. "I don't see the harm. I mean, anybody tracking her already knows she's here, right?"

"Unfortunately, that's sound logic."

"Mine usually is, for better or worse."

I didn't like leaving Phil to fend for himself and had to remind myself that he was capable. He had survived on Earth for decades, and his tech was more advanced than even the smartest humans on Earth would fathom for millennia. Still, he would always be the gawky kid trying to cover his alien body in a gawky holosuit…and doing a horrible job of it.

I could have simply portaled over to the house, but I needed to clear my head. Driving did that for me. I didn't mind when I ended up hitting traffic. I wasn't sure what my plan would be when I reached the apartment, and I had the whole ride to figure it out. Even in the dead of night, gridlock happened in Los Angeles, which was part of its charm and frustration.

There were six apartments in the complex, but only one had a series of wards and hexes on the door to prevent somebody from disturbing them. The "bust in and take what I want" approach was off the table unless I wanted five years of bad luck and a nasty case of diarrhea as a kicker. Luckily, I was used to dealing with criminals.

I put on my brightest smile and knocked lightly. A heavy knock would sound like cops, and I didn't want them on edge. I heard mumbling from inside the apartment and several pairs of feet shuffling around. Finally, a fit man in a form-fitting tank top opened the door. He rubbed his bald head at the sight of me.

"Hey, mama. What can I do for you?"

"Two rather large men would have come here to unload something a couple of weeks ago. I'm looking for that something." They were changelings, one of the easiest types of monsters to blend into the scenery. They were lucky because no matter what happened, all they had to do was slip on a new skin and disappear.

"I'm not int—" He tried to close the door, but I slammed my hand against it to stop it. Changelings were wily but weak. "Get off."

"Do you know who I am, son? My name is Ollie, and I can be your best friend or your worst nightmare. It's your choice."

"Yeah, I heard of you." He scratched his chin. "All right, all right. I'm listening."

"What's your name?"

"Carl. That's the only name I'm giving you."

"Smart." Some fae bartered in names, and he was too smart to give me anything I could use against him. "Two men came here several weeks ago, on the Solstice, late at night, with something to trade, something very powerful, and very rare. It was not theirs to give. It was mine. And I would like it back."

He sighed. "I knew that story was too good to be true. Yeah, I got it. Come in." He moved aside so I could step inside. Six other guys dressed so similarly that I couldn't tell them apart sat on worn sofas watching *Jaws* in Spanish. "They told me they found it in a shipping container they stole." He crawled over the other men and pulled a hollow box off a bookshelf empty except for different bits and bobs. He opened the box and pulled out a wand—my wand. "This it?"

I nodded. "It is. If you give it to me, I'll keep my end."

He shook his head. "Afraid I can't do that. You help me, and then, when it's all done, you can have your stupid wand."

"Maybe I'll just kill you now."

Carl laughed. "You can try. Even if you get through all my associates, this place is spelled up the ass to protect me. If you touch me, it will destroy you."

Was he bluffing? Probably not. He probably worked with lots of dangerous people, and warding his house for protection made sense. I wasn't in a place to take a chance. "What can I do for you?"

The smile spread slowly across his face. "You probably know this, but you have a bit of a reputation on the street. Word is you have a price on your head, two million. So, I figure you owe me five million for the wand and then another two on top for not turning you in, plus interest, of course, so let's make it an even ten."

"Ten million dollars? That's your price? I don't have that kind of money."

"That's okay. You can pay us in product. Not just any product, either. We had a shipment confiscated by the cops. I hear you can open portals anywhere you want, whenever you want, wherever you want. I want you to get me into that warehouse so we can get back our product. Zip in, zip out, then we're even, and you can have your wand back."

Criminals think so small, but I wasn't complaining. "Draw me a map and get me an address, and I'll get you inside."

CHAPTER 29

Carl forced me to finish watching *Jaws* before we started the job, which didn't bother me one bit. I needed a moment of big, dumb fun since my life recently had been filled with too much big, dumb idiocy and danger. When it was done, he wrote down the address for me and sent his men to get their weapons, just in case. When he handed me the address, I laughed.

"Do you think I'm stupid?" I asked.

"What do you mean?"

"This isn't a police impound. This is Jing Hai's warehouse, biggest heroin dealer in Los Angeles."

"All right." He shrugged. "You got me. So what? Are you going to tattle on me or something?"

"That depends. Is there any other way to get my wand back from you without killing you?"

He held the wand at either end between his hands. "I guess if you want it broken. Otherwise, you get the wand when we get the goods."

Jing Hai wasn't going to like this one bit. Ten million dollars in product was nothing to his multibillion-dollar operation, but word that somebody stole from him would get out, especially when he started to find his H on the street when he hadn't gotten his cut. I'd had a good working relationship with Jing Hai for years. I never used him for drugs, but his boats smuggled all kinds of things. His people were experts at evading law enforcement, which was advantageous for getting rare magic into the country.

Worse yet, if I helped Carl and his idiots, one of them would talk, probably more than one, even if it was just pillow talk with an overeager escort, and it would come back to me eventually. There were only so many portal-jumping women who wore sunglasses and a long trench coat and who could make it past all of his guards unseen.

But I couldn't let that wand out of my sight either. I would never find another like it.

"I'll play your game, Carl," I said. "But you better not break that wand."

"As long as we get ten million in H, I'll be happy, and then—" He pointed the wand to me. "You'll be happy."

"Then let's go. *Porth i warwa Jing Hai.*"

One problem with portals was they were imprecise. While somebody like Kimberly could home in on an exact location, portals were more like subways. The barrier between time and space wasn't thin everywhere, and portals could only materialize where the thinnest of membranes existed, which meant that you didn't always get as close as you wanted to your target.

Another problem was that portals were big and loud. Anyone guarding, say, a secluded heroin warehouse would be able to see it. I hoped to use that to my advantage and alert the guards to my presence before we got far.

It worked.

By the time Carl's crew came through the portal, we ended up in the far corner of the warehouse. Three of Jing Hair's men rushed toward us, forcing us to put up our hands.

Theirs was a big, bad, stupid plan, and it failed spectacularly in a matter of moments. Mine was just as risky and only slightly less stupid, and it relied on Jing Hai liking me a lot more than he let on and trusting that I would never screw him.

The eight of us were led into a pitch-black room and tied to chairs. I could have easily broken free, but I didn't want to piss off yet another dealer. My business relied on them all liking me, or at least tolerating me.

I kept a stiff upper lip when I heard the screams of Carl's men around me in the darkness. Somebody must have told them not to hurt me, or maybe that I couldn't be hurt because they never came for me.

I didn't know how long I was under the black hood they stuffed over my head. Eventually, two men pulled me from the chair and led me across the warehouse. It had been a long time since I heard any other voices or even the sound of breathing. That could not have been a good sign.

When the guards slammed me down again in a chair, they pulled off my mask, and Jing Hai, dapper, suave, graceful Jing Hai, was waving my wand in front of his face. When he saw me looking at him, he turned and smiled.

"Ah, Ollie. Long time no see. I hoped we would meet again, but under different circumstances."

"Me too, Jing Hai." I bowed my head. "It's an honor to see you again."

"Is it?" He stopped playing with the wand and placed it on the table in front of him. "Because it would seem you are working with a group of changelings to steal from me."

I shook my head. "They weren't smart enough to steal from you—I assume it's were and not are. They were impulsive, and they blackmailed me into helping you."

"How the mighty have fallen. Tsk tsk tsk." He sounded genuinely disappointed. "I thought so highly of you."

"I didn't want to work with them. I have had a terrible time of it since December. I lost my car. I lost my money."

I took a breath. "And I lost my wand, which is on your desk. I was just trying to get it back."

Jing Hai sat down in a high back rolling chair across from me. "Why should I believe you?"

"We both know that if I wanted to, I could rip all of your heads off and escape. I'm not doing that because I respect you."

"But not enough to refrain from stealing my property."

"Please, if you heard those idiots' plan, you would have known they had no chance of actually stealing even a kilo of H from this warehouse. They were clowns."

Jing Hai laughed. "I did hear it while I tortured the life out of them." He tented his hands in front of him. "This is the cost of doing business, I suppose. I'm ashamed of you, Ollie. I thought you were a better class of villain."

I shrugged. "I'm sorry to disappoint you."

He pushed the wand across the table. "You got what you came for. You can take this."

I picked up the wand. "Thank you. Are we cool?"

He shook his head. "No. I only give people one chance with me, and you burned that. However, since I can't kill you, I'll have to ask you to respect staying out of my business." Because I was half angel, he thought killing me would offend God. I wasn't about to tell him that God didn't care about me. I'll let the good Christian drug smuggler have his virtuosity as it suited my needs. "I can't destroy you, but I can destroy your reputation, which I will if I ever hear you interfere with me again."

"I'm sorry it's come to this," I said, bowing my head again. "But I understand."

"I knew you would." He gestured me to leave. "And Ollie, be careful. I hear there's a two-million-dollar price on your head."

I nodded. "Yeah, that's the word on the street."

There was honor among thieves, but it only went so far. I had to figure out how to stop this stupid hit before somebody was less forgiving than Jing Hai.

CHAPTER 30

"Yes, there does seem to be a two-million-dollar bounty on your head," Phil said. It had taken him all of five minutes of sitting behind his computer before he pulled that information. "I've heard five substantiated reports across my whisper network."

"Who called the hit?" I asked.

"It would seem Benny's number two put out the hit, but you have to understand how primitive this technology is—I had to interrupt phone signals and combine that with scattershot data from several disparate sources before I could even cobble this much information together… but yes, that is my best guess."

"How confident are you in that?"

Phil shrugged. "Seventy-three percent, give or take. Enough to confidently say it, but not enough to recommend you reign hellfire down upon them, just in case I am wrong."

"Can I reign hellfire on anyone?" I asked. "Because this is seriously hurting my reputation, and I am pissed off."

"That's not the thing I would be most concerned about," Phil said. "There is a Firestarter out there, and she can actually kill you. That's where my concentrations would lie at present if I were you."

"That bitch took a passive role in trying to kill me, as far as I know. She didn't attack until I showed up. This hit, though, it's actively trying to take me down, and while there aren't that many ways to kill me, there are enough monsters with enough know-how that I need this hit taken off me first. The Firestarter is next."

"Umm… speaking of…" Phil tapped on his keyboard a few times. "There seems to be a contingent of assassins approaching your mother's house as we speak."

He turned his monitor so I could see it. The video showed a green, hazy image where a group of masked monsters with assault rifles were milling around Mom's house.

"What?" I said. "How would they—" It came to me. I haven't had my name on a lease in a decade or more. My last known address was my mother's house, which didn't matter until somebody called a hit out on me. *"Porth i dŷ mam."*

"Where are you going?" Candy said, entering the room, covered in a towel. "Didn't you just get here?"

"Wow, you are getting comfortable," I replied.

"Phil said I could use his shower. It has very good pressure."

"Thank you," Phil replied with a smile. "I calibrated it myself."

"It was nice." She touched her stomach. "I couldn't rub the black stain where you removed my tag, though."

"It will fade away with time," I said. "Just stay here. Things are getting dicey out there."

"You mean they're staying dicey out there, don't you?" Candy asked.

I rolled my eyes behind my sunglasses without replying and disappeared into the portal. All the lights were off in the house when I entered my mom's living room. I tiptoed up the stairs. Family was a weird thing. I hated my mother, but I also loved her. I certainly didn't want her to die, even though I sometimes did, in short bursts. There was a familiarity there and a deep bond. I wasn't sure there was anything else there, but I couldn't stand the thought of losing her.

She birthed me. She made up half of my DNA. She didn't deserve what God did to her, and she didn't deserve to be hunted like an animal. I learned long ago that I could want her to pay for the way she treated me without wanting her dead and that sometimes, it was okay to wish her dead without actually wanting her dead.

I rushed down the hall when I reached the top of the stairs. Mom's door was the second on the right, with my old room being the first. She turned it into an art studio after I moved out, and then an exercise studio, and then it devolved into a cluttered storage unit.

I heard moaning from the room, and when I flipped on the lights, I saw her on top of a man—a boy, really. He couldn't have been more than twenty-two. I wasn't judging her for that, but no kid ever wanted to see their mom in that position.

"Mom!" I shouted, turning away.

Her tone was nonchalant. "Well, hello, Oleander. What a surprise to see you. As you can see, I'm a bit busy now. If you could—"

I ran to the window. The bushes rustled under me, and I watched movement in the darkness of the front lawn. "I'm sorry, Mom, but I can't. There are bad men outside."

"Always ruining my good time." Mom rolled away from her lover. "I'm sorry, Gill, but we'll have to finish this another time."

"But—" Gill tried to say.

"No buts, Gill. I would rather not have you die today. I'll call you, okay?" She snapped her fingers, and Gill vanished. "You know, this barging in is getting to be a problem."

I wheeled on her. "Would you rather I let you die?"

Mom scoffed. "Please. Many have tried in my life, none have succeeded. I think you forget I carried a flaming sword during the Rebellion. I reigned hellfire on Sodom—I can handle myself."

"There weren't assault rifles back then, Mom."

"Oh, piffle." She pulled a shirt over her head.

"Not piffle. These killers know what I am, and I'm sure they're prepared with black bullets forged from demonic weapons—and I came across a woman, mom. A Firestarter that could control the flames of Hell. We are not invulnerable to pain or death. Don't forget that."

"I suppose you're—"

All at once, the bullets rained down throughout the house. I pulled Mom to the ground as something large smashed through the front door. Glass broke on the other side of the hall, and two demons appeared in the doorway.

"Get out of my house!" Mom screamed, blue fire blazing in her eyes. She clasped her hands together, and an inferno of fire exploded in front of her, a power I never mastered. The two demons rushing toward us lit on fire. "Do you know how long I spent making this house perfect?"

I tried to pull Mom back, but she ripped her hand away from me. She turned down the hallway where a cadre of dwarves with long beards fired at us. Without blinking, Mom created a forcefield around herself that ricocheted the bullets back on the group, sending them to the ground. The dwarves sprawled all over the floor, bleeding.

"Look at this place! It's a disaster!" Mom growled. "And do you know what kind of problem I'm going to have with the homeowner's association about this noise?"

She stepped over them as I followed. Two demons with Uzis fired up at her when she reached the landing. She stopped the bullets with a glance and pushed them back at the demons. Behind her, the door opened. The monster behind it didn't have a chance to attack. Mom snapped her fingers, and it exploded into a pile of goo.

"Do you know how hard it is to get guts and blood out of carpet? This is unacceptable!"

Mom leaped down to the living room. Lights shone at her from outside the house. She pulled her hands together, and the demons on either side of the house smashed through the windows and crashed together in the center of the room. Mom looked down and pulled off both of their heads as if it were as easy as breathing.

And then she was done. Her body was covered in blood, and her chest heaved with wild and reckless abandon. She wiped the green blood off her cheek and licked it off. Mom had told me stories, but I had never seen her being a total and complete badass before.

She caught my eye as I stepped over the dead demons toward her. "I'm surprised you were afraid of these demons, my love. I barely broke a sweat beating them. I really should have trained you better."

I grabbed her hand. "Later, Mom. There will be more, and I have to get you to safety."

"Safety." She laughed. "They are the ones who should be going for safety. I'm not going anywhere. I have to clean all this up."

"Please, Mom."

"Give me one good reason."

I sighed. "You may be right. These demons can't hurt you, but they are still going to try. Until I get this hit called off me, they'll keep coming, over and over. Not just for you, but for everyone I care about."

"So, yourself."

"I care about more than just myself!" I yelled. "Not now, Mom!" I steadied my breath. "They'll come for Phil, too. If you don't care about leaving for me, then come to help Phil. You like Phil, right?"

"He's fine, I suppose."

"My recklessness got him kidnapped before. I can't let it happen again."

"Fine." She brushed her hands together, and as she did, the demons vanished, and her house repaired itself. "Hrm. I suppose that wasn't as hard as I made it out to be, was it, darling? Very well, let's go protect your friend." She smiled at me. "It's so nice to see that you still need your mommy."

CHAPTER 31

Phil didn't love the idea of my mother hanging out with him and Candy, especially since the two of them were clearly growing close, but he conceded that having a frigging angel for protection until this all blew over would be a logical move.

"I hope she does not interfere in my bonding with your friend," he said while walking me to the door. "I am becoming quite fond of Candace."

"You dog," I replied with a smile.

"I am very clearly not a dog. You would call me an alien, but that is not fair either, as my race is called—"

"It's just an expression," I said. "Just remember, Candy lied to me. She is a liar."

"I have taken that into consideration. Don't worry about that."

I placed my hand on his shoulder. "I will always worry about you. That's what friends do. They worry and look out for each other." I pulled my hand away. "Now, did you find out where they took Benny's body?"

Phil nodded. "They have moved it to their central medical examiner's office. They are very concerned with figuring out what happened to him."

"You would have thought they already knew what happened with how they are after me."

Phil shrugged. "I think that was more of a show of strength. A mob can't allow their boss to be killed without decisive action. It would undermine their credibility."

"If only we didn't all have to swing our dicks around all the time, maybe this would be a better world."

"Neither of us have penises in the traditional sense, Ollie. I think I understand your point, though. If we were more able to act with restraint and without blowing up at each other immediately, perhaps cooler heads would prevail. A better but less likely world, given the nature of humanity."

I sighed. "Guess we have to live with the hand we're dealt, huh?"

"Precisely."

I said my goodbyes and portaled to the medical examiner's office. I pulled the wand out of my long trench coat. "*Trawsnewid.*" With a tap from my wand, the trench coat transformed into the same white lab coats worn around the offices inside. Someone was leaving the office, and I ran up the stairs to grab the door before it latched behind her.

Inside, a security guard tapped their key card on the edge of the door. A green light popped up to grant her access to the back of the facility. I pulled a magazine from the rack in the front of the office and sat down as if I was waiting for an appointment. When the door opened again, an old man came out, palming his key card into his pocket. I stood up and "accidentally" bumped into him, swiping the key card out of his outside pocket as I did.

"*Trawsnewid.*" I tapped the key card and the face changed to mine, as did the information on the card. I tapped the key card against the door and entered without issue. Inside the door, a woman stood behind a pane of glass.

"Excuse me," I said. The woman looked up from her book. "I was just assigned to the Ratinger Drug shooting. Any idea where I should go?"

She rolled her eyes. "Man, they are bringing everyone onto that case. I don't blame them. It is strange. Who guns down fifty rats and three people, right?"

"Definitely weird," I replied. "But that's why they brought me in. Weird is my middle name."

"Weird." She gave me directions and returned to her book. I continued down the hallway until I reached the room that held the bodies. Inside were four long metal gurneys. On two were the troglodytes, except nobody knew them as that, obviously. Our disguises—the good ones, at least—worked even in death. On a third gurney was the poor pharmacist who didn't deserve to die, even if she was a catty wench.

In the center of the room was a fourth gurney with the bodies of dozens of little rats on them. They were all the same, brown with red eyes, riddled with bullets. It was a massacre. I looked through each little rat body, searching for a clue, and before I walked from one side of the gurney to the other, I found one. There were almost exactly fifty rats—forty-nine, to be exact, and one foot. There was at least one rat missing. I needed to find it.

The door opened, and two men with lab coats entered. They didn't look like the others I saw milling around. These two were built more like federal agents than scientists. They were wearing shoulder-strapped guns, and their jaws were stiff and square.

"What are you doing in here?" one of them asked. His coat said Dr. Ullman, while the other's said Dr. Overton.

Dr. Overton went for his gun immediately. Definitely not a scientist move. I held up my hands. "Easy, easy.

Look, it's a weird case, and I couldn't help but take a look. I mean, who guns down fifty rats, right?"

"Let me see your card." Dr. Overton demanded.

I held my card out to him. He flicked the sides of it and then tapped the top. When he looked at me, he looked even less polite than before, which I didn't think was possible. "This card has been magically altered. Who are you really?"

"How did you know that—" But I didn't want to stay and find out. I tossed a tray of tools into the air toward Dr. Overton as I spun and roundhouse kicked Dr. Ullman in the chest. I grabbed the severed rat leg and stuffed it in my pocket. Before the two men could regain their footing, I pushed open the door and ran out into the hallway.

"*Trawsnewid.*" I tapped my forehead, and my body turned into a dark-skinned woman with long, straight black hair. My lab coat returned to my trench coat form, and I took off to conceal myself in the darkness.

Who were those people? They weren't monsters, that was for sure. I would have been able to tell their true form if they were, which meant at least two humans, government agents probably, knew about magic. I did not like that idea at all.

CHAPTER 32

Before I headed into the sewer to chase down a mangled rat, I needed equipment. I stopped by a pet shop and picked up a carrier, some rat food, and bandages to tie up the animal's wound. The attack happened almost a day ago, which meant that if the rat was bleeding out, it might be dead already, and that would complicate things. I was not a master necromancer, and I preferred not to hang around those weirdos.

"You want some bedding?" the cashier asked. "Rats really love our empty nester bedding."

"No, thank you," I replied. "Just the carrier and the feed."

"What about some hay? Or a toy? We have a really nice wheel. Usually for hamsters but rats—"

"No," I said more forcefully. The happy cashier's face dropped to an intimidated scowl. I looked at the counter and saw a little fluffy plush cow. I placed it on the register. "All right, maybe just one."

She perked back up. "Excellent. And thank you for shopping at Pet Stop."

Police tape lined the perimeter of Ratinger Drug, but there were no officers nearby, just an empty squad car with its lights on. I ducked under the police tape and made my way down the corridor toward Benny's office. The stench of the sewer still permeated everything, and blood coated the floor in a layer of sticky red goo. I stepped into the office and toward Benny's desk.

All the blood had coagulated into one disgusting mess. I dug into my pocket and found the rotting rat paw. I would have to get my coat professionally cleaned when all this was over, but I would be lying if I said it was the most disgusting thing I had ever kept in my pocket.

"Paru."

I tapped the tip of the foot and then pointed my wand at the ground. After a moment, the foot began to glow a haunting green, and when I placed it on the ground, I saw a trail of blood lead into the tunnel behind me. I hopped into the sewer and followed the trail of blood, impossible to discern from the sludge outside from the glow of my spell. The trail turned right, then left, then right, and another right before I saw a barely breathing rat glowing brightly. I rushed down toward it and scooped the rat into the carrier. It would die soon, and healing spells were not my forte. Luckily, I knew somebody who could help me. Somebody who loved all sorts of animals, even the disgusting ones that didn't seem worthy of love.

I opened a portal to the Happy Smiles Animal Clinic in Las Vegas. A city known for debauchery, there was plenty of heart, too, if you knew where to look. I had once helped a vet named Claudia to rescue a rare, pygmy, white rhinoceros in the jungles of Kenya. She moved to the states shortly afterward, and we'd remained friends since.

It wasn't that humans didn't know about magic. Some did, but I was always wary of them, especially when they traveled in packs. Most humans wanted magic for the power, not for the potential to help, which was why I liked Claudia so much.

Her clinic was small, without even a receptionist out front to welcome me when I opened the door. The smell of dog, cat, and rabbit crashed upon my nose when I took a step into the place. After the sewer, it was an improvement, but not by much.

"Be right there!" Claudia said sweetly as two dogs barked in the distance. A minute later, she walked up, her bright smile illuminated the whole room. Her magic was small but beautiful. She could mend animals in a way that the medical community could only dream of, which meant she had to stay under the radar. She didn't want to explain herself, after all, and draw attention.

"Ollie!" She ran forward to wrap me in a big hug. "It's so good to see you. Sorry, I smell like dog, but—I mean, look around."

"No, I get it. It's good to see you, too."

Claudia bent down to the cage in my hand. "And who is this little guy?"

"A small piece of a big puzzle. I'm hoping you can help me figure some of it out by putting him back together."

"Of course I can. It would be my pleasure." Claudia smiled at me. "I assume you have the leg? This will be much harder without it."

She brought me into the back room of her practice and laid the rat down on a metal exam table. She brought over a hose and carefully washed the rat until it was clean, taking extra care to sanitize the wound. She did the same with the leg and then placed it right under the rat's amputation wound.

"Emantur ligna membri."

It was exhausting for humans to use magic, and even the smallest spell could zap them for hours or days, but Claudia fell into it like a pro. She had some fae running through her, which increased her magical well. She held her hands over the leg, and they began to glow. I heard a snap and a crack, and the rat yelped.

"Shhh," she said. "You'll be okay." She lifted her head toward me. "Somebody did quite a number on this little guy. Who would do such a thing?"

"That's what I'm trying to figure out. Any chance you speak rat?"

She held up her fingers very close together. "Just a little bit." She pressed her hand on the rat's chest. "It needs to rest now, but when it wakes up, I'll see what I can do."

CHAPTER 33

"How are you feeling, little guy?" Claudia asked as the rat started to wiggle around. She placed a plate of water under its nose, and it lapped it up. The red-eyed rodent was hideous, but she found love and beauty in it, which I found endearing in a way. I didn't see many humans that way. "Yeah, you drink up, okay? That's a good boy. You had a big day, huh?"

While the rat had still been sleeping, I told Claudia everything I knew about the murder. Doing so was a risk, but she'd proved herself trustworthy in the time we'd spent together. If she was going to translate for me, she needed to know everything that I knew.

The rat squeaked to her, and she smiled. "Well, you're welcome. I think you're quite handsome, too."

"Ask him who he thinks killed his friends."

They squeaked to each other for a couple of seconds, and Claudia's face turned down. "He's not a snitch."

I bent down. "Listen here, you almost died. How could you have any loyalty to anyone?"

The rat squeaked, and Claudia cocked her head. "I think he said that when you've lost everything, all you have is loyalty to your own internal code."

I threw up my arms. "This is great. I met the one rat who isn't a rat in the whole world." I turned to him. "Find out if he's seen what those monsters did to the rest of Benny."

She scrunched up her nose. "We're wasting time, doing it this way. How about I just—can I use your wand?" I gave it to her hesitantly, and she placed the tip against her temple. "*Vinculum.*" She handed it back to me. "Touch it on your temple and say it too."

I touched the wand to my temple. "*Vinculum.*"

"What's going on here?" the rat said.

Holy crap. I suddenly understood rat.

"You don't understand rat. I understand rat, and I paired that skill with you. It will only work for about an hour, but I have other patients and can't be your translator." She stood. "Go with the gods."

I smiled and picked up the cage. I was going to take Benny's rat and leave. "I'm going to show you exactly how those monsters treated you."

I called a portal to the medical examiner's office and stepped through. I had a different face this time, and I hoped I would be able to break in again. Luckily, finding a key proved easy, like way too easy. I was surprised they weren't raided all the time. Maybe it's because they were in a crappy profession that insulated them from being infiltrated mercilessly.

"*Trawsnewid,*" I said, touching the keycard to the tip of the wand until it transformed into my new face.

I stepped through the doors and past the keycard entry. I marched forward with purpose, passing right past the guard dug deep in her book and toward the room. I found that if you walk with purpose and conviction, you could do just about anything.

Finally, we got to the exam room, which was much as I left it except that somebody had cleaned the mess I made and moved the two troglodytes and the pharmacist, probably into the freezers in the back of the room. I didn't care much about them. I was there for Benny.

I moved the cage toward the dead rats. "Do you see?" I swung the cage toward the spot where I found the foot. "That's where I found your leg. The leg you gnawed off in order to escape the hive."

"Stop!" the rat squealed.

"Then tell me what happened?"

"I don't know, okay?" the rat screamed. "They were in and out in less than a minute. I only survived because I was in the back of the body, under the desk. They slaughtered all of us, or so they thought. I waited until they left, and I gnawed off my leg to escape. I thought they would come back, and I had to—I escaped and hid, like a coward. So, I don't know what happened, okay?"

I was tired of running into dead ends. But then I had an idea. If he was alive and a part of the rat king, then he could vouch for me with whoever was leading the organization now—that stupid little Elkman who was trying to kill me.

"Where is your hideout?" I asked.

"You saw it, toots."

"No, where would you go if it all went to pot?"

"Gino's," he replied. "But God help us if we're there. It means things are really bad. Way worse than I *squeak squeak squeak.*"

The connection between us had broken. I had to hope he was telling the truth and that I wasn't walking into a trap. I would never live down getting tricked by a frigging rat.

CHAPTER 34

Gino's was close to the water across Seattle from Ratinger's Drug in the circuitous maze that was Pike Place Market, a mesh of poorly planned buildings where buskers sold everything from fish to jellies.

People looked at me funny as I walked through the marketplace with the rat carrier. Shop owners would be fined and downgraded by the health inspector if they came across a rat in their store, and here I was swinging one gently like it was my pet. It wasn't, but none of them knew that. I took the stairs down to the basement and passed onto a rickety walkway with a perfect view of the water. The rat squeaked. I didn't have to speak its language to know that it wanted to see the water, too.

"It's pretty," I said to him, even though I knew the rat couldn't understand me. After a moment, I continued on the path past a used bookstore and several other shops. Every few dozen feet, the architecture changed completely, from mod to art deco to the bones of a condemned building. Eventually, we snaked around to the Italian restaurant cliché that was Gino's. Two burly ghouls stood on either side of the door, blocking the entrance with their brute bodies.

"Can I get inside, please? I have something your boss really needs to see." I lifted the rat carrier. "Do you recognize Benny? Because this is all that's left of him."

A piece of Benny was clearly worthy of their boss's attention. The ghouls looked at each other and nodded, then led me into the wood-paneled restaurant where two more monsters took their place. Several dozen monsters lurked around, all carrying weapons that could have iced me or at least caused a lot of pain. Finally, the room broke open, and I saw the elk at a table in its center, drinking a glass of sherry. Behind him, the windows showed off all the harbor.

His face rose into a slight smile when I approached. He clapped his hands together, which surprised me since he should have hooves. "I do so love when the prey comes right to me."

"I'm not prey, and I didn't kill your boss." I slammed the rat carrier on the table. "And here is the proof. I assume you recognize him."

The Elkman cocked its head. "Benny?"

The rat squeaked something, and it seemed like the Elkman understood him.

"I see, but how do I know you are really Benny?" The Elkman sighed. "I'm afraid you'll have to give me the password. The one you gave me in case of emergencies."

The rat squeaked again, and I thought it sounded indignant, somehow.

"I know that it seems like overkill, but you were once fifty rats, and you are all that is left of that glorious being who led us so bravely for so long and died like a—"

The rat squeaked.

"I was not going to say rat! I was going to say pig, or maybe dog, but I would never insult you like that."

The rat squeaked.

"I understand." The Elkman looked up at me. "It seems I may have made a mistake. Please sit down."

"Does that mean you'll call off your bounty?" I pulled up a chair across from him and sat down. The Elkman snapped his fingers, and a demon porter approached to pour another glass of sherry for me. I covered my glass. "No, thanks. I'm more a whiskey girl myself."

"I can arrange you a glass if you would like."

"What I would like is for people to stop trying to kill me."

"We are in a dangerous business." The Elkman sipped his sherry. "I'm afraid there's always somebody trying to kill us." The rat squeaked. "But Benny says that far from killing him, you actually saved his life. I'm sure you are aware that while one rat of the rat king exists, he can be rebuilt. We thought him dead. Seeing him alive is a great injustice righted."

"I didn't know that, but I'm glad you're happy." I slammed my hands on the table. "All I really care about is that those jagweeds stop trying to kill me."

The Elkman waved his arm dismissively. "Yes, yes. Done." The elk made a sign with his hand, and two demons walked to the other side of the bar. "See, it's already in process. I'll clear your bounty on the dark network, and it will all go away."

"Good," I replied. "Second thing. I think you should make good on your reward and pay me the two million."

The Elkman squealed with delight. "That is delicious, but no. I'm being generous not to kill you right now, you know. It's only fair since you've done this town a great service."

I pulled the rat carrier off the table and stood. "Then I think we're done here. I came to prove my innocence, and I've done that. Getting the rat back will cost you two million."

"That's kidnapping," the elk said.

"That's business."

"I like you." The Elkman clapped his hands together. "Perhaps we can come to an arrangement."

"We already have. Two million for the rat."

"Counteroffer." The Elkman snapped his fingers, and all the guns rose toward me. "I've had my men load their guns with obsidian bullets for just this eventuality. Thank you for giving us that information when we attacked the demons, by the way. Expensive, but worth it, so maybe you just give me the rat and walk away."

I smirked. This was my kind of negotiation. "Counter-counteroffer. I find the real killer, and you pay me five million."

"Why would I pay you when I could let the police do their job?"

I stepped toward him. "Because if they're on your payroll, they are clearly incompetent, as is everybody you work with. They've let this hit happen and forced you to hole up here. You need somebody new, somebody outside. Somebody Benny trusted." I pulled up the rat carrier. "Tell them."

The rat squealed.

"Yes—I understand—" The Elkman sighed. "Very well. Your terms are acceptable."

"Great," I replied, making for the door. "Meanwhile, I think Benny will stay with me. After all, none of you can be trusted to protect him."

Two orcs stepped in front of the door, blocking my exit. I held up the rat carrier again. A full minute of squealing later, and the Elkman snapped his fingers.

"Let him go." His voice was constrained and resigned. Five minutes ago, he was on top of the world, and now, he was being played by a girl and her rat.

CHAPTER 35

I returned to Claudia's vet clinic again because if I was going to find out who put out a hit on Benny, I needed to be able to talk to him. She was significantly less excited about seeing me than she had been the first time, but she agreed to extend the bond between us so I could communicate with the rat.

"I can give you twenty-four hours this time," she told me. "It wears me out to be the link in the bond, and I'll need a couple of days to recover from it. I'm sorry, but that's all I can do."

I agreed to send her on vacation anywhere in the world she wanted once I was paid so she could recover. I recognized the irony of accruing more debt on the promise of another payment from another shady mobster, but she had done so much for me that I would happily find a way to pay for it even if the Elkman's money fell through and it had to come out of my pocket. Now I had a hostage, though, which should have improved my chances of getting my money.

After we were bonded and I could speak to him, I took the rat to Phil's house. He was busy in the office working on some formula or another while my mother and Candy watched *The Dark Crystal* on VHS in the living room. I headed to the kitchen, where I could have some privacy.

"All right, rat. Do you have a name?"

"I was number thirty-seven," he replied, his voice thick. "I suppose now I am the one and only."

"But now you are free, right?"

The rat thought for a moment. "I suppose so."

"And if you're a free rat, you'll need a name. I could just call you Benny."

"NO!" it screamed. "That was OUR name, not my name."

"Well, I really don't want to call you rat, so if you have a better option, I'm all ears."

"Hrm," he said. "I always liked the name Dexter."

"I'll call you Dexter, then." He seemed satisfied with that answer. "Who wants to kill you, Dexter?"

"Who doesn't? That's not the right question. The question you must ask is who had the balls to enter my place of business, kill my guards, and gun me down like I was some two-bit criminal."

"You're right," I replied. "I'll bet you have a lot of enemies."

"The powerful always do. There are rival gangs trying to bring you down, rogue thugs trying to make a name for themselves, and even members of my own organization looking to move up. Any one of them had means, motive, and opportunity."

I stroked my chin. "Well, we have to start somewhere to find Benny's killer, and your guess is as good—well, probably better than mine. So, you tell me where to go first. Who has the biggest reason to kill you?"

"Scarpucci." Dexter's lip curled. "She always hated that I owned all of Seattle. We've had our spats in the past, but we respect each other. A couple of weeks ago, a lieutenant of ours killed one of her best men. I thought we resolved it, like professionals, but maybe not. If I had to bet on one mobster with the guts to carry out something like this and the muscle to get away with it, she's the one I would bank on."

"Okay, that's where I'll start."

"I'm coming with you," Dexter said.

"I don't—"

"They killed me!" he shrieked. "I want to watch them squirm."

I opened the cage. "All right." I placed my hand on the counter, and Dexter ran along my arm onto my shoulder.

Scarpucci's base was in Tacoma, just south of Seattle. A decade before, Benny had pushed the crime lord out of Seattle, and she retreated there. I didn't know exactly where we would go in the city, so when I called a portal, I made sure it was big enough for Lily and brought her with me.

The city of Tacoma was nice, even if it kind of smelled like raw sewage. Not all the time and not everywhere, but in enough places that you really didn't want to drive with your window open if you could help it. Even if you kept them closed, every once in a while, especially near the water, you got a pungent whiff of crap and muck as bad as anything I'd smelled in Benny's office.

Before we left Los Angeles, Dexter called the Elkman and told him to find where Scarpucci was operating her business from these days. "We have people in her organization," Dexter said. "And she has some in ours. It's supposed to be one, big, dysfunctional family…until something like this happens."

It was no secret that criminal organizations paid informants and double agents to do inside work, dismantling those that falsely professed their loyalty. Criminals didn't just pay off police officers, they paid off other criminals, too. There was a code, and you weren't supposed to hit another family without permission. I learned that from *The Godfather*, but it tracked with the reality that I lived. Nobody said boo if you got your beak wet, as long as you didn't go against the family in a way that crossed a line. Killing the boss was certainly across that line.

An abnormally high number of criminal organizations operated out of restaurants. Scarpucci ran hers out of a small Thai restaurant on the south edge of the city, close enough to the docks that the trucks had to pass along the highway but not close enough to be downwind of the worst of the "Tacoma Aroma," as residents called it.

The restaurant was built on the end corner of an unassuming strip mall, and the sign extended and wrapped around the edge of the building. I noticed the bulletproof glass on the windows as I walked in; hard to detect except for the subtle warp when looking through it into the restaurant. Scarpucci was a careful one.

The room was dark when we entered, just some candles and mood lighting to give it a hint of atmosphere. In the back, a fat, pasty man with a circular face and long jowls shoveled a pile of egg rolls into his mouth, disregarding the fork and chopsticks on either side of him.

"Scarpucci!" I shouted, and the man looked up. "I need to talk to you."

"Idiot!" the rat said. "That's not Scarpucci."

"He's the only person in here."

"Exactly. 'He.' Scarpucci is a woman!"

Of course. "He's also the only human in here. If not him, then who—"

Before I could finish, an orange tabby jumped down from a pillow on the counter. It ran along the railings and across three sets of tables before stopping at the man's side.

The dead-eyed man reached up, robotically, and began to pet the cat. The tabby purred.

"Good to see you, Ratinger," the cat cooed in a light, airy feminine sound. "Much thinner these days."

"Meanwhile," Dexter said. "You've gained enough weight for both of us."

"That's not very nice, Benny," she said, shaking her head sadly. "I can't help who I am, and I love my body."

"I don't like that name. It was my slave name. I go by Dexter now."

"I like that name, Dexter." Scarpucci raised her butt in the air for more pets. "See, I can be civil. Can you do the same?"

"I will try, I suppose," Dexter growled. He muttered to me under his breath, "Bring me over to the table."

I walked over to the table and sat down across from them. Dexter ran down from my shoulder to the table, where he and the cat spent a long moment circling each other. Scarpucci hissed, and I noticed a long scar running across her neck, jagged and uneven.

"Did you try to kill me, Scarpucci?" Dexter said.

The cat swatted at Benny before making its way back to the fat man's paw. "Of course not. I don't like you, but I don't hate you enough to kill you."

"Bull!" Dexter shouted. "You've always wanted Seattle. Maybe you decided to take your shot."

"I wish I could take credit for it, Dexter. In truth, I've grown very comfortable in Tacoma. In Seattle, it was always a gang war or a territorial pissing contest. Here, it's simple, and I've grown to love it."

"I don't believe that. You were always a manipulative, conniving, power-hungry bitch."

"Not anymore." She licked a paw. "I'm old. I only have a year or so left. I can feel my body shutting down, and I don't want to live my last days in battle with you or anyone else. I would like my children to inherit a peaceful operation, not one at war." The kitty purred as the man found a particularly nice spot under her chin. "I don't expect you to believe me, but that is the truth."

"And how can I trust you?" Dexter asked.

"You don't need to trust me. You should ask yourself why they were able to take you down so easily, though. The Benny I knew would never be so careless. Even if I wanted to hurt you, Dexter, could I really do so? Isn't that why you keep so many little birds in my organization? So they can fly away and tell you what I'll do?"

"You're not wrong," Dexter said. "But—"

"No buts," Scarpucci said. "When was the last time you heard me plot against you? Months? Years? Haven't you wondered yet if your money is better spent somewhere else? I have. It was only your death that reinforced to me why we keep informants. To prevent something getting the jump on us. So, I ask you…why did your little birds fail you?"

Dexter thought for a moment. "I—don't know."

Scarpucci sat. "And perhaps, that is why your precious rat king is dead. I can't say. I can say that I didn't kill him. I am perfectly happy to fight you, though I would prefer not to." She bared her teeth. "If you don't want a battle—" she meowed, and a slight woman brought out three white cartons filled with food. "Take these as my parting gift, from one old friend to another. I do hope you get back on your feet again."

CHAPTER 36

"Do you believe her?" I asked, turning onto the 5 freeway back up toward Seattle. It was the same freeway from Los Angeles, extending all the way from the border of Mexico to the border of Canada. One long, unbroken, stretch of road.

"I don't know." Dexter paused, lost in thought. "Part of me does, but another part of me feels stupid for believing her. We are mortal enemies, and she has every reason to lie…but I don't think she was lying."

"I agree," I replied. "She seemed sincere. She is also a cat, and they are ever only so sincere."

"I have never met a cat I liked."

"If it's not her, then who? Maybe somebody within your organization."

"Possible." Dexter sighed. "But my men are loyal to a fault. I'm more inclined to believe it's some new upstart trying to muscle in on my territory. Let's head to the docks. See if anyone's been scaling up their operations over the last few months, bringing in new weapons, hiring additional people. Somebody would need an army to take Seattle from me."

"What if it's not that?" I asked.

"Then we'll look inward, but not until I've ruled out everyone else first."

Dexter had a dock manager named Gordon on his payroll who worked at the top of a tall building overlooking the whole of the dock. Inside his office, a set of controls allowed him to reach out to anyone in the yard throughout the day. Kalle had the same setup in his office, though he preferred a more hands-on approach, zipping between the ships as they came in and handling everything by sight. It was a bygone method for a rapidly disappearing age, but I liked Kalle's type—dinosaurs. They were so much easier to bribe. When somebody embraced technology and accountability, there were books to fudge and regulators to worry about. It was a big headache.

Gordon wasn't a monster, and he'd never learned to speak rat, so I translated while Dexter whispered into my ear about what to say. After I told him what I needed, Gordon walked over to his filing cabinet and flipped through his files for ten minutes, scratching his head and butt in equal measure as he looked through his records.

"Sorry about this," he said. "I don't keep the best records."

"That's an asset, far as I'm concerned. Good records bring lots of questions in our line of business."

He smiled. Two of his top teeth were missing like he'd gotten on the wrong side of a fight at some point. "Ain't that the truth." He finally pulled two files and pushed the cabinet closed. "Here it is. These two companies have upped their shipment tenfold in the past couple of months—Jingle Junk and Panda Penny, Inc."

I took the folders from him. "Anything unusual in the shipments?"

He scratched his head, then his butt. "I don't know. They kind of pay me to look the other way."

Dexter screeched a series of obscenities I decided not to repeat. "Do they have anything in port right now?"

He nodded. "Jingle Junk has three containers on the west side of the port. Panda Penny picked one up yesterday, and has another shipment coming in three days."

"Can you take me to Jingle Junk's shipment?" I asked.

"I shouldn't," he replied with a grimace. "It's kind of against policy and—well you know I'm not against breaking the rules or nothing, but it puts me in an awkward spot, ya know?"

"I understand." I slid closer and pressed my finger deep into his fat stomach. "But you do understand that if Benny ever found out you were two timing, he would gut you like the pig you are, right?"

"I—I—"

"Stepping out on him with another company is a big no-no. Pick your loyalty—him or them, and please know that in one of these choices, you end up face down in the river by tomorrow."

"When you put it like that—" He gulped. "Follow me."

"Good choice."

We hopped into a cart and headed across the docks with Gordon, enjoying the crisp, winter, salt air. Fifteen minutes later, we were in front of the containers.

Gordon looked down at his feet. "You gotta promise me that if we find something—that this won't come back to me."

"I can't promise that," I said. "I can only promise not to kill you if you open this container, and I can't make the same promise if you don't."

Gordon bit his lip. It was a no-win situation, and he knew it. Sighing, he opened the first container, which held several different types of counterfeit Cabbage Patch Kids. The next container had similar counterfeit toys: Transformers and G.I. Joes. The third container didn't have anything more interesting than some light counterfeiting.

Shady, yes. Illegal, probably. Worth killing Benny for? Probably not.

Jingle Junk probably wasn't responsible for the attack on Benny, unless toys were somehow more valuable on the black market than I thought. I didn't know if Panda Penny, Inc. was responsible for the attack either. I doubted it. My money was still on it being an inside job, but it was as good a place as any to turn our attention until we had a better lead.

CHAPTER 37

Panda Penny, Inc. didn't have an address we could find in any public record, and they generally came to pick up their shipments themselves. However, the dock manager was able to pull up a recent shipment they'd delivered to a warehouse across the city.

I always liked driving in new towns. While I had been to Seattle several times, I never brought Lily with me, so I never drove. She purred so pretty taking the corners and exploring the streets.

It didn't take long to cross Seattle. Compared to LA, just about every other city was tiny, and you could make it across any of them in less than half an hour. Once, in Ithaca, I walked across the whole city in fifteen minutes. You don't understand scale on a map or a Thomas Guide. A city's size only sunk in when you were there.

"This is a bad idea," Dexter said, looking out on the dark warehouse from the dashboard. "I'll wait here."

"I don't think so," I replied.

"Where am I going to go?" he said. "If you lock the doors, how can I get out?" He held up his little claws. "Remember, I have no thumbs."

I didn't like it, but I agreed. I pressed the lock down on the passenger side, locked my door, and then shoved the key in my pocket.

A thick combination lock bound two ends of a bulky metal chain together at the metal sliding door to the warehouse. Luckily, it wasn't runed, which meant I could open it without brute force. I didn't want to break the lock and give anyone proof that I had been there.

"*Clo agored.*" I touched my wand to the lock, and it fell open for me. I placed the lock in my pocket and pulled open the sliding door. The light wasn't any better inside the warehouse, but I was blessed with very good night vision, a gift from my supernatural parents. Boxes and pallets littered the ground of the warehouse, but most of them were empty. They must have moved the last shipment already, and the shelving in the warehouse was equally sparse.

I needed to find the office, specifically the manifest of what was included in their last shipments. After investigating for a couple of minutes, I found it up a set of rusty stairs. The office was sparsely decorated with only a couple of filing cabinets, a metal desk, and two uncomfortable-looking chairs. The desk was piled high with papers, in no discernable order, which I rummaged through. Most of them were invoices, either paid or owed. The descriptions didn't mean anything to me. Still, I stuffed everything I found from the docks in the pocket of my trench coat. Maybe Phil could decode it. When I reached the bottom of the stack, I found a picture frame.

It was a picture of a blonde woman in a yellow sun dress, smiling, standing in front of the sliding door holding a sign that said, "First day." It would almost be sweet if the object of the picture weren't associated with an awful human. I shouldn't say human. She could have easily been a monster groupie. There were plenty of those.

The sound of metal falling on the concrete below put me on alert. I pocketed the picture and walked to the door. The metal stairs were noisy, so I hopped down from the ledge to the first floor.

"I thought you would be here sooner," I heard a voice say from behind me.

I recognized the voice as the Firestarter I'd met earlier—the one who had tried to blow me up when we attacked the demon compound. I turned around slowly. A light flickered in the woman's left hand, revealing the bottom half of her face under a dark hoodie.

"I thought they were connected—your bombing and Benny's death. Now I guess I don't have to wonder anymore."

"I wouldn't say that." Her voice was raspy. "I'm a contract killer and a good one. I work both sides of the aisle, wherever the money takes me."

"A mercenary, then."

"We're all just trying to get along in the world, using the skills God gave us. I was made in his image, and it would be a betrayal not to use those gifts to the best of my ability." She pulled her right hand from behind her back to reveal Dexter hanging by his tail, writhing as he tried to escape from her clutches.

"Let him go!"

"We thought we got them all, you know? But then, we found out we had missed one, and well, I do hate to leave a job undone."

"*Chwyth iâ!*" I shouted, pulling my wand out of my pocket and pointing it at her. An ice blast flew toward her head. I had to be careful not to hit Dexter. Elkman probably wouldn't pay up for a dead rat.

The Firestarter didn't even duck my blast. She simply raised her hand, and the ice melted before it could touch her. She retaliated with a blast of her own, one which sent the wall up in flame.

"You'll burn it all down!" I screamed.

"That's the point!" She fired again, and it hit a pallet behind me. Next, she hit a shelving unit lined with boxes. Before long, the whole of the warehouse was going up in flames. "I do so love the fire. A cleansing blaze can be so freeing, and then you rise from it, like a phoenix."

"*Pig dŵr!*" I screamed. A waterspout shot out of my wand toward her, but the fire she controlled wasn't just any fire. It was hellfire she carried—hellfire from the bowels of Hell, hotter and more powerful than anything on Earth.

"*Nodwydd haearn!*" Iron needles shot from my wand, a thousand of them, toward her. She dodged them and threw up a heat blast to protect against them, but just enough of the needles got through and embedded in her arm that she howled, dropping Dexter to the ground on impulse.

"Go!" I screamed. "*Pig dŵr!*"

My waterspout mixed with the heat of the warehouse to create a fog of steam around us, which blinded the Firestarter for a moment. Dexter sprinted toward me but then stopped, hesitating. Realizing he was free, he tore off in another direction.

"Stupid rat!" I hissed. I wanted to chase after him, but the fire was licking at me. Hellfire was one thing that petrified me with fear. It could burn down to your soul and evaporate it. I sprinted out of the warehouse, hopped through Lily's now-busted passenger side window, and peeled off, having lost Dexter to the night as he scampered away.

CHAPTER 38

"So, what you're telling me," the Elkman said, tenting his fingers, "is that you lost all that remained of Benny and burned down the warehouse that was your only lead to find his killer?"

"I think you're picking and choosing my words. I didn't burn down that warehouse. Some psycho Firestarter did, and it was the same psycho that nearly blew me up and killed two dozen of Benny's men in Los Angeles. What I'm saying is that whoever killed Benny is working with the demon that set me up. They're connected."

"Hrm." The Elkman leaned back. "It seems like a bit of a leap."

I pushed out my chair and stood up. As I did, several guns locked on me from around the restaurant. "Are you kidding me? It's the same chick both times!"

The Elkman furrowed his brow. "Understood, but if I'm not mistaken, you also worked for those demons, didn't you? I mean, didn't they hire you to retrieve the dagger?"

"Well yes, but—"

"And you also worked for us. By your logic, you are working to betray us, too. Is that right?"

"Well, no." I had to admit his logic made some sense. Even the Firestarter had said she was working both sides of the aisle. "But—I see your point, I guess, I just don't like it."

"And isn't it just as likely that this 'Firestarter,' as you call her, simply has contracts with two different organizations, just as you did?"

"You're twisting my words again."

He sighed. "This is the problem with people like you." He straightened his red tie, which was at most a centimeter off dead center. "You follow your gut. You shoot from the hip." The Elkman tapped his temple. "I think with my head, and I try not to go off half-cocked. That's why I'm leading this organization, and you have a dozen guns trained on you." His eyes narrowed as a waiter placed a salad in front of him then skittered off, away from the fray. "Now, unless you have anything else, I will ask you to leave. You're ruining a perfectly good lunch."

I did have more. I had the photo I'd taken from the warehouse. But the Elkman made a great point. He was in charge. He had means, motive, and opportunity to put a hit on Benny, and he had just become suspect number one.

If it was true, I certainly didn't want to share that I was onto him until I had more data to support my claim. I decided to cut my losses and leave. He had all the power at the moment, and power was as good a motive for murder as anything. Now, I just had to prove it.

I left Lily in Seattle and went back to Phil's house in Los Angeles. Candy was curled up in Phil's bed as he typed away with one hand while stroking her hair with the other, and Mom was asleep on the couch. Phil turned to me when I entered his room.

"That is surprisingly sweet," I said, sitting down on the bed next to his desk.

"Candy is surprisingly sweet, it turns out, and incredibly helpful. She has the dexterity of a Tyibion Mytril, and that is a great compliment where I am from."

I tried not to roll my eyes. "You know she's probably playing you."

"I calculate that at a fourteen percent likelihood, down from forty-three percent yesterday. By tomorrow it will be statistically insignificant."

"And what if your calculations are off?"

He shrugged. "That is the problem with predicting the future. There are just too many variables to isolate any single one. Eventually, you can use the modeling, but you must also have something else."

"What's that?" I asked.

"Trust."

"Never been a strong suit of mine."

"No, and I appreciate having earned it," Phil said. "Now, I assume you have not come to discuss the possibility of Candace being a black widow. What do you need?"

My lip twitched at his question. "Do I really just come here when I need something?"

"You would like me to say that you do not, and yet I cannot say that, which means I should not say anything, though you can likely infer the truth from my silence."

"I'm sorry."

"I would like to believe you, but this interaction happens often enough and is never followed by any action to correct it, so you have to forgive me for not believing you."

"That's a fair hit. I'm a bad friend."

"You are not a bad friend. Otherwise, I would have bad taste in friends. We simply have a specific kind of friendship, and I prefer it to not seeing you at all. Besides, I do very much love when you present me with a puzzle to solve, which is what I assume you have come to me with."

I nodded, pulling the picture out of my coat. "I took this from a warehouse before it burned down. I need to know who the woman is."

He looked at it. "She looks like a standard human female to me. Her blonde hair is somewhat unique, in that only about three percent of women in the world have blonde hair. Accounting for the same ratio in Seattle, a city of roughly 500,000 people, that would mean there are 7,500 women with naturally blonde hair in Seattle." He paused. "Though that is significantly lower than the number of women that dye their hair blond. Upwards of sixty percent of women color their hair." He handed the image back to me. "I appreciate that you think I can work miracles, but I cannot."

"But—you're Phil. Can't you just hack into something and pull down information?"

"Only if that information is available and connected to the internet. Unfortunately, at present, there is no repository of photographs of every human on the planet. Soon, I hope, but not today, which limits my analysis in this matter."

"So, you're saying I need to do boots on the groundwork, then?" I said. "I thought you were magic."

"No, but you are. If only there were a spell to track a human by face alone." Phil frowned. "But wouldn't it be easier to just wait at the location for the owner to show up or follow the police as they conduct their investigation?"

"Yes. Yes, it would." I smiled. "Phil, you are a genius."

CHAPTER 39

What a convoluted mess. All I wanted was for Benny's people to call off the hit on me, and now I was running around Washington State like a chicken with my head cut off, trying desperately to do what? Find a murderer? I wasn't an investigator. Nowhere close to it, and yet—here I was, sitting in front of a stupid warehouse, waiting for somebody to come that I could interrogate and hopefully, mercifully, get a lead on finding the blonde from the photo. Yes, Ollie, you really stepped in it. Just remember, five million dollars are waiting for you at the end of this—*assuming you get to the end of this.*

I didn't love stake-out work, but it was an essential component of any good investigation. Still, in desperate times we took desperate measures, and these were desperate times, with five million dollars on the line.

When I reached the warehouse, the fire had been quelled into a smoking ember. Fire trucks and ambulances were beginning to disburse, leaving only the police officers at the scene. By now, they would have found out who owned the lease to the building. If my hunch was correct, they would run into a dead-end, as the individual likely paid in cash under the table to remain anonymous.

That didn't change the fact, though, that somebody worked in that warehouse, and eventually, they would return, maybe tonight, maybe tomo—*oh, that looks like an interesting candidate.*

A scruffy-looking man walked up toward the warehouse, scratching his head. The cops circled around him, peppering him with questions, but it was clear that he didn't know much about anything. He had the body of a grunt warehouse worker, stocky and strong, wearing a back brace for heavy lifting—somebody who was told where to go and went there, gladly, not somebody who ran the warehouse.

Still, he should be able to lead me up the chain of command. After about fifteen minutes of questioning the worker, it seemed the officers had pulled as much information as they could from the man, and he headed back to the parking lot.

He was opening his car door when I appeared in front of him. "I have questions for you."

He jumped back in fright. "Who are you?"

"I'm sorry, I thought I was clear. I have questions. You have answers. Not the other way around." Gain the upper hand, and don't lose it. That was the key to effective negotiation. "Understand?"

He tried to brush past me. "Get out of here, lady."

It was funny to watch big men realize that I was stronger than they were. It's not something they ever expect. They were used to pushing everyone, so when I dropped him to the ground with just a finger, he was none too happy, but he finally got the point.

"Who is your boss?"

He grunted. "I don't—"

I twisted his arm behind his back, careful to stop before he yipped and alerted the police. "I know you don't have any part in this. You're just collecting a paycheck. Tell me who hired you and who runs this warehouse, and I'll let you go."

"Gina." He struggled unsuccessfully to break free. "Gina Feretti."

I released him. "Give me her number, and I'll let you go."

The man scribbled a number on a piece of paper and handed it to me before scrambling into his car and tearing out of the lot. *Poor shlub.*

I could have waited around for Gina at the warehouse, but who knew if that was even her real name or if she would ever come back to the scene of the crime when she was alerted her warehouse had been destroyed. She might have cut tail and run. In any case, I had a number and could reverse engineer an address from it, which was what Phil did, easily, for me.

The number traced to a house in West Seattle near Seacrest Park. The homes there were large but not gaudy, clean but not repressively so. Her house was a two-story colonial ten blocks from the water. A Corvette idled in the driveway with the trunk popped. Stupid car for a getaway. The trunk was way too small to carry a lifetime of possessions.

The front door was open when I walked up, which was never a good sign. Frank Sinatra blared over the speakers in the living room, and a series of glamour shots on the stairs confirmed whoever owned this house was the same woman from the picture I snatched in the warehouse.

I heard the muffled sounds of frantic feet above me. I stepped up the stairs slowly, not wanting to spook Gina. Then, I heard a scream, and my slow plod turned into lunging up to the second floor. The screams came from the bedroom at the end of the hall. I pulled out my wand.

When I opened the door to the room, Gina was lying on the ground, bleeding from multiple stab wounds to her stomach. Somebody wearing a ski mask stood over her, ready to impale her with the knife again.

"*Diarfogi*!" I screamed, and the spell knocked the knife out of the attacker's hands. They turned to me and then took off like a bolt toward the window, but they didn't jump through it. Instead, they took a headfirst dive into the shadows on the edge of the room, disappearing from sight. "Goddamn it!"

Gina was hyperventilating as the blood flowed out of her. I knelt next to her. "*Trwsio.*"

The spell was meant to mend her wound, but it did nothing except make the blood gush harder. I picked up the knife from the ground and studied it. It was covered in runes. A magical wound blocked my mending. There were plenty that could, including many that I'd procured in my career.

"Gina, Gina, Gina," I said to her. "Listen to me. I need you to tell me who you work for. Who hired you to oversee the warehouse?"

She choked for every breath of air. Blood pooled under her. She only had a few moments left. She dug into her pocket and pulled out a beeper. With her last act, she placed it into my hand.

"Last… number." That was it. She was dead. I heard the police sirens in the distance, and I had to get out of there before they harassed me like I had a part in this. Somebody was tying up loose ends, and I had to figure out what was going on before they managed to do so.

CHAPTER 40

The number led to a pay phone outside of a laundromat. Another dead end, or so I thought until I watched a cockroach-faced monster walk out of the laundromat every time the phone rang and jot down notes on a pad of paper before returning inside.

By the end of a single day, the phone must have rung a dozen times, and the cockroach diligently answered every single one but never made an outbound call. The bug never talked to anyone except customers who asked for change, and the notepad never left his pocket.

Around six in the evening, just when I thought I couldn't look at a stupid roach anymore, an oversized lizard ambled into the laundromat. The cockroach nodded to the lizard, pulled out the notepad, and handed it over.

The lizard thanked the man and left. *Finally, some action.*

I turned Lily's ignition and followed the lizard from laundromat to car dealership to donut shop around the city until it must have collected a dozen notebooks. Once the lizard was done, it wound its way back to the water, where a large yacht was moored at the end of a long pier. The lizard wasn't the only monster to walk down the pier that evening. Three more lumbering beasts, a great ape, a slimy otter, and a Bengal tiger, all headed down to the dock as well. I counted three guards visibly stationed around the dock, with more likely below deck. If there were answers, they were inside that boat.

It was a common misconception that boats were good protection. Their defenses were easily breached with the right spell. I stripped down to my underwear and left everything except my wand in the car. Then, I dove into the water.

"*Poced aer*," I said, tapping my head before dipping under the water. The air pocket that formed around me was as important for allowing me to cast spells as for breathing. It was nearly impossible to cast spells underwater otherwise. I kicked under the pier until I reached the boat.

"*Turio twll.*" A drill shot out of the wand and bore into the bottom of the ship until it had made a two-inch hole, big enough to fill the boat with water and give the bad guys just long enough to run out before it sank. I bored two more holes in different places in the underside of the boat, then swam back to shore.

By the time I dried off, the pier was in chaos. Monsters scrambled all over, trying to stop the leak and figure out what was going on. I had just enough time to get dressed and make it to the head of the dock before the monsters realized there was no way to save their ship.

They rushed off the ship and toward me, one after another. "Evening, boys and girls."

"Who are you?" the great ape shouted.

"Now, see, you probably don't know how this works. I have questions, and you have answers. Understood?"

The monsters went for their guns, and I pulled my wand again. "*Cwymp!*" The pier under them collapsed, sending them all into the water. "*Swigen ddŵr!*" I spun my wand in a quick circle, and each of the dozen monsters became cocooned in their own water bubble, with only their heads rising from it. "*Codi!*" The bubbles rose into the air all around me as I moved backward into the street. "Now, I will ask you again—who is the boss here?"

For a moment, none of them spoke, then the weasel cleared its throat. "It's the frigging rabbit, okay? Now let me go!"

"You rat!" the rabbit screeched. "I'm gonna kill you, traitor!" I moved forward, and the man-sized rabbit with long, furry ears growled at me.

"Is that true?" I said. "Are you the boss?"

"What's it to you?"

"Well, if that's true, then you've tried to kill me a bunch of times, and that makes me mad. You've already seen what I can do when I'm not mad. Care to see what I can do when I am?"

The rabbit gulped. "I ain't scared of you."

I pulled off my glasses, my blue and red eyes swirling independently from each other. "You should be. Now, I will ask you again. Are you the boss?"

The rabbit's nose twitched, trying to fight my power, but it was impossible for a feeble mortal to withstand me for long. "No, I'm not."

"Good," I said. "Now we're getting somewhere. Who is your boss?"

"I ain't no rat," the rabbit said, squeezing his eyes shut.

I reached into the water bubble and pulled him out by the throat. With my other hand, I twisted my wand, and all the bubbles fell to the ground. "You are all free to go. If you stay, you'll suffer the same fate as this bunny here." The rest of the cadre didn't think twice before disappearing into the dark night. "You can't even buy good help these days, can you?"

The bunny kicked his feet in the air. "Let me down."

"I will," I replied. "The minute you tell me who hired you." I squeezed his throat tighter. "Or you die, whichever comes first. Will anyone care about your loyalty in Hell?"

"Fine, fine, fine!" the bunny said. "Aw geez, he ain't gonna like this."

"It's a he? Good. Now we're getting somewhere. What does he look like?"

"A frigging elk man. I mean, his real form is an elk. He kind of looks like a business prick without it."

"An Elkman?" I said. "And where can I find him?" I already knew the answer, but I needed confirmation that I wasn't leaping to the wrong conclusion.

"In Pine Street Market. Gino's. All right? Now let me down."

I pulled the bunny close. "If you're lying to me, I'll fillet you. I haven't had rabbit stew in a long time." I dropped him to the ground. "Now, I need proof that this elk is behind all of this."

The bunny pointed behind him toward the dock. "Good luck. All of that stuff is in that boat, and it's headed to the bottom of the ocean."

I smiled. "I don't think that will be a problem."

CHAPTER 41

It took a half-hour to raise the boat and for the bunny to recover the information I needed, but it was well worth the wait. Transcriptions of phone calls between the Elkman and the bunny, wire transfers between accounts, signatures on checks, and more. Aside from a signed confession or a picture of him ordering the hit on Benny, it was everything I needed to bring him down.

There was just one problem—he was also the one who promised me five million dollars to catch the killer, a feat he must have thought I would never be able to pull off. Even if I did, I would have to make a decision whether to blackmail him or call him out, and if I chose the former, then five million would be a small price to pay to control an empire.

I had to talk with him, alone. I slipped the incriminating papers inside a satchel and headed to Pine Street Market. The Elkman was under lock and key at all times, except, of course, when he was using the bathroom. Bodily functions killed more monsters than any other. You couldn't avoid them, no matter how powerful you were.

"*Myfyrio,*" I said, touching the wand to my wrist when I reached the corridor near Gino's. There was a complete invisibility spell, but it was tricky and required absolute concentration to maintain, something I didn't have much of at the moment, or ever. A cheap substitute was a mirror spell, which reflected everything behind you back at the person in front of you. It fell apart during close inspection due to the refraction, but it was fine in a pinch if you moved quickly.

I had cased out the joint pretty well on my last two times inside Gino's. Enough to know that the bathroom was on the right when you walked in, on the other side of the restaurant from where the Elkman held court.

I slid past the two guards at the door easy enough and spun around another on my way to the bathroom. I waited until somebody opened the door and slipped inside. The worst part would be the wait. I needed the Elkman alone, and I had no idea when he would need the bathroom, which made for the grossest couple of hours I'd had in a long time. I heard things in that bathroom no being should ever have to hear, and the smell—my nose plugs could only do so much…but eventually, the Elkman showed and sidled up to the urinal, which was when I placed my wand on his neck and revealed myself.

"I know it was you," I replied. "Don't scream, or everyone will know."

He chuckled. "I'm not scared of you, and I have no idea what you're talking about."

"I know you owned the warehouse that burned. I know you were working with the demon that betrayed me. Tell me his name, and I'll let you pee in peace."

"I would, my dear, except you couldn't be more wrong."

"I have documents, checks, transcripts, and more proving you, and you alone were responsible for Benny's death."

"Ah, I see. And I suppose this is when you try to extort me for the five million dollars with your doctored evidence." This was not how I expected it to go. "Of course, all of that is preposterous. After all, Benny isn't even dead, is he? Once we find that rat, assuming he's still alive, then he will be back."

"So you'll be able to betray him again, is that it?"

"Can I wash up?" the Elkman asked. I nodded and led him over to the sink. "Nice to know you haven't lost all civility." He wiped his hands and turned to me. "Now, if you would like to tell your lies to my men, I am sure they would love to hear it."

"I will then."

I followed him out of the bathroom. When the men saw me, the Elkman held up his hands. "It's okay. She's with me." He walked to his normal table and slid into his chair, gesturing for me to continue. "You were saying?"

"This man!" I started, pulling a pile of files out of my satchel. "Killed Benny! And here is the proof." I tossed the wet files on the table.

"Soggy papers, probably with runny ink that would absolve me. How convenient. I don't see how this proves anything."

"Think about it!" I said. "Who had the most to gain by Benny's death?" I pointed. "Him! The frigging Elkman!"

"My name is Heath, actually."

"I don't care!" I shouted. "You are a murderer."

"We're all murderers here, love."

"Yes, but only you murdered Benny."

"That is—"

"ENOUGH!" A sound quaked through the restaurant. The shriek came from five different octaves at once. I smirked when I saw a reformed rat king come around the corner. "I have heard enough!"

"Benny!" I screamed.

The rat king shook its head. "We don't go by that name anymore. We are Dexter."

"Well, then, it's good to see you, Dexter," I said. "I thought you were dead."

"While one of us is alive, we are never dead, only changed." The rats moved around to make the mouth scowl. "And I find you guilty, Heath. Guilty of my attempted murder…and I sentence you to death!"

"What?" Heath shouted. "You can't—I've always served you loyally!"

"GUARDS!" Dexter turned to the guards stationed around the restaurant. "Take him away!"

The guards took a moment to consider their loyalties, then advanced on Heath. The Elkman tried to gallop away but he didn't make it far, and Dexter's guards pulled him back, kicking and screaming.

"You have done well," Dexter said, looking at me. "I owe you a great debt."

"The five million dollars would be nice."

The rat king howled. "Yes, it would be nice. Now, go."

"So, the money?"

Dexter simply looked out the window at the water.

"You know what? We'll talk about it later."

CHAPTER 42

I tried to put it out of my mind for the next week, but something didn't sit right with me about how things ended in Seattle, and it wasn't just missing out on five million dollars. I portaled to Ratinger Drug to have it out with Benny—I mean, Dexter.

The whole place had been remodeled and refinished. A new, bright-faced woman stood behind the counter. Even though she'd never met me, she looked at me like she had and pressed the button under her counter. There was a buzz, and the hidden door behind her swung open. A burly demon stood inside with a shotgun. He nodded at the woman and moved out of the way so I could move past.

I passed several more guards on my way down to Dexter's office at the bottom of the ramp, where he sat behind the desk, just like Benny had done every time I saw him.

"Ollie!" He shouted. "I'm so glad you're here."

Two guards stood on either side of him as I walked toward him. "Security has been beefed up, I see."

"After last time, can you blame me?"

I shook my head. "That's why I'm here. Something doesn't sit right with me about how it went down. I can't shake it."

"What's to shake? The bad guy got what he deserved. It so rarely happens we should take the win when we can."

"That's just it. The bad guy almost never gets it, and it's never so clean, you know? It's too clean." I didn't want to beat around the bush, so I decided to come out with it.

"You said Benny was your slave name. What did you mean?"

"I would rather not talk about it."

"I know, but humor me."

Dexter snapped his fingers, and the guards left. He waited until they were all gone before he spoke again. "Only one of us is allowed to control the hivemind. Before, it was Benny. I had to do everything he said. I didn't have my own thoughts or feelings. I just—existed."

"And now—?"

A grin rose on the rat king's face. "Now I have the power, and it's glorious."

"Yes, that's what I was thinking." I paced across the room. "This whole time, I was wondering who had a reason to kill Benny. I kept coming back to power. I thought the Elkman—Heath—wanted power, but who would want power more than someone who had none?"

"What are you accusing me of?" Dexter asked.

"I just want to know if it's true because if that someone worked with the demon who betrayed me, they would be an enemy to me."

"Heath was an enemy to me. He plotted against me at every turn. The world is better off without him."

"You mean he plotted against Benny, don't you? Benny was the brains, after all. He was the master."

Dexter slammed his hand on the table. "And now the master is me." He calmed himself and slid a piece of paper across the table. "To think, I was so excited to see you and give you this." I picked up the sheet of paper. "It took me some time to get ahold of all our finances, but I wanted to make good on our deal."

It was a check for five million dollars. I nearly choked on my spit. "Holy shit."

"There is just one catch. If you keep that money, I would ask you not to speak of anything so unpleasant again, to anyone. It gives me indigestion, and it sends the wrong message."

"Blood money."

"No. The fee my weasel number two agreed to, that I am making good on because I like you. However, it does seem to cover your original fee from the demon who betrayed you, with interest, so perhaps you could put that whole matter to bed."

I nodded. "I'll accept this on two conditions."

"Name them."

"First, admit that it was all a wild goose chase. That Heath was an innocent pawn. That you used me to frame him—you know what—scratch that. I don't want to know. I just have one condition."

"Well, that was easy."

"Tell me his name. The demon that betrayed me, and please don't insult me by saying you don't know it."

"I'm afraid I don't know because I did not betray you."

I held up the check. "If you think this will buy me off, believe me, it won't. Tell me his name or make an enemy this night."

"That would be a big mistake."

"I agree. Tell me his name, and I will leave here, and you will never see me again. I will fade into the background. Deny me, and I will kill you. Not tonight, but someday, after I have taken everything from you."

Dexter thought for a moment. "Et'atal."

I turned on my heels. It was all I needed to know. "Thank you."

BOOK 3

"Black Hearted Heroine"

CHAPTER 43

Money really was the great equalizer.

Whenever my clients complained that things were taking too long, I would remind them that if they paid more, it would go faster. Most thought it was a ploy to squeeze more money from their grubby little hands.

It wasn't.

Money greased squeaky wheels in every language and every country around the world. Everybody had a price, and if you hit it, then they would betray all their beliefs. For some people, the price might be steep, but if you gave the most pious man in the world ten million dollars, I'm supremely confident that he would punch his dying mother in the mouth. Most people would strangle her to death for a tenth of that.

Even I had a price.

I vowed to rain Hellfire down on anyone who worked with the demon jerk Et'atal that betrayed me, but when Dexter offered me five million dollars to spare his little rodent life, I agreed. It was a betrayal of my own values. The thing was, I was broke, and I needed money to track down Et'atal if I was going to make him pay for trying to kill me.

It had only been a month since Dexter's money cleared, and I had already used a third of it to clear my debts and another third to pay off four dozen informants to squeal about Et'atal—hotel clerks in Amsterdam and Fiji, a bank manager in Bali, two ex-employees in Sudan, old clients all over the U.S.S.R. One thing was true across all of their accounts—Et'atal was a ghost.

Not one of them had met him in person. They delivered for him. They picked up for him. They received weapons, drugs, women, and more from him, but they were never in the same room as that son of a bitch. A month of my life and nearly two million dollars bought me very little in the way of tangible information.

It vexed me, and that was putting it mildly.

I had gleaned a whole lot of information about Et'atal's organization, tax records from every country in Europe, and reams upon reams of papers that were useless to me for anything but kindling. Phil's house was filled with papers that he spent all day and night scouring through for me, but the more information I gathered, the further away from the truth I felt.

When my beeper buzzed with the number from a contact in South Africa, I was skeptical that I should even meet my contact down there. Marcus was not known for handing over pertinent information, and I doubted the lynchpin I needed would come from him. However, I was desperate, so I agreed to his price and portaled down to Cape Town to meet with him.

South Africa was really two different countries. One for white people who had access to all of the excess the 1980s was known for, and another for the Black African majority they ruled over. Marcus was the city manager of Cape Town and thus had access to all the housing records, land deeds, and zoning requests that flowed through the city. Criminals liked South Africa because in it, they found a government as corrupt as their cold, dead hearts.

We met at a restaurant overlooking the cape. Marcus sat against the edge of the patio in the back when I arrived, having already ordered two Bloody Marys for himself. He expected me to pay, of course, and indulging their decadence was part and parcel of dealing with corrupt politicians. Sometimes, you could get them to flip just by paying a couple of hundred dollars for their meals. Not Marcus, though. He was savvier than that.

Marcus was dressed in a white linen suit and thumbed a manila folder on the table. I slid into the chair across from him, and immediately his panic washed over me. He was usually a cool customer, having spent his life steeped in underhanded dealings, but he was tapping his leg and darting his eyes back and forth like it was his first time on the take.

"I see you started already," I said, pointing to the Blood Mary glasses.

He nodded and took a sip. "Just need to calm my nerves. You have no idea what you asked me to dig up."

"I think I have a pretty good idea." The waitress brought a tray of curly fries and laid them on the table. I ate one before speaking again. "What do you have for me?"

He leaned forward. "I need more money, Ollie." Marcus loved negotiating for more money and then underdelivering.

"Tell me what you have, and if it's worth it, I can go up to seventy-five."

"I need a hundred."

"Are you going to bang me with a gold dildo, too?" I had never paid Marcus more than fifty thousand for information before. "Or are you just trying to screw me metaphorically?"

He gripped the sides of the folder, bending up the sides. "My house was shot up last night." He crunched the folder together. "I need that money to get out of Cape Town because of you. Agree to a hundred, or I'll burn this folder."

I laughed. "Well, if what you're saying is true, you need my fifty thousand to escape." I leaned back in my chair. "I doubt you'll burn it."

"I'm serious," Marcus said through clenched teeth. "You owe me."

"You better have something good. Okay. If you lead me to Et'atal, then I'll give you a hundred thousand."

I grabbed the folder and pulled it toward me. He fought me for a second, his iron grip warping the folder before he relented with a sigh and released it. I opened it to see pictures of a tall, gangly man. Or at least I thought it was a man, the images were blurry and had been enhanced poorly.

"What am I looking at here?" I said.

"Do you know the looks you get when you say the name Et'atal?" he said, taking a long sip of his drink. "Half of Cape Town must be on his payroll."

"And this is him?"

Marcus shook his head. "I—d—" He grabbed his throat and started choking, gasping for air, and convulsing. He fell out of his chair and onto the floor as foam spewed from his mouth.

"Marcus!" I shouted, dropping to the ground to help him, but it was too late. His glassy eyes looked at me for a moment, then all the life drained from him.

He was dead. Maybe he really was on to something. He wouldn't die in vain.

CHAPTER 44

The address inside Marcus's folder led me to a big house on the hill overlooking Cape Town. A squad of demons patrolled the perimeter and roof of the walled building. It wasn't abnormal for complexes in South Africa to have their own security, but it was unusual for that security to be demons.

Demons were the most expensive monsters to hire, and they were rare, so it was uncommon to find more than one on a payroll, let alone the ten I counted patrolling the complex, and likely more inside. I had only ever seen that many demons once before—at the demon complex in the Hollywood Hills during my botched attack, which made it a good bet that Et'atal was hidden inside this place right now. Poor Marcus might have stumbled on something real this time and died for it.

I cased the place for three weeks, looking for weaknesses, and was quite upset that I didn't find a single one. It would take an army to storm the building, and the last time I did something like that, I ended up nearly burnt by Hellfire. No, I would have to take a more subtle tact than when I attacked Et'atal's Los Angeles house.

Luckily, he left every day at 11 am, like clockwork, in a black stretch limo flanked by motorcycles, to meet up one of his many mistresses around the city. He would finish with them by 12:15 pm, then go to lunch at the same spot every day. The apartments of his lovers were guarded by their own squads of demons, and there was no hope of getting into the restaurant, which exclusively employed high-level monsters and demons.

It was a flawless routine, save for one tiny kink in his route. About five minutes into his drive, the limo turned down a tight street. Three motorcycles went ahead of the limo, and three stayed behind, each guarding one side of the road, preventing anyone from getting through the tight alley until the limo was through the bottleneck. It was the perfect place to abduct him. There was only one demon guard inside the car with him and an imp driver. If I worked quickly, I could send both of them back to Hell before they could retaliate.

It was another week before I finished constructing a prison for him, complete with foot-thick titanium he couldn't burn through and warded to prevent him from snapping to safety. The morning I finished its construction, I followed the motorcade from the roofs high above the street. Three of the motorcycles broke off and zoomed ahead through the alley as I crouched over the lip, watching the limo ease its way through.

"*Porth i garchar cythaul*," I whispered under my breath.

I pointed my wand in front of the limo and a green portal opened before the driver could react. I leaped down onto its roof as it disappeared and closed the portal behind us. The room on the other end was tight, and the limo crashed into the titanium wall at the far end, smashing the imp and demon through the front window. Demons never used seat belts.

"*Pigyn obsidian.*" My wand shot spikes through the demon's forehead, killing it instantly. I sent another one into the imp's brain, dispatching it back to Hell.

"*Agored!*" I shouted, and the back door of the limo swung open. A red-faced demon fell out onto the ground, bleeding green ooze from its head. I grabbed him by the collar and threw him onto a metal chair I had stashed in the corner of the room.

"*Ei glymu I funy!*" I twirled the wand in my hand, and the enchanted iron chains spun around Et'atal's arms and chest. "*Yn dunn!*"

The chains clasped tightly around him, and he let out a yelp of pain as they constricted him like a boa. I rushed forward and grabbed his head, pushing it back as I ripped off my sunglasses, so he had no choice but to look into my eyes.

"You're a tough one to find, Et'atal. I swore I would track you down after what you did to me, and I am a woman of my word."

Et'atal laughed weakly. "If you believe I am Et'atal, then you are a fool." He coughed green blood on my trench coat, and I punched him across the mouth for it.

"Don't lie to me," I hissed. "I know—"

"You know nothing!" the demon barked. "Et'atal has been trapped in Hell for eons. His father refuses to let him leave, and no matter how many we enlist to worship him, none can conjure him."

"You're lying. I spoke to him!" I screamed.

"And did his voice sound like mine?"

I had to admit that it didn't. Et'atal's voice was smooth and confident, while the imposter's voice was harsh and gritty. "That doesn't mean anything."

The red-faced demon looked at me, deeply, in the eyes, so much so that it was uncomfortable. "Then look me in the eyes and ask your truth. I will not fight you."

It was an elegant solution if you could trust a demon, which I didn't. I did trust my own power, though, so I grabbed him by the neck and looked deeply into his eyes. "Are you Et'atal?"

His eyes swirled with my influence. "No."

"Is Et'atal on Earth?" I asked.

"No."

"Is he in Hell?"

"The last I saw him, yes, unable to leave on order from his father."

I could feel the demon trying to worm its way into my brain. "Who is his father?"

"The dark lord, Lucifer."

My head began to throb, and I let go of the demon. I didn't know what kind of power he had but he was doing something to burrow into my brain, using my own power against me. Beyond the edges of the room, something banged loudly on the walls. Many somethings, actually. They smashed against it from every angle in a deafening chorus.

The demon grinned. "Oh good, they're here."

"Who's here?" I asked.

He chuckled. "You must know that my car was tagged so my people could find me, given that this eventuality was bound to happen."

I shook my head. "No, I runed it from sight."

The titanium glowed red, and the heat in the room was rising. "Not well enough. In mere moments, my men will melt this place to the ground, with you in it. I suggest you run."

I stomped forward. "How do I get to Et'atal?"

"You would have to enter Hell itself, and even you don't seem stupid enough to do that."

The heat was becoming unbearable, even for me. "*Pigyn obsidian.*"

I fired an obsidian spike into the imposter's head. He was of no more use to me. I opened a portal and left the prison before it became a tomb. One more dead end, but at least I didn't leave empty-handed. I had my first real lead. Now, I just had to decide if my vengeance was worth a trip to Hell.

CHAPTER 45

"Well, I guess that settles it," Phil said as he spun from his chair.

"What does it settle?" I asked, confused.

"All of it," Candy said, looking up from an X-Men comic book she was reading. She had been staying with Phil for weeks now, and while they wouldn't admit it, they were clearly seeing each other. "It's not like you are dumb enough to go into Hell, right?"

"I'm not?"

Phil furrowed his brow. "I'm worried you phrased that like a question instead of a statement."

I shrugged. "I mean, being stuck in Hell didn't prevent Et'atal from screwing up my whole life, so I doubt it would prevent him from doing it again. If anything, it's keeping him insulated from me."

"Wait," Candy said, matching Phil's expression but with two eyes instead of one. Couples really did start to mimic each other. "You are really thinking about going into Hell? Is that even possible?"

"Why not? It's possible to get out of Hell. Stands to reason I should be able to get in there, too."

Candy scoffed. "Yeah, if you die."

"Please don't die," Phil said matter-of-factly.

"I don't want to die!" I shouted. "I just want to teach Et'atal a lesson."

"No, you want to kill him," Candy said.

"Yes, I want to kill him. It's a very powerful lesson."

"But he's already in Hell," Phil said. "I don't understand this. How much more dead could somebody be if they are already in Hell?"

"I don't know!" I flung my arms in the air. "Dead enough, so I feel safe for you and Candy."

"Well, you won't have to worry about that for long," Candy said, and then she looked like she just told a big secret and clasped her mouth tightly with both hands.

"What does she mean?" I said, cocking my head to Phil.

"Nothing," Phil said, his eye darting to avoid my gaze.

"No lies, Phil. I've had quite enough of them for one lifetime."

He sighed. "Fine. We weren't going to tell you yet, but we've almost finished rebuilding the ship, finally, and I'm going to be leaving Earth pretty soon."

"And I'm going with him," Candy said, wrapping her fingers inside Phil's. At least they weren't hiding it anymore.

"You're leaving Earth?" I took a deep breath, trying to control my seething rage. "And when were you going to tell me about this?"

"Soon," Phil replied. "We were going to help you figure this whole thing out, square you away, and then—"

"We'd be off."

It was equally disgusting and adorable that they finished each other's sentences, which was a pretty good summation of love, too. Equal parts nauseating and beautiful, depending on when and how you looked at it.

"I'm happy for you," I said, trying to add as much excitement in my voice as possible, which wasn't much, even in the best of times.

"You don't sound happy," Phil said.

"Cuz I'm furious!" I said. "But I'm also happy for you, as long as you are happy for you."

He looked over at Candy, smiled, then back at me. "I'm happy."

"Good," I replied. "Now, if you'll excuse me, I need to—not be here."

I was used to being abandoned, but I never thought I would be abandoned by Phil. It was stupid, I guess. I thought maybe when he finally finished that ship, he would ask me to go with him. I would've liked him to at least ask me. There was no way I could go with him now, not while he was canoodling with his girlfriend.

And there was another thing.

They barely knew each other. Now they were going to travel the universe together in Phil's ship? They would be at each other's throats in a week. And then what will Phil do? Jettison her out of an airlock…

I actually quite liked that idea.

No, I didn't. Despite everything that Candy had done to me, I liked her, and I liked the two of them together. Phil deserved to be happy. That's all I had ever wanted for him, and he could never be truly happy on Earth. His life was beyond the stars, not living among glorified chimps. I still hated it, though, in practice, even if I approved of it in the abstract.

I needed to get out of there and focus on the task at hand. I had a demon to bitch slap.

I left Lily in front of Phil's house and walked over to my mom's house. It wasn't a long walk, and the crisp, winter air whipping against my face helped me forget my troubles. I had a plan, or at least the inklings of one, though it required my mom to give me something she'd never been willing to part with before—a way to contact my father to see if he could help me get into Hell. I wasn't swimming in reliable demon contacts. Every time I met one, they tried to kill me.

After the Elkman and Dexter called off the hit on me, Mom went back home and resumed her previous life. After catching her having sex last time I barged in on her, I was sure to knock. She answered a few minutes later, dressed in a pink bathrobe and wearing a green beauty mask.

"You knocked," she said. "I didn't think you would actually respect my wishes."

"Well, last time I walked in on you—"

"Please, say no more about it. As much as a child does not want to walk in on their parents, parents equally dread being found by their children." She looked at me for a moment. "So, what do you want?"

"When was the last time you saw Dad?" I asked bluntly.

She leaned against the doorframe. "Please don't use that name in this house."

"I'm not in the house," I said. "I'm on the front stoop, and I need to see him."

"Why?" she asked.

"If I tell you, promise not to freak out?"

"Absolutely not," she said, standing up straight again. "In fact, I promise whatever you tell me to freak out double now."

I turned away from her. "Forget it."

She sighed and grabbed my arm. "Wait, now I'm curious. If it's something foolish, which I'm sure it is, I would rather you did it with my help."

I turned back to her. "I need to find a way into Hell, and the only demon I know that doesn't actively want me dead is Dad."

She laughed at that. She laughed until she saw on my face that I wasn't joking, and then her face turned sour. "Why on Earth would you want to go to that terrible place?"

"I found out who's trying to kill me. A demon named Et'atal, and he's in Hell right now."

"And you're sure about that?" she asked. When I nodded, she stepped outside onto the porch with me. "How?"

"A demon told me."

"Well, that's not a very reliable source." She scoffed. "Demons are known liars, you know."

She was right, which pained me to admit, but that didn't change the facts. "I don't have a lot of options. That's why I was asking about Dad. I thought—"

"He is NOT reliable."

"At least he's not actively trying to kill me. Look, Mom, you have been hiding my dad from me for years, and I've never pushed back on it before now, but unless you have a way into Hell, then I need his help. If you have another plan, I'm all ears."

"Ugh, you have that look in your eyes like you are going to do something stupid whether I help you or not." She groaned. "I know a way into Hell that doesn't involve him."

I waited for her to add conditions, but she didn't. Instead, she turned and went into the house, leaving the door open for me to walk inside after her. Before I could, though, I heard a rustle in the bushes in front of the porch. I spun on my heels and pulled out my wand, only to see Blezor fall out of the bushes, burned half dead, and carrying the gnarled dagger I once stole from him in his hand.

"Ollie," he said, whimpering. "Help me."

CHAPTER 46

I helped Blezor into the house and laid him on the couch in the living room, then ran into the kitchen and brought back water for him. He drank voraciously and begged for more.

"What happened?" I asked after replacing his water for the third time. "You look horrible."

"A girl—woman—she came to my house, looking for the dagger." Blezor took a deep breath and winced in pain. "I told her it wasn't for sale, and she—she—"

The char on his face gave away that the Firestarter had visited him. I sat back and frowned. "Let me guess. She snapped her fingers and burned everything down?"

"How did you—" Blezor paused, then nodded. "Of course you know her. Friend of yours?"

I shook my head. "Not a friend. Definitely not a friend." I took a damp rag and dotted his head with it. "I'm sorry you got involved. How did you know where I lived, though?"

"After you left me, I had—you know, I have friends too, okay? I had one of them track down your last known address."

"Well, well, well," my mother said from the top of the stairs. "You do love your strays."

"This wasn't me. He just came here on his own."

"They all just come here, dear," she said, rolling her eyes. "You're like a magnet for them." She sighed as she walked down the stairs with the grace of a gazelle. "And why did you have to lay him on my nice, clean couch?"

I saw the black stains all over the couch. "I'll buy you a new one."

"Money is nothing." She knelt next to me. She was no longer in her robe and mask. Instead, she wore a glistening white toga with a golden headband pulling her hair back from her face. "I wanted a change anyway."

"You are her mother?" Blezor asked. "Or her sister? Or her lover?"

"Her mother, and thank you, but also, ew." Mom pressed her hand against his chest. "You are in a bad way. I'm afraid—"

He nodded. "I know I'm going to die. I don't fear it." He placed the knife into my hand. "I wanted you to have this. Whatever you do, don't let them take it from you."

"So dramatic." Mom stood. "Actually, I was going to say that I'm afraid I'll have to save another one of Oleander's friends. I am an angel, after all. I have some bit of magic left for miracles."

"Oh," Blezor said. "I never thought that—"

"If you want to be saved, that is. I hear monsters like you are put to work in Hell for the pleasure of the demons, and God...he doesn't much like your kind."

Blezor shook his head. "I wouldn't go to Heaven anyway. Not after what I've done." He coughed. "If you could save me, that would be wonderful."

"Ollie?" She looked at me. "Should I?"

"Don't put this on me!" I threw my hands in the air. "I don't want his life in my hands."

"I'm afraid it's on you, my love. Does this orc need a miracle? You know how much they wear me out, and you also need my help."

She was right. Mom would need a week to recover from performing a miracle, especially one as big as saving a life, which meant it would prevent her from helping me unless I wanted to wait for a week, and I really, really didn't. Still, even though I didn't like Blezor, I couldn't be the one responsible for his death. Not when I could save him.

"He needs it," I said, standing up. "He probably doesn't deserve it, but you should do it, I think."

"Let's not equivocate here," Mom said. "Either the man deserves a miracle or not."

I turned back to Blezor. "Do you promise to clean up your act if my mom saves you? You're putting me in a really inconvenient spot."

Blezor growled. "I'm sorry to put you out, but yes. I promise to clean up my act."

"This is non-negotiable." Mom's eyes narrowed. "Miracles are conditional. If you don't clean up your act, you'll be hit by a bus or drown in the tub, or some other horrible thing, and there will be nothing to save you then."

"I will clean up my act."

She nodded. "You can start by helping my Ollie find the demon trying to kill her."

"Of course, I'll help her."

"Then I suppose I lied to you, Ollie. I can't help you right now." Mom took off her headband and handed it to me. "In the small Scottish town of Plockton, on the western coast, there is a bar that is unlike any bar you have ever seen. You cannot tell somebody the address. You must be led there by another who already knows the way. Take this headband to a place called The Seamus in the town center and give it to the bartender. Tell him you are my child and ask him to bring you to The Bar. He will make a stupid joke, and when he does, say 'Muriel would hate that joke.' He will then do as you ask."

"Muriel is a nice name," Blezor said. He was shaking now, one step closer to death.

"Thank you. When we fell in love, it was the one I used."

"Wait," I said. "Are you trying to tell me the person you're sending me to is my father?"

Mom sighed. "Unfortunately, yes. I have been shunned by the angels who once welcomed me, and…he's the only demon I even partially trust."

"How long have you known where he is?"

"I lost track of him when he went back to Hell after your birth, but he's been back for fifteen years, and I've known where he was that whole time. I'm sorry—I just didn't think—"

"This is exactly like you, Mom." I was livid, but I didn't have time to yell at her. "Just fix him so we can go."

She wanted to say something, probably to defend her case, but she didn't. Instead, she simply bent down and placed her hand on Blezor's face. She began to glow a brilliant yellow, and then Blezor radiated with her, the same color.

A minute later, it was over, and Mom collapsed into me. Blezor no longer looked charred; he was exactly as he was last time I saw him and just as ugly. If anything, the char covered his hideous face and covered up the smell of old cheese that normally wafted off him.

CHAPTER 47

I didn't make it to small towns very often. Most of my work centered on major cities and their surrounding suburbs. Every now and again, an object or potion led me to one of the world's smaller towns, and Plockton was one of the smallest I had been to in recent memory.

One thing about small towns that was consistent across my experience was that there was a dearth of monsters and magical people in them since it was easier to blend in with the milieu in denser populations. Plockton was different in that respect. It was overrun with monsters everywhere I looked. You could toss a rock from one side of the city to another without much effort, but you would certainly hit some monster or another with it.

We walked down the town's main and only street until we found a pub called The Seamus in the town square, just like Mom said it would be, sitting on an unassuming corner. The Seamus might have been impressive by small-town Scotland standards, but wasn't much more than a two-bit saloon in Los Angeles. Fewer than a dozen monsters speckled the bar, all drinking by themselves, staring off in silence.

"That him?" Blezor asked, whispering to me.

"Unclear," I replied.

"What can I get you?" A brightly-colored demon said, wiping down the end of the bar. Most demons were a dull red, orange, or burnt yellow. However, this one shimmered like a diamond. I could see what my mother saw in him, I guess. If I were to picture an angel with a demon, he would be the type I would imagine them with—also, gross.

"Ummm…I'm looking for The Bar?" I said.

"You found it," the bartender replied. "Unless you think all this liquor is just for show."

Groan. Dad jokes. I held up the golden headband and showed it to him. "Muriel would hate that joke."

The demon's face dropped, and his eyes went wide. He rushed around the bar and grabbed me by the shoulders. "Ollie? Ollie, is that you?"

I nodded. "Yeah, but I don't like being touc—"

He didn't care that I didn't like being touched. He grabbed me around the waist and pulled me into the air, laughing. "Everyone, look. It's my daughter!"

They all looked at me for a moment and muttered under their breath an unimpressed huzzah, raising their glasses in tacit acknowledgment and tempered enthusiasm.

"I really don't like attention. So, now you're oh for two."

"Sorry, sorry," he said, dropping me to the ground. "I just…never thought I would see you, is all. This is incredible. I'm a little taken aback."

"Yeah," I replied. "The feeling is mutual. I thought you were in Hell."

"I was, but you know. I'm a pretty popular demon to summon. Easy on the eyes, and I'm supposed to grant you the power of luck. Complete bologna, but it's good marketing, which means I'm never down there for long." He walked back behind the bar. "Can I get you a drink?"

"I'll take a triple whiskey," Blezor said.

"No," I said. "We're not here for a social visit. We need to find The Bar."

"Why would you need that stupid place? I make a great Manhattan. It's to die for." He slapped a ghoul lightly on the arm. "Tell her, Angus."

"It's great." The ghoul raised his glass to his lips and took a long, enchanted sip.

"That sounds good," Blezor said.

"Dad…" God, it felt weird saying that word. "Please."

"No," he said. "I haven't seen you in decades, and that's all you can say to me? Please?"

"She's very self-centered that way," Blezor said.

"Shut up," I snapped. It was a fair hit, but still.

Dad pursed his lips. "I'll tell you what. I'll take you to The Bar if you first indulge me in an old Scottish pastime."

"What is it?" I asked.

He poured a glass of whiskey for me. "Getting sloshed."

I could think of worse ways to spend an evening. "And then you'll take me. Swear?"

"I swear." He crossed his heart. "Hope to die."

"I can make that happen if you're lying to me." I grabbed the glass and downed it in one gulp. "Deal."

"Slangevar!"

It turned out my father was a pretty fun hang. He told me stories about Hell and his time in Plockton, where he always returned after cavorting around the world. He had traveled the world since the beginning of humanity.

"There was one time when I met Lot, okay, you know Lot, right? Lotta bitterness in Lot, you know, with the wife who turned to salt? So, I turn to him one time after he's moaning about something, and I say to him, 'you seem salty.' Get it? Salty? Cuz of his wife?"

"Oh, I get it, Mr. White," Blezor said. "It's not funny, plus you already told that story three hours ago."

I rimmed my whiskey glass with my finger. "He makes a good point. We've been good sports and had plenty of drink with you. Now, you need to take us to The Bar."

Dad finished his drink, which was just a bottle of Scotch he'd pulled from behind the bar, so he didn't have to clean a glass. His face was full of scorn, not directed at me or Blezor. "Why do you want to go there? I don't—I don't like it there."

"You don't have to go in," I said. "Just bring us to the entrance, and we'll handle the rest."

"Why do ya—why do ya wanna go there? I mean, I am a demon. Maybe I could help. Maybe your dear old dad could help, ya know?" He burped. "You ever think of that?"

"Fine," I replied, slamming my hand on the table. "Tell me everything you know about Et'atal then. Is he still in Hell? How is he communicating with his demons on Earth?"

Dad blinked profusely. "You don't—ya don't wanna deal with that one. He's—he's crazy, man. Even for a demon he's—he's crazy."

"I don't want to deal with him." I pulled the dagger out of my pocket and stuck it deep into the table. "I aim to kill him, and if you don't help me, then I'm inclined to kill you too."

"Threatening your own dad?" Blezor said. "That's low, even for you. I love it."

I pointed my finger at my dear dad's chest. "I've never met this demon before today, and since I've known him, all he's been is a prick. At least Mom was a prick that stuck around."

"Is that what this is about? Listen, your mom forced me out of Los Angeles. She warded the crap out of that city to prevent me from seeing you. I tried—I did…I really did."

"How hard?" I asked.

"What?" Dad asked.

"How hard did you try?" I said, making sure to hit every single syllable. "How hard did you try to see me?"

"I mean—" He flailed his arms wildly. "Hard enough."

I pulled the dagger from the table. "I don't believe it. If you had tried hard enough, you would have seen me. Nothing would have stopped you. God—"

"Don't bring him into this," Dad said.

"You have any idea what I went through?" I stood up and kicked the chair out of the way and lunged toward him. "Do you have any idea what kind of psychopath you left me with?"

"I do," Dad said. "That's what I love about her."

I threw my hands in the air. "You two really do deserve each other. Never mind, I'll find this place myself."

Dad's face turned deathly serious. "You really don't want to go after Et'atal. He's as connected as any demon in Hell. Even Lucifer is scared of him." He looked up at me. "I'm trying…to protect you. That's what a dad is supposed to do."

"I don't need a dad," I snapped. "I need a guide. Are you going to show me or not? Last chance. If I walk out of that door without you, I'm not coming back, ever. If I see you again—" I held up the knife, "I will end you, permanently."

"And if I help you?" he asked.

"Who knows?" I shrugged. "I only know what will happen if you don't help me."

He pushed up from his chair and slammed the bottle on the bar so hard it shattered. "I'll get that later." Then he turned to me, trying hard to put one foot in front of the other and failing miserably. "Let's go."

CHAPTER 48

Dad stumbled down the streets of Plockton, using the lamp posts and edges of houses to steady himself. I thought he would vomit, and twice he stopped to dry heave, but he was able to hold it back.

"I have to admit," Blezor said, trying to keep Dad upright. "I thought a demon would be able to hold their liquor better."

"That—that was Fyre—" Dad hiccupped. "Brewed in Hell. I only—only use it on special—special occasions—" He smiled at me. "Like seeing my da—my daughter—"

"It would have been nice if you remembered it," I said under my breath, but loud enough for him to hear. "Instead of getting blackout drunk."

"I'll rember—remember—" He poked his forehead. "Mind like a—steel—Oh god—" He heaved again, leaning against the side of a quaint cottage that didn't deserve a drunken expectoration from a demon. Blezor rubbed his back until Dad slapped him away. "Get off—I don't needyer pity—I'm good."

"We don't pity you," I said, grabbing him by the arm. "We pity ourselves for having to put up with you."

"I pity him," Blezor said. "I mean, look at the guy. He's clearly in pain."

"What do you know?" I asked.

"I've dealt with my own unrequited love from you." Blezor wrapped Dad's other arm around his shoulder. "I know about pain."

"Enough!" Dad flapped his arms and fell backward away from us. "Whadid—What did I say—no pity for me."

I pressed my fingers to the bridge of my nose. "Are we almost there?"

Dad walked forward, but instead of stumbling further down the street, a purple spark knocked him backward. A giant orb of light sparked for a moment and then vanished. Where there had been nothing a moment before, an abandoned building materialized in front of me. It was shrouded in darkness, but when I looked again, hundreds of fireflies lit the cozy-looking house behind the forcefield.

"What the—" Blezor said.

"We're here," Dad said, rubbing his forehead.

I helped him stand up. "So, that's why Mom forced me to find you. It's enchanted, so only somebody who's been before can lead somebody to it."

"Precisely," he replied. "It's a dumb—I don't like it—"

"How do we break the forcefield?" I asked.

"Walk with gusto—determi—detona—detriment—"

"Determination?" Blezor offered.

"Bingo." Dad slipped back down to the ground like all his bones were made of jelly. "Bango."

"You stay here and help him get back to the bar," I said to Blezor. "Maybe get him some coffee or something. I'll meet you back at the bar when I'm done."

"So I'm a babysitter, then?"

"Yup. A glorified one, at least. You can take some pride in that."

I took a deep breath and pushed through the forcefield, channeling all the will and determination in my body. An electrical charge rushed over every inch of my skin as the forcefield tried to prevent me from moving through it like I was fighting against the ocean current.

With a loud pop, I was finally through. I stumbled toward the door, trying to slow the momentum I'd built up through the forcefield. I latched onto one of the pillars holding up the porch roof. After I had regained my composure, I looked back. It was hard to make out Blezor helping Dad to his feet through the warped translucence of the magical barrier.

I made my way up the steps to the door and pushed it open. Inside was a sight I never thought I would witness—dozens of angels and demons, cavorting together across long, wooden picnic tables, laughing and humming together, as a musician played a piano in the corner. *Weren't demons and angels on opposite sides?*

I made my way past a couple of demons making out together and toward the bar at the far end of the room where a man with thick, red hair covering every corner of his face poured a glass of grog for an imp waiting impatiently nearby.

I could see whether somebody was a monster, and there was no doubt the bartender was a human—just a normal, everyday human, surrounded by monsters and angels.

"What can I get for ya, stranger?" He spoke with a thick Scottish brogue.

"What…is happening here?" I asked, my face scrunching in confusion.

The man laughed. "First time, is it?"

I nodded. "Obviously."

"Well, you caught me on a busy night, so I'll give you the short version. My great-great-great great-grandpa accidentally summoned a demon while making himself a snack."

"How do you accidentally—"

The man continued, like he had told this story a million times, and wouldn't be stopped for anything. "They got to talking, and learned they had a lot in common. Grandpa asked if he wanted a beer, and over a hundred years later, here we are."

"How do you go from one demon to this place?"

"That part's easy. One demon tells another, and then another, and then another. Soon enough, whenever a demon was summoned to Earth, they came to pay respects to Grandpa. That brought the angels, who wanted to keep tabs on the demons, and Grandpa offered them a beer, too. Eventually, this became a sort of waystation for angels and demons alike. A safe spot where they can let down their hair and grab a beer between missions."

"This is the craziest thing I've ever seen," I said, looking around.

"Then you must not have been around long."

"No, I've been around plenty, and still, this is the weirdest thing."

The man smiled through his red beard. "Then you need a weirder life."

"I guess so."

"Now," he said. "What can I get you? Beer, grog, ale, mead?"

"I'm looking for information on Et'atal."

At the utterance of the demon's name, everything stopped. The piano ceased, as did the chatter, and all eyes turned to me.

"Where did you learn that name?" one of the demons said from his spot at the bar next to me.

"From a rat king in Seattle."

"We don't talk about him here," the bartender said. "There's no more feared name in all of Hell. I'm gonna have to ask you to leave."

I shook my head. "I can't do that. My mother, Muriel, told me I could find out information on where to find Et'atal here and how to find him, so I can kill him."

The bartender chuckled. "I'm 'fraid we don't plot the murder of demons here. Like I said, this is a safe space. Besides, you kill a demon, they just go back to Hell."

I reached into my coat and slammed the dagger into the bar. "I vaporized plenty of demons with this dagger last time I used it. They didn't die. They just disintegrated. I plan to do it to Et'atal and any demon or angel that comes between us."

"We don't take kindly to threats here," the bartender said, his voice edged. "Now, leave before we force you to leave."

I looked around at the demons and angels, all staring at me with fear and anger in their eyes. I pulled the dagger out of the bar and turned toward the door. "I don't know what Et'atal could have done to make you so scared of him, but he betrayed me once and nearly killed me a half dozen times, and I still chase after him. If any of you are not too pussy to tell me where he is and how to find him, I'll be waiting outside the forcefield for you." I stomped toward the door and flung it open. "My mom told stories of demons and angels when I was a kid, of their great battles, and how they feared nothing. She would be ashamed of what you've become, shells of your former glory."

I slammed the door behind me on my way out.

CHAPTER 49

I waited out front of the bar until the next morning, watching angelic and demonic pairs leaving the bar together like old friends. It threw everything I knew about the universe into stark relief. My mother taught me that her love was unique with my father, and that part of the reason it was so looked down upon was because the angels and demons were on two sides of an eternal war, with nothing but bad blood between them. I didn't see any bad blood in that bar.

The one consistency between all the denizens of the bar was their distaste for me. When they saw me after walking outside, they turned the other way, not wanting to distort the balance they kept between each other. I threatened their fragile peace.

Finally, when the sun was high overhead, I stood up and began walking back toward Dad's pub, feeling like a complete failure. I was passing a blind alley when I felt a tug on my sleeve. I turned to see a thin, red arm pulling me toward it. I allowed the arm to lead me behind a dumpster, where I found it was attached to an imp crouched low, hidden from sight.

"Get down here," a voice hissed, pulling me toward it. "If any of those mooks found out I was talking to you— forget about it."

I knelt down, tucking myself small so that I was hidden from the street. "Who are you?"

"Unimportant. You can just call me the wind because nothing I tell you can be traced back to me ever, understood? You heard it from a man who heard it from a man who heard it on the wind. You got me?"

"I got you. I never met you."

"Good girl. Now, you wanted to know about Et'atal, right?"

I nodded. "That's right."

"First thing you gotta know is he's crazy."

"Yeah, I heard. Aren't all demons, though?"

"No, he's psychopathic because he's a mutt. Half demon, half human. He was disrespected his whole life, which made him overcompensate. His cruelty knows no bounds."

"I thought I had a messed-up childhood."

"Well, you weren't born by the seed of the Devil in the pits of Hell. He believes the throne is his birthright and aims to take it, by force if necessary."

I grabbed the hilt of my dagger. "He won't because I aim to kill him."

"That's another thing," the imp said. "You can't go around saying you're going to vaporize demons. Do you know how many objects in the solar system can vaporize a demon from existence? Five. Sure, plenty can kill us, but vaporize us out of existence? Very few, which means you have something real powerful there. If you advertise it, they're gonna take it from you, which puts you in danger."

"I thought that bar was a safe space?"

"Yeah, inside its walls. Out here, we're still all scheming against each other, and I promise you at least one demon in that bar told Et'atal you were coming for him, which means he'll be ready. Good job, genius."

"Does that mean he's in Hell, then?"

"Yeah, he's still in Hell. Lucifer put him in charge of the expansion."

"What's the expansion?"

"You'll see if you go there, which I don't recommend if you can avoid it."

"Whatever," I replied with an eye roll. "So, Et'atal can't escape Hell, then?"

"He hasn't found a way yet, but he's looking for one and a way to get revenge on Daddy."

"That must be why he wanted to start an Apocalypse."

"Bingo. That's one surefire way around Daddy's rules." The imp pointed at the knife. "And that dagger—I'll bet you dollars to donuts it can kill Lucifer, which is the second part of his plan. So, if you plan on entering Hell to teach Et'atal a lesson, then you'll be walking that dagger right into his welcoming arms."

"Do you have a better plan?"

"Any other plan!" the imp said before catching himself yelling. "Stay up here. Hide the dagger. Keep a low profile. Thank your lucky stars that he's not able to come up and take it himself. Hell is a nasty place. Why do you think demons are all trying to stay up here on Earth?"

"And if he finds the dagger anyway? What if he starts the Apocalypse? What then?"

"That's a problem for future you. I can see in your eyes you won't listen to me, so I wish you bad luck. I hope you fail miserably and never find a way into Hell."

"Does that mean you won't tell me how to get there?"

"Absolutely not," the imp replied. He snapped his fingers and vanished from sight. Frigging imps. As helpful as a wet sponge. I guess he did confirm that Et'atal was still in Hell, though, which was something. And he probably wasn't wrong when he said I shouldn't be broadcasting my plans to every demon under the sun.

There was one that could still help me, assuming he wasn't still hungover.

I made my way back to Dad's pub, where he was sitting at the counter with Blezor drinking a heaping pot of coffee. When Blezor saw me enter, he ran behind the counter and got another cup for me and poured coffee into it for me.

"Thank you," I said, sitting next to Dad. "How do you feel?"

"Stupid," Dad said. "I was so excited to see you, and I made a fool out of myself."

I smirked. "Honestly, it was nice. Mom is so worried about being perfect all the time, it was nice to see that one of my parents was a screw-up. Showed me where I got it from."

He took a sip of coffee. "Glad I could contribute in some way."

"You can contribute in another way, too, if you're willing to help me."

"I can tell by your tone I'm going to hate it, but if I can help you, I will. I suppose it's the least I could do."

"No, the least you can do is nothing, which is what you've been doing my whole life."

"That's because—"

I held up my hand to stop him. "I don't care. I need a way into Hell. Can you take me?"

He laughed, and then when he saw I was serious, his face dropped. "You can't be serious. Do you have any idea what's happening in Hell right now?"

"None, and I don't care."

"It's packed nuts to butts down there. It's absolutely disgusting. There's no way I'm going back there. Not until…"

"Until what?" Blezor asked.

He sighed. "Until I'm forced to, after the Apocalypse."

"We're not going to let that happen. There will never be an Apocalypse."

"That's cute," Dad said. "There are literally dozens of demons trying to start one right now. You can stop ninety-nine out of a hundred, and still, one day, somebody will find a way to succeed where everyone else fails. Until then, I am keeping my nose clean and my head down." He looked over at me. "I suggest you do the same."

I made a face. "I never took demons to be such cowards. Fine, you don't have to take me, just tell me how to get there, and I'll go without you."

"I wish you wouldn't." He went back to his coffee. "But you have the same look of determination as your mother." He sighed. "There are spots on this Earth where the fabric that separates our dimensions is weak."

"Like portals," I said. "I know about them."

"Exactly. These are the only spots on Earth where you can travel between Earth and Hell—unless, of course, you die." He gave me a long look while he poured another cup of coffee. "When you find one of these spots, you need to call upon the fires of Hell and melt the divide, and you can walk right in."

"Melt?" I asked.

"With Hellfire."

As he spoke, a plan formulated in my head. I already knew of a spot in Hawaii they called the Gateway to Hell. I needed a Firestarter who could call forth the flames of Hell, which meant enlisting an old nemesis. I just hoped she was as much a mercenary as she let on.

CHAPTER 50

"Are you sure about this?" Blezor asked after I filled him in on everything the imp told me.

"I'm not sure about any of this, but if you want to get some rest, then the best way is to make sure that the demon trying to kill you is dead, or at least sufficiently spooked, so they know we mean business."

"I suppose that makes some bit of sense," he said. "Though I'm not sure any of this makes any sense. I mean, she just tried to kill me. I don't know how I feel about asking for her help."

"That's the most sensible thing I've ever heard you say. Unfortunately, unless you know any other people who can burn the fabric between Earth and Hell with Hellfire, our options are pretty limited."

"I'm at a loss," he said. "I won't stop you from going—"

"Yeah, you can't—"

"But I can't go with you, either."

"Fair enough. Stay here and drink yourself into a stupor, then."

"I will!"

There was only one person who I knew had hired the Firestarter before, and I'd sworn the next time I saw that smarmy rat, I'd kill him. These extreme circumstances called for extreme measures and extreme flexibility to my usually rigid moral code.

I portaled to Ratinger Drug in Seattle and made my way inside. The pharmacist rolled her eyes and let me inside the hidden door behind the register. Gone were the half dozen monster guards protecting Dexter on our last visit, replaced by remote surveillance machine guns that followed my movements down the ramp toward his office.

"I thought we had an agreement," Dexter said when we finally reached the bottom of the ramp. "You should know that these guns are filled with black metal and obsidian-tipped bullets. They will rip you apart with extreme prejudice. Thanks for that idea, by the way."

"I'm not here to fight you, Dexter."

"Oh, thank god," the Rat King said, letting out a breath. "I was totally kidding about those bullets. They are crazy expensive. If you're not here for revenge, then what can I do for you?"

"I need you to get in touch with the Firestarter for me."

"I'm not going to set up one of my best contractors for you to kill."

"I'm not going to kill her. I need her help."

"You are full of surprises today." Dexter thought for a moment. "Very well, I will set up a meeting. But if you kill her, then—"

"You could just trust me, Dexter. I'm not the one who betrayed you, remember?"

"And when has trust ever ended up well for anyone?" The rats that made up Dexter's eyes narrowed them. "If the Firestarter dies, so do you."

"I wouldn't expect anything less."

The Firestarter would only agree to meet with me under Dexter's protection, so we chose a location that both of us knew well: Gino's in Pine Street Market. Even though it was no longer used by the Elkman as a stronghold for his troops, there were monsters loyal to Dexter throughout the restaurant, from the boxer busboy strapped with a Glock to a pair of tigers dining near the window. As I spied the layout, looking for threats, an iguana hostess led me to a table in the middle of the restaurant.

Five minutes after I sat down, the Firestarter did as well, dressed in a hoodie and sliding into the chair with her hands deep inside her pockets.

"It's good to see you," I said. "Thank you for coming."

"Skip the pleasantries," the Firestarter said with a hoarse voice like she hadn't had any water in days. "I'm only here because Dex asked nicely, and he's a good client."

"Fair enough. I'm glad we don't have to pretend to like each other."

"I don't like or dislike you. You were just a job to me. When the job ended, I never thought about you. Sorry to disappoint you."

"I'm not disappointed. Relieved, maybe." I didn't break my eye contact with her. "That must be nice, to have the ability to turn off like that, not think about all the people you hurt."

"There's no other way to get through the day. We all have our coping mechanisms. Some of us forget. Some lie to ourselves." She hit the last line hard like it was meant for me.

"What's that supposed to mean?"

"I studied your file. I watched you work. I know your clients, and yet you look down on what I do and who I am like you aren't exactly the same."

"I'm not—I don't—I don't hurt people."

"Not directly, maybe, but the money you give to bad people lets them do bad things."

I closed my eyes and took a breath. "I'm not here to fight."

"No, you want me to believe that you need my help. Excuse me for being skeptical, given our past."

"I'm willing to put all of that behind us if you help me."

"How magnanimous of you." She leaned forward. "And what if I don't want you to forgive and forget. What if I want you to hate me? What then?"

I pulled out a wad of twenty thousand dollars in hundred-dollar bills and slammed it on the table. "Then I would hope you are as mercenary as you claim and take the money in front of you as a down payment for services rendered."

"What services will I render?" she asked, casually flipping through the stack of bills as if this wasn't her first time holding that much cash.

"I need you to burn a gateway to Hell for me, and then come with me so I can get back through to Earth when I'm done."

"You want me to go to Hell with you?"

"In a very literal way."

"That's funny," she said, even though she didn't laugh.

"Why?"

"Well, plenty of people have told me to go to Hell in my life, including you, if I remember correctly. Two hundred and fifty thousand—"

"That's crazy!"

"I wasn't finished. Two hundred and fifty thousand in advance, another five hundred when we get back."

"You're insane."

"Maybe," she said. "But you're asking for crazy, and I know you wouldn't be coming to me if you had any other options."

"You're not the only Firestarter on the planet. I could find—"

"Good luck." She kicked out her chair and stood. "I hope you do go to Hell, and I mean that in every conceivable context."

"Wait!" I said, biting my lip. "I'll pay it."

"Good," she said. "I knew you would. Now, come with me."

"Where are we going?" I asked.

"To cement our bond in fire."

CHAPTER 51

The Firestarter led me through the woods south of Seattle. We were deep in the thicket with only the sounds of nature for company, and she wasn't much of a talker. She insisted on walking, even though I could have portaled us anywhere on Earth in a matter of seconds. I hated hiking, especially when I didn't know where I was going, but I went along with it because it was easier than finding another Firestarter. She was pushing it, though.

"It's just up here," she said after a long silence.

I reached the top of a hill and looked down into a chasm below us, full of black char and adorned with a pentagram in its center.

"This isn't ominous at all," I said, following the Firestarter to the bottom of the hill.

"Stand over there," she said, pointing to the other side of the pentagram. It was made of rock and bone. "And hold out your hand."

She reached behind a rock and pulled out a long, serrated black knife, runed up the hilt in a language spoken by demons and written in unholy texts.

"I know I said I wanted to go to Hell, but I don't want to be sacrificed to do it."

"What?" she said and then half-laughed in spite of herself. "Oh, don't be stupid. I'm not going to sacrifice you. I'm just going to draw a little blood. You do bleed, don't you?"

"I can," I said. "I don't like to."

"I force all my clients to make a blood pact that they won't harm me, and in turn, I won't harm them. If either of us break that pact, the offending party burns up, soul and all. Do you agree?"

I knew all about blood magic. I had entered into these sort of pacts before and initiated my fair share of them. They were unbreakable, even between the most powerful of magic kind.

"Do I have a choice?"

"No," she said, walking toward me with the knife. "Do you want to hurt me?"

"So badly," I replied. "But I won't."

"Swear it on my name and yours." She was emphatic as she held my palm open. "By the fire of creation."

"What is your name?"

"My name is Aimee. Aimee Donovan."

"Really?" I said, surprised. "That's such a normal name."

"I was normal once, before I was cursed with this. Now, swear it on my name and yours."

"I swear I will not hurt you, Aimee Donovan, on my name, Oleander White…by the fire of creation."

She cut my palm, and it bled onto the center of the pentagram. Each drop sizzled on its surface.

"Good," she said.

"Where did you get that knife?" I asked.

"Funny story," she said. "I swiped it from somebody that got it from you, actually. A decade ago." She cut her palm. "I swear I will not hurt you, Oleander White, on my name, Aimee Donovan by the fire of creation." Her blood sizzled on the rock. When it stopped, she reached down and placed her hand on the center of the pentagram. "Step back." She lit the rock on fire, and the pentagram burned brightly for several seconds, then extinguished abruptly.

"It's done," Aimee said. "Our pact is sealed."

"Out of curiosity, can I watch somebody else injure you without doing anything, or is this a 'you can never be harmed when you're around me type of situation'?"

"You can never intentionally cause me harm or allow harm to befall me, and I cannot let any harm knowingly befall you, either. I'm sure you know that magic has its own rules about what is intentional or not. I would err on the side of caution."

"Always good advice."

It took us another hour to get back to the edge of the woods and to Lily. I had insisted on driving if Aimee was going to force me to join her on a weird journey through the woods. She reluctantly agreed. We weren't five minutes into our return trip before I noticed a black sedan behind us.

There weren't many cars between where we had stopped and the highway. This particular one followed us back to the 5 North and changed lanes whenever we did once we got there. I started making jerkier motions with Lily, trying to make sure I wasn't losing my mind, but the car kept close behind, no matter what moves I made.

"What are you doing?" Aimee said, grabbing her stomach. "I get motion sickness."

"We're being followed," I said, spinning the wheel toward the exit coming up on our right, cutting across three lanes in the process. When we turned off the highway, I watched the sedan swerving through the streets as I made it further into the depths of the city.

"What is going on?" I asked. "Are you setting me up?"

"Please," she replied. "If I was trying to kill you, wouldn't I have done it already? I mean, you literally let me cut you and burn the ground around you. How much harder do you think I would have to work to make it fatal?"

"I don't know. It doesn't make sense. It's too much coincidence."

"Speak. Plain. English." Aimee said.

"We're being followed, or at least I'm being followed, and the only thing I've done today is meet with you, so—"

"Maybe you have a tag," she said.

"Never. I'm runed up the ass, and so is Lily."

"Then maybe you're just low-jacked. Ever think about that?" I hadn't. I never thought of non-magical ways to hurt me. "You magical creatures are almost always taken down by some piece of normie tech."

I slid into a parking lot and jumped out of the car. Sure enough, when I dropped to the ground, I found a little tracker on my undercarriage. "Well, I'll be. Look at that."

It was a simple black box with a red blinking light. I pulled it off of Lily, smashed it on the ground and crushed it with my boot. Once I was done, I heard a helicopter overhead. It was heading right toward us.

"Hang on," I shouted as I jumped back into the car and sped out of the lot. "Let's see what Phil's upgrades can do."

I flipped open the button on the gearshift and pressed the red button. A second later, Lily began to overclock her engine and grunt as she gained speed. I swerved around the other cars on the road.

"It's still following us!" Aimee shouted.

I was far less worried about the helicopter than the blockade of black sedans in front of me.

"*Tonnau sioc*!" I screamed, and the cars broke out of the way. We passed them with ease, but I didn't see the hole they had dug into the street. When I finally skidded to a stop, it was too late, and Lily slid down the ramp into the hole.

A woman in a black suit leaned over the edge, looking at us. "*Prope*," she said.

The hole covered over, leaving us in darkness. I felt us start to move, like we were on a conveyor belt.

"Get us out of here!" Aimee shouted.

"*Porth i Ratinger Drug*!" But a portal didn't open. Instead, runes on the edges of the tunnel glowed green, absorbing my magic.

"Do something!"

"The portal's not working!" I yelled.

"Can't you demons snap your fingers and vanish to anywhere at will?"

Yes, it was something that demons could do, but I didn't move like that. I couldn't. When I was a teenager, I'd almost gotten lost in the abyss when I lost concentration for a second—the dark, inky blackness of nothingness that existed between the snap of your finger and arriving at your location. I couldn't do it. I just couldn't…I—couldn't—

"Screw this!" Aimee said, fire glowing in her eyes.

"Wait!" I said. "You don't know what's above us right now or what will happen if you collapse this tunnel."

"So what, we're just supposed to let this happen?"

"For the moment, it would seem so," I replied, keeping my voice even. "And then, when they let us out, we rain down hellfire on them."

"I like that last part, at least," she growled. "Fine. We'll do it your way, but if I get arrested, I'm gonna be so pissed."

I smiled. "I don't think it's that kind of abduction. It feels like they want something from us. If that's true, we listen, figure out how to double-cross them, and then we kick their asses."

"Yeah, yeah. I like that plan."

There was nothing left to do except let ourselves be pulled through the darkness into the great unknown.

CHAPTER 52

Twenty-three minutes later—according to my watch—a light appeared at the end of the tunnel. A couple of minutes after that, the conveyor belt track ended inside a white, seamless room, with nothing but a large metal door directly in front of us.

The tunnel had collapsed behind us and the track beneath us disappeared, leaving Lily to crash two feet onto the ground. My head smashed against the roof when we landed.

"Ow."

A woman's voice spoke over an intercom. "Sorry about that."

"You should be," I snarled. "Lily is an innocent in all of this!"

"Show yourself, asshole!" Aimee added, pushing herself out of the car and banging on the door.

"Patience. We would like to speak with you in a civilized manner. I promise that if we cannot, we have ways of neutralizing you."

"All right!" I said, exiting the car. "We'll be good. What do you want?"

"You say that," the voice said, "but your heart rate is still elevated. Once you have returned to calm, the door will open, and you will be led to the truth. And please don't try to use magic in this room. It is 'warded up the ass,' to use your expression, Ms. White."

"Goddamn it!" Aimee shouted. "This is bull!"

"I know," I said. "But they hold all the cards here, and we can either play their game and find a way to cheat, or we'll be stuck in here."

"I like cheating," Aimee said.

"Then we have to play the game."

Aimee took a deep breath and let it out. It wasn't enough on its own, but another five minutes of deep breathing must have been enough, because the door clicked open with a loud buzz.

"Please follow the hallway until the end and take a seat at the table there," the voice said. "Don't be cute about it, or we'll zap you."

Aimee ripped open the door and stomped down the hallway. I followed behind. I knew enough to know you never wanted to be the first person to enter a room in a new, weird place, so I let Aimee be the guinea pig. However, we reached the next room without incident and sat down in the only two chairs.

"Very good," the voice said. "Now, I appreciate that you are not interested in hearing what I have to say, but I promise you we are on the same team."

"People on the same team don't kidnap each other!" I muttered.

"Now, now. You and Dexter were on the same team, and didn't you kidnap him?"

"I just took him for a little bit!"

"Marvelous," the voice said. "Then you agree that 'taking you for a little bit' isn't kidnapping. When you've heard us out, we will let you go if you so choose."

I grumbled under my breath and then said, "Who are you, anyway?"

"You have surely heard of us, though never our name. We are the same agency that conspiracy theorists have placed behind Area 51, among other things. In the simplest terms possible, we are here to protect humanity against all things that go bump in the night, big and small."

The intercom clicked again, and then the voice continued. "For the past decade plus, we have been mostly concerned with preventing an Apocalypse and have become increasingly concerned with the dagger you keep on your person, Ms. White."

"This one?" I held it up. "Come close, and I'll show you just how dangerous it is."

"Pass," the voice replied. "However, yes, to answer your question, that is the dagger in question. We believe it to be the most likely cause of the Apocalypse, and we need it destroyed."

I put the dagger away. "Well, I'm using it right now."

"And we're definitely not giving it to you!" Aimee added.

"Oh, perish the thought. We have heard of your plans, due to Ms. White's outburst in Scotland, and make a proposal to you both. Help us destroy the dagger, and we will give you a pardon of all your past crimes and give you a chance to start your life over again."

"What if we like our lives?" Aimee asked.

"Then you will at least not have to hide from us at every turn, Ms. Donovan. Really, it must be exhausting."

"I'm used to it by now."

The voice sighed. "Fine. I don't wish to be crass, but we are prepared to give you each ten million dollars for helping us. I know money, as you say, 'talks.' Am I speaking loudly enough for you?"

"I'm listening," I said.

Aimee gave me a shocked look. "Come on, Ollie!"

"You come on. You're supposed to be the heartless contractor here. That's ten million dollars apiece. That's 'screw you' money. That's 'never have to work a day in your life' money."

"I mean…" She faltered. "I guess. I don't like it, though."

"I don't either, but…ten million dollars."

"What do we have to do?" Aimee asked, settling into her chair.

"Much like you were going to do, go into Hell, and throw that dagger into the lake of fire in front of Lucifer's castle."

"What about Et'atal?"

"He is one of ours, on our payroll, and we prefer him to remain unharmed."

"That's a deal breaker for me," I said. "He needs to pay."

There was a pause, and another sigh before the voice spoke again. "What happens to him is not our concern, so long as the dagger is destroyed."

"I can live with that plan," I said.

Aimee sighed. "If I can break my morals for five hundred grand, I guess I can do it for ten million. I hate all of this."

"We do not like this, either," the voice said. "It's most untoward to involve civilians in our business. But, drastic times and all." The voice went silent for a moment. "Welcome to the U.S. Armed Forces."

CHAPTER 53

My mother would say I was a damned fool for working with the government, but I had been a fool for less than ten million dollars before—a lot less.

I could have entered Hell by myself, of course; gotten out of the underground prison, found the gateway, and entered the Hellmouth. But the government drones that captured us seemed to have all sorts of information we didn't have about the layout of Hell, a team of soldiers to accompany us, and plenty of tech that would make entering Hell much easier than if we were going to do it ourselves.

Of course, going with them meant we wouldn't be able to sneak around like we could if it were just the two of us. In exchange for treating this like a paramilitary operation, we got access—and of course, ten million dollars, half of which had already been wired into my offshore accounts, as confirmed by Phil in a quick but terse phone call.

"It's a bad idea," he told me. "But perhaps it is the best idea."

"What do you give my odds?" I asked.

"With the troops, you have a seventeen percent chance of success. Without them, that chance drops to three percent."

The military gave me almost a six times better chance of success, even if my odds weren't good either way. A scruffy-looking nerf herder might have said to never tell him the odds, but they comforted me. I was probably going to die in Hell, or be captured, and I wanted to go in with a clear head about it. *Was killing Et'atal enough to risk my life? What good was ten million dollars if you weren't around to spend it?*

"It's no good," Aimee replied when I asked her the same question. "But that's not the real question. The real question is whether you can live with yourself if you don't take the chance. That's all life is—a series of chances, high probability ones that don't have much of a payoff and low probability ones with high rewards if you succeed. The key is finding the ones with the best odds and best payoffs."

"I'm not very good at that one," I said with a sigh. "At least not these days. I used to be a lot better, but recently— recently I'm taking a lot of stupid chances. I can't stop myself."

She laid on Lily's hood next to me. "Because the reward is so high?"

I nodded. "I knew getting into business with the government was a bad idea, but the money—god, it was so much money, and it kept getting better and better, so I kept making dumber and dumber choices, which led me here."

"I've been around a lot of rich people in my life. The best ones are real risk-takers. They talk about hedging their bets and trying to make high percentage plays, but they're only guessing. They say things like 'this is a good bet' and 'that's a bad bet,' but they don't know. They're gambling, just like we are with our lives. But ten million dollars? That's enough money that I don't have to work for them anymore. I can be one of them."

"Yeah, and what if we die getting it?"

She laughed. "Dude, we're both going to Hell either way eventually. We might as well die trying to get back out—to do something good for once. I've worked for a lot of horrible people and a lot of shady organizations. None of them have ever wanted to do anything good with my skills. This is at least a good thing."

"Is it?" I asked. "What if they're wrong? What if the dagger doesn't matter at all?"

She shrugged. "It's the intention, you know?"

"And if their intentions are bad?"

"Mine are good, and I have to think that's a far cry better than usual." She turned to me. "I'm sorry for trying to blow you up. Twice."

I sighed. "Since we're probably going to die, I am going to forgive you. I'm not forgetting, but I don't want to go into Hell with any of that baggage." I pushed myself up and off of Lily's roof. "In fact, there are some things I need to do before we leave."

The head of the agency, Director Chapman, had introduced herself to us several days ago after the money transfer was complete and our irritation had subsided. She was a tough woman with a stern scowl permanently plastered on her face, and as of yet, she had refused to allow me to leave the bunker.

That needed to change.

Forgiving Aimee convinced me I needed to make amends with the other people in my life. I wanted to say goodbye in case I never saw them again. If I had less than a one in six chance of returning to Earth, I needed to make my peace.

Director Chapman looked up from her computer when I knocked and beckoned me over. Her hair was pulled up in a tight bun, and she pushed her thick glasses up on her head as I sat down.

"I need to see my family," I said.

There was a long moment of silence as she sized me up. "No," she replied, finally. She was not a loquacious speaker, but when she spoke, her words had weight.

"I'm not asking." I squeezed the edges of my armrests. "If you want me on this mission, you will let me go to see my family before we leave."

"It's too dangerous."

"We're going into Hell," I said. "There's not a place more dangerous, and since I'm probably not coming home—"

"Why would you say that?"

"Because it's Hell."

"If you don't have faith in this operation, why would you agree to it?"

"You gave me ten million dollars." My lip twitched. "Which you wouldn't do if you didn't know the danger of this mission, so don't play coy with me."

She sat back and gave me another one of those long, appraising looks. "Request denied."

I rose from my chair, fury coursing through my veins. "You might have warded this place to prevent me from using magic, but I can rip your pitiful human body apart with my bare hands."

She wasn't scared in the least, or if she was, her face didn't show it. "This is not civilized, and I don't appreciate it."

My ire subsided in the face of her calm. "Please."

"You don't even like your parents," she said, turning back to her computer. "You have been estranged from your father until recently, and your mother—well, your relationship with your mother is cantankerous at best, if not openly hostile. Why would you even want to say goodbye to them? They have done nothing for you."

"Because I love them, okay? You can't stop who you love, no matter how screwed up it is. I've agreed to help you. I'm willing to die for this mission if that's what is required of me, and we both know there's a good chance of that. All I want is some time to say goodbye to the people I love."

"And ten million dollars," Director Chapman added curtly.

"I won't vanish. If you have a file on me, you have to know that I will honor my debt, no matter the cost."

She nodded. "Very well. The mission will commence tomorrow at five a.m. Hawaii Standard Time. You have until then to make your final goodbyes."

"And Aimee?" I asked. "Will you give her the same courtesy?"

"I doubt there's anyone she loves, but if she comes to make the same request, I will honor it."

I turned to walk out of the door. "Thank you."

CHAPTER 54

"You're a damned fool," my mom said when I told her what I had planned. *I knew it.* "You know that angels weren't meant to survive in Hell, right? That's kind of the whole point."

"I thought the point of Hell was to punish the wicked."

She bit her lip. "Actually, neither of those is the point, but that's not the point. Suffice to say, I'm worried you won't be able to survive the heat, my love. I'm worried about so much more than that, but I'm worried—I'm worried about all of it."

I clasped Mom's hands inside of mine. "I appreciate that. We've had our—I'll just call them differences for the sake of time, and I thought we would have time to get over them. That's the thing with eternity, you always have more time. Now, I don't know if I do, so I have to get this out."

"Dear, you don't—"

"Yes, I do. This isn't for you. It's for me. I'll never forget what you did to me, but I can forgive you."

She smiled. "As you know, I don't think that I did anything to warrant forgiving, but I appreciate the sentiment."

I pulled my hands away. "Even now, at the end, you can't just admit you did anything wrong in our relationship?"

She shrugged. "I did the best I could, and I am an angel, so that's quite good."

I stood up from the table. "It's fine. I'm not forgiving you for you. I'm doing it for me, but…oh my god. You make it nearly impossible to be the bigger person."

"I love you," she said, still smiling at me. "No matter what, always know that."

"I know, Mom." It wasn't enough. It was never enough just to love somebody if you treated them terribly, but that was her cross, and the minute I stepped out of her house, I promised myself I wouldn't think about it again. I still had two stops to make.

The first was Phil's house. No one answered when I knocked on the door. Instead, a hologram dropped from the door, a perfect representation of Phil, except translucent.

"I always know your knock, Ollie," he said. "Unfortunately, you are late. We are ready to leave. Fortunately, I would never leave without saying goodbye. Meet me at the coordinates below." A string of numbers scrolled across his hologram chest, and I wrote them down. "I'll be waiting for you, but please don't make me wait long."

The coordinates were in Death Valley, in the center of a rock formation that kind of looked like it was giving me the middle finger. Phil's ship shimmered silver at the top of the mesa, and I lifted myself up on it to find him and Candy waxing the outside of the craft. It was as circular as the drawing he showed me, with a cockpit smaller than I imagined would be comfortable for two people, even if one of them was an alien.

"Ollie!" Candy shouted when she saw me, running up and wrapping her arms around my neck. "Can you believe it? Isn't it beautiful?"

"It is," I said, looking past her to Phil, who finished buffing the outside of the ship and turned to me. "I can't believe you guys are going."

"I've talked about it for a long time, no?" he said. "I didn't know the exact date, but I was always very clear about my desire to leave this place. With your impending trip, I thought it was best for me to leave now. One less thing to regret leaving behind."

Candy let go of me, and I walked over to Phil. I placed my hand on his shoulder. "I'm glad you waited for me. Thank you."

"I knew you would find a way to say goodbye." He didn't catch my eyes, which was good, so he wouldn't see me crying. "I have always appreciated our friendship."

"How long have you had it finished?"

"A week, give or take," Candy started and then looked down at her feet. "But you weren't asking me. I'll go inside and get ready." She hopped up the ramp leading inside the ship, leaving Phil and me alone outside.

"You will be careful, won't you?" Phil asked.

"I can't promise that," I said. "And without you to temper my mood, who knows what I'll get into."

"I could run those calculations for you, but I'm afraid I left most of my equipment in my house, which is now your house."

"No way, Phil. I couldn't—"

He held up his hand. "The deed is done. It's in your name. You need a safe place to conduct your business, and I made sure that my house is as safe a lair as anywhere on Earth. Please take it. It will make me feel better that I have done my part to protect you, as you have always tried to protect me."

"I'll take it," I said. "But I'll never tell my mother about it."

"Oh god, no."

I laughed and wrapped Phil in a hug. "You are my best friend."

"And you are mine."

We held each other for another moment, and then he stepped away and walked into the ship. The ramp raised, and the jets under the ship kicked up enough sand that I retreated up the hill to watch the rest of the launch from there. I stared after it until it was out of sight, then collapsed on the ground and cried until I had nothing left in my eyes, and I was caked in a thin layer of sand.

The last stop was to see my father. He and Blezor were sharing a drink behind the bar when I walked inside. Nothing had changed since I saw him last. Not for him, at least. Everything changed for me.

"I'll be in the back," Blezor said when he saw me, leaving me to talk with my father.

"Did you find what you were looking for?" Dad asked.

"Yes, Et'atal is still in Hell, and we are going in after him."

"Dangerous business, that," he said. "Is there really no other way?"

"I'm sure there is, but this is the one that presented itself first."

He nodded into his drink. "Impetuous. You get that from me."

"Mom would beg to differ, I think. Though she does blame every unflattering thing about me on you."

"She would."

I stepped closer to him. "I have a favor to ask you. I know we just met, but I can't trust Mom with it."

"Anything."

"If I get stuck in Hell, I need you to find a way to summon me back. I'm half demon, so there must be some spell that can get me back to Earth if I get stuck."

Dad nodded. "Count on it."

"Thank you. Now, it's time to do something stupid."

CHAPTER 55

"Wait!" Blezor said as I set out into the streets of Plockton. I turned to see him chasing after me.

"What do you want?" I asked. "I'm late."

"You've been gone for weeks. I've been waiting here for you, just like you said. Like a frigging puppy, and you didn't even say two words to me."

"I don't have time for hysterics. *Porth i West Kamokuna*." I pointed my wand, and a portal opened. I was walking toward it when I felt his tug on my arm. I shrugged it off. "Let me go."

"Take me with you," Blezor pleaded. "I don't know what stupid thing you are going to do, but I want to be there to save you."

I rolled my eyes. "I don't need some stupid orc to save me. Go home, Blezor."

"I don't have a home! In case you forgot, my home got burned down by that crazy Firestarter."

"Aimee," I replied. "Her name is Aimee."

"Of course. I guess you found her, then."

"I did. She's helping me get into Hell."

Blezor snarled. "So, you'll work with her, but not with me. You treat me like a child, somebody who doesn't even deserve an ounce of respect."

"You told me you didn't want to work with her!" I screamed.

"That was weeks ago! I've evolved since then."

"This is so stupid." I pulled myself away from him. "You want to risk your own life, who am I to stop you? But I have to go. Come if you want."

He blinked a few times. "Really?"

"I'm not your mother. But you can't piss off Aimee, okay? We need her to get to Hell and to get back."

He held up his hands. "I'll be cool if she can be cool."

"No, you need to be cool either way. Otherwise, I'm leaving you here."

"Fine." He threw his arms around his chest in a huff. "I'll be cool."

My watch vibrated again. Now I was late. I stepped through the portal and arrived on West Kamokuna. On one side of us, the ocean crashed into the shore of the mighty volcano. On the other, the ash and dust rose high into the air, toward the caldera thousands of feet above us. In front of us, the red mouth of the portal to Hell spewed red light into the night air. It was still pitch dark, with only the half-moon shimmering above us for light. The gateway to Hell glowed an ominous red.

Blezor joined me on the obsidian ground at the edge of the great volcano, and together we walked across the uneven terrain toward the mouth of Hell. My last visit there hadn't been for pleasure, and I hadn't seen the gateway to Hell up close. As we neared, I understood why it was called that. The lava made it look like dozens of souls were fighting to escape the clutches of Hell. Perhaps they were.

"Thought you wouldn't show," Director Chapman said, standing a hundred yards from the red gateway. Three monsters were at the volcanic base, loading up gear. Aimee stood before the crater, her arms extended, bathing in the heat.

"Who is this?" Director Chapman asked.

"Blezor. He insisted on coming."

"That's stupid." She turned to him. "Did she tell you how stupid that was? She's going into Hell, not Disneyland."

"She told me," Blezor said, determined. "I don't care."

Chapman shrugged. "If you don't care, then I don't care." She lifted an eyebrow and glanced in my direction. "But it's coming out of your share."

"He's not getting any money. He's here for the sheer love of it."

"That's even dumber," she said flatly. "Come on."

Blezor trotted behind us to catch up. "There's money?"

"Not for you, it appears," Chapman said.

She turned and led us toward the gateway. The heat was unbearable even a hundred feet from the entrance. Aimee was already standing there, next to three commandos—an ogre, a troll, and an inferi. They were dressed in black, chain mail armor, with crossbows and swords slung on their backs. There were no demons among them.

"This is your team," Chapman said, pulling an amulet out of her pocket. "Wear this. It will help allay the heat of Hell." I draped the amber necklace over my neck. She dug into her pocket and gave another one to Blezor. "Here's one for you. Luckily, I come prepared."

"Do I get some weapons or armor or anything?" he asked.

Chapman pointed to a table to her right, piled high with swords, axes, armor, and an assortment of other weapons, all made from the black metal of Hell. "Go nuts." Blezor hopped over to the table as Chapman led me down the line.

"This is your team. The ogre's name is Drownt. The inferi is—well, we call him Igor, and the Troll is Bob. Aimee, you know. There's one other member of your team, meeting you in Dis, an imp who will be your guide."

"I hate imps," I said.

"And this one gives imps a bad name. Don't trust anyone or anything you see in Hell, even Charlie when you meet him. From my research, everything is a trap."

"Your…research?" Aimee said. "Haven't you ever been in Hell before?"

"Well, no…" Chapman trailed off.

"What?" I scoffed. "I thought—"

"It doesn't matter what you think," Chapman said, each syllable uttered with force. "We have as much knowledge of Hell as even Lucifer. We've just never performed a field operation there. This is the perfect opportunity, and we believe we are prepared enough to deal with any eventuality."

"And if you're not?" I said.

"We trust you to improvise."

"Jesus Christ. This is nuts. I thought you guys had more experience than me. I—"

"Your job is still the same, either way. Toss that dagger into the lake of fire surrounding Lucifer's castle. That will destroy it."

I gripped the dagger at my side. "Are you even sure that will work?"

"…as sure as we are about anything." Director Chapman turned to the team. "Igor's been. He grew up there."

"It's true," Igor said.

"This is totally—wow—" Aimee said. "We're totally, totally screwed."

Chapman whipped around to face her. "Which is why we have offered you so much, as well as a pardon for all your crimes. It's not something we offer easily, or often. This is a special circumstance, and thus, we have made—" Blezor, now clad in full armor and holding a war hammer, clanked past Chapman. "—we have made allowances."

"Whatever," Aimee said. "Let's just get this over with. Sooner we get into Hell, the sooner we get out."

"Or die inside," Blezor said. "But let's not start out with that kind of negativity."

"Well said, orc," Chapman said.

"It's not negativity to point out the obvious," Aimee retorted, turning to the mouth of the volcano. "Do I have to do anything special to open this gateway? Or is simply using my Hellfire enough to open a path to Hell?"

"According to our research," Chapman said, "that should be enough. See if it works, and if not, we'll go from there."

Aimee stared at the Director for a few moments before finally saying, "This is just peachy."

Then she closed her eyes and took a deep breath. She could call the Hellfire without saying a word, and as she moved her hands in a circular pattern, the fire pulsated between them. When she had enough to cover her fists, she aimed it at the entrance and pushed the fire toward it. As the fire shot from her hands, the red glow of the volcano was replaced by the image of a dark cavern.

"Oh, good. It's working," Chapman said. "I was worried there for a second. Good luck to you all."

CHAPTER 56

We arrived in Hell inside a sewer pipe filled with bile and sludge. It wasn't unlike a sewer pipe on Earth, except that it was made of clay instead of concrete. I knew we had arrived in Hell by the smell. The air was tinged with sulfur and brimstone and was so dry it hurt to breathe.

Drownt the ogre studied the map he'd pulled from inside his armor. "This way."

He led us through the slop until we reached a ladder. He pointed at Igor and Bob to go ahead of us, then Blezor, before he grasped the ladder and began to climb.

"After you," I said to Aimee as we looked up at the open manhole. "Please."

"What do you think is up there?" she asked.

"Whatever it is, it won't be good."

"That's a given."

She pulled herself up the ladder, and I made my way behind her. When I rose above the sewer, a big, orange hue lit the air. Aimee gestured from the end of the alley, and I walked toward her until the alley broke into a busy and bustling street. Hundreds of monsters walked around just like people did on Earth, completely nonchalant and effortless. A market lined either side of the street, with vendors of all sorts selling shoes, weapons, tools, and all kinds of products.

The monsters did not have to hide their true faces. Not one of them wore an illusion charm. I had never seen anything like it. Even when I found a pocket of monsters on Earth who seemed truly free, they still were forced to wear a fake face to prevent humans from finding them. Here, in the middle of a bustling city, these monsters were unrestricted in a way I had never seen before.

"Where are we?" I asked.

"Dis," Igor said with a wistful tone. "This is where most of the monsters and demons that work the pits live. Think of it as your New York City, except instead of working stocks and bonds, these monsters work pits."

The pits. "Is that what it sounds like?"

The inferi nodded. "Where they torture away the sins of humanity."

"Fun," Aimee said.

"Work is work," Blezor said with a shrug. "I've done torture before. It's not my favorite thing to do, but it's fine."

Igor snorted. "True enough. After centuries, it becomes rote. I barely thought about it in the end."

"Why did you leave?" I asked.

"Would you stay?" Igor asked. "This is my home, but it's also Hell."

I chuckled. "I know exactly what you mean, actually. You can love a place and want to escape it at the same time."

"Exactly."

"Enough gabbing," Bob said. "Let's get this over with. This place gives me the creeps."

Drownt nodded and walked out into the street, where we were quickly swept away by the ocean of monsters. After five blocks, he pulled us out of the flood and into a side street where the traffic was much lighter.

"We should stay on the back streets to keep from splitting up," Bob said.

The rest of us agreed, and Drownt led us through the back streets and alleys that wrapped around the city. Most of the monsters in Dis wore simple robes, which made our armor and weaponry stick out. A few of the monsters were wearing armor, though they clearly hadn't repaired it for many battles. It was full of dents and holes and hadn't been polished in ages. We looked like we had just rolled off the assembly line.

Eventually, we made it to the waypoint on the map where we were supposed to meet Charlie, at a bar called the Old Hat. Before Blezor could grab the door handle, two centaurs lunged out of the entrance, grappling with each other in combat. A small cadre of various types of monsters flooded into the street to catch a glimpse of the scuffle, but none did anything to stop it.

"You Ollie?" I heard behind me. I spun to see a familiar face. It was the same imp that talked to me outside of The Bar on Earth. "Oh, hey. I recognize you. Small world, eh?"

"You're Charlie?" I asked.

"That's right." He nodded, gesturing us to follow him. "Let's go. We got a long way to go and a short time to get there."

We turned down an alley, and Charlie stopped to grab a robe from a clothesline. As he moved through the alley, he kept looking back, mumbling to himself, and then pulling different sized robes off the lines.

"Is that legal?" I asked.

"Legal don't mean much around here, at least not these days." He tossed the robes at us. "You guys look terrible. First, only demons wear that kind of armor, and then— there's everything else wrong with this picture. Everybody, strip down and put on the robes instead. I'll pull some sheets to carry the armor."

"I'm not stripping down," I said.

"You look like a human, and in case you haven't figured it out yet, humans aren't welcome in Dis." He grabbed my sunglasses and pulled them off my head. "These are a big no-no here, too." He looked at my swirling eyes before stuffing the sunglasses into my chest. "That actually helps." He turned to Aimee and looked her up and down. "You, though. God, you are just the living end. I hear you're a Firestarter. That true?"

She nodded. "It's true."

"Can you light yourself on fire or something to cover your body?"

"Oh yeah, duh."

Aimee lit herself on fire until she glowed like the inferi. We all finished changing while Charlie packed our armor into sheets and tied them off. None of us liked the fact that we were pretty much defenseless, but we were also not on our home turf, so we had to go with the flow. The last thing we wanted was to blow our cover because we didn't understand the customs.

When we were done, Charlie scratched his chin and nodded. "Well, you look pathetic, so you'll fit right in. Welcome to Dis."

CHAPTER 57

Dis was nothing like I had imagined. I wouldn't go so far as to say it was a happy place, but the monsters living there certainly didn't seem any more miserable than they did on Earth. I even saw several of them laughing and smiling. It was a complete and utter mind screw.

Blezor must have felt the same way. "How can these monsters be…happy?" he said as we followed Charlie through the city.

"What's not to be happy about?" Charlie answered. "They get to punish the same humans that hunted them to extinction. They get a place to live. They get friends. They have steady work. It's kind of a paradise if you think about it the right way."

"I never want to think that way," Bob said as the street widened into a city square. A high wall served as a backdrop while monsters streamed in and out of the gate cut into it. Huge piles of black muck swayed back and forth across the horizon, blocking my view of anything past them.

"What is that?" I pointed to the wobbling black towers.

"Souls," Charlie said. "You all have been breeding like rabbits out there, and we're running out of places to put you, so we end up just shoveling you into big piles while you wait. It's becoming a problem, and it's getting worse."

Souls. What a horrible end. Charlie didn't give me time to let it sink in before he started moving again. He led us to a large wooden wagon yoked to a pair of oxen near the wall, then reached into the back of the hay-lined wagon and grabbed a quill.

"Roll up your sleeve," he said. We did, and he wrote *8-431* on our right arms. "Anybody asks, you are new recruits for pit eight, annex 431, got it?"

I nodded. "Got it." The others nodded dumbly as well.

"Lovely," he said. "Get in the back. Hide your armor and weapons under the hay." He pointed at me. "You, up front with me."

When we were all loaded up, he snapped the reins, and the oxen began to move forward, slowly.

"Where are you taking these…monsters?" A glowing blue banshee said as we neared the gate.

"New recruits for pit 8," Charlie said.

The banshee looked down at her clipboard. "We don't have any recruits scheduled for travel today."

Charlie reached into his pocket and pulled out a roll of parchment. "I don't know what to tell you. We're short-staffed, as you know, so lots of things are slipping through the cracks." He handed the parchment to the banshee. "I think you'll see that the paperwork is in order."

The banshee unrolled the parchment and read through it. "I see. Very well. You know the way. The pit annexes are—"

"Yeah, yeah. I know. I've been there before." Charlie snapped the reins again, and we started moving through the gates.

"What are the annexes?" I asked as we pulled away from the banshee.

"The main pits on the other side of Dis have been filled for years, so we started digging annex pits out—well, there's quite a bit of unused space in Hell. Unfortunately, as fast as we build pits, there are still more humans coming than we can handle. Thus, the towers of souls."

There was a sound on the air, a gurgle, low but persistent, that filled my ears as we moved closer to the souls. "What's that noise?"

"The worst part of this whole thing," he said. "That's the sound of souls waiting for their final rest."

Aimee shuddered. "It's horrible."

"It's Hell," Charlie replied with a shrug. "Now, in about ten miles the road forks. You take the high path to the Black Gate and Lucifer's castle. The low road leads to the lava river Styx, where Charon ferries people to Lucifer's castle. We have a stop to make first." He looked back at the team. "All of this fuss seems like a bit of overkill, honestly. Hell's not that dangerous a place."

"I beg to disagree," I rasped. The dry air of Hell was burning my throat.

"Well, I'll beg you to shut up about things you don't know about."

He had a point.

"And where is Et'atal's castle?" I asked.

He chuckled. "I was wondering when you'd ask that." He pointed to his right. "Opposite side of Hell. He's leading the expansion efforts right now, and he's none too happy about it. It's not glamorous work. If somehow you could see past all these bodies, that's where Et'atal's castle is."

I filed that away for later.

"Now, just sit back and relax. You're with Charlie now. Nothing can go wrong."

CHAPTER 58

The stench of charred flesh filled my nostrils as we made our way down the dirt roads of Hell. Even with my nose plugs, it permeated my mouth and spread deep into my lungs. Coal miners often got black lung from breathing coal dust. I wondered if there was an equivalent for demons working the ambered fires.

Even without the stench, Hell was a bleak place. I thought the stacks of souls were depressing when I first saw them from the streets of Dis, but it was nothing compared to seeing them close up. Thousands of souls layered one on top of each other like a shawarma spit, each crushing the one below it, which was, in kind, flattened by the one above it. On and on like that for hundreds of feet into the air, a wobbling skyscraper of pain and misery.

As we passed, the demons stopped their work to eye our caravan. The dead-eyed souls inside the towers reached out their arms and moaned at us, but there would be no help for them—not today.

"This is miserable," I said.

"You get used to it," Charlie said finally. Even though I never asked him a question, he must have seen the pained look on my face.

"How?" I asked, catching the face of a child, no older than twelve, screaming for help, reaching out with its stubby arm, the only appendage not crushed into submission by the souls above it, hoping against hope that maybe I would take pity.

"I mean, what are you going to do? Complain to management?"

"Yeah, man," Aimee said. "Maybe bring it up with Lucifer. It couldn't be any worse than this depressing stuff."

"That's funny, coming from a human."

"What does that mean?" she asked, insulted.

"It means you acclimate to terrible situations better than any other being. That's probably why you've survived as a species as long as you have. Think about it. You guys went through two world wars, and now you're stuck in a nuclear arms race with the Soviet Union. That is crazy. Any single second you could be blown to oblivion by a thousand nuclear warheads, and yet you still go to school, go to work, eat, screw, and complain, like it's not bonkers that you live in a world that could be annihilated any second. How is this any different?"

"Because you can see it," Bob said. "Everywhere."

"So, out of sight, out of mind?" Charlie pulled the reins. "Lying to ourselves is exactly how we get through it, too."

We came to a fork in the road far before the cliffs, and Charlie turned the oxen to the right, down a smaller dirt road, and into the abyss filled with cubes of souls in every direction.

"Where are we going?" I asked.

"Pit 8, annex 431, remember? I said you were new recruits, and they'll be waiting for you. If you don't show up, they'll send a search party for you, and you don't want that. Don't worry, I got a friend inside who'll fudge the books after you check in, but you still have to put in an appearance."

"This wasn't part of the plan."

"How do you know the plan?" Charlie asked. "I told you we had a stop to make, didn't I?"

"I guess so," I mumbled. "I don't like it, though."

"Noted. Now, they are going to search you when you get into the pit, and if they find that dagger, they'll know you aren't a new recruit. Give it to me, and I'll keep it safe until we meet again."

"And when will that be?" Igor asked.

"Once you're through processing, my friend will come and get you out. These pits are like a labyrinth, connected by all sorts of corridors. She'll lead you through, and I'll meet you on the other side."

"I don't like this," Drownt said.

"This is Hell, you're supposed to hate everything about it. But your boss trusted me, so maybe you should, too."

"Chapman is an idiot," Aimee said. "She barely knows how to tie her shoes."

"She knew enough to get you this far."

"No," I replied. "Aimee and I did that."

Charlie pulled the reins of the oxen and stopped the carriage. "You can get out right now if you want. I already told you how to get to the Black Gate. If you think you can navigate Hell without me—if you have the balls to think you can do this better than me—then go."

I looked back at the rest of my team, and they all shook their heads. I saw the distrust blazing in their eyes, but the imp was right. We were in a new place, and we had no idea what any of the customs were. We had to trust that Charlie had our best interests at heart. Trusting a demon. What was the world coming to? *An end, if we didn't destroy the dagger.*

"Okay." I reached into my robe and pulled out the dagger. "I'm sorry. You're right. We're with you."

He grabbed the dagger from me and snapped the reins, prodding the oxen to move again. "Good."

The road jutted dozens of times before we reached our turnoff. At the end of each road, there were a series of mounds that looked like ant hills, black bile spewing out of them into the air, like the exhaust from a coal plant.

Eventually, Charlie turned onto one of the smaller roads, then to a smaller road still. By the time he pulled up to the edge of a pit, the Black Gate was little more than a speck in the distance.

"Come on. Leave the armor and weapons. I'll keep them safe." Charlie jumped down from the wagon. "Can't keep your new job waiting."

We followed him toward the pit's entrance. A crook-nosed hobgoblin sat behind an obsidian desk at the edge of it. A squad of demons stood behind her, clad in full battle armor, carrying huge swords on their belts.

"Morning, Gl'adr'e," Charlie said, walking up to the hobgoblin. When she saw him, she let out a mournful sigh.

"More scrubs today," she said. "I am so sick of the B-team. I remember when the pits were an honor, and demons fought each other for the honor of working them."

"I think we're on the D-team now, Gladys. These ones might be the F-team, actually."

My lip twitched. I didn't like to be insulted, even if it was part of a ploy. I decided to eat my pride, just this once.

"These three are 4-6," Charlie said, pointing to Drownt, Igor, and Bob. He thumbed over his shoulder at Blezor. "6-1-2." He pointed to Aimee and me. "These ones are 9-7-8."

The hobgoblin chuckled as she wrote into her book. "Well, well, well. Prisoner labor. That's a new one." She looked at us. "What must you monsters have done to piss off Et'atal? The pits are bad enough, but prison labor…welcome to Hell, I guess." They both chuckled.

"Prisoners?" I shouted. "What's going on here, Charlie?"

He tipped the dagger to me. "Et'atal will very much appreciate this gift. He's been searching for it for ages, and here, you brought it right to him."

"*Pigyn obsidian!*" I shouted, but nothing happened. "*Pigyn obsidian!*"

"Your magic don't work down here, toots," Charlie said.

"Mine does!" Aimee snapped her fingers, and the fire of Hell rose into her hand and spewed towards the imp. He opened his hand, and the fire danced in his hand playfully before he snuffed it out. "Cute." He turned to Gladys. "Be careful with these ones. They're trouble."

I had no power except my fists. When the demons gathered around us, I prepared to attack. Aimee stood at my back, and the others stood ready to fight, as well. However, the demons moved faster than I had ever seen them do on Earth, and before I knew what was going on, I was on my knees, head slammed onto the ground along with the others.

A demon stood me up and shoved me onto a slanted ramp leading into the pit. As I made my way forward, I vowed vengeance on Charlie and Et'atal.

CHAPTER 59

We had descended for miles before they finally threw Aimee and me into our cells. They had already separated us from the rest of our pack, tossing Igor and the other members of the swat team, including Blezor, in cells far above us. Millions of moaning monsters and souls called out from their own prisons as we passed, begging for salvation, but we were as damned as they were.

"You're not going to get away with this!" I screamed through the bars on my cell as our demon jailers walked away.

"What are you talking about?" Aimee asked, still glowing with fire. "They already did. We're trapped. I can't imagine there's any water down here, so we'll be dead in what, three to five days, max?"

"I didn't even think of that." I turned from the bars. "I mean, I'm a half angel-half demon so I don't have to eat or drink, but yeah, you're kind of screwed if we don't get out of here."

She bounced her head off the back of the cell. "And then I'll wind up back here, getting tortured in some other horrible way."

I shook my head. "I'm not going to let that happen."

She shrugged. "I mean, it's bound to happen eventually, right? Someday I'm going to die, and then I'll be right back here, maybe in this exact pit for all I know."

I placed my hand on her knee, hoping it might reassure her. "On the plus side, maybe the Apocalypse will start by then."

She laughed. I didn't expect her to, and the laugh came from deep in the depths of her belly. She went on so long that a snarling demon banged on the bars. "Quit it in there! No laughing."

But that just made her laugh longer and harder. In Hell, laughing seemed like an act of rebellion. Keys jangled outside, and the door creaked open. The demon raised his club in the air. "We must not be torturing you hard enough!"

He dropped the club to Aimee's face. I wouldn't let him get away with hurting her. I spun on my heels and grabbed his wrist with one arm and the club with the other. I smashed his hand over my knee until the club fell.

Aimee grabbed it and used it to knock the demon across the face. When he slid to the ground, she leaped on top of him and beat him until green blood oozed from his head, and he fell back, limp.

"That's enough," I said, grabbing the club. "Well done, though."

Panting, she grabbed the keys from the demon's belt. "I have anger issues."

"Who doesn't? Come on. We're getting out of here."

We covered the guard with the thin sheet from our cots and hoped it would buy us time to get some distance from the pits after we found the others. Once we were outside the cell, I closed it behind us and snapped off the key in the lock.

I glanced around. "Where are the others?"

I don't kn—" Aimee pointed about the gate. "Look."

Above the cell were the numbers 9-7-8. It was where Charlie assigned us when we came into the prison. "Quick, what did he say about the others? It was like 4-9 or—"

"4-6," Aimee replied. "And then Blezor was in 6-1-2, I think."

"Let's hope they are above us and not below."

It took us about an hour to climb from the nine hundred level cells up to the seven hundred level. There were plenty of other monsters working the pits, and they were all wearing the same type of disgusting robes as we were, so it wasn't hard to fit in with them. Whenever a demon passed our way, we ducked into the nearest cell or busied ourselves with some sort of menial chore. There seemed to be a lot of maintenance to do on an old, disgusting pit to prevent it from collapsing, especially one with such shoddy construction.

"We're getting close to Blezor," I said. The sign on the cage we were passing said 7-8-1. The horribly deformed man inside of it whimpered like a wet dog. His arms had been sawed off at the elbows, exposing the bone on his biceps.

"Go away!" He shouted to a rat trying to gnaw on his arm. "I said go away!"

"Quiet down over there!" a coarse voice grumbled. "Some of us are trying to sleep." It was the first conversation I'd heard since we started to climb.

The occupants of each cell were going through a different type of torture. Some had their eyes gouged out, or their teeth pulled, or their fingers cut off. The prisoners were on a spectrum from screaming in agony to whimpering in pain to numbly resigned. The one who had yelled at the sawed man, though, looked barely gaunt and no worse for wear than any of the chronically homeless people that made Los Angeles their home.

"I'm sorry about him," he said. "It's hard—It's hard."

"Doesn't seem that hard for you," Aimee said.

"That's because I'm at the end of a cycle. He's in the middle."

"A cycle?" I asked.

"We are tortured until the edge of our sanity and then allowed to rest until—until we are whole again."

"Why not just torture you forever?" I asked. "That's what I would do."

"Not a good idea," the man said. "You can't torture somebody at the same level forever, or they acquiesce. They give us a break to recover and remember that there is a world outside of pain, and then, once we are comfortable without the pain, that's the moment they bring it back again."

"Seems like you know a lot about torture," I said.

He nodded. "I've been here a long time. And in my old life, it was a vocation of mine." I heard the clink of demon armor coming closer, and the man's cool demeanor changed to one of terror. "They are coming for me. Please, let me out. Please, please." He grabbed at my clothes, and I batted him away. "PLEAAAAASSSEE!"

I turned from the man and continued up the ramp. I passed the demon, and it growled at me but didn't say a word. I watched as it pulled the man from his cage and dragged him away, kicking and screaming.

We kept climbing until we reached cell 6-1-2. Blezor was on a cot, looking up at the ceiling. I opened the door to his cell and walked inside.

"Don't you da—" He sat up when he saw me. "Ollie? You are a sight for sore eyes."

"It's good to see you, too. Quick, let's go."

When I locked the door behind us, I heard a loud growl behind me. "Stop!"

I turned in time to see the demon charging at us. We started to run, but it didn't take long for the ruckus to alert other demons. They rushed toward us from all directions. What was it that Charlie said? The pits were a big honeycomb network. I pulled Aimee and Blezor into a corridor, hoping that it wasn't just another one of his lies.

CHAPTER 60

We were lost, and no closer to getting out of the god-forsaken ant farm that was the confusing labyrinth of tunnels and corridors deep underneath the pit annexes.

"Everywhere looks the same!" I screamed, popping out of a corridor inside another pit that spewed the same disgusting black smog into the air. "I have no idea where we are."

"Four hundred this time, though," Blezor said, looking at the numbers above the cell. He was right. Somehow, we had made our way from the 600s in the original pit to the 400s in this new one, which was something, though there was still a long way to go if we wanted to escape.

I looked down at the demons climbing the ramp below. By this point, every demon in Hell knew we had broken out of our cell and were on the lookout for us. I turned to the cell nearest us and grabbed the key ring. I opened the cell and pushed Blezor and Aimee inside before locking the door behind me.

"Everybody, look pathetic," I said.

"Done and done," Aimee said, sliding to the ground next to me. I heard the clatter of demons outside the cell. They stopped for a moment before grumbling to themselves and moving on.

"Who are you?" a voice said from the cot in the back of the cell. The sheet moved, and an ancient demon emerged. He had long, brittle white hair and was shaking. "New roommates?"

"Quiet," I hissed, watching the demons through the bars.

"Hrm," the demon said. "No, not new roommates. Prisoners?"

"Please be quiet, old man," Aimee grumbled. "I didn't even know demons could get old."

He smacked his lips. "Usually, they can't, but this is my punishment for defying Et'atal. There is not much we fear but losing our faculties—that is a fear across all sentient beings, I think, even demons."

"Wait," I said, absorbing the old demon's words. "Did you say you defied Et'atal?"

He nodded. "Screw that guy. He doesn't own me or Hell, no matter what he would try to have you believe. I am loyal to the true ruler of Hell."

"Lucifer," Blezor said.

"Oh, you're sweet. No, Velaska."

"What's a Velaska?" Aimee asked.

"She was beautiful, magnanimous, and would never have let any of this unpleasantness happen." He smacked his lips again. "No, no. I will never worship Et'atal—or his father—and I certainly don't approve of these annex pits. Complete travesty, and poorly constructed. Of course, maybe I shouldn't belittle my own design."

"You designed this pit?" Blezor asked.

"I did. I mean, it wasn't all my design—kind of design by committee, but I was on the committee, for sure."

I said, moving toward him, "Do you know how to escape this pit, then?"

He pointed to the ceiling. "By going up, of course."

I looked outside again. Another pair of demons walked past. "That's not an option. We were told there was a back entrance. Somewhere that led back to the plains of Hell. Do you know of it?"

"Of course I know of it. How do you think we bring in supplies, carrying them down a million flights? Don't be stupid. You just have to turn out of here and go left, left, left, straight, straight, right, left, left, right, left, straight, left, right...or was that right left straight? I would know it if I saw it." He tapped his forehead. "The old noggin ain't what it used to be."

"If we helped you escape, could you find your way out of this place the back way?"

He nodded. "I thought you would never ask." He pushed himself to stand on rickety legs, wobbling as he moved to the door. "These old bones."

"Jesus Christ, this is going to take forever," Blezor said.

"Would you carry him, please?" I asked.

"I'm not an invalid!"

"You actually are," Aimee touched his shin lightly with her foot, and he collapsed against the wall. "See?"

"All right." He grabbed onto Blezor's back. "I suppose I am an invalid. I used to be the greatest demon in Hell, and now...and now I'm nothing—"

I opened the cell door. "I'll listen to all your prattle if you get us out of here, but first, let's get out of here."

"You got it, missy. First, turn left, and then another left." I led them out of the cell when the coast was clear, and we ducked inside the corridor again. "This is the better way to go, after all, since demons don't use the corridors much."

"Why?" Blezor asked.

"They're mostly for moving supplies from one place to another, which is one job demons won't do. Imps, sure. Monsters, of course, but not demons. They think menial labor is beneath them. They were built for torture, and that's the only job they'll accept." He sighed. "I was like them, once."

"Not anymore?" Aimee asked.

"Monsters and imps have been kind to me. They've brought me food and talked to me when I was convalescing. Demons abandoned me. I am nothing but a worm to them, unworthy of a second thought. Turn right."

We turned the corner and came face to face with a penitent ogre. She was kind-faced, for a monster, and she looked at the demon with wide eyes.

"Shi'lo," she said. "You are out of your cell. Does that mean—"

"I'm breaking free, gorgeous," he said. "You won't tell on an old demon, will you?"

She shook her head. "Your secret is safe with me."

"Thank you, doll face." Shi'lo smiled at her as we walked past. When we were free, he turned to me. "See, a demon would have ripped us apart. I was such a fool."

I let Shi'lo take the lead since he was the one who knew the way. Every time we passed someone in the hall, he greeted them like an old friend, and they waved us by, content to keep his secret.

"How long have you been in here?" Aimee eventually asked.

"I don't know. I was a lord of Hell until I spoke ill of Et'atal. They moved me here then, and I've been here since. First, they forced me to help construct these same corridors that I designed, and then, when they were done, I was brought to the cell to rot."

"Is that where you met all of these people?" I asked.

"Yes," Shi'lo said. "We worked the land together and built a bond. They took pity on me since I was left here."

When we turned down the next hallway, light blinded me. It took a moment for my eyes to adjust, but I was sure it was a way out. I ran forward, and as I neared the end of the tunnel, a shadow overcame the light.

"You aren't going anywhere," a demon growled. Two more demons rushed toward us.

"Run!" I shouted, turning in the other direction. A half dozen guards entered the hallway. "Not good."

"Let me down!" Shi'lo shouted from Blezor's back. "I'll take them all on."

"Ummm…I appreciate your enthusiasm but—"

"You don't understand. I've been gaining strength since we left the cell. Let me down!"

Blezor knelt, and Shi'lo hopped off his back. His knees were less wobbly than before, though he still looked quite pathetic.

"Bonzai!" Shi'lo said, rushing toward the demons. Before he reached them, he leaped into the air at the top of the hallway and smashed into it with full speed, only to be bounced back to Blezor, who caught him in his arms. "Well, you get the point. Smash the walls so they crumble!"

"Okay!" Blezor said.

He slammed his hands against the edges of the hallway so hard that they started to quake and shudder around us.

He spun with Shi'lo and rushed toward us as the corridor collapsed, separating us from the demons.

"Great idea," I said. "Got anything left for these demons blocking the exit?"

Shi'lo held out his hands and grabbed dirt from the edges of the wall. "Duck and close your eyes!" He blew the dirt into the eyes of the demons. They swiped, blinded, as we slid under them to the other side of the cavern. When we were past them, Blezor destroyed the corridor, and they collapsed under its weight.

"That was fun!" Shi'lo said. "What's next?"

"What's next is you get to go back to whatever you want to do, and we go on without you."

"I don't like that story," he said. "Come on, I can be helpful to you! Let me come with you."

"You can't even stand!" I said. "How can you be helpful?"

"Hello!" Shi'lo said, pointing to the cavern. "You never would have gotten out of there without me. I know this place better than you."

"He's got a point," Aimee said. "We need a guide."

"What about Igor and the others?" Blezor asked.

"We barely got out of there with our lives," Aimee said. "They're on their own for the time being. We have to look out for ourselves, and the mission, I guess, too."

"Fine," I said. "How do we get to Et'atal's castle?"

Shi'lo smiled. "Oh, I know that place well. It used to be mine, you know."

"Right, because you were a duke or something?" Blezor asked.

"Oh no, nothing like that, just a lord of Hell, with a little plot of land. When I refused to bend the knee to Et'atal, all of that was taken from me."

"He took something from me, too, and I aim to get it back," I said.

CHAPTER 61

"There it is!" Shi'lo said as he pointed to a black castle across a lake of black bile. "Though this lake wasn't here the last time I was here."

I bent down closer to the bile lake. It smelled as foul as the souls piled high all through Hell. I touched my finger to it, and the bile stuck to my finger like tar. It wouldn't rub off on the ground, either.

"Um—" in fact, far from wiping it off, the bile grew on my finger until it consumed my whole hand. "Ew. Ew. Ew. Get it off."

"Don't look at me," Aimee said. "Unless you want it burned off."

"I don't really care how it goes away—" I remembered that Aimee's fire burned through souls. "Actually, no. Please don't touch me." I turned to Shi'lo. "What is this stuff?"

"Hrm," Shi'lo said. "It looks like runoff from the pits coalesced in this spot." He tapped his finger on his chin. "It's like liquid soul. I'm not sure if that's the right way to describe it, but…" He leaned in close, and the bile tried to leap onto his nose. He backed away. "Yes, if I had to guess, then that would be my answer. Though, I'm afraid I was never much of a guesser."

The black bile kept creeping up until it covered my whole forearm. I held my hand as far away from the rest of my body that I could. "Somebody think of something."

"Well," Aimee said. She had long since dropped the fire around her body. "My fire burns through souls, so technically, if it's really just liquid soul, my fire should be able to burn it off, but it's hella dangerous."

"How hella dangerous?" I asked.

"Like, hella hella dangerous. I would not recommend it, though it's probably our only option."

"Awesome." I sighed. "Just do it."

"All right." She snapped her fingers, but nothing happened. "Come on."

She snapped her fingers again and again, but there was nothing coming out of her.

"What's happening?" she asked.

Shi'lo looked at her. "You haven't eaten or slept since you entered Hell, have you?"

"No."

"I thought not. The magic is the first to go. I can help you gain more power, though," he said. "If you'll allow it."

"How?" Blezor replied. "Are you magic now?"

"Well, yes, but so are all demons."

"Less talking," I yelled as the black bile reached up my arm. "More fire."

"Will you allow me?" Shi'lo asked Aimee.

Aimee nodded. She looked weaker, suddenly. "Just do it."

Shi'lo beckoned her forward and touched her on the arm, and muttered something under his breath. "Okay, try it now."

Aimee snapped her fingers, and this time, a spark of fire appeared. "Wicked." She turned to me. "I need you to stay really still. It's super hard to keep a controlled burn. Easy to light a big fire or a tiny ember, but what you're asking takes a huge amount of concentration."

Staying still while being burned by Hellfire, sure. I held my arm in the air and knelt down, planting myself with as much of my body on the ground as I could. The goop oozed down. "Hurry!"

Aimee took a deep breath, and when she let it out, a tiny stream of flames shot from the end of her finger and hit the sludge on my arm. I felt it shrink against my skin immediately, and scatter away from the fire. The burning smell from the putrid bile nearly caused me to pass out, but I knew if I collapsed, I'd lose my arm.

"It's working!" Aimee said.

"I can feel it. It's really gross."

A few minutes later, the ooze no longer throbbed on my fingers. I looked up and saw that the bile was gone.

"All done," she said. "That was lucky. I've never actually done that before."

"What?" I said. "Please tell me that isn't true."

"I mean, I don't know where I would have the occasion to move black soul bile off somebody but look." She slapped me on the back. "It all worked out."

I smiled. "And I think we have a way through the black bile lake, too."

"My fire?" Aimee looked out upon the lake. "That is going to take one hell of a controlled burn."

"Can you do it?" I asked.

"I don't know. Usually, I start the fire, and then it takes care of itself. You're basically asking me to keep a flame going consistently for an hour or more until we get across the lake, right?"

"Less if we run," I said. "Plus, you used that fire for a long time to create the illusion you were an inferi."

"Yeah," Aimee replied. "And look at me now. Completely out of juice. I can't do it alone." Aimee turned back to Shi'lo. "Do you have that much energy left to give me, old man?"

He hesitated for a second, then nodded. "Absolutely."

"Awesome." Aimee turned to the lake and clapped her hands together. "Then let's try it. Worst case, we drown in soul juice. Get close to me."

We gathered around her while she closed her eyes and pressed her hands together. She pushed the flame out in front of her and moved her hands around her head in a circle, encasing us in a cocoon of fire.

She stepped forward, and the black bile jumped back where the flame touched it. Once we were completely inside the lake, Aimee picked up her pace. I could see her struggling. She was strong, but the human body was not meant to conduct Hellfire against such overwhelming odds.

"I'm half demon," I said to Shi'lo when we were halfway across the lake. "Why doesn't my power work?"

"The magic you use is Earthen magic and doesn't come from angels or demons. You have that power, especially the demon one, though. It's just buried deep."

"That's funny," I replied. "My mom says I'm all demon."

"She's wrong. You need to embrace your demon side if you hope to—"

Aimee dropped to her knee.

"Aimee!"

The fire collapsed closer to us as I bent down to pick her up. She was burning up, sweating, and shaking like she had the flu.

"I'm okay," she whimpered, but I knew she was wrong. The edge of the lake was close, but we couldn't run for it.

"Here, child," Shi-lo said from behind, placing his hand on Aimee's back. With his touch, Aimee's breathing returned to normal and she stopped shaking.

"Thank you."

We continued across the lake, and when we were finally safely on the other side, Aimee collapsed, white as a sheet.

"Shi'lo!" Blezor said, and when I looked over, Shi'lo was equally weakened. I left Aimee and walked over to him.

"What did you do, you old fool?"

He smiled. "I tried…to do something good…in the end. I wonder what is on the other side…for me."

His eyes closed, and he fell to the ground with one last breath. I wanted to cry. Shi'lo was nothing to me, and yet, I felt a deep sadness for him. There wasn't a chance to mourn for him before the door to the castle opened. A small turtle skeleton wearing tuxedo tails and a monocle ambled outside.

"Et'atal requests the pleasure of your company. Attendance is compulsory."

CHAPTER 62

The turtle skeleton led us down an ornate hallway. I didn't know how Et'atal managed to get gold to hold together as a solid in Hell since it had an incredibly low boiling point, but he basically painted the whole of his castle with it. Gold rugs, gold tapestries, paintings trimmed in gold—it was like Donald Trump's apartment threw up on every wall, gaudy and ugly as anything I'd ever seen.

At the end of the long entry hall, a throne with a high back rose ten feet into the air and featured two dragons locked in an epic battle. A demon draped in a black suit with a golden cape sat there. He looked considerably less monstrous than any I had seen before, except maybe my father. He stroked a thin goatee as we walked toward him, and I noticed him twirling the dagger in his hand.

"Your majesty," the turtle skeleton said. "The prisoners you requested."

"Ah, there you are. I was wondering when you would arrive." Et'atal descended the marble steps. "The minute you got away from the pits, I knew I had to meet you." He pointed at Blezor. "You must be Blezor." Then, he spun to Aimee. "And you, then, are the Firestarter. So nice to meet you finally." He shook Aimee's hand before he reached me. "Oleander White. You are a legend here in Hell. You've sent many of my best men back here with their tails between their legs." He snapped his fingers, and Balaam and Moloch, the two mooks I iced on the Solstice, walked out of doors on either side of the throne.

"Did you plan that?" I asked. "Because that kind of coordination is impossible without some kind of rehearsal."

He chuckled. "You caught me. I'm a bit of a showman. I love a good bit of theater, and you three have been more than a little entertaining." He returned to his throne and sat down. "Tell me, was it hard to leave your friends behind, knowing what we would do to them when we learned you escaped?"

"Yes," I replied, a bit of regret in my voice. "But it was the right choice for the mission and to get my revenge on you."

"Revenge is a funny word," he said, gesturing toward Balaam and Moloch. "These two have been thinking about nothing else but getting revenge on you. When I told them you were coming, they were thrilled."

"Charlie told you, I assume?" Aimee said. "Where is the little bastard?"

"I don't keep imps on the payroll. He delivered my prize, told me about you, collected his payment, and left."

"Too bad," I replied. "I would have liked to take revenge on him, too."

"Oh, you'll have the chance. He has a knack for returning to Earth, even against my father's wishes. Me, on the other hand," Et'atal slammed his hand on the throne. "I'm stuck here, forever—or I was, at least, until now." He held up the dagger. "You have delivered to me the means of my escape."

"Over my dead body," I said.

"No," he pointed at Aimee. "Over hers. Her body is needed for the sacrifice." He snapped his fingers. "Bring the Firestarter to me, kill the orc, and do what you will with the Nephilim." Balaam and Moloch stepped toward us. "They're much stronger in Hell, but I'm sure you already learned that."

Balaam threw a haymaker, and I ducked to avoid it, socking him in the stomach. Moloch grappled with Blezor, while Aimee stood there, frozen, pale as a sheet. After Shi'lo's death, she had no power. She was just a frightened human surrounded by demons. I wasn't going to let her die. I dropped my shoulder and tossed Balaam up the steps. Et'atal ducked to avoid being hit but stayed seated as the demon slid off the throne.

"Hide!" I screamed to Aimee, and she hobbled for the door.

I ran across the throne room and grabbed Moloch by his neck, slamming him down hard enough to crack the stone floor.

"Do you know how much it costs to replace—" Et'atal shouted. "Not cool."

Balaam had recovered and rushed me again. I tried to block him, but he was faster than I could parry, and he grabbed me around the neck.

"NO!" Blezor screamed, ramming his head into Balaam's stomach hard enough to cause him to release me.

I kicked off the ground just in time to see Balaam rip Blezor in half with his bare hands and toss him across the room. Blood flew everywhere. It was two on one with two demons that didn't look fazed at all while I was sweating bullets, barely able to stand against them.

"This is delightful," Et'atal said. "Nothing is sweeter than watching a dream dashed at my feet. Moloch. Balaam! Finish her off."

I leaped over their attack and rolled onto the ground. When I popped up, I rushed up the stairs as fast as I could. Et'atal raised the dagger in his hand, but I dodged his arm and grabbed for it, pulling the knife from his hand just as he smacked me back across the room.

"She has the dagger! Get her!"

What was that thing that Shi'lo said? I needed to embrace my demon side? That sounded good just about now. Moloch attacked first, and I spun around him and stabbed him in the back. He yelped for a moment and then disappeared into dust.

"Moloch!" Balaam yelled. He went in a berserker rage, swinging wildly. I had seen it in a demon's eyes before. They were never as powerful and never as reckless. He scratched, clawed, and rushed at me, but if I could find an opening—*ah, there it is.* He swung high, and I jabbed the dagger into his side. He looked at me, scared, for a second, before he turned to dust.

"You can't do this!" Et'alal screamed. "I'll have a hundred demons here in a second, and you'll be sorry."

I knelt next to Blezor's face—wide-eyed, tongue hanging out, glassy-eyed, lifeless. He followed me everywhere I went and did everything I asked, and some things I didn't, and I never gave him his due. I was sorry about that. I looked into his eyes one last time and then shut them forever. One day, I might see him in Hell again, but I hoped that day was a long time away.

"I don't think this was a very good plan," I said, walking back toward the throne.

"Can I come out now?" Aimee asked.

"I think so. He doesn't look like much of a threat anymore." It was true. Et'atal was shaking in fear. In the end, he was nothing but a coward. "And you'll never hurt another again."

"That's what you think. Right now, every demon in Hell is on its way here. If you kill me, my father will take no mercy on you." He smiled. "If you spare me, then I can have a very interesting impact on your fate."

I pulled the dagger back. "You already have."

"Wait, wait, wait!" Et'atal shouted. "If you spare me, I'll tell you how to get to the lake of fire and destroy the dagger."

"We already know how to destroy it!"

"Ha!" Et'atal said. "We told you what we wanted you to know. The Black Gate will destroy you, and Charon will never let you into the lake with that dagger. No, there is only one way into the lake—through the castle, a secret back door right into the throne room, and then you can walk out the front door. If you go quickly, you might even make it before my minions descend on you."

"Speak quickly!" I snapped.

"First, your word!" He was a sniveling coward. "Your word you will not kill me. You are nothing but a woman of your word."

I nodded. "I swear it, but just remember. I can get to you anywhere, any time."

"Oh, I am painfully aware."

"In exchange, I have several requests. You will release the rest of my team. They will meet us at the Old Hat in Dis tomorrow morning, or you will die."

"Yes," he said. "I will make it so."

I ran the dagger along Et'alal's chin. A bit of his blood oozed onto the blade.

"Swear it!"

"What good is the word of a demon?" Aimee said. "Kill him."

I didn't listen to her. Instead, I pointed at Blezor. "And you will give him an exalted position. Do you hear me? Swear to it all!"

"I swear to it!"

"Swear you will never try to start an Apocalypse again, content to live out your miserable life here, in Hell, without interfering with the machinations of Earth in any way."

"I swear to it. However, should an Apocalypse happen…I will find you and destroy you."

"Fair." I cut my finger and blended it with his. "Swear to it on the blood of your ancestors and with your life."

"I swear it."

The blood glowed as it mixed. I wiped it from the blade and used it to make an X on his forehead. The blood glowed for a moment then absorbed into his skin.

"There is no magic more powerful than blood magic. Its bond is unbreakable. However, if you somehow find a way not to keep up your end, I will come back to you. I will find you, and I will kill you. Count on that."

He held up his hands in defense. "It will be done. I swear it."

"Good, now tell me where this entrance is."

CHAPTER 63

"This is a dumb idea," Aimee said as we stared up the side of the sheer cliff. High above us, a small rock formation jutted out, leaving a plateau for a tall black door carved into the rock. "You should have just killed him."

"Yes, you've said that before, and you might be right," I replied. "But he's not worth it. He's just a sniveling coward."

We had been staring up at the rock for an hour, having trudged across the plains in the direction that Et'atal gave us. He hadn't lied. There was a hidden door, high up on a ledge, crafted to blend into the rock face until you were right on top of it. Whether it led into Lucifer's castle or not was some measure of speculation.

"The absolute worst people on Earth, the vilest of the vile, are all cowards in the end. Cowardice has nothing to do with evil or how much terrible somebody can put into the world."

I looked over at her. "If he comes back again, I'll kill him then."

"In my experience, you only get one chance at a thing like that." She shook her head. "Not to mention, you took his word—"

"He made a blood pact." I raised my hand to show her the scar from the one she and I had made. "You know better than anyone the kind of power that has."

"I still don't trust him."

"Me either." I gestured at the empty land around us. "There haven't been demons chasing us this whole time, though, have there?"

"No." She narrowed her eyes. "But you're assuming there really were demons on their way. I don't take that as truth, either."

We had already tried scaling the cliff with our hands, with magic, and with everything at our disposal, and were no closer to reaching the ledge. We had gotten as high as a hundred feet before slipping and falling back down. Aimee almost broke her neck in the fall, and since then, I'd been cautious about trying to scale the cliff.

"I have no idea what to do now, and that is not easy for me to say."

"I mean, let's just try the boat, you know? Worst case scenario, Et'atal was right, and then we go back to Dis and find some climbing supplies or hire a sherpa or something that will get us up the cliff."

It wasn't a terrible idea, and it was better than staring up at a cliff until an answer magically presented itself. "Okay."

The lava river was a half day's hike from the cliffs, and if we traversed it long enough, we'd likely find a dock eventually. Aimee kept looking out at the horizon, back at Et'atal's castle, as we walked, sure that we would be attacked at any moment.

We made it to a dock several miles upriver from where we started. "Thank god," Aimee said, grasping her stomach. "I need to sit."

We hadn't had anything to eat or drink since we left the prison. Even if I didn't need to eat or drink, the heat of Hell left my mouth miserably parched. I couldn't imagine how hard it must be for her.

"How long do you think we'll need to wait?" I asked.

She shrugged. "Who knows?"

My question was answered less than an hour later when a gondola pushed through the smoke of the lava. The gondolier wore a black robe, tattered and ragged like it hadn't been changed in a million years.

"State your business," the black-robed gondolier croaked. He had no face, save for two glowing yellow eyes that bore into my soul as he stared.

"We seek the lake of fire," I said, holding up the dagger. "To destroy this weapon."

"No body may pass." The words were harsh as they came out of him. "And no weapon may pass the Black Gate."

"Isn't that gate up on a high hill?"

"The gate…sees all. It knows all. Once…it held off fifty legions of angelic guard that wished harm on the dark lord."

"Charon, right?" I asked him calmly.

He nodded. "Correct."

"We don't wish him harm," I said. "We just want to destroy this stupid thing so Et'atal can't start an Apocalypse."

Charon thought for a moment. "I detect no deception in your voice, but you will never pass through the Black Gate." He stopped, looking me up and down. "There is another…way."

"Yes," I said. "The door on the cliff. We tried that, too. However, we can't find a way to climb up the cliff. We've tried."

"You…are a demon," Charon said, a combination of statement and question.

I nodded. "Half a demon. Half an angel."

"May I…touch you?"

I nodded, and he reached his hand up to my face. There was no skin on it. It was simply bone, and when he touched me, a jolt went through my body.

"Two sides—creation and destruction—at war in you." Charon took a deep breath, even though it was clear he didn't breathe. "I sense that you fear the demon inside of you. If you release it, you have powerful magic available to you."

I gulped. "You are talking about a demon's ability to transport themselves at will. They say that if you don't do it right, you can vanish into the abyss forever."

"If you do it right, you might just save everyone."

I knew he was right, but I didn't want him to be. I liked portals. They made sense to me, and they didn't take complete concentration to execute correctly. Charon was right, though, and there weren't other options.

I turned to Aimee. "I can't do this with you. Go back to Dis. Find the Old Hat. Wait for me until tomorrow. If I don't make it by then, go back. Don't die here."

"This is stupid," Aimee said. "So stupid."

I couldn't argue with her. "All of this is stupid. But I can't let anyone else die because of me, and I can't concentrate on breaking through the abyss and keep you safe at the same time."

When I was sixteen years old, on my first job, I thought I could simply snap my way into this rich prick's house and grab what I wanted. I had a partner then until I lost them in the abyss. I barely made it out and promised myself never to use that method again. Here I was, about to go back on my word…but I wouldn't risk somebody else.

"Okay," Aimee said. "I will do this."

I looked up at Charon. "Will you bring her to Dis? Please? She is weak from lack of food and water."

"I'm not weak!" The effort of raising her voice made her stagger, and she dropped to her knees. "Okay, maybe I'm a little weak."

"I'm not a chauffeur." Charon looked at her. "There are secret ways into the city that my beloved once told me about. I will see she gets in safely."

"Thank you."

I walked a few yards away and gathered my thoughts, clutching the dagger. I knew the spell. My mother taught it to me. Close your eyes and imagine where you want to travel. Imagine every inch of it. Make it real in your mind…and then…disappear.

I had only done it once before, but I recognized the feeling in the pit of my stomach after I visualized the door in my mind's eye. Everything went cold, and I felt the whip of a freezing wind, and then, the cold snapped, and I felt the heat of Hell on my face again.

When I opened my eyes, I was in front of the gigantic door. I had done it.

I looked back across the plains of Hell. Under me, the lava river ran into the distance, where I could make out the walls of Dis. I pushed open the doors. There was nothing but darkness in front of me, and I stepped inside. I felt in my gut that my quest was almost over.

CHAPTER 64

Inky blackness collapsed all around me. My eyes generally adjusted to the darkness quickly, but the blackness in this place was unyielding. Something whooshed behind me. It didn't feel like the wind. It felt like something, or someone, swiped against the back of my leg.

I turned to look, but it was no use. I couldn't see anything. I tried to turn back, but when I whipped around, I lost my sense of where I was going.

"Think, Ollie," I said.

"Yes, Ollie," a voice grumbled in the darkness. "Think."

A laugh echoed all around me.

"Who did that?" I growled. "Show yourself."

The darkness broke in front of me, and the smoky image of my mother stood in the light. "I'm so disappointed in you."

"You have to know I don't care about her at this point," I said, looking around. "I don't know what you're trying to do, but I have been immune to my mother for a long time."

"You can lie to yourself, Oleander," Mom said. "But I know that you still hurt because of me. I can feel it inside of you. I never loved you."

I shook my head. "That's not true. She didn't know how to show it, but she loved me." I felt wetness on my face, and I realized I was crying. "I wish you didn't because it would make it so much easier to hate you. The worst part about you is that you loved me. It made you even more sadistic."

The smoke morphed into Blezor's face. His eyes were white with death. "Just like you treated me, with contempt."

"I never loved you, Blezor. I told you that. I was very clear. I was mean to you. I manipulated you. I never loved you, so it's not the same thing."

"You killed me!"

"No, a demon killed you!" I laughed. "This is not real. None of this is real."

"You have so little empathy for your fellow beings. Is that because Daddy didn't love you?" The smoke transformed into my father. "Is it because I didn't love you?"

I scratched my chin. "This is pathetic now. Honestly, I don't know what game you are playing, but let me out of here. I am not a plaything, and I'm getting pissed off now."

There were murmurs all around me. Whatever was toying with me wasn't one being, it was many—maybe hundreds.

"What manner of creature are you?" I asked. "I know many that live in the darkness. Most are friendly, or at least not malicious. Do you want something from me? Memories? Pain? Joy? Hate? Love? Whatever it is, just take it from me so I can get going."

"You…offer it…freely…"

I nodded. "I do if you promise not to take more than you need, and you let me go afterward."

"Or, we could leave you here…yes, leave you…and feast for longer…more fun."

"I have been around long enough to know that I'm not a fun hang. Tell me I'm not already irritating to you. You can't, can you? Seriously, if you want me to stay around and we can play this dance forever, I can't stop you, but I will never stop being this annoying."

There was a moment of silence, and then I felt a cold gust of wind smash against me—no, not against me, into me. It wound its way through my arms and legs, up to my heart, and finally into my brain.

I felt a surge of pain in my skull, and I dropped to the ground. Every good memory in my life flashed before me—dancing, hanging out with Phil, meeting Anjelica—all of it—I watched all of it and then felt them drain from me, all at once, and then the gust of wind shot out of me, and left me on the ground, crying and sobbing.

"Across the grotto, down the stairs, left along the dungeon, and then up, through the dining room and into the throne room, and you will find what you seek."

From the corner of my eye, I saw a pinprick of light and crawled toward it. I followed it until I found myself in a dilapidated grotto. The grass was burnt brown, and the gazebo in the center was falling apart, its white paint chipped, and wood rotted through. Weeds cracked through the stone flooring, and I followed the crack until I found the door on the other side, just like the voice had said.

I stood, gathered what strength I had left, and followed the steps beyond the door. The wear on the castle continued through the corridor toward the dungeon. The cracks in the floor splintered up the walls and the ceiling. I imagined that at some point, the groans of prisoners echoed through the pristine halls, but now, there was only silence. Several doors were flung wide open, hanging off their hinges as I walked through them. Those that were closed had rusted shut.

Next to a room filled with corroded and discarded tools of torture, a set of stairs led me to what would have been an elaborate and ornate hallway once but had fallen into as much disrepair as the rest of the castle. Dust and muck coated the blue walls, and the paintings on them had so much grime caked on them it was hard to make out the art underneath.

Following the hallway as it moved left and then right, I passed a dining room that hadn't been used in ages, and finally, I pushed open a door, and the hallway broke into a throne room.

"Hello," I heard a voice coo next to me. I turned to see a ratty demon, potbellied, sitting atop a throne of skulls. "Why, isn't this interesting. Have you come to bargain with the Devil?"

It was Lucifer.

CHAPTER 65

"Are you here to bargain?" Lucifer asked. His gaze settled on the dagger at my hip. "Or have you come to kill me? My, my, my. This is very interesting indeed."

"I'm not here to kill you," I said, holding up my hands in submission. "I'm not here to fight anyone. I just want to destroy this knife, and I need your lake to do so."

He stood. "Ah, I see. Well then, let me escort you to your final destination."

I furrowed my brow. "Wait, there are no follow-up questions to that?"

Lucifer shook his head. "None that I can think of." The skulls cracked, hissed, and popped as he walked down to me. "Do I have any reason to doubt your sincerity?"

"I guess not. I don't know why you have any reason to trust me, either, though."

He laughed. "Oh, I don't trust you. I just…don't care. I figure if you want to kill me, you will do so." He looked down at the dagger. "After all, unless I am wrong, that is one of very few weapons in the universe that can do so." He beckoned me forward. "Come now."

The entrance of the castle was guarded by nothing but several empty suits of armor, as dusty and discarded as the rest of the castle. Black bones and skulls adorned the huge doors. The motif continued around the room, up its pillars, and around the ceiling.

"Cheery."

Lucifer pushed open the door, and the bright light of Hell fell upon me once again. I had not noticed how little light came into the castle until that moment, but as I looked up at the ceilings, I noticed that all the windows were blacked out.

"I hope you'll excuse the mess. I don't entertain much."

What seemed like a thousand steps separated us from the lake of lava below. "Where are all your guards?" I asked as we descended.

He chuckled. "Once, I had hundreds in my personal army. Those numbers have dwindled as the attempts on my life stopped."

"Demons tried to kill you?"

"Oh yes. Every time I sought to do anything to better Hell, it was met with resistance, and eventually, one assassination attempt or another."

"I don't understand. Aren't you the Devil? Can't you just smite them?"

He rolled his eyes, looking exasperated. "I wish. It's mostly a ceremonial position and filled with bureaucracy. Non-stop bureaucracy. You have never known boredom like a ten-hour meeting with the Dukes about resource allocation." He looked at the dark stacks of souls teetering over Hell. "It's getting worse, isn't it?"

"I don't know how bad it was, but it's pretty terrible out there."

"I have asked for help, you know. So far, my requests have been unheeded." He sighed. "It doesn't have to be this way." A sadness filled his eyes. "God has truly abandoned me."

We walked in silence for a long time until we finally reached the dock, and he sat down upon it, his cloven hooves dangling over the edge. "You know, I haven't been out of my castle in decades. I really hate it here."

I sat down on the dock next to him. "You sound like your son."

"Which one?" He laughed. "The one nice thing about being the Devil is the groupies."

"Et'atal." I looked over at him. "He's trying to start an Apocalypse, you know."

Lucifer nodded. "That sounds like him. He's very proactive." He sighed. "A few more centuries in Hell will break him, and he'll realize the only true path is to do nothing and accept your fate." He pointed to the dagger. "Are you sure you're not here to kill me with that?"

I nodded. "Just want to destroy it."

"Well, unfortunately, that's impossible. Even if you leave it at the bottom of the lake, it will not be destroyed. This isn't Mordor, and that is not the one ring, Frodo." He laughed at the shocked look on my face. "I do love reading. That dagger was made from a material so ancient that— let's just say that nothing can destroy it. All we can do is make it harder for people to find it."

"So, I will always have to be on the lookout for it?"

He shrugged. "I have tried to destroy that dagger many times. So many times." He looked over at me. "It really is the bane of my existence, and yet I fear I will never be rid of it."

"That sucks."

"I'm sure you are ready to leave, then, if there is nothing else."

"I could stay here a little longer if you wanted."

He nodded. "That would be nice. Charon won't be here for a while yet."

We sat on that pier until Charon came for me, which was the better part of a day.

"You made it," Charon said, looking at a very not-dead Lucifer. "And the Devil is still very much alive. It looks like I was right to trust you."

"Looks that way." I stood up. "And Aimee?"

"I connected her with an old friend and am confident she will make it to the Old Hat to meet with you."

"Then it looks like all of this worked out," Lucifer said. "Are you satisfied?"

I shook my head. "Never." I clutched the dagger. "You're sure this lake won't destroy it?"

Lucifer chuckled and looked at Charon. "What do you think, old friend?"

"Oh no," the boatman said. "This lake is nowhere near powerful enough."

I flung the dagger into the middle of the lake. "Well, I guess I'll keep my eye out for it."

"Give it about forty years Earth time," Lucifer said. "Unfortunately, for immortals like you and I, that's the blink of an eye."

"It was…interesting to meet you, Satan."

"Please," Lucifer said with a crooked smile. "Call me Lou."

I stepped onto Charon's gondola and watched Lucifer from the boat as we disappeared into the smoke. In time, we arrived back in Dis. I said my goodbyes to Charon and stepped into the secret passage that would lead me back into the city. From there, it was a simple matter to find my way to the Old Hat. Aimee and the others were waiting for me at a table in the back.

"Thank god," Aimee said. "I don't think I could have drunk one more glass of this warm piss."

"And in Hell," I replied, "that might actually be piss."

She pushed her glass away. "Gross."

Drownt still had his map of the city, and we used it to find our way back to the sewers where we began our journey. Aimee closed her eyes and set fire to the barrier between our worlds, and then we fell back into the Gateway where the Commander was waiting for us.

"Back already?" she said.

"Already?" I said. "We've been gone for days."

She tapped the watch on her wrist. "Not according to this. Were you successful?"

I looked back at my team. "As successful as we could hope to be, I think."

"And the dagger?"

"You won't have to worry about it anymore."

It was true. Somebody would have to worry about it, but not her. She would be long retired by the time the dagger made its way back. I would have to be vigilant, though, because I would very much still be alive, and I was okay with that being my lot in life.

Until then, though, I would be taking a much-needed vacation.

***

You just finished *Magic*, but the adventure isn't over yet. Keep reading after the author's note for a sneak peek of *Evil*, which follows Anjelica's adventures right after she leaves Ollie.

AUTHOR'S NOTE

This is a very weird experience because even though you will likely be reading this as one of the first books in The Godsverse Chronicles, it's actually the EIGHTH Godsverse Chronicles book.

What the what is happening here?

Well, after writing the first seven books, I decided to produce a graphic novel called *Black Market Heroine*.

When I produce a graphic novel in the Godsverse, I find it helpful to write an expanded universe novel with a novelization of that book AND a couple of new stories. I've been doing that since 2017 when I wrote *Death* to complement my graphic novel *Katrina Hates the Dead* and *Hell* as the expansion of my graphic novel *Pixie Dust*.

It might have been easier to make this the ninth book, but as I was writing it, I realized that this was the PERFECT way into the Godsverse Chronicles. I was just about through with the first part of the story when I realized it, so that's what I've done. My plan is to write a ninth book following Anjelica and a tenth book which is a team-up book with Anjelica, Ollie, Kimberly, and another character to be named later.

Did I mention this is really confusing? However, if I do it right, I think it will make the Godsverse make all sorts of sense.

I have been writing this series for years now, and it's always been a messy experiment. When I started the first four books, my idea was to release them in four separate series, and then I combined them into one series, and then I added three more books, and now these first few books, and well, it's never been easy.

Ever.

But I wouldn't change anything. Despite every crazy thing that has happened while I've been writing this series, I am so proud of how this book turned out, and the Godsverse in general. I thought I was done with this universe until Ollie and Anjelica burrowed their way into my heart. I hope they find their way into yours as well.

***

Now, enjoy a preview of Anjelica's book, *Evil,* and follow her adventure after the events of this book.

EVIL

Book 2 of The Godsverse Chronicles

By
Russell Nohelty

Edited by:
Leah Lederman

Proofread by:
Katrina Roets
Toni Cox

Cover by:
Psycat Covers

Planet chart and timeline design by:
Andrea Rosales

CHAPTER 1

Bronard, Missouri wasn't on my list of top 10,000 cities in the world to visit, and yet that was where I found myself, sitting across from a magical pixie, a mere twenty-four hours after a crazy monster had tried to use my blood to start the Apocalypse...all because I was a demon.

No, I wasn't just a demon. I was the antichrist. Actually, that's not right, either. I'm *an* antichrist. One of dozens, hundreds, thousands. I had no idea how many little demon babies were growing up around the world waiting to explode and cause the Apocalypse, just that I wasn't the only one. According to Kimberly, whatever crazy potion I drank last night had diffused the part of my blood that was capable of ending the world...but that only neutralized the antichrist part of me.

I was still a demon and would be for the rest of my hopefully rather long life. On top of that, demons and other evil creatures would continue to pop out of the woodwork and cause trouble for me if I stayed in Los Angeles.

Which meant I was a danger to myself and my mother until I figured out how to control my powers and could defend myself at least, and that fact brought me to Bronard, Missouri, a small town in the middle of nowhere, hours outside of St. Louis, where cows outnumbered people ten to one—according to a proud sign outside of town.

"You're not eating," Kimberly said to me with a small smile. "This isn't going to suck any less with an empty stomach."

How was she my age? She wasn't big, but she commanded a room with confidence and poise. Even with half the diner staring daggers at her, she didn't cower or fold to them. Bronard wasn't the kind of place that welcomed dark-skinned teenagers. Maybe it was because there was a very good chance she could kill everybody in this restaurant all at one time with both hands tied behind her back and not break a sweat.

"I'm not hungry." That was strange in and of itself. I was always hungry.

Kimberly reached over and pulled a fry from my plate. "That's too bad. If there's one thing Bronard does well, it's diner food. This town runs on pancakes and ribs." She popped the whole fry in her mouth and smiled at me. After a few seconds, her face fell. "They're nice people. You'll see."

She was talking about my new "parents," Carl and Junebug. "I'm sure they are, but like, I just wanna go home."

"If you go home, you're putting everyone in danger, including your mother. I can't protect you in Los Angeles. I can protect you here."

"But you really aren't protecting me, are you?" My eyes narrowed. "You're dumping me here and leaving so that Junebug and Carl can protect me."

Kimberly leaned forward. "There's a lot of fairy folk in this town, and they look out for each other. I'm leaving you in the best hands I can, given the circumstances."

After I'd said goodbye to my savior Ollie and left the coast of Hawaii with Kimberly, I was filled with excited adrenaline, ready for a new challenge, thrilled to start a fresh adventure. However, in the hours that followed, that excitement drained from me, and I realized the ramifications of my decision. I was relegated to a small-town life, cut off from everything I ever knew, and I would have to build from nothing again.

"I don't want to seem ungrateful," I started. "But—"

"You can stop there. Nobody has ever looked good after they started a sentence like that." She shook her head. "Listen, this is your decision. I can tell Junebug you had a change of heart and take you back to Los Angeles right now, let you fend for yourself. We both know how well that worked last time."

"Hey!" I said. "I survived."

"You survived because you lucked into finding Ollie, and that somehow Ollie knew Phil, and Phil contacted me. If any of those things didn't happen, you would be dead, and you know it."

I started to argue but stopped. She was right, of course, and any argument I formulated seemed stupid in comparison. "I do appreciate it."

Kimberly yawned. We had been up for over a day now, and it was wearing on both of us. "You could do a better job showing it, but like I said, I know this sucks."

I popped a fry in my mouth. I had to admit, they were really good. Just the right amount of salt. I thought for a second, chewing slowly before I finally looked at her again. "Why did it have to happen to me?"

"I don't know," Kimberly said as if she expected the question. "Life sucks. Did I ever tell you how I was kidnapped by a banshee when I was eight?"

I shook my head. "No, I would have remembered that kind of story."

"Well, it happened," she said. "It brought me to Hell, like real-life Hell, and I was rescued by my mentor, Julia, who I watched die in front of me some years later."

"That sucks."

"Yeah, and I go to bed most nights wondering why all this happened to me. I just want to play soccer, graduate, and go to college. Here I am, helping you instead. Do you know I have an exam today? Like, a hard one, too. I am woefully underprepared."

"Why are you doing it then?" I asked.

"Because we all gotta deal with our lot in life. We can't run from it. Destiny doesn't care what we want."

"Sure you could, you could run away."

"Then you would be dead," she replied. "I can't have that on my conscience. I have these powers for a reason, and it's my responsibility to use them to help people. Especially because everything else in the world is working to hurt them."

"Crud," I replied. "When you put it like that, I guess I should just shut my mouth."

Kimberly took another fry. "That was my polite way of saying as much. Now, if you're done having a pity party, finish eating so I can introduce you to your adopted parents."

I swallowed my sadness and dug into the food. The salty, deep-fried chicken sandwich made me feel better. It really was some amazing diner food. Kimberly was right about that, even if I had my doubts about everything else.

***

After stuffing ourselves with a second helping of fries, Kimberly and I left the diner and began walking down the street. It was mid-morning, and the sun beat down, protecting us from the winter cold.

"Why don't we just flash directly to the house? I mean, you can literally teleport from one place to another at will."

"I can," she replied. "As long as I know exactly where I'm going. Otherwise, I'll get lost in the ether, and I absolutely do not want that."

"No, I imagine you wouldn't." The rocky ground crunched under our feet as we walked. "Doesn't walking seem boring by comparison, though?"

She kicked a rock through the white fence next to us, and we watched it skid into a thatch of corn stalks. "Honestly, no. When you can flash anywhere you want, walking is a luxury. Besides, another reason we're walking is for you to get a sense of the town—your town." She pointed to a big silo painted to look like Big Bird. "That's the Henson Silo. Aside from the water tower, it's the highest place in town, so you get your bearings if you need it. Sun sets right over the silo from your house." She pointed over to the other side of the road, where a big blue water tower loomed over everything else. "That's the Bronard water tower, tallest structure in town. Sun rises behind it, directly east."

"A silo and a water tower are my two biggest landmarks. Jesus Christ, what did I sign up for?"

"It's not like Los Angeles has a lot of big buildings, either."

"No, but it has more than here."

"Fair enough." She laughed. "Small-town life takes getting used to, but there's a calmness to it. You're not going to get a lot of high-profile celebrities rolling through, but everyone will know your name. For our purposes, that's important." We reached a stop sign, and she pointed to the right. "This way."

"What if I hate it?" I said, following her. "This is a big change for me."

She thought for a moment. "Did you like Los Angeles?"

I nodded. "Of course. What's not to like?"

"So much stuff." Kimberly kicked another rock off the side of the road. "I mean, it's dirty. The people…suck. Plus, everything costs a ton of money. It smells like smoke everywhere you go…did I mention the people suck?"

"I'm from Los Angeles. So is Ollie. Do we suck?"

"Ollie most definitely sucks," she said playfully. "But you're okay, I guess. I'm just saying, this place has its charm if you let yourself see it. It's not as progressive as the big city, but it's beautiful country. You can actually smell the freshness in the air."

That I couldn't deny. As we walked, the sun glimmered in gold, orange, and yellow, over the wheat fields, rippling from the wind. There was a tranquility to it that I never had in Los Angeles. I loved LA, but the city felt slapped together in a hurry. Even "new" roads felt a hundred years old, and taking a stroll without a destination just didn't happen there, not unless you had a death wish.

After a twenty-minute walk, with the water tower behind us in the distance, we turned down a dirt road. "Here we are."

A rusted shed sat offset to the right of the driveway. An old tractor rested inside, covered by a dirty, rusted, metal overhang. Some farm equipment stood against the wall of the shed. I recognized a hoe and a shovel, but the rest were foreign to me. Wild grass grew in thick patches and several large trees arched over the road. At the end of it was a big white house with a pick-up out front. Two rocking chairs sat on the porch, and on them, a black man and white woman sat, drinking from coffee cups.

When Kimberly saw them, she smiled. "Hi, Carl! Junebug!"

"There she is," Carl said, standing. "We thought you had a change of heart, girl. Where you been?"

"Took her to Cheryl's for breakfast."

"Last supper," Junebug said with a smile. "Just kidding, kid. Cheryl's is pretty good for an out-of-towner. You must be Anjelica."

I nodded. "Yes, ma'am."

"Good manners," Carl said. "Better than the last one you brought 'round."

"The last one?" I asked, confused.

June set her cup down and walked toward me. I placed my hand out to shake hers, but she wasn't interested in my hand. Instead, she wrapped me in a big hug. "Don't you worry about that none. All you gotta know is that you're safe here."

I wanted to protest, but something about her energy made me collapse into her bosom, and suddenly, all the pain of the last day, everything that I had been through, burst out of me. I fell into her, crying.

"It's okay, child," Junebug said. "You let it all out. There's no shame in crying. None at all."

"Kimberly," Carl said, waving her forward. "Why don't you come inside for some coffee. Leave those two outside for a moment."

Kimberly patted me on the back as she walked past. The weight of my legs became too heavy a burden to carry, and I slid to the ground. Junebug came with me, settling onto her knees. I collapsed into her lap and cried, and cried, and cried, for my mother, for myself, and for the life that I left behind.

CHAPTER 2

I laid on the dirt road in front of Junebug and Carl's house until all my tears dried up and my back stopped heaving.

"You feel better?" Junebug asked when my whimpers fell silent.

"I don't think I'm ever going to feel better again."

She sighed. "You will. Someday you'll wake up, and you'll barely feel the pain at all."

"How?" I asked hopefully. "How do you know?"

"I'm quite a bit older than you, and I've lost a lot in my years. Most people have a lifetime to get comfortable with that much sadness. You just got too much thrown on you too soon. You left your mom, right?"

I nodded, wiping my face. "Uh-huh."

"I lost my mom to cancer about a decade ago. Lost my dad, too, and my brother. It's awful every time. You have any siblings?"

I shook my head. "No, I was an only child. My mom called me a spoiled…brat…" When I said that last word, the tears came again. "Brat…because of…because of it." I sputtered out through my tears.

Junebug rubbed her hand through my hair. "It's going to come in waves like that. Over time, those crashing waves recede and finally just leave a little wake behind them. That's when it gets survivable, though none of us get out of this life alive."

I looked up at her. For the first time, I saw June's bright green eyes and her soft skin. Age hadn't hit her hard, and she barely had any wrinkles on her face, though there was great wisdom in it all the same. "Thank you." I took a deep breath. "When did you find out you were different?"

"Different?"

"You're a fairy, right?"

She laughed. "Oh yeah. Sorry, 'round here that doesn't make me very different from most of the people." She thought for a moment. "It was later in life, when my mom was sick. I don't have much fairy blood, just a drop, so I can't do much. Not like Carl. He's more like Kimberly. He can move through the ether at will. Very handy for vacations."

I wiped my nose on my sleeve. "I think I'm ready to go inside now."

"Oh good," she said. "This road was not meant for sitting."

Junebug stood up with a small groan and brushed the dirt off her flower dress, then held out her arm to help me up. I wiped myself off and followed her inside. The wooden steps up to the porch creaked as my weight pressed down upon them, and I made sure to note that for later in case I needed to leave unnoticed.

She pulled the storm door open and held it open for me. The hardwood foyer was cluttered with shoes and coats. A mirror hung over a little table filled with keys, and I had my first look at myself since before I was kidnapped.

I was a wreck. My freckled face was blotchy and red, and my red hair frayed like wild thatch. It hadn't been combed in two days. My green eyes were cracked with red veins from crying, and my nose was as puffy as the bags under my eyes.

"I look terrible."

"No," Junebug said, pulling a hair tie from her wrist. "Well, yes, but we can fix that."

She handed it to me, and I pulled my hair back into a ponytail. "Thank you." I still looked terrible, but slightly less so now. "I feel like I'm just going to keep saying that forever now."

"Well, don't thank me until I show you around." She pointed me to a room set off the main foyer. Ruddy old couches were arranged in front of a TV at the far end. "This is the TV room." She turned to the left, where Kimberly and Carl waved from a long table. "That's the dining room." She pointed to another door. "Behind there is the kitchen. That's where I spend a lot of time."

"You a cook?"

"I have a little bakery in the middle of town, sells everything from bread to pies. Pretty popular, too, if I do say so. Most of the ingredients I use come right from this farm or from trading our produce for whatever we need."

"Sounds nice," I said. "Quaint even."

"There isn't much around here, but we like it. You'll get used to it in a while. Or you won't, and then it's good you only have a couple of years before you're off on your own." In front of us, the wooden staircase matched the grain of the foyer.

She beckoned me to followed her up the stairs, which led to another short hallway with four doors. She pointed to the one on the far left. "There at the end is our room." She moved her attention to the door next to it. "That's the office. Carl likes to putz around in there when he's not out in the fields." She walked to the furthest door on the right and knocked. "Lizzie, open up!"

"Coming!" The door opened, and a light-skinned girl opened it. She was every bit the mix of Carl and Junebug, with June's green eyes and Carl's stern jaw. Her hair was buzzed short, and she wore a bullring in her nose.

"Take that out," June said, pulling on the bullring. I gasped, thinking it might rip her septum out, but instead, it slid off like nothing. June glanced in my direction. "It's just a clip-on. She's twelve and just getting to that rebellious stage."

I chuckled. "I remember it well."

"Who's this?" Lizzie asked, studying me.

"Lizzie, meet Anjelica."

"Hi," I said, with a little wave.

"She's staying with us for a while," Junebug replied.

"Another one?" Lizzie rolled her eyes. "Nice to meet you, I guess. Can I go now?"

"Yes, but next time I see you, I expect a better attitude, yes? Otherwise, don't bother coming out 'til school tomorrow."

"Fine," Lizzie said over her shoulder as she shut the door.

"She's nice," I said.

"Usually, at least," Junebug turned back to me. "I wish I could beg my mother's forgiveness for how I treated her at that age. I guess this is my punishment."

"I heard that!" Lizzie called from behind her door.

"Good!" Junebug said, the smile never leaving her face. She pointed to room next door. "This is your room."

She held the door for me, and I walked through. At home, the walls of my room were painted a dark green and covered in posters. This room had boring, plain, white walls that were bare, save for a single flower painting near the window. On the wall closest to Lizzie was a long closet with double doors. The furniture was plain. A writing desk, a dresser, and a mirror. Near the window on the other side was a small curio. Along the far wall was a queen size bed, covered in a similar floral pattern as Junebug's dress, along with a small, whitewashed vanity.

"We'll go to the store and get you some proper clothes later today, but I'll leave you to settle for now."

"Actually," I said. "Could I have some coffee?"

"You sure you don't want to sleep?"

"I know I should, but…can I have some anyway?"

***

There was a simple reason why I wanted coffee. Kimberly was downstairs, and once she left, I had no idea when I would see her again. She was the only anchor to my past life. When she left, I would have nothing left, and no choice but to literally start from scratch.

I sat at the dining room table listening to Kimberly and Carl swap stories, each more fantastical than the last, until my second cup of coffee was gone.

"And then," Carl clapped his hands together. "Just like that, I was gone, and the chonchon was left flying toward an empty space in the forest." He laughed. "I would have paid to see its face when I just vanished in thin air."

"You say that now," Junebug said. "But I was there when you tumbled home—you were shook."

"It's basically a human face with bat wings." He looked directly at me when he said that. Kimberly must have told him I didn't know anything about magical life. Either that, or my confusion was etched deep on my face. "And I don't want to meet the person who isn't scared of something like that. Ugly little buggers."

Kimberly took a final sip of coffee and then leaned back in her chair, stretching. "I could stay here all day swapping stories, but as I've told Anjelica, I have an exam today, and my mom is going to freak out that I was gone all night without calling."

"You're gonna get so grounded," I said, smiling.

She stood. "You laugh, but I will."

It sounded nice, to have a mother that cared about you enough to ground you, even when you were a powerful pixie who could slaughter demons. I would be lucky if my mom even noticed I was gone before next weekend when she finally got a day off, and even then, it's not like we kept the same schedule. She might literally go weeks before realizing I was gone.

"I'll walk you out," Carl said.

I pushed my chair out. "Mind if I do it?"

Carl shrugged. "Fine with me. I need to go feed the hogs anyway."

"Don't take too long, dear," Junebug said, catching my eye. "If you're not going to sleep, you can help me bring some food to the bakery, and we'll get you those clothes."

"Well, I didn't say I wasn't going to sle—" I looked over at Kimberly, and she shook her head. "I mean, that sounds great."

Kimberly led me outside and gave me an apologetic smile. "This is your life now." She dropped her head. "Don't get me wrong, it's a good life. They're nice people, but I know it's not what you signed up for." She leaped forward and hugged me tightly. "I'm glad you aren't dead."

"Me too." I patted her on the back. "And I have you to thank for it, for all of this."

"I don't think you understand how lucky you are." She pulled back from me. "You will, though. In time."

"I hope so."

She squeezed my arms before turning from me. "You saved the world, Anjelica."

"All I did was not die."

Kimberly raised her eyebrows slightly. "Sometimes, that's all it takes." She reached into her pocket and pulled out a black opal pendant on a silver necklace. "Don't ever take this off, no matter what. Understand?"

I put on the necklace. "I won't."

"Good." With that, she dropped a pinch of the pink pixie dust she kept in a pouch on her belt, vanishing in a puff of pink smoke.

The dust tickled my nose. When it had settled, I turned back to the house. Junebug was already bringing a plate of donuts down the steps toward the pick-up truck.

"You ride in the back, love. The wind will wake you right up."

That couldn't be a safe way to travel, but I hadn't been making very safe choices lately. I shrugged and hopped into the bed of the pick-up, ready for a new adventure.

CHAPTER 3

"How you doin' back there, hon?" Junebug asked from the front of the cab as we rattled down the street. "It's not much further."

"I'm fine!" I screamed back. I was not fine. I was struggling not to slide around the back of the cab, clinging tight to a tray of muffins June asked me to hold after she stuffed the cab full of trays. It was freezing, and the wind whipping over the hood made it worse.

I did my best to focus on the route from June's house. We made a right from the main road, away from the water tower, and across two train tracks until we arrived at a crossroad, where we took two lefts, and a right before I lost the thread. The roads were winding and undulating, and I cheered inwardly when we finally reached the center of town and Junebug slowed to a crawl after having gunned it irresponsibly fast on the country roads.

"This is Main Street," Junebug said. "You'll get to know it well."

Junebug pulled up to a small strip mall on the main drag. The town was out in full force, even though it was a workday, and dozens of people scurried down the sidewalks on either side of the street. I had seen quaint little towns in movies, but I had never been in one. The colorful vinyl siding alternated between every building, from forest green to powder blue to burgundy. All of the buildings had adorable white shutters on their windows.

"Can you help me?" Junebug said, pulling a tray out of the front seat after lowering the bed so I could scoot out of the truck. I centered the tray of muffins and she placed another into my hands before I could answer. "It's over there. Dessertation."

She pointed to a powder blue shop across the street with *Dessertation* scrawled on the window in pretty cursive. "That's funny. Like dissertation?"

"What?" Junebug said, kicking the door closed after filling her hands with trays. "No, like dessert vacation, hon. The heck is a dissertation?"

"Like a PhD? You're kind of like a doctor of baking."

She looked at me, deadpan. "I like you, but that was a real dumb thing you said."

"Sorry," I replied, hanging my head.

"Don't drop yer head, kiddo," she said, crossing the street. "You need your head on a swivel at this intersection. People drive like maniacs through it. Come on, then."

Junebug scooted the door to the bakery open with her butt, and the bell atop the entrance rang to welcome us. She placed the trays on a glass counter filled with bakery goodness and walked around it to give a middle-aged woman in a white apron a hug. "Sorry, Betty. We had a busy morning."

"Oh, it's okay," Betty said. "Hasn't been busy yet, but Earl's going to come in for another two-dozen glazed in about fifteen minutes."

Junebug pointed to a set of trays. She had made exactly two dozen glazed donuts. "I had a feeling."

"How do you always know?" Betty said.

"Intuition." Junebug winked at me.

I had a feeling that one of the gifts she had been given as a pixie was some sort of magical perception or something like that.

"Who's your friend?" Betty said. "And why is she standing in the doorway like a fool?"

"This is Anjelica. She's…staying with me for a while."

"Ah, another one of your strays." Betty raised her hand. "Well, nice to meet you. Anybody ever tell ya that you make a better door than a window?"

"Huh?" I said.

"Come in out of the doorway, sweetie," Junebug said softly.

I took a few steps into the shop and was overwhelmed by the smell of bread. I loved that smell. There was a bakery not far from my house, Randy's, and every time I passed it, I literally wanted to eat everything inside after one whiff…and that paled in comparison to the heavenly scents here at June's place.

"It smells great in here," I said, setting down the trays.

"It better," Betty said. "I've been baking since four."

"In the morning!" I breathed, incredulous. I was pretty sure I had been fighting demons at that time. The thought that people were going about their lives while mine was about to end left me shook for a moment.

"Every morning," Betty said with a smile that said she truly loved it.

"We've grown a little too big for this space, so every morning, I have to supplement our supply with some of my own." Junebug covered her mouth with a finger. "We're not supposed to, but what the health inspectors don't know won't hurt them."

I had to admit, Junebug was more fun than I expected. I worried that her rustic, down-home charm was going to wear on me quickly, but she was spunky, and she made cookies, which, in a mom, were two things that I highly valued.

Junebug must have seen me eyeing the eclairs because she pulled a pair of tongs and handed me one. "Take one."

"Oh no, I couldn't," I said.

"Girlie, you had a night. You could probably eat this whole place down to the floorboards and still deserve another one. Now, eat. I insist."

"Don't insult her," Betty said. "Trust me, denying food from a Campbell is an insult."

"Darn tootin' it is," Junebug said as I took the éclair.

"It's my favorite," I said, taking a bite. It was unlike anything I had eaten before. I thought I'd had delicious eclairs before, but this one set a new standard for everything else in my life. "Oh my god."

Junebug watched me with a knowing smile. "Kind of makes all that crap you dealt with worth it, eh?"

A bit of gooey vanilla cream slid down my throat. "Not even a little bit, but this is pretty amazing."

"Go wait outside for me. I'll be done in a second, and then we'll go shopping."

I didn't argue. I couldn't. Junebug's food had driven me to complacency. I would have done anything she asked me to as long as she kept feeding me her delicious goodies.

***

Dana's Dress Barn was not Melrose or Beverly Hills, but it was…a woman's clothing shop…and the things she stocked technically counted as clothes. I wasn't trying to be picky, especially since Junebug was paying the bill, but not many items spoke to me. After over an hour of searching through the racks, I pulled out four blouses, two pairs of jeans, a jacket, and three dresses that I wouldn't be mortified to wear. Mostly, I just enjoyed talking to Junebug.

"That one makes your butt look big," she said with a scrunched-up nose after I came out of the dressing room one last time. "I guess we'll just go with what we have and hope we can go to the mall this weekend."

"You guys have a mall?"

She grabbed the clothes we chose from a chair where she stashed them. "Well, it's an hour away, but it's a nice drive. We do a lot of driving out here, that's for sure. Not much is close."

"So did I, back in LA."

I never had a mother to do girlie things with, and my mom was an only child, which meant I didn't have aunts or cousins, or really anybody to hang out with that was family. Besides, it's not like she was going to have two demon spawn babies. I'm sure I was enough of a handful in that department. I didn't blame her, of course, at least not much, for being an absentee parent. Mom worked as a nurse, and she was pretty much always on call. When she wasn't, the odd hours she worked always made her tired.

"So, can I ask why Lizzie is home today? I mean, I know it's a school day and all." I set down the clothes on the counter. The over-makeuped teller started ringing us up.

A curt smile from Junebug told me it was a sore subject. "That girl," she muttered. "She skipped school, so they suspended her…which is letting her miss another day of school. I swear they are idiots at that school. Why would you keep a kid home from school as punishment for them not wanting to go to school?"

"I gotta say, I agree with them," the woman behind the counter said. "Being in your house is the worst punishment I could imagine."

"Good for you, Dana." She threw a credit card onto the counter. "Just ring us up, already. I don't need your lip." She turned to me. "Where was I?"

"You were complaining about the school and suspensions."

"Right." She pressed her finger to the bridge of her nose. "They are idiots, all of them. But you'll find that out soon enough. You start there next week, assuming all your paperwork is in order."

Oh yeah. School. That would be…fun? No. That wasn't the right word, was it?

***

If you liked that preview, make sure to pick up *Evil* today.

ALSO BY RUSSELL NOHELTY

NOVELS
My Father Didn't Kill Himself
Sorry for Existing
Gumshoes: The Case of Madison's Father
Invasion
The Vessel
The Void Calls Us Home
Worst Thing in the Universe
Anna and the Dark Place
The Marked Ones
The Dragon Scourge
The Dragon Champion
The Dragon Goddess
The Obsidian Spindle Saga

COMICS and OTHER ILLUSTRATED WORK
The Little Bird and the Little Worm
Ichabod Jones: Monster Hunter
Gherkin Boy
How NOT to Invade Earth

www.russellnohelty.com

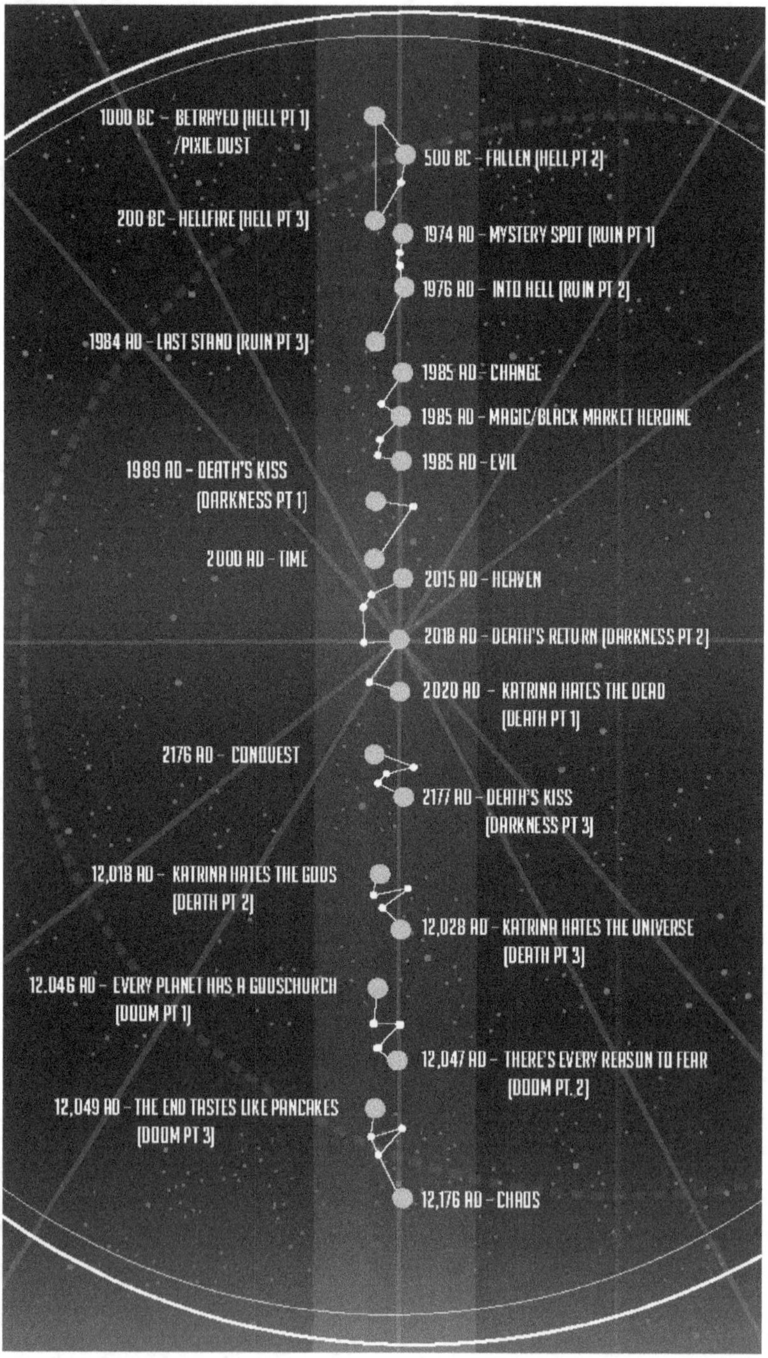

1000 BC – BETRAYED [HELL PT 1] /PIXIE DUST
500 BC – FALLEN [HELL PT 2]
200 BC – HELLFIRE [HELL PT 3]
1974 AD – MYSTERY SPOT [RUIN PT 1]
1976 AD – INTO HELL [RUIN PT 2]
1984 AD – LAST STAND [RUIN PT 3]
1985 AD – CHANGE
1985 AD – MAGIC/BLACK MARKET HEROINE
1985 AD – EVIL
1989 AD – DEATH'S KISS [DARKNESS PT 1]
2000 AD – TIME
2015 AD – HEAVEN
2018 AD – DEATH'S RETURN [DARKNESS PT 2]
2020 AD – KATRINA HATES THE DEAD [DEATH PT 1]
2176 AD – CONQUEST
2177 AD – DEATH'S KISS [DARKNESS PT 3]
12,018 AD – KATRINA HATES THE GODS [DEATH PT 2]
12,028 AD – KATRINA HATES THE UNIVERSE [DEATH PT 3]
12,046 AD – EVERY PLANET HAS A GODSCHURCH [DOOM PT 1]
12,047 AD – THERE'S EVERY REASON TO FEAR [DOOM PT. 2]
12,049 AD – THE END TASTES LIKE PANCAKES [DOOM PT 3]
12,176 AD – CHAOS